PENSION VAUQUIER, GORIOT'S HOUSE

THE HARVARD CLASSICS
SHELF OF FICTION
SELECTED BY CHARLES W ELIOT LL D

FRENCH FICTION

HONORÉ DE BALZAC — GEORGE SAND
ALFRED DE MUSSET — ALPHONSE DAUDET
GUY DE MAUPASSANT

EDITED WITH NOTES AND INTRODUCTIONS
BY WILLIAM ALLAN NEILSON PH D

P F COLLIER & SON COMPANY
NEW YORK

MANUFACTURED IN U. S. A.

CONTENTS

M—1

APPENDIX

ALFRED DE MUSSET

ALPHONSE DAUDET

GUY DE MAUPASSANT

THE NOVEL IN FRANCE

THE French, not without reason, pride themselves on the skillful technique of their works of fiction. During the whole period of modern French literature, the authors, whether of five and ten volume romances like Mlle. de Scudéry, or of short tales like Alphonse Daudet and Guy de Maupassant, have been conscious literary artists. Moreover, except during the romantic outburst of our first half of the nineteenth century, which produced the exuberant fantasies of persons like Alexandre Dumas the elder, they have usually sought psychological analysis and the presentation of character. This aim has, on the whole, been consistently pursued in both divisions of French fiction, the idealistic and the realistic novels.

Works of these two types appear, judging from their names, to move in different planes. But the connection of both kinds with life has been fairly close, and, in the seventeenth century, discussion of popular romances was so much the preoccupation of social circles such as the Hôtel de Rambouillet, that not only did the novelist try to portray characters he saw, but the leisure classes often sought to model their life after the pattern of the fiction they read.

At the threshold of the seventeenth century we come upon one of the most important novels ever written in France because of its influence, even if to-day unread except by specialists, the great pastoral romance "Astrée." Though the scenes of the story take place in a world impossible and unreal by its anachronisms, and though the characters are as untrue as can be to the civilization of the Gaul in which they are supposed to live, nevertheless the author, Honoré d'Urfé, would have us see in his creations human beings, perhaps in some cases to be identified by a key. Their language, highflown and sentimental though it be, fulfills the author's desire to analyze feelings. So the shepherds and the shepherdesses, the knights and the nymphs of the story, discuss love in all its actions and reactions, and try to define the various kinds of love, faithful, fickle, or Platonic. "My shepherdesses are not needy ones who have to earn a living," D'Urfé admitted. But he supposed, at least, that their sentimental experiences were those of human beings.

The same purpose may safely be attributed to the successors of D'Urfé down to the middle of the seventeenth century and to the novels of Mlle. de Scudéry. In their stories of fantastic experience and of Romanesque incident, or of romantic adventure in distant lands, the authors would have us believe in the verisimilitude, if not in the truth of the characters they describe. So the novels of Mlle. de Scudéry, though they are supposed to take place in the days of the great Cyrus or of early Rome, are nevertheless intended to be read in the light of history contemporaneous with the author.

If this statement be true of the professionally idealistic romance, it is the more so of the realistic novel. The "Roman bourgeois" of Furetière and the "Roman comique" of Scarron are most useful documents for the knowledge of life in the seventeenth century and the character of individual people.

We come to the same conclusion about Madame de la Fayette's "Princesse de Clèves," which, as a reaction against the long romance of fantasy and chivalry, has been called the "first modern French novel." Certainly no better example of the literary spirit of its period could be found. Brief and to the point in its descriptions, it is the psychological analysis of a woman's heart written by a woman, and is no less truthful than the great tragedies of Racine.

The eighteenth century was, on the whole, very matter of fact. It was an age of rationalism and of science. Consequently its novels have much the same quality. A satirical writer like Voltaire permits himself whimsical unrealities in his stories, but most writers pose as truthful chroniclers. Lesage's picaresque novel "Gil Blas," Marivaux's "Marianne," and the Abbé Prévost's "Manon Lescaut" seek to impart the effect of reality. Even Rousseau's emotional "Julie" would fain be a painstaking and accurate picture of human nature.

Rousseau is looked upon as the source of the romantic school which, after his death, occupied so important a place in the literary history of the earlier nineteenth century. This school consciously reacted against what it considered the cut-and-dried rationalism of the hitherto reigning literature, and advocated the cult of feeling and a return to nature. This nature included the outer world of mountains and rivers, and intellectual descendants of Rousseau such as Bernardin de Saint-Pierre, author of "Paul and Virginia," and Chateaubriand run riot amid the flora and fauna of exotic landscapes. But, strange as it sometimes seems now, the romanticists thought themselves better portrayers of human nature than their opponents had been. It is true that to us the fiction of the romantic age is apt to appear a chaos of imaginative weavings. But if we eliminate the vagaries of which has been called the "lower romanticism," with its fantastic and melodramatic incidents often foreign in origin, if we omit also the exuberance of Dumas, we find that the French romantic novelist was usually intent on portraying human nature, just as the classicist before him. We are prone to call the heroes of romanticism a motley herd of eccentrics. The romanticist said that life consists of varied experiences, that souls are multiform, and that the drab monotony of classicism portrays only commonplaces which do not make up the whole of life.

In such a novel as Victor Hugo's "Notre Dame" we have a characteristic example of romantic fiction. Here the author has sought to reconstruct the Paris of the late Middle Ages, though modern scientific objective historians may say he has not succeeded; he has tried to people this city of his imaginative reconstruction with varied characters, each one intended to show more individuality and more vigor than the anaemic kings and heroes of late neo-classic tragedy. Something new and different was always the aim, because life and character are protean. But so it also comes about that this novel, engrossing as it may be to the reader, seems a gallery of curiosities more than a collection of human beings. Victor Hugo would not have understood that his novels might, after his time, derive their chief interest less from this portrayal of character than from their incidents, and particularly from their tearful emotionalism and the vague humanitarianism which is in the spirit of modern democracy.

Of George Sand we are less justified in saying that she tries to copy life exactly. The object of art, she says in the first chapter of "La Mare au Diable," is to make us love the objects of its interest and it need not be blamed if it occasionally flatters.

"Art is not a study of positive reality; it is a quest for ideal truth, and the *Vicar of Wakefield* was a more useful and a healthier book than the *Paysan perverti* and the *Liaisons dangereuses*."

In some of her novels she tries to reconstruct social Utopias and indulges in a semirhapsodic mysticism, in others like the "Marquis de Villemer" she at least means to portray life. But in stories like "La Mare au Diable" and "La Petite Fadette" she frankly idealizes the existence of the peasants in her native Berry and composes pretty prose pastorals with an individuality of charm that we do not find elsewhere.

The effect of a novel by Balzac is totally different from that of one by Hugo. Yet Balzac, the realist, like Hugo, the romanticist, is trying to portray human nature. But though Balzac had passed through a brief romantic discipleship in youth, his great literary production belongs to a very different school. Instead of seeking exceptional heroes, apt therefore to appear morbid eccentrics, instead of making these characters vehicles for the author's moralizings and his views on civilization, Balzac aimed at the close and painstaking study of the men and women of his time. His plan of composition illustrates his careful method. No longer handling his pen, as Hugo did, like a broad brush, Balzac corrected and recorrected his work in proof until the original text was unrecognizable in its final form.

Balzac's men and women are, in their way, as individual as any character of romanticism. Nobody is likely to forget old man Goriot, or the miser Grandet, or to confuse them with other characters in fiction. But Balzac, if we neglect the epic sweep of his constructive imagination in devising and harmonizing the multitudinous characters of his "Comédie humaine," helped to initiate the new realistic school which succeeded romanticism. This was the method of the photograph or of the daguerreotype, the close reproduction of details of life and manners. Consequently, the novels of Balzac are most valuable documents for the study of the period they chiefly describe, the reign of Louis Philippe, when the moneyed bourgeoisie or middle-class was in control, and when material interests were much more prevalent than one would infer from reading the romanticists alone. Balzac's stories are apt to deal with the selfish and sordid side of life, but that results rather from the social conditions of the time or from the bias of his mind than from the inherent demands of his method.

The perfection of realism is to be found in Gustave Flaubert, in a such a book as "Madame Bovary." There the accurate portrayal is faithfully carried out, and the men and women of the Norman province whom he seeks to describe are not only photographic in their exactness but live by the touch of genius.

Realism might appear in theory the perfect literary method in fiction, if verisimilitude be accepted as the author's goal. Yet the personal bias of the writer may, no less than in romanticism, make the novel deviate from the truth of life through the cult of the exceptional. Much of the moral disapprobation which has been expressed for the modern French novel during the past generation is based on dislike for the "naturalism" of authors like the Goncourt brothers and Emile Zola. The naturalists delighted in description of vice and disease, the dramshop, the hospital and the brothel.

That such a literary treatment of life does not necessarily belong to realism can be seen in the works of Alphonse Daudet and in some of those of Guy de Maupassant. Both of them wrote novels, but some of the best work of both, certainly of Maupassant, was done in the short story, or *nouvelle*. Alphonse Daudet has often been called the "French Dickens," and his realism has much that is akin to that of the English writer. His characters stand out as individualities to be remembered, they have their little peculiarities and idiosyncrasies, and his narrative is interwoven with constant sentimental and pathetic incidents to touch the reader's feelings. Moreover, as in "Le Petit Chose," like Dickens in "David Copperfield," he writes from the full memory of his own youthful hardships. In his short stories he has composed little masterpieces of grace and tenderness, as well as often of brisk wit and good-humored satire.

Guy de Maupassant was the literary disciple of Flaubert, consequently a more objective realist than Daudet. Some of his writings unfortunately astound by the crudeness and brutality of the narrative and descriptions, but yet when he wishes, no author in French literature portrays more faithfully and more unerringly.

Thus it may be inferred that the great masters of French literature have generally aimed to copy life. This does not imply that the fanciful and the whimsical have been banished—Alfred de Musset's "White Blackbird" is a proof of the contrary. But the romantic tendency, however popular, has been less genuinely French in its sources and influence, and the various complicated schools of art for art's sake have almost always had a transient rather than a permanent effect. But the great writers of realism have been masters in creating children of the brain whose actions and characters we may discuss almost with the vivid interest we feel for men and women of history.

C. H. C. W.

OLD GORIOT

BY

HONORÉ DE BALZAC

BIOGRAPHICAL NOTE

HONORÉ DE BALZAC was born at Tours on May 20, 1799. His father, Bernard François Balssa, who adopted the form of the family name made familiar by the novelist, came of peasant stock from the south of France. Honoré went to school at Vendôme, Tours, and Paris, later proceeding to study law, and spending three years in a solicitor's office. But when his father wished him to devote himself definitely to the practice of law he revolted, and at the age of twenty-one took up with determination the profession of letters. For five years he lived in very straitened circumstances, producing unsuccessful dramas and a large number of equally unsuccessful novels, chiefly after the pattern of the English "School of Terror."

The prospect of making a living by his pen remaining dark, he went into business in 1825 as a publisher, printer, and type-founder; but all he seems to have gained from this enterprise was a large debt, which burdened him ever after, some experience of life, and a knowledge of the details of business, of which he availed himself in his later writings.

In 1829 he again began to publish, and his historical novel, "Les Chouans," marks the real beginning of his literary career. This work is influenced by Scott, whom Balzac greatly admired, and is of a distinctly romantic type. The "Physiologie du mariage," published in the same year, is as distinctly realistic. For the next twenty-one years, Balzac continued to produce with unexampled fertility. About 1842 he set about planning his books as part of a vast "Comédie humaine," into which scheme he fitted, as far as possible, the works already issued. This was subdivided into scenes from private life, from provincial life, from political life, from military life, and from country life; and outside of these groups were philosophical and analytical studies. Among the most important titles are "La Peau de chagrin," "Le Curé de Tours," "Eugénie Grandet," "L'Illustre Gaudissart," "La

Recherche de l'absolu," "La Femme de trente ans," "Le Père Goriot," "Séraphita," "Histoire de la grandeur et de la décadence de César Birotteau," "Ursule Mironet," and "La Cousine Bette."

In spite of the amount and popularity of his work, Balzac was continually in financial straits, partly because of his bad business management, partly because his habit of rewriting his books after they were in proof increased enormously the cost of production. No man ever labored more persistently in his profession. He would write sixteen hours a day, and keep it up for weeks; and it is little wonder that ultimately his constitution broke down. For the last eighteen years of his life he was devoted to a Madame Hanska, a wealthy Polish countess, with whom he corresponded and whom he occasionally visited. They were finally married in March, 1850; but scarcely had Balzac settled down to enjoy the long-deferred fulfillment of his desires than he was seized with heart disease, and died on the 17th of August of that year. Victor Hugo delivered the eulogy over his grave.

Balzac's two great gifts were a colossal imagination and a capacity for minute observation. From the first came the romantic tendency which predominates in a number of his works and crops out here and there throughout; from the second the realism which makes his "Comédie" so wonderful a picture of France in the second quarter of the nineteenth century. "Old Goriot," an acknowledged masterpiece, gives an excellent idea of his power of portraying a section of society, of presenting memorable—if seldom wholly admirable—types, and of moving us with the picture of a passion like parental love turned into a fatal weakness and the source of intolerable suffering.

W. A. N.

CRITICISMS AND INTERPRETATIONS

I

By Arthur Symons

THE novels of Balzac are full of electric fluid. To take up one of them is to feel the shock of life, as one feels it on touching certain magnetic hands. To turn over volume after volume is like wandering through the streets of a great city, at that hour of the night when human activity is at its full. There is a particular kind of excitement inherent in the very aspect of a modern city, of London or Paris; in the mere sensation of being in its midst, in the sight of all those active and fatigued faces which pass so rapidly; of those long and endless streets, full of houses, each of which is like the body of a multiform soul, looking out through the eyes of many windows. There is something intoxicating in the lights, the movement of shadows under the lights, the vast and billowy sound of that shadowy movement. And there is something more than this mere unconscious action upon the nerves. Every step in a great city is a step into an unknown world. A new future is possible at every street corner. I never know, when I go out into one of those crowded streets, but that the whole course of my life may be changed before I return to the house I have quitted. . . .

For Balzac is the equivalent of great cities. He is bad reading for solitude, for he fills the mind with the nostalgia of cities. When a man speaks to me familiarly of Balzac I know already something of the man with whom I have to do. "The physiognomy of women does not begin before the age of thirty," he has said; and perhaps before that age no one can really understand Balzac. Few young people care for him, for there is nothing in him that appeals to the senses except through the intellect. Not many women care for him supremely, for it is part of his method to express sentiments through facts, and not facts through sentiments. But it is natural that he should be the favourite reading of men of the world, of those men of the world who have the distinction of their kind; for he supplies the key of the enigma which they are studying.—From "Studies in Prose and Verse" (1899).

II

By G. L. Strachey

THE whole of France is crammed into his pages, and electrified there into intense vitality. The realism of the classical novelists was a purely psychological realism; it was concerned with the delicately shifting states of mind of a few chosen persons, and with nothing else. Balzac worked on a very different plan. He neglected the subtleties of the spirit, and devoted himself instead to displaying the immense interest that lay in those prosaic circumstances of existence which the older writers had ignored. He showed with wonderful force that the mere common details of everyday life were filled with drama, that, to him who had eyes to see, there might be significance in a ready-made suit of clothes, and passion in the furniture of a boarding house. Money in particular gave him an unending theme. There is hardly a character in the whole vast range of his creation of whose income we are not exactly informed; and it might almost be said that the only definite moral that can be drawn from "La Comédie humaine" is that the importance of money can never be overestimated. The classical writers preferred to leave such matters to the imagination of the reader; it was Balzac's great object to leave nothing to the imagination of the reader. By ceaseless effort, by infinite care, by elaborate attention to the minutest details, he would describe *all*. He brought an encyclopædic knowledge to bear upon his task; he can give an exact account of the machinery of a provincial printing press; he can write a dissertation on the methods of military organisation; he is absolutely at home in the fraudulent transactions of money-makers, the methods of usurers, the operations of high finance. And into all this mass of details he can infuse the spirit of life. Perhaps his masterpiece in realistic description is his account of La Maison Vauquer—a low boarding house, to which he devotes page after page of minute particularity. The result is not a mere dead catalogue: it is a palpitating image of lurid truth. Never was the sordid horror which lurks in places and in things evoked with a more intense completeness.

Undoubtedly it is in descriptions of the sordid, the squalid, the ugly, and the mean that Balzac particularly excels. He is at his greatest when he is revealing the horrible underside of civilisation—the indignities of poverty, the low intrigues of parasites, the long procession of petty agonies that embitter and ruin a life. Over this world of shadow and grime he throws strange lights. Extraordinary silhouettes flash out and vanish; one has glimpses of obscure and ominous movements on every side; and, amid all this, some sudden vision emerges from the darkness, of pathos, of tenderness, of tragic and unutterable pain.—From "Landmarks in French Literature" (1912).

III

By Leslie Stephen

PERHAPS the most striking example of this method is the "Père Goriot." The general situation may be described in two words, by saying that Goriot is the modern King Lear. Mesdames de Restaud and de Nucingen are the representatives of Regan and Goneril; but the Parisian Lear is not allowed the consolation of a Cordelia; the cup of misery is measured out to him drop by drop, and the bitterness of each dose is analysed with chemical accuracy. We watch the poor old broken-down merchant, who has impoverished himself to provide his daughters' dowries, and has gradually stripped himself, first of comfort, and then of the necessaries of life to satisfy the demands of their folly and luxury, as we might watch a man clinging to the edge of a cliff and gradually dropping lower and lower, catching feebly at every point of support till his strength is exhausted, and the inevitable catastrophe follows. The daughters, allowed to retain some fragments of good feeling and not quite irredeemably hateful, are gradually yielding to the demoralising influence of a heartless vanity. They yield, it is true, pretty completely at last; but their wickedness seems to reveal the influence of a vague but omnipotent power of evil in the background. . . .

Hideous as the performance appears when coolly stated, it must be admitted that the ladies have got into such terrible perplexities from tampering with the seventh commandment, that there is some excuse for their breaking the fifth. Whether such an accumulation of horrors is a legitimate process in art, and whether a healthy imagination would like to dwell upon such loathsome social sores, is another question. The comparison suggested with "King Lear" may illustrate the point. In Balzac all the subordinate details which Shakespeare throws in with a very slovenly touch are elaborately drawn and contribute powerfully to the total impression. On the other hand we never reach the lofty poetical heights of the grandest scenes in "King Lear." But the situation of the two heroes offers an instructive contrast. Lear is weak, but is never contemptible; he is the ruin of a gallant old king, is guilty of no degrading compliance, and dies like a man, with his "good biting falchion" still grasped in his feeble hand. To change him into Goriot we must suppose that he had licked the hand which struck him, that he had helped on the adulterous intrigues of Goneril and Regan from sheer weakness, and that all his fury had been directed against Cornwall and Albany for objecting to his daughter's eccentric views of the obligation of the marriage vow. Paternal affection leading a man to the most trying self-sacrifice is a worthy motive for a great drama or romance; but Balzac is so anxious to intensify the emotion, that he makes even paternal affection morally degrading. Everything must be done to heighten the colouring. Our sympathies are to be excited by making the sacrifice as complete, and the emotion which prompts it as overpowering, as possible; until at last the love of children becomes a monomania. Goriot is not only dragged through the mud of Paris, but he grovels in it with a will. In short, Balzac wants that highest power which shows itself in moderation, and commits a fault like that of an orator who emphasises every sentence. With less expenditure of horrors, he would excite our compassion more powerfully. But after all, Goriot is, perhaps, more really affecting even than King Lear.—From "Hours in a Library."

OLD GORIOT

To the great and illustrious Geoffroy Saint-Hilaire,
a token of admiration for his works and genius.
De Balzac.

MME. VAUQUER (*née* de Conflans) is an elderly person, who for the past forty years has kept a lodging-house in the Rue Neuve-Sainte-Geneviève, in the district that lies between the Latin Quarter and the Faubourg Saint-Marcel. Her house (known in the neighborhood as the *Maison Vauquer*) receives men and women, old and young, and no word has ever been breathed against her respectable establishment; but, at the same time, it must be said that as a matter of fact no young woman has been under her roof for thirty years, and that if a young man stays there for any length of time it is a sure sign that his allowance must be of the slenderest. In 1819, however, the time when this drama opens, there was an almost penniless young girl among Mme. Vauquer's boarders.

That word drama has been somewhat discredited of late; it has been overworked and twisted to strange uses in these days of dolorous literature; but it must do service again here, not because this story is dramatic in the restricted sense of the word, but because some tears may perhaps be shed *intra et extra muros* before it is over.

Will anyone without the walls of Paris understand it? It is open to doubt. The only audience who could appreciate the results of close observation, the careful reproduction of minute detail and local color, are dwellers between the heights of Montrouge and Montmartre, in a vale of crumbling stucco watered by streams of black, and a vale of sorrows which are real and of joys too often hollow; but this audience is so accustomed to terrible sensations, that only some unimaginable and well-nigh impossible woe could produce any lasting impression there. Now and again there are tragedies so awful and so grand by reason of the complication of virtues and vices that bring them about, that egoism and selfishness are forced to pause and are moved to pity; but the impression that they receive is like a luscious fruit, soon consumed. Civilization, like the car of Juggernaut, is scarcely stayed perceptibly in its progress by a heart less easy to break than the others that lie in its course; this also is broken, and Civilization continues on her course triumphant. And you, too, will do the like; you who with this book in your white hand will sink back among the cushions of your armchair, and say to yourself, "Perhaps this may amuse me." You will read the story of Old Goriot's secret woes, and, dining thereafter with an unspoiled appetite, will lay the blame of your insensibility upon the writer, and accuse him of exaggeration, of writing romances. Ah! once for all, this drama is neither a fiction nor a romance! *All is true,*—so true, that everyone can discern the elements of the tragedy in his own house, perhaps in his own heart.

The lodging-house is Mme. Vauquer's own property. It is still standing at the lower end of the Rue Neuve-Sainte-Geneviève, just where the road slopes so sharply down to the Rue de l'Arbalète, that wheeled traffic seldom passes that way, because it is so stony and steep. This position is sufficient to account for the silence prevalent in the streets shut in between the dome of the Panthéon and the dome of the Val-de-Grâce, two conspicuous public buildings which give a yellowish tone to the landscape and darken the whole district that lies beneath the shadow of their leaden-hued cupolas.

In that district the pavements are clean and dry, there is neither mud nor water in the gutters, grass grows in the chinks of the walls. The most heedless passer-by feels the depressing influences of a place where the sound of wheels creates a sensation; there is a grim look about the houses, a suggestion of a jail about those high garden walls. A Parisian straying into a suburb apparently composed of lodging-houses and public institutions would see poverty and dullness, old age lying down to die, and joyous youth condemned to drudgery. It is the ugliest quarter of Paris, and, it may be added, the least known. But, before all things, the

Rue Neuve-Sainte-Geneviève is like a bronze frame for a picture for which the mind cannot be too well prepared by the contemplation of sad hues and sober images. Even so, step by step the daylight decreases, and the cicerone's droning voice grows hollower as the traveler descends into the Catacombs. The comparison holds good! Who shall say which is more ghastly, the sight of the bleached skulls or of dried-up human hearts?

The front of the lodging-house is at right angles to the road, and looks out upon a little garden, so that you see the side of the house in section, as it were, from the Rue Neuve-Sainte-Geneviève. Beneath the wall of the house front there lies a channel, a fathom wide, paved with cobble-stones, and beside it runs a graveled walk bordered by geraniums and oleanders and pomegranates set in great blue and white glazed earthenware pots. Access into the graveled walk is afforded by a door, above which the words MAISON VAUQUER may be read, and beneath, in rather smaller letters, "*Lodgings for both sexes, etc.*"

During the day a glimpse into the garden is easily obtained through a wicket to which a bell is attached. On the opposite wall, at the further end of the graveled walk, a green marble arch was painted once upon a time by a local artist, and in this semblance of a shrine a statue representing Cupid is installed; a Parisian Cupid, so blistered and disfigured that he looks like a candidate for one of the adjacent hospitals, and might suggest an allegory to lovers of symbolism. The half-obliterated inscription on the pedestal beneath determines the date of this work of art, for it bears witness to the widespread enthusiasm felt for Voltaire on his return to Paris in 1777—

"Whoe'er thou art, thy master see;
He is, or was, or ought to be."

At night the wicket gate is replaced by a solid door. The little garden is no wider than the front of the house; it is shut in between the wall of the street and the partition wall of the neighboring house. A mantle of ivy conceals the bricks and attracts the eyes of passers-by to an effect which is picturesque in Paris, for each of the walls is covered with trellised vines that yield a scanty dusty crop of fruit, and furnish besides a subject of conversation for Mme. Vauquer and her lodgers; every year the widow trembles for her vintage.

A straight path beneath the walls on either side of the garden leads to a clump of lime-trees at the further end of it; *line*-trees, as Mme. Vauquer persists in calling them, in spite of the fact that she was a de Conflans, and regardless of repeated corrections from her lodgers.

The central space between the walks is filled with artichokes and rows of pyramid fruit-trees, and surrounded by a border of lettuce, pot-herbs, and parsley. Under the lime-trees there are a few green-painted garden seats and a wooden table, and thither, during the dog-days, such of the lodgers as are rich enough to indulge in a cup of coffee come to take their pleasure, though it is hot enough to roast eggs even in the shade.

The house itself is three stories high, without counting the attics under the roof. It is built of rough stone, and covered with the yellowish stucco that gives a mean appearance to almost every house in Paris. There are five windows in each story in the front of the house; all the blinds visible through the small square panes are drawn up awry, so that the lines are all at cross purposes. At the side of the house there are but two windows on each floor, and the lowest of all are adorned with a heavy iron grating.

Behind the house a yard extends for some twenty feet, a space inhabited by a happy family of pigs, poultry, and rabbits; the wood-shed is situated on the further side, and on the wall between the wood-shed and the kitchen window hangs the meat-safe, just above the place where the sink discharges its greasy streams. The cook sweeps all the refuse out through a little door into the Rue Neuve-Sainte-Geneviève, and frequently cleanses the yard with copious supplies of water, under pain of pestilence.

The house might have been built on purpose for its present uses. Access is given by a French window to the first room on the ground floor, a sitting-room which looks out upon the street through the two-barred windows already mentioned. Another door opens out of it into the dining-room, which is separated from the kitchen by the well of the staircase, the steps being constructed partly of wood, partly of tiles, which are colored and beeswaxed. Nothing can be more depressing than the sight of that sitting-room. The furniture is covered with horsehair woven in alternate dull and glossy stripes. There is a round table in the middle, with a purplish-red marble top, on which there stands, by way of ornament, the inevitable white china tea-service, covered with a half-effaced gilt network. The floor is sufficiently uneven, the wainscot rises to elbow height, and the rest of the wall space is decorated with a varnished paper, on which the principal scenes from *Télémaque* are depicted, the various classical personages being colored. The subject between the two windows is the banquet given by Calypso to the son of Ulysses, displayed thereon for the admiration of the boarders, and has furnished jokes these forty years to the young men who show themselves superior to their position by making fun of the dinners to which poverty condemns them. The hearth is always so clean and neat that it is evident that a fire is only kindled there on great occasions; the stone chimney-piece is adorned by a couple of vases filled with faded artificial flowers imprisoned under glass shades, on either side of a bluish marble clock in the very worst taste.

The first room exhales an odor for which there is no name in the language, and which should be called the *odeur de pension*. The damp atmosphere sends a chill through you as you breathe it; it has a stuffy, musty, and rancid quality; it permeates your clothing; after-dinner scents seem to be mingled in it with smells from the kitchen and scullery and the reek of a hospital. It might be possible to describe it if someone should discover a process by which to distill from the atmosphere all the nauseating elements with which it is charged by the catarrhal exhalations of every individual lodger, young or old. Yet, in spite of these stale horrors, the sitting-room is as charming and as delicately perfumed as a boudoir, when compared with the adjoining dining-room.

The paneled walls of that apartment were once painted some color, now a matter of conjecture, for the surface is incrusted with accumulated layers of grimy deposit, which cover it with fantastic outlines. A collection of dim-ribbed glass decanters, metal discs with a satin sheen on them, and piles of blue-edged earthenware plates of Touraine ware cover the sticky surfaces of the sideboards that line the room. In a corner stands a box containing a set of numbered pigeon-holes, in which the lodgers' table napkins, more or less soiled and stained with wine, are kept. Here you see that indestructible furniture never met with elsewhere, which finds its way into lodging-houses much as the wrecks of our civilization drift into hospitals for incurables. You expect in such places as these to find the weather-house whence a Capuchin issues on wet days; you look to find the execrable engravings which spoil your appetite, framed every one in a black varnished frame, with a gilt beading round it; you know the sort of tortoise-shell clock case, inlaid with brass; the green stove, the Argand lamps, covered with oil and dust, have met your eyes before. The oilcloth which covers the long table is so greasy that a waggish *externe* will write his name on the surface, using his thumb nail as a style. The chairs are broken-down invalids; the wretched little hempen mats slip away from under your feet without slipping away for good; and finally, the foot-warmers are miserable wrecks, hingeless, charred, broken away about the holes. It would be impossible to give an idea of the old, rotten, shaky, cranky, worm-eaten, halt, maimed, one-eyed, rickety, and ramshackle condition of the furniture without an exhaustive description, which would delay the progress of the story to an extent that impatient people would not pardon. The red tiles of the floor are full of depressions brought about by scouring and periodical renewings of color. In short, there is no illusory grace left to the poverty that reigns here, it is dire, parsimonious, concentrated, threadbare poverty; as yet it has not sunk into the mire, it is only splashed by it, and though not in rags as yet, its clothing is ready to drop to pieces.

This apartment is in all its glory at seven o'clock in the morning, when Mme. Vauquer's cat appears, announcing the near approach of his mistress, and jumps upon the sideboards to sniff at the milk in the bowls, each protected by a plate, while he purrs his morning greeting to the world. A moment later the widow shows her face; she is tricked out in a net cap attached to a false front set on awry, and shuffles into the room in her slipshod fashion. She is an oldish woman, with a bloated countenance, and a nose like a parrot's beak set in the middle of it; her fat little hands (she is as sleek as a church rat) and her shapeless, slouching figure, are in keeping with the room that reeks of misfortune, where hope is reduced to speculate for the meanest stakes. Mme. Vauquer alone can breathe that tainted air without being disheartened by it. Her face is as fresh as a frosty morning in autumn; there are wrinkles about the eyes that vary in their expression from the set smile of a ballet-dancer to the dark, suspicious scowl of a discounter of bills; in short, she is at once the embodiment and interpretation of her lodging-house, as surely as her lodging-house implies the existence of its mistress. You can no more imagine the one without the other, than you can think of a jail without a turnkey. The unwholesome corpulence of the little woman is produced by the life she leads, just as typhus fever is bred in the tainted air of a hospital. The very knitted woolen petticoat that she wears beneath a skirt made of an old gown, with the wadding protruding through the rents in the material, is a sort of epitome of the sitting-room, the dining-room, and the little garden; it discovers the cook; it foreshadows the lodgers—the picture of the house is completed by the portrait of its mistress.

Mme. Vauquer at the age of fifty is like all women who "have seen a deal of trouble." She has the glassy eyes and innocent air of a trafficker in flesh and blood, who will wax virtuously indignant to obtain a higher price for her services, but who is quite ready to betray a Georges or a Pichegru, if a Georges or a Pichegru were in hiding and still to be betrayed, or for any other expedient that may alleviate her lot. Still, "She is a good woman at bottom," said the lodgers, who believed that the widow was wholly dependent upon the money that they paid her, and sympathized when they heard her cough and groan like one of themselves.

What had M. Vauquer been? The lady was never very explicit on this head. How had she lost her money? "Through trouble," was her answer. He had treated her badly, and left her nothing but her eyes to cry over his cruelty, the house she lived in, and the privilege of pitying nobody, because, she was wont to say, she herself had been through every possible misfortune.

Sylvie, the stout cook, hearing her mistress's shuffling footsteps, hastened to serve the lodgers' breakfasts. Beside those who lived in the house, Mme. Vauquer took boarders who came for their meals; but these *externes* usually only came to dinner, for which they paid thirty francs a month.

At the time when this story begins, the lodging-house contained seven inmates. The best rooms in the house were on the first story, Mme. Vauquer herself occupying the least important, while the rest were let to a Mme. Couture, the widow of a commissary-general in the service of the Republic. With her lived Victorine Taillefer, a schoolgirl, to whom she filled the place of mother. These two ladies paid eighteen hundred francs a year.

The two sets of rooms on the second floor were respectively occupied by an old man named Poiret and a man of forty or thereabouts, the wearer of a black wig and dyed whiskers, who gave out that he was a retired merchant, and was addressed as M. Vautrin. Two of the four rooms on the third floor were also let—one to an elderly spinster, a Mlle. Michonneau, and the other to a retired manufacturer of vermicelli, Italian paste, and starch, who allowed the others to address him as "Old Goriot." The remaining rooms were allotted to various birds of passage, to impecunious students, who, like "Old Goriot" and Mlle. Michonneau, could only muster forty-five francs a month to pay for their board and lodging. Mme. Vauquer had little desire for lodgers of this sort; they ate too much bread, and she only took them in default of better.

At that time one of the rooms was tenanted by a law student, a young man from the neighborhood of Angoulême, one of a large family who pinched and starved themselves to spare twelve hundred francs a year for him. Misfortune had accustomed Eugène de Rastignac, for that was his name, to work. He belonged to the number of young men who know as children that their parents' hopes are centered on them, and deliberately prepare themselves for a great career, subordinating their studies from the first to this end, carefully watching the indications of the course of events, calculating the probable turn that affairs will take, that they may be the first to profit by them. But for his observant curiosity, and the skill with which he managed to introduce himself into the salons of Paris, this story would not have been colored by the tones of truth which it certainly owes to him, for they are entirely due to his penetrating sagacity and desire to fathom the mysteries of an appalling condition of things, which was concealed as carefully by the victim as by those who had brought it to pass.

Above the third story there was a garret where the linen was hung to dry, and a couple of attics. Christophe, the man-of-all-work, slept in one, and Sylvie, the stout cook, in the other. Beside the seven inmates thus enumerated, taking one year with another, some eight law or medical students dined in the house, as well as two or three regular comers who lived in the neighborhood. There were usually eighteen people at dinner, and there was room, if need be, for twenty at Mme. Vauquer's table; at breakfast, however, only the seven lodgers appeared. It was almost like a family party. Everyone came down in dressing-gown and slippers, and the conversation usually turned on anything that had happened the evening before; comments on the dress or appearance of the dinner contingent were exchanged in friendly confidence.

The seven lodgers were Mme. Vauquer's spoiled children. Among them she distributed, with astronomical precision, the exact proportion of respect and attention due to the varying amounts they paid for their board. One single consideration influenced all these human beings thrown together by chance. The two second-floor lodgers only paid seventy-two francs a month. Such prices as these are confined to the Faubourg Saint-Marcel and the district between La Bourbe and the Salpêtrière; and, as might be expected, poverty, more or less apparent, weighed upon them all, Mme. Couture being the sole exception to the rule.

The dreary surroundings were reflected in the costumes of the inmates of the house; all were alike threadbare. The color of the men's coats was problematical; such shoes, in more fashionable quarters, are only to be seen lying in the gutter; the cuffs and collars were worn and frayed at the edges; every limp article of clothing looked like the ghost of its former self. The women's dresses were faded, old-fashioned, dyed and re-dyed; they wore gloves that were glazed with hard wear, much-mended lace, dingy ruffles, crumpled muslin fichus. So much for their clothing; but, for the most part, their frames were solid enough; their constitutions had weathered the storms of life; their cold, hard faces were worn like coins that have been withdrawn from circulation, but there were greedy teeth behind the withered lips. Dramas brought to a close or still in progress are foreshadowed by the sight of such actors as these, not the dramas that are played before the footlights and against a background of painted canvas, but dumb dramas of life, frost-bound dramas that sear hearts like fire, dramas that do not end with the actors' lives.

Mlle. Michonneau, that elderly young lady, screened her weak eyes from the daylight by a soiled green silk shade with a rim of brass, an object fit to scare away the Angel of Pity himself. Her shawl, with its scanty, draggled fringe, might have covered a skeleton, so meager and angular was the form beneath it. Yet she must have been pretty and shapely once. What corrosive had destroyed the feminine outlines? Was it trouble, or vice, or greed? Had she loved too well? Had she been a second-hand clothes dealer, a frequenter of the backstairs of great houses, or had she been merely a courtesan? Was she expiating the flaunting triumphs of a youth overcrowded with pleasures by an old age in which she was shunned by every passer-by? Her vacant gaze sent a chill through you; her shriveled face seemed like a menace. Her voice was like the shrill, thin note of the grasshopper sounding from the thicket when winter is at hand. She said that she had nursed an old gentleman, ill of catarrh of the bladder, and left to die by his children, who thought that he had nothing left. His bequest to her, a life annuity of a thousand francs, was periodically disputed by his heirs, who mingled slander with their persecutions. In spite of the ravages of conflicting passions, her face retained some traces of its former fairness and fineness of tissue, some vestiges of the physical charms of her youth still survived.

M. Poiret was a sort of automaton. He might be seen any day sailing like a gray shadow along the walks of the Jardin des Plantes, on his head a shabby cap, a cane with an old yellow ivory handle in the tips of his thin fingers; the outspread skirts of his threadbare overcoat failed to conceal his meager figure; his breeches hung loosely on his shrunken limbs; the thin, blue-stockinged legs trembled like those of a drunken man; there was a notable breach of continuity between the dingy white waistcoat and crumpled shirt frills and the cravat twisted about a throat like a turkey gobbler's; altogether, his appearance set people wondering whether this outlandish ghost belonged to the audacious race of the sons of Japhet who flutter about on the Boulevard Italien. What kind of toil could have so shriveled him? What devouring passions had darkened that bulbous countenance, which would have seemed outrageous as a caricature? What had he been? Well, perhaps he had been part of the machinery of justice, a clerk in the office to which the executioner sends in his accounts,—so much for providing black veils for parricides, so much for sawdust, so much for pulleys and cord for the knife. Or he might have been a receiver at the door of a public slaughter-house, or a sub-inspector of nuisances. Indeed, the man appeared to have been one of the beasts of burden in our great social mill; one of those Parisian Ratons whom their Bertrands do not even know by sight; a pivot in the obscure machinery that disposes of misery and things unclean; one of those men, in short, at sight of whom we are prompted to remark that, "After all, we cannot do without them."

Stately Paris ignores the existence of these faces bleached by moral or physical suffering; but, then, Paris is in truth an ocean that no line can plumb. You may survey its surface and describe it; but no matter what pains you take with your investigations and recognizances, no matter how numerous and painstaking the toilers in this sea, there will always be lonely and unexplored regions in its depths, caverns unknown, flowers and pearls and monsters of the deep overlooked or forgotten by the divers of literature. The Maison Vauquer is one of these curious monstrosities.

Two, however, of Mme. Vauquer's boarders formed a striking contrast to the rest. There was a sickly pallor, such as is often seen in anæmic girls, in Mlle. Victorine Taillefer's face; and her unvarying expression of sadness, like her embarrassed manner and pinched look, was in keeping with the general wretchedness of the establishment in the Rue Neuve-Sainte-Geneviève, which forms a background to this picture; but her face was young, there was youthfulness in her voice and elasticity in her movements. This young misfortune was not unlike a shrub, newly planted in an uncongenial soil, where its leaves have already begun to wither. The outlines of her figure, revealed by her dress of the simplest and cheapest materials, were also youthful. There was the same kind of charm about her too slender form, her faintly colored face and light-brown hair, that modern poets find in mediæval statuettes; and a sweet expression, a look of Christian resignation in the dark gray eyes. She was pretty by force of contrast; if she had been happy, she would have been charming. Happiness is the poetry of woman, as the toilet is her tinsel. If the delightful excitement of a ball had made the pale face glow with color; if the delights of a luxurious life had brought the color to the wan cheeks that were slightly hollowed already, if love had put light into her sad eyes, then Victorine might have ranked among the fairest; but she lacked the two things which create woman a second time—pretty dresses and love-letters.

A book might have been made of her story. Her father was persuaded that he had sufficient reason for declining to acknowledge her, and allowed her a bare six hundred francs a year; he had further taken measures to disinherit his daughter, and had converted all his real estate into personalty, that he might leave it undivided to his son. Victorine's mother had died broken-hearted in Mme. Couture's house; and the latter, who was a near relation, had taken charge of the little orphan. Unluckily, the widow of the commissary-general to the armies of the Republic had nothing in the world but her jointure and her widow's pension, and some day she might be obliged to leave the helpless, inexperienced girl to the mercy of the world. The good soul, therefore, took Victorine to Mass every Sunday, and to confession once a fortnight, thinking that, in any case, she would bring up her ward to be devout. She was right; religion offered a solution of the problem of the young girl's future. The poor child loved the father who refused to acknowledge her.

Once every year she tried to see him to deliver her mother's message of forgiveness, but every year hitherto she had knocked at that door in vain; her father was inexorable. Her brother, her only means of communication, had not come to see her for four years, and had sent her no assistance; yet she prayed to God to unseal her father's eyes and to soften her brother's heart, and no accusations mingled with her prayers. Mme. Couture and Mme. Vauquer exhausted the vocabulary of abuse, and failed to find words that did justice to the banker's iniquitous conduct; but while they heaped execrations on the millionaire, Victorine's words were as gentle as the moan of the wounded dove, and affection found expression even in the cry drawn from her by pain.

Eugène de Rastignac was a thoroughly southern type; he had a fair complexion, blue eyes, black hair. In his figure, manner, and his whole bearing it was easy to see that he either came of a noble family, or that, from his earliest childhood, he had been gently bred. If he was careful of his wardrobe, only taking last year's clothes into daily wear, still upon occasion he could issue forth as a young man of fashion. Ordinarily he wore a shabby coat and waistcoat, the limp black cravat, untidily knotted, that students affect, trousers that matched the rest of his costume, and boots that had been re-soled.

Vautrin (the man of forty with the dyed whiskers) marked a transition stage between these two young people and the others. He was the kind of man that calls forth the remark: "He looks a jovial sort!" He had broad shoulders, a well-developed chest, muscular arms, and strong square-fisted hands; the joints of his fingers were covered with tufts of fiery red hair. His face was furrowed by premature wrinkles; there was a certain hardness about it in spite of his bland and insinuating manner. His bass voice was by no means unpleasant, and was in keeping with his boisterous laughter. He was always obliging, always in good spirits; if anything went wrong with one of the locks, he would soon unscrew it, take it to pieces, file it, oil and clean and set it in order, and put it back in its place again: "I am an old hand at it," he used to say. Not only so, he knew all about ships, the sea, France, foreign countries, men, business, law, great houses, and prisons,—there was nothing that he did not know. If anyone complained rather more than usual he would offer his services at once. He had several times lent money to Mme. Vauquer, or to the boarders; but, somehow, those whom he obliged felt that they would sooner face death than fail to repay him; a certain resolute look, sometimes seen on his face, inspired fear of him, for all his appearance of easy good-nature. In the way he spat there was an imperturbable coolness which seemed to indicate that this was a man who would not stick at a crime to extricate himself from a false position. His eyes, like those of a pitiless judge, seemed to go to the very bottom of all questions, to read all natures, all feelings, and thoughts. His habit of life was very regular; he usually went out after breakfast, returning in time for dinner, and disappeared for the rest of the evening, letting himself in about midnight with a latch key, a privilege that Mme. Vauquer accorded to no other boarder. But then he was on very good terms with the widow; he used to call her "mamma," and put his arm round her waist, a piece of flattery perhaps not appreciated to the full! The worthy woman might imagine this to be an easy feat; but, as a matter of fact, no arm but Vautrin's was long enough to encircle her.

It was a characteristic trait of his generously to pay fifteen francs a month for the cup of coffee with a dash of brandy in it, which he took after dinner. Less superficial observers than young men engulfed by the whirlpool of Parisian life, or old men, who took no interest in anything that did not directly concern them, would not have stopped short at the vaguely unsatisfactory impression that Vautrin made upon them. He knew or guessed the concerns of everyone about him; but none of them had been able to penetrate his thoughts, or to discover his occupation. He had deliberately made his apparent good-nature, his unfailing readiness to oblige, and his high spirits into a barrier between himself and the rest of them, but not seldom he gave glimpses of appalling depths of character. He seemed to delight in scourging the upper classes of society with the lash of his tongue, to take pleasure in convicting it of inconsistency, in mocking at law and order with some grim jest worthy of Juvenal, as if some grudge against the social system rankled in him, as if there were some mystery carefully hidden away in his life.

Mlle. Taillefer felt attracted, perhaps unconsciously, by the strength of the one man, and the good looks of the other; her stolen glances and secret thoughts were divided between them; but neither of them seemed to take any notice of her, although some day a chance might alter her position, and she would be a wealthy heiress. For that matter, there was not a soul in the house who took any trouble to investigate the various chronicles of misfortunes, real or imaginary, related by the rest. Each one regarded the others with indifference, tempered by suspicion; it was a natural result of their relative positions. Practical assistance not one of them could give, this they all knew, and they had long since exhausted their stock of condolence over previous discussions of their grievances. They were in something the same position as an elderly couple who have nothing left to say to each other. The routine of existence kept them in contact, but they were parts of a mechanism which wanted oil. There was not one of them but would have passed a blind man begging in the street, not one that felt moved to pity by a tale of misfortune, not one who did not see in death the solution of the all-absorbing problem of misery which left them cold to the most terrible anguish in others.

The happiest of these hapless beings was certainly Mme. Vauquer, who reigned supreme over this hospital supported by voluntary contributions. For her, the little garden, which silence, and cold, and rain, and drought combined to make as dreary as an Asian *steppe,* was a pleasant shaded nook; the gaunt yellow house, the musty odors of a back shop had charms for her, and for her alone. Those cells belonged to her. She fed those convicts condemned to penal servitude for life, and her authority was recognized among them. Where else in Paris would they have found wholesome food in sufficient quantity at the prices she charged them, and rooms which they were at liberty to make, if not exactly elegant or comfortable, at any rate clean and healthy? If she had committed some flagrant act of injustice, the victim would have borne it in silence.

Such a gathering contained, as might have been expected, the elements out of which a complete society might be constructed. And, as in a school, as in the world itself, there was among the eighteen men and women who met round the dinner table a poor creature, despised by all the others, condemned to be the butt of all their jokes. At the beginning of Eugène de Rastignac's second twelvemonth, this figure suddenly started out into bold relief against the background of human forms and faces among which the law student was yet to live for another two years to come. This laughing-stock was the retired vermicelli-merchant, old Goriot, upon whose face a painter, like the historian, would have concentrated all the light in his picture.

How had it come about that the boarders regarded him with a half-malignant contempt? Why did they subject the oldest among their number to a kind of persecution, in which there was mingled some pity, but no respect for his misfortunes? Had he brought it upon himself by some eccentricity or absurdity, which is less easily forgiven or forgotten than more serious defects? The question strikes at the root of many a social injustice. Perhaps it is only human nature to inflict suffering on anything that will endure suffering, whether by reason of its genuine humility, or indifference, or sheer helplessness. Do we not, one and all, like to feel our strength even at the expense of someone or of something? The poorest sample of humanity, the street arab, will pull the bell handle at every street door in bitter weather, and scramble up to write his name on the unsullied marble of a monument.

In the year 1813, at the age of sixty-nine or thereabouts, "Old Goriot" had sold his business and retired—to Mme. Vauquer's boarding-house. When he first came there he had taken the rooms now occupied by Mme. Couture; he had paid twelve hundred francs a year like a man to whom five louis more or less was a mere trifle. For him Mme Vauquer had made various improvements in the three rooms destined for his use, in consideration of a certain sum paid in advance, so it was said, for the miserable furniture, that is to say, for some yellow cotton curtains, a few chairs of stained wood covered with Utrecht velvet, several wretched colored prints in frames, and wall papers that a little suburban tavern would have disdained. Possibly it was the careless generosity with which old Goriot allowed himself to be overreached at this period of his life (they called him Monsieur Goriot very respectfully then) that gave Mme. Vauquer the meanest opinion of his business abilities; she looked on him as an imbecile where money was concerned.

Goriot had brought with him a considerable wardrobe, the gorgeous outfit of a retired tradesman who denies himself nothing. Mme. Vauquer's astonished eyes beheld no less than eighteen cambric-fronted shirts, the splendor of their fineness being enhanced by a pair of pins each bearing a large diamond, and connected by a short chain, an ornament which adorned the vermicelli maker's shirt front. He usually wore a coat of corn-flower blue; his rotund and portly person was still further set off by a clean white waistcoat, and a gold chain and seals which dangled over that broad expanse. When his hostess accused him of being "a bit of a beau," he smiled with the vanity of a citizen whose foible is gratified. His cupboards (*ormoires,* as he called them in the popular dialect) were filled with a quantity of plate that he brought with him.

The widow's eyes gleamed as she obligingly helped him to unpack the soup ladles, tablespoons, forks, cruet-stands, tureens, dishes, and breakfast services—all of silver, which were duly arranged upon the shelves, besides a few more or less handsome pieces of plate, all weighing no inconsiderable number of ounces; he could not bring himself to part with these gifts that reminded him of past domestic festivals.

"This was my wife's present to me on the first anniversary of our wedding day," he said to Mme. Vauquer, as he put away a little silver posset dish, with two turtle-doves billing on the cover. "Poor dear! she spent on it all the money she had saved before we married. Do you know, I would sooner scratch the earth with my nails for a living, madame, than part with that. But I shall be able to take my coffee out of it every morning for the rest of my days, thank the Lord! I am not to be pitied. There's not much fear of my starving for some time to come."

Finally, Mme. Vauquer's magpie's eye had discovered and read certain entries in the list of shareholders in the Funds, and, after a rough calculation, was disposed to credit Goriot (worthy man) with something like ten thousand francs a year. From that day forward Mme. Vauquer (*née* de Conflans), who, as a matter of fact, had seen forty-eight summers, though she would only own to thirty-nine of them—Mme. Vauquer had her own ideas. Though Goriot's eyes seemed to have shrunk in their sockets, though they were weak and watery, owing to some glandular affection which compelled him to wipe them continually, she considered him to be a very gentlemanly and pleasant-looking man. Moreover, the widow saw favorable indications of character in the well-developed calves of his legs and in his square-shaped nose, indications still further borne out by the worthy man's full-moon countenance and look of stupid good-nature. This, in all probability, was a strongly-built animal, whose brains mostly consisted in a capacity for affection. His hair, worn in *ailes de pigeon,* and duly powdered every morning by the barber from the École Polytechnique, described five points on his low forehead, and made an elegant setting to his face. Though his manners were somewhat boorish, he was always as neat as a new pin, and he took his snuff in a lordly way. like a man who knows that his snuff-box is always likely to be filled with maccaboy; so that when Mme. Vauquer lay down to rest on the day of M. Goriot's installation, her heart, like a larded partridge, sweltered before the fire of a burning desire to shake off the shroud of Vauquer and rise again as Goriot. She would marry again, sell her boarding-house, give her hand to this fine flower of citizenship, become a lady of consequence in the quarter, and ask for subscriptions for charitable purposes; she would make little Sunday excursions to Choisy, Soisy, Gentilly; she would have a box at the theater when she liked, instead of waiting for the author's tickets that one of her boarders sometimes gave her, in July; the whole Eldorado of a little Parisian household rose up before Mme. Vauquer in her dreams. Nobody knew that she herself possessed forty thousand francs, accumulated *sou* by *sou,* that was her secret; surely as far as money was concerned she was a very tolerable match. "And in other respects, I am quite his equal," she said to herself, turning as if to assure herself of the charms of a form that the portly Sylvie found molded in down feathers every morning.

For three months from that day Mme. Veuve Vauquer availed herself of the services of M. Goriot's coiffeur, and went to some expense over her toilet, expense justifiable on the ground that she owed it to herself and her establishment to pay some attention to appearances when such highly-respectable persons honored her house with their presence. She expended no small amount of ingenuity in a sort of weeding process of her lodgers, announcing her intention of receiving henceforward none but people who were in every way select. If a stranger presented himself, she let him know that M. Goriot, one of the best known and most highly respected merchants in Paris, had singled out her boarding-house for a residence. She drew up a prospectus headed MAISON VAUQUER, in which it was asserted that hers was *"one of the oldest and most highly recommended boarding-houses in the Latin Quarter."* "From the windows of the house," thus ran the prospectus, "there is a charming view of the Vallée des Gobelins [so there is—from the third floor], and a *beautiful* garden, *extending* down to *an avenue of lindens* at the further end." Mention was made of the bracing air of the place and its quiet situation.

It was this prospectus that attracted Mme. la Comtesse de l'Ambermesnil, a widow of six-and-thirty, who was awaiting the final settlement of her husband's affairs, and of another matter regarding a pension due to her as the wife of a general who had died "on the field of battle." On this Mme. Vauquer saw to her table, lighted a fire daily in the sitting-room for nearly six months, and kept the promise of her prospectus, even going to some expense to do so. And the Countess, on her side, addressed Mme. Vauquer as "my dear," and promised her two more boarders, the Baronne de Vaumerland and the widow of a colonel, the late Comte de Picquoisie, who were about to leave a boarding-house in the Marais, where the terms were higher than at the Maison Vauquer. Both these ladies, moreover, would be very well to do when the people at the War Office had come to an end of their formalities. "But Government departments are always so dilatory," the lady added.

After dinner the two widows went together up to Mme. Vauquer's room, and had a snug little chat over some cordial and various delicacies reserved for the mistress of the house. Mme. Vauquer's ideas as to Goriot were cordially approved by Mme. de l'Ambermesnil; it was a capital notion, which for that matter she had guessed from the very first; in her opinion the vermicelli maker was an excellent man.

"Ah! my dear lady, such a well-preserved man of his age, as sound as my eyesight—a man who might make a woman happy!" said the widow.

The good-natured Countess turned to the subject of Mme. Vauquer's dress, which was not in harmony with her projects. "You must put yourself on a war footing," said she.

After much serious consideration the two widows went shopping together—they purchased a hat adorned with ostrich feathers and a cap at the Palais Royal, and the Countess took her friend to the Magasin de la Petite Jeannette, where they chose a dress and a scarf. Thus equipped for the campaign, the widow looked exactly like the prize animal hung out for a sign above an à la mode beef shop; but she herself was so much pleased with the improvement, as she considered it, in her appearance, that she felt she lay under some obligation to the Countess; and, though by no means open-handed, she begged that lady to accept a hat that cost twenty francs. The fact was that she needed the Countess's services on the delicate mission of sounding Goriot; the Countess must sing her praises in his ears. Mme. de l'Ambermesnil lent herself very good-naturedly to this maneuver, began her operations, and succeeded in obtaining a private interview; but the overtures that she made, with a view to securing him for herself, were received with embarrassment, not to say a repulse. She left him, revolted by his coarseness.

"My angel," said she to her dear friend, "you will make nothing of that man yonder. He is absurdly suspicious, and he is a mean curmudgeon, an idiot, a fool; you would never be happy with him."

After what had passed between M. Goriot and Mme. de l'Ambermesnil, the Countess would no longer live under the same roof. She left the next day, forgot to pay for six months' board, and left behind her her wardrobe, cast-off clothing to the value of five francs. Eagerly and persistently as Mme. Vauquer sought her quondam lodger, the Comtesse de l'Ambermesnil was never heard of again in Paris. The widow often talked of this deplorable business, and regretted her own too confiding disposition. As a matter of fact, she was as suspicious as a cat; but she was like many other people, who cannot trust their own kin and put themselves at the mercy of the next chance comer—an odd but common phenomenon, whose causes may readily be traced to the depths of the human heart.

Perhaps there are people who know that they have nothing more to look for from those with whom they live; they have shown the emptiness of their hearts to their housemates, and in their secret selves they are conscious that they are severely judged, and that they deserve to be judged severely; but still they feel an unconquerable craving for praises that they do not hear, or they are consumed by a desire to appear to possess, in the eyes of a new audience, the qualities which they have not, hoping to win the admiration or affection of strangers at the risk of forfeiting it again some day. Or, once more, there are other mercenary natures who never do a kindness to a friend or a relation simply because these have a claim upon them, while a service done to a stranger brings its reward to self-love. Such natures feel but little affection for those who are nearest to them; they keep their kindness for remoter circles of acquaintance, and show most to those who dwell on its utmost limits. Mme. Vauquer belonged to both these essentially mean, false, and execrable classes.

"If I had been here at the time," Vautrin would say at the end of the story, "I would have shown her up, and that misfortune would not have befallen you. I know that kind of phiz!"

Like all narrow natures, Mme. Vauquer was wont to confine her attention to events, and did not go very deeply into the causes that brought them about; she likewise preferred to throw the blame of her own mistakes on other people, so she chose to consider that the honest vermicelli maker was responsible for her misfortune. It had opened her eyes, so she said, with regard to him. As soon as she saw that her blandishments were in vain, and that her outlay on her toilet was money thrown away, she was not slow to discover the reason of his indifference. It became plain to her at once that there was *some other attraction,* to use her own expression. In short, it was evident that the hope she had so fondly cherished was a baseless delusion, and that she would "never make anything out of that man yonder," in the Countess's forcible phrase. The Countess seemed to have been a judge of character. Mme. Vauquer's aversion was naturally more energetic than her friendship, for her hatred was not in proportion to her love, but to her disappointed expectations. The human heart may find here and there a resting-place short of the highest height of affection, but we seldom stop in the steep, downward slope of hatred. Still, M. Goriot was a lodger, and the widow's wounded self-love could not vent itself in an explosion of wrath; like a monk harassed by the prior of his convent, she was forced to stifle her sighs of disappointment, and to gulp down her craving for revenge. Little minds find gratification for their feelings, benevolent or otherwise, by a constant exercise of petty ingenuity. The widow employed her woman's malice to devise a system of covert persecution. She began by a course of retrenchment—various luxuries which had found their way to the table appeared there no more.

"No more gherkins, no more anchovies; they have made a fool of me!" she said to Sylvie one morning, and they returned to the old bill of fare.

The thrifty frugality necessary to those who mean to make their way in the world had become an inveterate habit of life with M. Goriot. Soup, boiled beef, and a dish of vegetables had been, and always would be, the dinner he liked best, so Mme. Vauquer found it very difficult to annoy a boarder whose tastes were so simple. He was proof against her malice, and in desperation she spoke to him and of him slightingly before the other lodgers, who began to amuse themselves at his expense, and so gratified her desire for revenge.

Towards the end of the first year the widow's suspicions had reached such a pitch that she began to wonder how it was that a retired merchant with a secure income of seven or eight thousand livres, the owner of such magnificent plate and jewelry handsome enough for a kept mistress, should be living in her house. Why should he devote so small a proportion of his money to his expenses? Until the first year was nearly at an end, Goriot had dined out once or twice every week, but these occasions came less frequently, and at last he was scarcely absent from the dinner table twice a month. It was hardly to be expected that Mme. Vauquer should regard the increased regularity of her boarder's habits with complacency, when those little excursions of his had been so much to her interest. She attributed the change not so much to a gradual diminution of fortune as to a spiteful wish to annoy his hostess. It is one of the most detestable habits of a Liliputian mind to credit other people with its own malignant pettiness.

Unluckily, towards the end of the second year, M. Goriot's conduct gave some color to the idle talk about him. He asked Mme. Vauquer to give him a room on the second floor, and to make a corresponding reduction in her charges. Apparently, such a strict economy was called for, that he did without a fire all through the winter. Mme. Vauquer asked to be paid in advance, an arrangement to which M. Goriot consented, and thenceforward she spoke of him as "old Goriot."

What had brought about this decline and fall? Conjecture was keen, but investigation was difficult. Old Goriot was not communicative; in the sham countess's phrase, he was "a curmudgeon." Empty-headed people who babble about their own affairs because they have nothing else to occupy them, naturally conclude that if people say nothing of their doings it is because their doings will not bear being talked about; so the highly respectable merchant became a scoundrel, and the late beau was an old rogue. Opinion fluctuated. Sometimes, according to Vautrin, who came about this time to live in the Maison Vauquer, old Goriot was a man who went on 'Change and *dabbled* (to use the sufficiently expressive language of the Stock Exchange) in stocks and shares after he had ruined himself by heavy speculation. Sometimes it was held that he was one of those petty gamblers who nightly play for small stakes until they win a few francs. A theory that he was a detective in the employ of the Home Office found favor at one time, but Vautrin urged that "Goriot was not sharp enough for one of that sort." There were yet other solutions; old Goriot was a skinflint, a shark of a money-lender, a man who lived by selling lottery tickets. He was by turns all the most mysterious brood of vice and shame and misery; yet, however vile his life might be, the feeling of repulsion which he aroused in others was not so strong that he must be banished from their society—he paid his way. Besides, Goriot had his uses, everyone vented his spleen or sharpened his wit on him; he was pelted with jokes and belabored with hard words. The general consensus of opinion was in favor of a theory which seemed the most likely; this was Mme. Vauquer's view. According to her, the man so well preserved at his time of life, as sound as her eyesight, with whom a woman might be very happy, was a libertine who had strange tastes. These are the facts upon which Mme. Vauquer's slanders were based.

Early one morning, some few months after the departure of the unlucky Countess who had managed to live for six months at the widow's expense, Mme. Vauquer (not yet dressed) heard the rustle of a silk dress and a young woman's light footstep on the stair; someone was going to Goriot's room. He seemed to expect the visit, for his door stood ajar. The portly Sylvie presently came up to tell her mistress that a girl too pretty to be honest, "dressed like a goddess," and not a speck of mud on her laced cashmere boots, had glided in from the street like a snake, had found the kitchen, and asked for M. Goriot's room. Mme. Vauquer and the cook listening, overheard several words affectionately spoken during the visit, which lasted for some time. When M. Goriot went downstairs with the lady, the stout Sylvie forthwith took her basket and followed the lover-like couple, under pretext of going to do her marketing.

"M. Goriot must be awfully rich, all the same, Madame," she reported on her return, "to keep her in such style. Just imagine it! There was a splendid carriage waiting at the corner of the Place de l'Estrapade, and *she* got into it.'"

While they were at dinner that evening, Mme. Vauquer went to the window and drew the curtain, as the sun was shining into Goriot's eyes.

"You are beloved of fair ladies, M. Goriot—the sun seeks you out," she said, alluding to his visitor. *"Peste!* you have good taste; she was very pretty."

"That was my daughter," he said, with a kind of pride in his voice, and the rest chose to consider this as the fatuity of an old man who wishes to save appearances.

A month after this visit M. Goriot received another. The same daughter who had come to see him that morning came again after dinner, this time in evening dress. The boarders, in deep discussion in the dining-room, caught a glimpse of a lovely, fair-haired woman, slender, graceful, and much too distinguished-looking to be a daughter of old Goriot's.

"Two of them!" cried the portly Sylvie, who did not recognize the lady of the first visit.

A few days later, and another young lady—a tall, well-molded brunette, with dark hair and bright eyes—came to ask for M. Goriot.

"Three of them!" said Sylvie.

Then the second daughter, who had first come in the morning to see her father, came shortly afterwards in the evening. She wore a ball dress, and came in a carriage.

"Four of them!" commented Mme. Vauquer and her plump handmaid. Sylvie saw not a trace of resemblance between this great lady and the girl in her simple morning dress who had entered her kitchen on the occasion of her first visit.

At that time Goriot was paying twelve hundred francs a year to his landlady, and Mme. Vauquer saw nothing out of the common in the fact that a rich man had four or five mistresses; nay, she thought it very knowing of him to pass them off as his daughters. She was not at all inclined to draw a hard-and-fast line, or to take umbrage at his sending for them to the Maison Vauquer; yet, inasmuch as these visits explained her boarder's indifference to her, she went so far (at the end of the second year) as to speak of him as an "ugly old wretch." When at length her boarder declined to nine hundred francs a year, she asked him very insolently what he took her house to be, after meeting one of these ladies on the stairs. Old Goriot answered that the lady was his eldest daughter.

"So you have two or three dozen daughters, have you?" said Mme. Vauquer sharply.

"I have only two," her boarder answered meekly, like a ruined man who is broken in to all the cruel usage of misfortune.

Towards the end of the third year old Goriot reduced his expenses still further; he went up to the third story, and now paid forty-five francs a month. He did without snuff, told his hair-dresser that he no longer required his services, and gave up wearing powder. When Goriot appeared for the first time in this condition, an exclamation of astonishment broke from his hostess at the color of his hair—a dingy olive gray. He had grown sadder day by day under the influence of some hidden trouble; among all the faces round the table, his was the most woe-begone. There was no longer any doubt. Goriot was an elderly libertine, whose eyes had only been preserved by the skill of the physician from the malign influence of the remedies necessitated by the state of his health. The disgusting color of his hair was a result of his excesses and of the drugs which he had taken that he might continue his career. The poor old man's mental and physical condition afforded some grounds for the absurd rubbish talked about him. When his outfit was worn out, he replaced the fine linen by calico at fourteen *sous* the ell. His diamonds, his gold snuff-box, watch chain and trinkets, disappeared one by one. He had left off wearing the cornflower blue coat, and was sumptuously arrayed, summer as winter, in a coarse chestnut-brown coat, a plush waistcoat, and doeskin breeches. He grew thinner and thinner; his legs were shrunken, his cheeks, once so puffed out by contented bourgeois prosperity, were covered with wrinkles, and the outlines of the jawbones were distinctly visible; there were deep furrows in his forehead. In the fourth year of his residence in the Rue Neuve-Sainte-Geneviève he was no longer like his former self. The hale vermicelli manufacturer, sixty-two years of age, who had looked scarce forty, the stout, comfortable, prosperous tradesman, with an almost bucolic air, and such a brisk demeanor that it did you good to look at him; the man with something boyish in his smile, had suddenly sunk into his dotage, and had become a feeble, vacillating septuagenarian.

The keen, bright blue eyes had grown dull, and faded to a steel-gray color; the red inflamed rims looked as though they had shed tears of blood. He excited feelings of repulsion in some, and of pity in others. The young medical students who came to the house noticed the drooping of his lower lip and the conformation of the facial angle; and, after teasing him for some time to no purpose, they declared that crétinism was setting in.

One evening after dinner Mme. Vauquer said half banteringly to him, "So those daughters of yours don't come to see you any more, eh?" meaning to imply her doubts as to his paternity; but old Goriot shrank as if his hostess had touched him with a sword point.

"They come sometimes," he said in a tremulous voice.

"Aha! you still see them sometimes?" cried the students. "Bravo, Father Goriot!"

The old man scarcely seemed to hear the witticisms at his expense that followed on the words; he had relapsed into the dreamy state of mind that these superficial observers took for senile torpor, due to his lack of intelligence. If they had only known, they might have been deeply interested by the problem of his condition; but few problems were more obscure. It was easy, of course, to find out whether Goriot had really been a vermicelli manufacturer; the amount of his fortune was readily discoverable; but the old people, who were most inquisitive as to his concerns, never went beyond the limits of the Quarter, and lived in the lodging-house much as oysters cling to a rock. As for the rest, the current of life in Paris daily awaited them, and swept them away with it; so soon as they left the Rue Neuve-Sainte-Geneviève, they forgot the existence of the old man, their butt at dinner. For those narrow souls, or for careless youth, the misery in old Goriot's withered face and its dull apathy were quite incompatible with wealth or any sort of intelligence. As for the creatures whom he called his daughters, all Mme. Vauquer's boarders were of her opinion. With the faculty for severe logic sedulously cultivated by elderly women during long evenings of gossip till they can always find a hypothesis to fit all circumstances, she was wont to reason thus—

"If old Goriot had daughters of his own as rich as those ladies who came here seemed to be, he would not be lodging in my house, on the third floor, at forty-five francs a month; and he would not go about dressed like a poor man."

No objection could be raised to these inferences. So by the end of the month of November 1819, at the time when the curtain rises on this drama, everyone in the house had come to have a very decided opinion as to the poor old man. He had never had either wife or daughter; excesses had reduced him to this sluggish condition; he was a sort of human mollusk who should be classed among the cap*ulidæ*, so said one of the dinner contingent, an employé at the Muséum, who had a pretty wit of his own. Poiret was an eagle, a gentleman, compared with Goriot. Poiret would join the talk, argue, answer when he was spoken to; as a matter of fact, his talk, arguments, and responses contributed nothing to the conversation, for Poiret had a habit of repeating what the others said in different words; still, he did join in the talk; he was alive, and seemed capable of feeling; while old Goriot (to quote the Muséum official again) was invariably at zero—Réaumur.

Eugène de Rastignac had just returned to Paris in a state of mind not unknown to young men who are conscious of unusual powers, and to those whose faculties are so stimulated by a different position, that for the time being they rise above the ordinary level.

Rastignac's first year of study for the preliminary examinations in law had left him free to see the sights of Paris and to enjoy some of its amusements. A student has not much time on his hands if he sets himself to learn the repertory of every theater, and to study the ins and outs of the labyrinth of Paris. To know its customs; to learn the language, and become familiar with the amusements of the capital, he must explore its recesses, good and bad, follow the studies that please him best, and form some idea of the treasures contained in galleries and museums.

At this stage of his career a student grows eager and excited about all sort of follies that seem to him to be of immense importance. He has his hero, his great man, a professor at the Collège de France, paid to talk down to the level of his audience. He adjusts his cravat, and strikes various attitudes for the benefit of the women in the first galleries at the Opéra-Comique. As he passes through all these successive initiations, and breaks out of his sheath, the horizons of life widen around him, and at length he grasps the plan of society with the different human strata of which it is composed.

If he begins by admiring the procession of carriages on sunny afternoons in the Champs-Elysées, he soon reaches the further stage of envying their owners. Unconsciously, Eugène had served his apprenticeship before he went back to Angoulême for the long vacation after taking his degrees as bachelor of arts and bachelor of law. The illusions of childhood had vanished, so also had the ideas he brought with him from the provinces; he had returned thither with an intelligence developed, with loftier ambitions, and saw things as they were at home in the old manor house. His father and mother, his two brothers and two sisters, with an aged aunt, whose whole fortune consisted in annuities, lived on the little estate of Rastignac. The whole property brought in about three thousand francs; and though the amount varied with the season (as must always be the case in a vine-growing district), they were obliged to spare an unvarying twelve hundred francs out of their income for him. He saw how constantly the poverty, which they had generously hidden from him, weighed upon them; he could not help comparing the sisters, who had seemed so beautiful to his boyish eyes, with women in Paris, who had realized the beauty of his dreams. The uncertain future of the whole family depended upon him. It did not escape his eyes that not a crumb was wasted in the house, nor that the wine they drank was made from the second pressing; a multitude of small things, which it is useless to speak of in detail here, made him burn to distinguish himself, and his ambition to succeed increased tenfold.

He meant, like all great souls, that his success should be owing entirely to his merits; but his was pre-eminently a southern temperament, the execution of his plans was sure to be marred by the vertigo that seizes on youth when youth sees itself alone in a wide sea, uncertain how to spend its energies, whither to steer its course, how to adapt its sails to the winds. At first he determined to fling himself heart and soul into his work, but he was diverted from this purpose by the need of society and connections; then he saw how great an influence women exert in social life, and suddenly made up his mind to go out into this world to seek a protectress there. Surely a clever and high-spirited young man, whose wit and courage were set off to advantage by a graceful figure, and the vigorous kind of beauty that readily strikes a woman's imagination, need not despair of finding a protectress. These ideas occurred to him in his country walks with his sisters, whom he had once joined so gayly. The girls thought him very much changed.

His aunt, Mme. de Marcillac, had been presented at court, and had moved among the highest heights of that lofty region. Suddenly the young man's ambition discerned in those recollections of hers, which had been like nursery fairy tales to her nephews and nieces, the elements of a social success at least as important as the success which he had achieved at the École de Droit. He began to ask his aunt about those relations; some of the old ties might still hold good. After much shaking of the branches of the family tree, the old lady came to the conclusion that of all persons who could be useful to her nephew among the selfish genus of rich relations, the Vicomtesse de Beauséant was the least likely to refuse. To this lady, therefore, she wrote in the old-fashioned style, recommending Eugène to her; pointing out to her nephew that if he succeeded in pleasing Mme. de Beauséant, the Vicomtesse would introduce him to other relations. A few days after his return to Paris, therefore, Rastignac sent his aunt's letter to Mme. de Beauséant. The Vicomtesse replied by an invitation to a ball for the following evening. This was the position of affairs at the Maison Vauquer at the end of November 1819.

A few days later, after Mme. de Beauséant's ball, Eugène came in at two o'clock in the morning. The persevering student meant to make up for the lost time by working until daylight. It was the first time that he had attempted to spend the night in this way in that silent quarter. The spell of a factitious energy was upon him; he had beheld the pomp and splendor of the world. He had not dined at the Maison Vauquer; the boarders probably would think that he would walk home at daybreak from the dance, as he had done sometimes on former occasions, after a fête at the Prado, or a ball at the Odéon, splashing his silk stockings thereby, and ruining his pumps.

It so happened that Christophe took a look into the street before drawing the bolts of the door; and Rastignac, coming in at that moment, could go up to his room without making any noise, followed by Christophe, who made a great deal. Eugène exchanged his dress suit for a shabby overcoat and slippers, kindled a fire with some blocks of patent fuel, and prepared for his night's work in such a sort that the faint sounds he made were drowned by Christophe's heavy tramp on the stairs.

Eugène sat absorbed in thought for a few moments before plunging into his law books. He had just become aware of the fact that the Vicomtesse de Beauséant was one of the queens of fashion, that her house was thought to be the pleasantest in the Faubourg Saint-Germain. And not only so, she was, by right of her fortune, and the name she bore, one of the most conspicuous figures in that aristocratic world. Thanks to his aunt, thanks to Mme. de Marcillac's letter of introduction, the poor student had been kindly received in that house before he knew the extent of the favor thus shown to him.

It was almost like a patent of nobility to be admitted to those gilded salons; he had appeared in the most exclusive circle in Paris, and now all doors were open for him. Eugène had been dazzled at first by the brilliant assembly, and had scarcely exchanged a few words with the Vicomtesse; he had been content to single out a goddess from among this throng of Parisian divinities, one of those women who are sure to attract a young man's fancy.

The Comtesse Anastasie de Restaud was tall and gracefully made; she had one of the prettiest figures in Paris. Imagine a pair of great dark eyes, a magnificently molded hand, a shapely foot. There was a fiery energy in her movements; the Marquis de Ronquerolles had called her a "thorough-bred," but this fineness of nervous organization had brought no accompanying defect; the outlines of her form were full and rounded, without any tendency to stoutness. "A thorough-bred," "a pure pedigree," these figures of speech have replaced the "heavenly angel" and Ossianic nomenclature; the old mythology of love is extinct, doomed to perish by modern dandyism. But for Rastignac, Mme. Anastasie de Restaud was the woman for whom he had sighed. He had contrived to write his name twice upon the list of partners upon her fan, and had snatched a few words with her during the first quadrille.

"Where shall I meet you again, Madame?" he asked abruptly, and the tones of his voice were full of the vehement energy that women like so well.

"Oh, everywhere!" said she, "in the Bois, at the Bouffons, in my own house."

With the impetuosity of his adventurous southern temper, he did all he could to cultivate an acquaintance with this lovely countess, making the best of his opportunities in the quadrille and during a waltz that she gave him. When he had told her that he was a cousin of Mme. de Beauséant's, the Countess, whom he took for a great lady, asked him to call at her house, and after her parting smile, Rastignac felt convinced that he must make the visit. He was so lucky as to light upon someone who did not laugh at his ignorance, a fatal defect among the gilded and insolent youth of that period; the coterie of Maulincourts, Maximes de Trailles, de Marsays, Ronquerolles, Ajuda-Pintos, and Vandenesses who shone there in all the glory of coxcombry among the best-dressed women of fashion in Paris—Lady Brandon, the Duchess de Langeais, the Comtesse de Kergarouët, Mme. de Sérizy, the Duchesse de Carigliano, the Comtesse Ferraud, Mme. de Lanty, the Marquise d'Aiglemont, Mme. Firmiani, the Marquise de Listomère and the Marquise d'Espard, the Duchesse de Maufrigneuse and the Grandlieus. Luckily, therefore, for him, the novice happened upon the Marquis de Montriveau, the lover of the Duchesse de Langeais, a general as simple as a child; from him Rastignac learned that the Comtesse lived in the Rue du Helder.

Ah, what it is to be young, eager to see the world, greedily on the watch for any chance that brings you nearer the woman of your dreams, and behold two houses open their doors to you! To set foot in the Vicomtesse de Beauséant's house in the Faubourg Saint-Germain; to fall on your knees before a Comtesse de Restaud in the Chaussée d'Antin; to look at one glance across a vista of Paris drawing-rooms, conscious that, possessing sufficient good looks, you may hope to find aid and protection there in a feminine heart! To feel ambitious enough to spurn the tight-rope on which you must walk with the steady head of an acrobat for whom a fall is impossible, and to find in a charming woman the best of all balancing poles.

He sat there with his thoughts for a while, Law on the one hand, and Poverty on the other, beholding a radiant vision of a woman rise above the dull, smoldering fire. Who would not have paused and questioned the future as Eugène was doing? who would not have pictured it full of success? His wandering thoughts took wings; he was transported out of the present into that blissful future; he was sitting by Mme. de Restaud's side, when a sort of sigh, like the grunt of an overburdened St. Joseph, broke the silence of the night. It vibrated through the student, who took the sound for a death-groan. He opened his door noiselessly, went out upon the landing, and saw a thin streak of light under old Goriot's door. Eugène feared that his neighbor had been taken ill; he went over and looked through the keyhole; the old man was busily engaged in an occupation so singular and so suspicious that Rastignac thought he was only doing a piece of necessary service to society to watch the self-styled vermicelli maker's nocturnal industries.

The table was upturned, and Goriot had doubtless in some way secured a silver plate and cup to the bar before knotting a thick rope round them; he was pulling at this rope with such enormous force that they were being crushed and twisted out of shape; to all appearance he meant to convert the richly wrought metal into ingots.

"Peste! what a man!" said Rastignac, as he watched Goriot's muscular arms; there was not a sound in the room while the old man, with the aid of the rope, was kneading the silver like dough. "Was he then, indeed, a thief, or a receiver of stolen goods, who affected imbecility and decrepitude, and lived like a beggar that he might carry on his pursuits the more securely?" Eugène stood for a moment revolving these questions, then he looked again through the keyhole.

Old Goriot had unwound his coil of rope; he had covered the table with a blanket, and was now employed in rolling the flattened mass of silver into a bar, an operation which he performed with marvelous dexterity.

"Why, he must be as strong as Augustus, King of Poland!" said Eugène to himself when the bar was nearly finished.

Old Goriot looked sadly at his handiwork, tears fell from his eyes, he blew out the dip which had served him for a light while he manipulated the silver, and Eugène heard him sigh as he lay down again.

"He is mad," thought the student.

"Poor *child!"* old Goriot said aloud. Rastignac, hearing those words, concluded to keep silence; he would not hastily condemn his neighbor. He was just in the doorway of his room when a strange sound from the staircase below reached his ears; it might have been made by two men coming up in list slippers. Eugène listened; two men there certainly were, he could hear their breathing. Yet there had been no sound of opening the street door, no footsteps in the passage. Suddenly, too, he saw a faint gleam of light on the second story; it came from M. Vautrin's room.

'There are a good many mysteries here for a lodging-house!" he said to himself.

He went part of the way downstairs and listened again. The rattle of gold reached his ears. In another moment the light was put out, and again he distinctly heard the breathing of two men, but no sound of a door being opened or shut. The two men went down stairs, the faint sounds growing fainter as they went.

"Who is there!" cried Mme. Vauquer out of her bedroom window.

"I, Mme. Vauquer," answered Vautrin's deep bass voice. "I am coming in."

"That is odd! Christophe drew the bolts," said Eugène, going back to his room. "You have to sit up at night, it seems, if you really mean to know all that is going on about you in Paris."

These incidents turned his thought from his ambitious dreams; he betook himself to his work, but his thought wandered back to old Goriot's suspicious occupation; Mme. de Restaud's face swam again and again before his eyes like a vision of a brilliant future, and at last he lay down and slept with clenched fists. When a young man makes up his mind that he will work all night, the chances are that seven times out of ten he will sleep till morning. Such vigils do not begin before we are turned twenty.

The next morning Paris was wrapped in one of the dense fogs that throw the most punctual people out in their calculations as to the time; even the most business-like folk fail to keep their appointments in such weather, and ordinary mortals wake up at noon and fancy it is eight o'clock. On this morning it was half-past nine, and Mme. Vauquer still lay abed. Christophe was late, Sylvie was late, but the two sat comfortably taking their coffee as usual. It was Sylvie's custom to take the cream off the milk destined for the boarders' breakfast for her own, and to boil the remainder for some time, so that Madame should not discover this illegal exaction.

"Sylvie," said Christophe, as he dipped a piece of toast into the coffee, "M. Vautrin, who is not such a bad sort, all the same, had two people come to see him again last night. If Madame says anything, mind you say nothing about it."

"Has he given you something?"

"He gave me a five-franc piece this month, which is as good as saying, 'Hold your tongue.'"

"Except him and Mme. Couture, who don't look twice at every penny, there's no one in the house that doesn't try to get back with the left hand all that they give with the right at New Year," said Sylvie.

"And, after all," said Christophe, "what do they give you? A miserable five-franc piece. There is old Goriot, who has cleaned his shoes himself these two years past. There is that old beggar Poiret, who goes without blacking altogether; he would sooner drink it than put it on his boots. Then there is that whipper-snapper of a student, who gives me a couple of francs. Two francs will not pay for my brushes, and he sells his old clothes, and gets more for them than they are worth. Oh! they're a shabby lot!"

"Pooh!" said Sylvie, sipping her coffee, "our places are the best in the Quarter, that I know. But about that great big chap Vautrin, Christophe; has anyone told you anything about him?"

"Yes. I met a gentleman in the street a few days ago; he said to me, 'There's a gentleman at your place, isn't there? a tall man that dyes his whiskers?' I told him, 'No, sir; they aren't dyed. A gay fellow like him hasn't the time to do it.' And when I told M. Vautrin about it afterwards, he said, 'Quite right, my boy. That is the way to answer them. There is nothing more unpleasant than to have your little weaknesses known; it might spoil many a match.' "

"Well, and for my part," said Sylvie, "a man tried to humbug me at the market, wanting to know if I had seen him put on his shirt. Such bosh! There," she cried, interrupting herself, "that's a quarter to ten striking at the Val-de-Grâce, and not a soul stirring!"

"Pooh! they are all gone out. Mme. Couture and the girl went out at eight o'clock to take the wafer at Saint-Étienne. Old Goriot started off somewhere with a parcel, and the student won't be back from his lecture till ten o'clock. I saw them go while I was sweeping the stairs; old Goriot knocked up against me, and his parcel was as hard as iron. What is the old fellow up to, I wonder? He is as good as a plaything for the rest of them; they can never let him alone; but he is a good man, all the same, and worth more than all of them put together. He doesn't give you much himself, but he sometimes sends you with a message to ladies who fork out famous tips; they are dressed grandly, too."

"His daughters, as he calls them, eh? There are a dozen of them."

"I have never been to more than two—the two who came here."

"There is Madame moving overhead; I shall have to go, or she will raise a fine racket. Just keep an eye on the milk, Christophe; don't let the cat get at it."

Sylvie went up to her mistress's room.

"Sylvie! How is this? It's nearly ten o'clock, and you let me sleep on like a dormouse! Such a thing has never happened before."

"It's the fog; it is that thick, you could cut it with a knife."

"But how about breakfast?"

"Bah! the boarders are possessed, I'm sure. They all cleared out before there was a wink of daylight."

"Do you speak properly, Sylvie," Mme. Vauquer retorted; "say a blink of daylight."

"Ah, well, Madame, whichever you please. Anyhow, you can have breakfast at ten o'clock. La Michonnette and Poiret have neither of them stirred. There are only those two upstairs, and they are sleeping like the logs they are."

"But, Sylvie, you put their names together as if——"

"As if what?" said Sylvie, bursting into a guffaw. "The two of them make a pair."

"It is a strange thing, isn't it, Sylvie, how M. Vautrin got in last night after Christophe had bolted the door?"

"Not at all, Madame. Christophe heard M. Vautrin, and went down and undid the door for him. And here are you imagining that——"

"Give me my bodice, and be quick and get breakfast ready. Dish up the rest of the mutton with the potatoes, and you can put the stewed pears on the table, those at five a penny."

A few moments later Mme. Vauquer came down, just in time to see the cat knock down a plate that covered a bowl of milk, and begin to lap in all haste.

"Mistigris!" she cried.

The cat fled, but promptly returned to rub against her ankles.

"Oh! yes, you can wheedle, you old hypocrite!" she said. "Sylvie! Sylvie!"

"Yes, Madame; what is it?"

"Just see what the cat has done!"

"It is all that stupid Christophe's fault. I told him to stop and lay the table. What has become of him? Don't you worry, Madame; old Goriot shall have it. I will fill it up with water, and he won't know the difference; he never notices anything, not even what he eats."

"I wonder where the old heathen can have gone?" said Mme. Vauquer, setting the plates round the table.

"Who knows? He is up to all sorts of tricks."

"I have overslept myself," said Mme. Vauquer.

"But Madame looks as fresh as a rose, all the same."

The door bell rang at that moment, and Vautrin came through the sitting-room, singing loudly—

"'Tis the same old story everywhere,
A roving heart and a roving glance . . ."

"Oh! Mamma Vauquer! good-morning!" he cried at the sight of his hostess, and he put his arm gayly round her waist.

"There! have done——"

"'Impertinence!' Say it!" he answered. "Come, say it! Now isn't that what you really mean? Stop a bit, I will help you to set the table. Ah! I am a nice man, am I not?

'For the locks of brown and the golden hair
A sighing lover.'

"Oh! I have just seen something so funny——

'. . . led by chance.'"

"What?" asked the widow.

"Old Goriot in the goldsmith's shop in the Rue Dauphine at half-past eight this morning. They buy old spoons and forks and gold lace there, and Goriot sold a piece of silver plate for a good round sum. It had been twisted out of shape very neatly for a man that's not used to the trade."

"Really? You don't say so?"

"Yes. One of my friends is expatriating himself; I had been to see him off on board the Royal Mail steamer, and was coming back here. I waited after that to see what old Goriot would do; it is a comical affair. He came back to this quarter of the world, to the Rue des Grès, and went into a money-lender's house; everybody knows him, Gobseck, a stuck-up rascal, that would make dominos out of his father's bones; a Turk, a heathen, an old Jew, a Greek; it would be a difficult matter to rob *him,* for he puts all his coin into the Bank."

"Then what was old Goriot doing there?"

"Doing?" said Vautrin. "Nothing; he was bent on his own undoing. He is a simpleton, stupid enough to ruin himself by running after——"

"There he is!" said Sylvie.

"Christophe," said old Goriot's voice, "come upstairs with me."

Christophe went up, and shortly afterwards came down again.

"Where are you going?" Mme. Vauquer asked of her servant.

"Out on an errand for M. Goriot."

"What may that be?" said Vautrin, pouncing on a letter in Christophe's hand. *"Mme. la Comtesse Anastasie de Restaud,"* he read. "Where are you going with it?" he added, as he gave the letter back to Christophe.

"To the Rue du Helder. I have orders to give this into her hands myself."

"What is there inside it?" said Vautrin, holding the letter up to the light. "A bank-note? No." He peered into the envelope. "A receipted account!" he cried. "My word! 'tis a gallant old dotard. Off with you, old chap," he said, bringing down a hand on Christophe's head, and spinning the man round like a thimble; "you will have a famous tip."

By this time the table was set. Sylvie was boiling the milk, Mme. Vauquer was lighting a fire in the stove with some assistance from Vautrin, who kept on humming to himself—

"The same old story everywhere.
A roving heart and a roving glance."

When everything was ready, Mme. Couture and Mlle. Taillefer came in.

"Where have you been this morning, fair lady?" said Mme. Vauquer, turning to Mme. Couture.

"We have just been to say our prayers at Saint-Étienne du Mont. To-day is the day when we must go to see M. Taillefer. Poor little thing! She is trembling like a leaf," Mme. Couture went on, as she seated herself before the fire and held the steaming soles of her boots to the blaze.

"Warm yourself, Victorine," said Mme. Vauquer.

"It is quite right and proper, Mademoiselle, to pray to Heaven to soften your father's heart," said Vautrin, as he drew a chair nearer to the orphan girl; "but that is not enough. What you want is a friend who will give the monster a piece of his mind; a barbarian that has three millions (so they say), and will not give you a dowry; and a pretty girl needs a dowry nowadays."

"Poor child!" said Mme. Vauquer. "Never mind, my pet, your wretch of a father is going just the way to bring trouble upon himself."

Victorine's eyes filled with tears at the words, and the widow checked herself at a sign from Mme. Couture.

"If we could only see him!" said the Commissary-General's widow; "if I could speak to him myself and give him his wife's last letter! I have never dared to run the risk of sending it by post; he knew my handwriting——"

"'Oh woman, persecuted and injured innocent!'" exclaimed Vautrin, breaking in upon her. "So that is how you are, is it? In a few days' time I will look into your affairs, and it will be all right, you shall see."

"Oh!" said Victorine, with a tearful but eager glance at Vautrin, who showed no sign of being touched by it, "if you know of any way of communicating with my father, please be sure and tell him that his affection and my mother's honor are more to me than all the money in the world. If you can induce him to relent a little towards me, I will pray to God for you. You may be sure of my gratitude——"

"The same old story everywhere," sang Vautrin, with a satirical intonation. At this juncture, Goriot, Mlle. Michonneau, and Poiret came downstairs together; possibly the scent of the gravy which Sylvie was making to serve with the mutton had announced breakfast. The seven people thus assembled bade each other good-morning, and took their places

at the table; the clock struck ten, and the student's footstep was heard outside.

"Ah! here you are, M. Eugène," said Sylvie; "everyone is breakfasting at home to-day."

The student exchanged greetings with the lodgers, and sat down beside Goriot.

"I have just met with a queer adventure," he said, as he helped himself abundantly to the mutton, and cut a slice of bread, which Mme. Vauquer's eye gauged as usual.

"An adventure?" queried Poiret.

"Well, and what is there to astonish you in that, old boy?" Vautrin asked of Poiret. "M. Eugène is cut out for that kind of thing."

Mlle. Taillefer stole a timid glance at the young student.

"Tell us about your adventure?" demanded Mme. Vauquer.

"Yesterday evening I went to a ball given by a cousin of mine, the Vicomtesse de Beauséant. She has a magnificent house; the rooms were hung with silk—in short, it was a splendid affair, and I was as happy as a king——"

"Fisher," put in Vautrin, interrupting.

"What do you mean, sir?" said Eugène sharply.

"I said 'fisher,' because kingfishers see a good deal more fun than kings."

"Quite true; I would much rather be the little careless bird than a king," said Poiret the ditto-ist, "because——"

"In fact"—the law-student cut him short—"I danced with one of the handsomest women in the room, a charming countess, the most exquisite creature I have ever seen. There was peach blossom in her hair, and she had the loveliest bouquet of flowers—real flowers, that scented the air—but there! it is no use trying to describe a woman glowing with the dance. You ought to have seen her! Well, and this morning I met this divine countess about nine o'clock, on foot in the Rue de Grès. Oh! how my heart beat! I began to think——"

"That she was coming here," said Vautrin, with a keen look at the student. "I expect that she was going to call on old Gobseck, a money-lender. If ever you explore a Parisian woman's heart, you will find the money-lender first, and the lover afterwards. Your countess is called Anastasie de Restaud, and she lives in the Rue du Helder."

The student stared hard at Vautrin. Old Goriot raised his head at the words, and gave the two speakers a glance so full of intelligence and uneasiness that the lodgers beheld him with astonishment.

"Then Christophe was too late, and she must have gone to him!" cried Goriot, with anguish in his voice.

"It is just as I guessed," said Vautrin, leaning over to whisper in Mme. Vauquer's ear.

Goriot went on with his breakfast, but seemed unconscious of what he was doing. He had never looked more stupid nor more taken up with his own thoughts than he did at that moment.

"Who the devil could have told you her name, M. Vautrin?" asked Eugène.

"Aha! there you are!" answered Vautrin. "Old Father Goriot there knew it quite well! and why should not I know it too?"

"M. Goriot?" the student cried.

"What is it?" said the old man. "So she was very beautiful, was she, yesterday night?"

"Who?"

"Mme. de Restaud."

"Look at the old wretch," said Mme. Vauquer, speaking to Vautrin; "how his eyes light up!"

"Then does he really keep her?" said Mlle. Michonneau, in a whisper to the student.

"Oh! yes, she was tremendously pretty," Eugène answered. Old Goriot watched him with eager eyes. "If Mme. de Beauséant had not been there, my divine countess would have been the queen of the ball; none of the younger men had eyes for anyone else. I was the twelfth on her list, and she danced every quadrille. The other women were furious. She must have enjoyed herself, if ever creature did! It is a true saying that there is no more beautiful sight than a frigate in full sail, a galloping horse, or a woman dancing."

"So the wheel turns," said Vautrin; "yesterday night at a duchess's ball, this morning in a money-lender's office, on the lowest rung of the ladder—just like a Parisienne! If their husbands cannot afford to pay for their frantic extravagance, they will sell themselves. Or if they cannot do that, they will tear out their mothers' hearts to find something to pay for their splendor. They will turn the world upside down. Just a Parisienne through and through!"

Old Goriot's face, which had shone at the student's words like the sun on a bright day, clouded over all at once at this cruel speech of Vautrin's.

"Well," said Mme. Vauquer, "but where is your adventure? Did you speak to her? Did you ask her if she wanted to study law?"

"She did not see me," said Eugène. "But only think of meeting one of the prettiest women in Paris in the Rue des Grès at nine o'clock! She could not have reached home after the ball till two o'clock this morning. Wasn't it queer? There is no place like Paris for these sort of adventures."

"Pshaw! much funnier things than *that* happen here!" exclaimed Vautrin.

Mlle. Taillefer had scarcely heeded the talk, she was so absorbed by the thought of the new attempt that she was about to make. Mme. Couture made a sign that it was time to go upstairs and dress; the two ladies went out, and old Goriot followed their example.

"Well, did you see?" said Mme. Vauquer, addressing Vautrin and the rest of the circle. "He is ruining himself for those women, that is plain."

"Nothing will ever make me believe that that beautiful Comtesse de Restaud is anything to old Goriot," cried the student.

"Well, and if you don't," broke in Vautrin, "we are not set on convincing you. You are too young to know Paris thoroughly yet; later on you will find out that there are what we call men with a passion——"

Mlle. Michonneau gave Vautrin a quick glance at these words. They seemed to be like the sound of a trumpet to a trooper's horse. "Aha!" said Vautrin, stopping in his speech to give her a searching glance, "so we have had our little experiences, have we?"

The old maid lowered her eyes like a nun who sees a statue.

"Well," he went on, "when folks of that kind get a notion into their heads, they cannot drop it. They must drink the water from some particular spring—it is stagnant as often as not; but they will sell their wives and families, they will sell their own souls to the devil to get it. For some this spring is play, or the stock exchange, or music, or a collection of pictures or insects; for others it is some woman who can give them the dainties they like. You might offer these last all the women on earth—they would turn up their noses; they will have the only one who can gratify their passion. It often happens that the woman does not care for them at all, and treats them cruelly; they buy their morsels of satisfaction very dear; but no matter, the fools are never tired of it; they will take their last blanket to the pawnbroker's to give their last five-franc piece to her. Old Goriot here is one of that sort. He is discreet, so the Countess exploits him—just the way of the gay world. The poor old fellow thinks of her and of nothing else. In all other respects you see he is a stupid animal; but get him on that subject, and his eyes sparkle like diamonds. That secret is not difficult to guess. He took some plate himself this morning to the melting-pot, and I saw him at Daddy Gobseck's in the Rue des Grès. And now, mark what follows—he came back here, and gave a letter for the Comtesse de Restaud to that noodle of a Christophe, who showed us the address; there was a receipted bill inside it. It is clear that it was an urgent matter if the Countess also went herself to the old money-lender. Old Goriot has financed her handsomely. There is no need to tack a tale together; the thing is self-evident. So that shows you, sir student, that all the time your Countess was smiling, dancing, flirting, swaying her peach-flower crowned head, with her gown gathered into her hand, her slippers were pinching her, as they say; she was thinking of her protested bills, or her lover's protested bills."

"You have made me wild to know the truth," cried Eugène; "I will go to call on Mme. de Restaud to-morrow."

"Yes," echoed Poiret; "you must go and call on Mme. de Restaud."

"And perhaps you will find old Goriot there, who will take payment for the assistance he politely rendered."

Eugène looked disgusted. "Why, then, this Paris of yours is a slough."

"And an uncommonly queer slough, too," replied Vautrin. "The mud splashes you as you drive through it in your carriage—you are a respectable person; you go afoot and are splashed—you are a scoundrel. You are so unlucky as to walk off with something or other belonging to somebody else, and they exhibit you as a curiosity in the Place du Palais-de-Justice; you steal a million, and you are pointed out in every salon as a model of virtue. And you pay thirty millions for the police and the courts of justice, for the maintenance of law and order! A pretty state of things it is!"

"What," cried Mme. Vauquer, "has old Goriot really melted down his silver posset-dish?"

"There were two turtle-doves on the lid, were there not?" asked Eugène.

"Yes, that there were."

"Then, was he fond of it?" said Eugène. "He cried while he was breaking up the cup and plate. I happened to see him by accident."

"It was dear to him as his own life," answered the widow.

"There! you see how infatuated the old fellow is!" cried Vautrin. "The woman yonder can coax the soul out of him."

The student went up to his room. Vautrin went out, and a few minutes later Mme. Couture and Victorine drove away in a cab which Sylvie had called for them. Poiret gave his arm to Mlle. Michonneau, and they went together to spend the two sunniest hours of the day in the Jardin des Plantes.

"Well, those two are as good as married," was the portly Sylvie's comment. "They are going out together to-day for the first time. They are such a couple of dry sticks that if they happen to strike against each other they will draw sparks like flint and steel."

"Keep clear of Mlle. Michonneau's shawl, then," said Mme. Vauquer, laughing; "it would flare up like tinder."

At four o'clock that evening, when Goriot came in, he saw, by the light of two smoky lamps, that Victorine's eyes were red. Mme. Vauquer was listening to the history of the visit made that morning to M. Taillefer; it had been made in vain. Taillefer was tired of the annual application made by his daughter and her elderly friend; he gave them a personal interview in order to arrive at an understanding with him.

"My dear lady," said Mme. Couture, addressing Mme. Vauquer, "just imagine it; he did not even ask Victorine to sit down, she was standing the whole time. He said to me quite coolly, without putting himself in a passion, that we might spare ourselves the trouble of going there; that the young lady (he would not call her his daughter) was injuring her cause by importuning him (*importuning!* once a year, the wretch!); that as Victorine's mother had nothing when he married her, Victorine ought not to expect anything from him; in fact, he said the most cruel things, that made the poor child burst out crying. The little thing threw herself at her father's feet and spoke up bravely; she said that she only persevered in her visits for her mother's sake; that she would obey him without a murmur, but that she begged him to read her poor dead mother's farewell letter. She took it up and gave it to him, saying the most beautiful things in the world, most beautifully expressed; I do not know where she learned them; God must have put them into her head, for the poor child was inspired to speak so nicely that it made me cry like a fool to hear her talk. And what do you think the monster was doing all the time? Cutting his nails! He took the letter that poor Mme. Taillefer had soaked with tears, and flung it on to the chimney-piece. 'That is all right,' he said. He held out his hands to raise his daughter, but she covered them with kisses, and he drew them away again. Scandalous, isn't it? And his great booby of a son came in and took no notice of his sister."

"What inhuman wretches they must be!" said old Goriot.

"And then they both went out of the room," Mme. Couture went on, without heeding the worthy vermicelli maker's exclamation; "father and son bowed to me, and asked me to excuse them on account of urgent business! That is the history of our call. Well, he has seen his daughter at any rate. How he can refuse to acknowledge her I cannot think, for they are as like as two peas."

The boarders dropped in one after another, interchanging greetings and the empty jokes that certain classes of Parisians regard as humorous and witty. Dullness is their prevailing ingredient, and the whole point consists in mispronouncing a word or in a gesture. This kind of argot is always changing. The essence of the jest consists in some catchword suggested by a political event, an incident in the police courts, a street song, or a bit of burlesque at some theater, and forgotten in a month. Anything and everything serves to keep up a game of battledore and shuttlecock with words and ideas. The diorama, a recent invention, which carried an optical illusion a degree further than panoramas, had given rise to a mania among art students for ending every word with *rama.* The Maison Vauquer had caught the infection from a young artist among the boarders.

"Well, Monsieur-r-r Poiret," said the employé from the Muséum, "how is your health-orama?" Then, without waiting for an answer, he turned to Mme. Couture and Victorine with a "Ladies, you seem melancholy."

"Is dinner ready?" cried Horace Bianchon, a medical student, and a friend of Rastignac's; "my stomach is sinking *usque ad talones.*"

"There is an uncommon *frozerama* outside!" said Vautrin. "Make room there, Father Goriot! Confound it! your foot covers the whole front of the stove."

"Illustrious M. Vautrin," put in Bianchon, "why do you say *frozerama?* It is incorrect; it should be *frozenrama.*"

"No, it shouldn't," said the official from the Muséum; "*frozerama* is right by the same rule that you say 'My feet are *froze.*'"

"Ah! ah!"

"Here is his Excellency the Marquis de Rastignac, Doctor of the Law of Contraries," cried Bianchon, seizing Eugène by the throat, and almost throttling him.

"Hallo there! hallo!"

Mlle. Michonneau came noiselessly in, bowed to the rest of the party, and took her place beside the three women without saying a word.

"That old bat always makes me shudder," said Bianchon in a low voice, indicating Mlle. Michonneau to Vautrin. "I have studied Gall's system, and I am sure she has the bump of Judas."

"Then you have seen a case before?" said Vautrin.

"Who has not?" answered Bianchon. "Upon my word, that ghastly old maid looks just like one of the long worms that will gnaw a beam through, give them time enough."

"That is the way, young man," returned he of the forty years and the dyed whiskers—

"The rose has lived the life of a rose—
A morning's space."

"Aha! here is a magnificent *soupe-au-rama,*" cried Poiret as Christophe came in bearing the soup with cautious heed.

"I beg your pardon, sir," said Mme. Vauquer; "it is *soupe aux choux.*"

All the young men roared with laughter.

"Had you there, Poiret!"

"Poir-r-r-rette! she had you there!"

"Score two points to Mamma Vauquer," said Vautrin.

"Did anyone notice the fog this morning?" asked the official.

"It was a frantic fog," said Bianchon, "a fog unparalleled, doleful, melancholy, sea-green, asthmatical—a Goriot of a fog!"

"A Goriorama," said the art student, "because you couldn't see a thing in it."

"Hey! Milord Gâôriotte, they air talking about yoo-o-ou!"

Old Goriot, seated at the lower end of the table, close to the door through which the servant entered, raised his face; he had smelt at a scrap of bread that lay under his table napkin, an old trick acquired in his commercial capacity, that still showed itself at times.

"Well," Mme. Vauquer cried in sharp tones, that rang above the rattle of spoons and plates and the sound of other voices; "and is there anything the matter with the bread?"

"Nothing whatever, Madame," he answered; "on the contrary, it is made of the best quality of corn; flour from Étampes."

"How could you tell?" asked Eugène.

"By the color, by the flavor."

"You knew the flavor by the smell, I suppose," said Mme. Vauquer. "You have grown so economical, you will find out how to live on the smell of cooking at last."

"Take out a patent for it then," cried the Muséum official; "you would make a handsome fortune."

"Never mind him," said the artist; "he does that sort of thing to delude us into thinking that he was a vermicelli maker."

"Your nose is a corn sampler, it appears?" inquired the official.

"Corn *what?*" asked Bianchon.

"Corn-el."

"Corn-et."

"Corn-elian."

"Corn-ice."

"Corn-ucopia."

"Corn-crake."

"Corn-cockle."

"Corn-orama."

The eight responses came like a rolling fire from every part of the room, and the laughter that followed was the more uproarious because poor old Goriot stared at the others with a puzzled look, like a foreigner trying to catch the meaning of words in a language that he does not understand.

"Corn? . . ." he said, turning to Vautrin, his next neighbor.

"Corn on your foot, old man!" said Vautrin, and he drove old Goriot's cap down over his eyes by a blow on the crown.

The poor old man thus suddenly attacked was for a moment too bewildered to do anything. Christophe carried off his plate, thinking that he had finished his soup, so that when Goriot had pushed back his cap from his eyes his spoon encountered the table. Everyone burst out laughing. "You are a disagreeable joker, sir," said the old man, "and if you take any further liberties with me——"

"Well, what then, old boy?" Vautrin interrupted.

"Well, then, you shall pay dearly for it some day——"

"Down below, eh?" said the artist, "in the little dark corner where they put naughty boys."

"Well, Mademoiselle," Vautrin said, turning to Victorine, "you are eating nothing. So papa was refractory, was he?"

"A monster!" said Mme. Couture.

"Mademoiselle might make application for aliment pending her suit; she is not eating anything. Eh! eh! just see how old Goriot is staring at Mlle. Victorine!"

The old man had forgotten his dinner, he was so absorbed in gazing at the poor girl; the sorrow in her face was unmistakable,—the slighted love of a child whose father would not recognize her.

"We are mistaken about old Goriot, my dear boy," said Eugène in a low voice. "He is not an idiot, nor wanting in energy. Try your Gall system on him, and let me know what you think. I saw him crush a silver dish last night as if it had been made of wax; there seems to be something extraordinary going on in his mind just now, to judge by his face. His life is so mysterious that it must be worth studying. Oh! you may laugh, Bianchon; I am not joking."

"The man is a subject, is he?" said Bianchon; "all right! I will dissect him, if he will give me a chance."

"No; feel his bumps."

"Hm!—his stupidity might perhaps be contagious."

The next day Rastignac dressed himself very elegantly, and about three o'clock in the afternoon went to call on Mme. de Restaud. On the way thither he indulged in the wild intoxicating dreams which fill a young head so full of delicious excitement. Young men at his age take no account of obstacles nor of dangers; they see success in every direction; imagination has free play, and turns their lives into a romance; they are saddened or discouraged by the collapse of one of the wild visionary schemes that have no existence save in their heated fancy. If youth were not ignorant and timid, civilization would be impossible.

Eugène took unheard-of pains to keep himself in a spotless condition, but on his way through the streets he began to think about Mme. de Restaud and what he should say to her. He equipped himself with wit, rehearsed repartees in the course of an imaginary conversation, and prepared certain neat speeches à la Talleyrand, conjuring up a series of small events which should prepare the way for the declaration on which he had based his future; and during these musings the law student was bespattered with mud, and by the time he reached the Palais Royal he was obliged to have his boots blacked and his trousers brushed.

"If I were rich," he said, as he changed the five-franc piece he had brought with him in case anything might happen, "I would take a cab, then I could think at my ease."

At last he reached the Rue du Helder, and asked for the Comtesse de Restaud. He bore the contemptuous glances of the servants, who had seen him cross the court on foot, with the cold fury of a man who knows that he will succeed some day. He understood the meaning of their glances at once, for he had felt his inferiority as soon as he entered the court, where a smart cab was waiting. All the delights of life in Paris seemed to be implied by this visible and manifest sign of luxury and extravagance. A fine horse, in magnificent harness, was pawing the ground, and all at once the law student felt out of humor with himself. Every compartment in his brain which he had thought to find so full of wit was bolted fast; he grew positively stupid. He sent up his name to the Countess, and waited in the ante-chamber, standing on one foot before a window that looked out upon the court; mechanically he leant his elbow against the sash, and stared before him. The time seemed long; he would have left the house but for the southern tenacity of purpose which works miracles when it is single-minded.

"Madame is in her boudoir, and cannot see anyone at present, sir," said the servant. "She gave me no answer; but if you will go into the dining-room, there is someone already there."

Rastignac was impressed with a sense of the formidable power of the lackey who can accuse or condemn his masters by a word; he coolly opened the door by which the man had just entered the ante-chamber, meaning, no doubt, to show these insolent flunkeys that he was familiar with the house; but he found that he had thoughtlessly precipitated himself into a small room full of dressers, where lamps were standing, and hot-water pipes, on which towels were being dried; a dark passage and a back staircase lay beyond it. Stifled laughter from the ante-chamber added to his confusion.

"This way to the drawing-room, sir," said the servant, with the exaggerated respect which seemed to be one more jest at his expense.

Eugène turned so quickly that he stumbled against a bath. By good luck, he managed to keep his hat on his head, and saved it from immersion in the water; but just as he turned, a door opened at the further end of the dark passage, dimly lighted by a small lamp. Rastignac heard voices and the sound of a kiss; one of the speakers was Mme. de Restaud, the other was old Goriot. Eugène followed the servant through the dining-room into the drawing-room; he went to a window that looked out into the courtyard, and stood there for a while. He meant to know whether this Goriot was really the Goriot that he knew. His heart beat unwontedly fast; he remembered Vautrin's hideous insinuations. A well-dressed young man suddenly emerged from the room almost as Eugène entered it, saying impatiently to the servant who stood at the door: "I am going, Maurice. Tell Mme. la Comtesse that I waited more than half an hour for her."

Whereupon this insolent being, who, doubtless, had a right to be insolent, sang an Italian trill, and went towards the window where Eugène was standing, moved thereto quite as much by a desire to see the student's face as by a wish to look out into the courtyard.

"But M. le Comte had better wait a moment longer; Madame is disengaged," said Maurice, as he returned to the ante-chamber.

Just at that moment old Goriot appeared close to the gate; he had emerged from a door at the foot of the back staircase. The worthy soul was preparing to open his umbrella regardless of the fact that the great gate had opened to admit a tilbury, in which a young man with a ribbon at his button-hole was seated. Old Goriot had scarcely time to start back and save himself. The horse took fright at the umbrella, swerved, and dashed forward towards the flight of steps. The young man looked round in annoyance, saw old Goriot, and greeted him as he went out with constrained courtesy, such as people usually show to a money-lender so long as they require his services, or the sort of respect they feel is necessary to show for someone whose reputation has been blown upon, so that they blush to acknowledge his acquaintance. Old Goriot gave him a little friendly nod and a good-natured smile. All this happened with lightning speed. Eugène was so deeply interested that he forgot that he was not alone till he suddenly heard the Countess's voice.

"Oh! Maxime, were you going away?" she said reproachfully, with a shade of pique in her manner. The Countess had not seen the incident nor the entrance of the tilbury. Rastignac turned abruptly and saw her standing before him, coquettishly dressed in a loose white cashmere gown with knots of rose-colored ribbon here and there; her hair was carelessly coiled about her head, as is the wont of Parisian women in the morning; there was a soft fragrance about her —doubtless she was fresh from a bath;—her graceful form seemed more flexible, her beauty more luxuriant. Her eyes glistened. A young man can see everything at a glance; he feels the radiant influence of woman as a plant discerns and absorbs its nutriment from the air; he did not need to touch her hands to feel their cool freshness. He saw faint rose tints through the cashmere of the dressing gown; it had fallen slightly open, giving glimpses of a bare throat, on which the student's eyes rested. The Countess had no need of the adventitious aid of corsets; her girdle defined the outlines of her slender waist; her throat was a challenge to love; her feet, thrust into slippers, were daintily small. As Maxime took her hand and kissed it, Eugène became aware of Maxime's existence, and the Countess saw Eugène.

"Oh! is that you, M. de Rastignac? I am very glad to see you," she said, but there was something in her manner that a shrewd observer would have taken as a hint to depart.

Maxime, as the Countess Anastasie had called the young man with the haughty insolence of bearing, looked from Eugène to the lady, and from the lady to Eugène; it was sufficiently evident that he wished to be rid of the latter. An exact and faithful rendering of the glance might be given in the words: "Look here, my dear; I hope you intend to send this little whipper-snapper about his business."

The Countess consulted the young man's face with an intent submissiveness that betrays all the secrets of a woman's heart, and Rastignac all at once began to hate him violently. To begin with, the sight of the fair carefully arranged curls on the other's comely head had convinced him that his own crop was hideous; Maxime's boots, moreover, were elegant and spotless, while his own, in spite of all his care, bore some traces of his recent walk; and, finally, Maxime's overcoat fitted the outline of his figure gracefully, he looked like a pretty woman, while Eugène was wearing a black coat at half-past two. The quick-witted child of the Charente felt the disadvantage at which he was placed beside this tall, slender dandy, with the clear gaze and the pale face, one of those men who would ruin orphan children without scruple. Mme. de Restaud fled into the next room without waiting for Eugène to speak; shaking out the skirts of her dressing-gown in her flight, so that she looked like a white butterfly, and Maxime hurried after her. Eugène, in a fury, followed Maxime and the Countess, and the three stood once more face to face by the hearth in the large drawing-room. The law student felt quite sure that the odious Maxime found him in the way, and, even at the risk of displeasing Mme. de Restaud, he meant to annoy the dandy. It had struck him all at once that he had seen the young man before at Mme. de Beauséant's ball; he guessed the relation between Maxime and Mme. de Restaud; and with the youthful audacity that commits prodigious blunders or achieves signal success, he said to himself, "This is my rival; I mean to cut him out."

Rash resolve! He did not know that M. le Comte Maxime de Trailles would wait till he was insulted, so as to fire first and kill his man. Eugène was a sportsman and a good shot, but he had not yet hit the bull's eye twenty times out of twenty-two. The young Count dropped into a low chair by the hearth, took up the tongs, and made up the fire so violently and so sulkily, that Anastasie's fair face suddenly clouded over. She turned to Eugène with a cool, questioning glance that asked plainly, "Why do you not go?" a glance which well-bred people regard as a cue to make their exit.

Eugène assumed an amiable expression.

"Madame," he began, "I hastened to call upon you——"

He stopped short. The door opened, and the owner of the tilbury suddenly appeared. He had left his hat outside, and did not greet the Countess; he looked meditatively at Rastignac, and held out his hand to Maxime with a cordial "Good-morning," that astonished Eugène not a little. The young provincial did not understand the amenities of a triple alliance.

"M. de Restaud," said the Countess, introducing her husband to the law student.

Eugène bowed profoundly.

"This gentleman," she continued, presenting Eugène to her husband, "is M. de Rastignac; he is related to Mme. la Vicomtesse de Beauséant through the Marcillacs; I had the pleasure of meeting him at her last ball."

Related to Mme. la Vicomtesse de Beauséant through the Marcillacs! These words, on which the Countess threw ever so slight an emphasis, by reason of the pride that the mistress of a house takes in showing that she only receives people of distinction as visitors in her house, produced a magical effect. The Count's stiff manner relaxed at once as he returned the student's bow.

"Delighted to have an opportunity of making your acquaintance," he said.

Maxime de Trailles himself gave Eugène an uneasy glance, and suddenly dropped his insolent manner. The mighty name had all the power of a fairy's wand; those closed compartments in the southern brain flew open again; Rastignac's carefully drilled faculties returned. It was as if a sudden light had pierced the obscurity of this upper world of Paris, and he began to see, though everything was indistinct as yet. Mme. Vauquer's lodging-house and old Goriot were very far remote from his thoughts.

"I thought that the Marcillacs were extinct," the Comte de Restaud said, addressing Eugène.

"Yes, they are extinct," answered the law student. "My great-uncle, the Chevalier de Rastignac, married the heiress of the Marcillac family. They had only one daughter, who married the Maréchal de Clarimbault, Mme. de Beauséant's grandfather on the mother's side. We are the younger branch of the family, and the younger branch is all the poorer because my great-uncle, the Vice-Admiral, lost all that he had in the King's Service. The Government during the Revolution refused to admit our claims when the Compagnie des Indes was liquidated."

"Was not your great-uncle in command of the *Vengeur* before 1789?"

"Yes."

"Then he would be acquainted with my grandfather, who commanded the *Warwick*."

Maxime looked at Mme. de Restaud and shrugged his shoulders, as who should say, "If he is going to discuss nautical matters with that fellow, it is all over with us." Anastasie understood the glance that M. de Trailles gave her. With a woman's admirable tact, she began to smile, and said—

"Come with me, Maxime; I have something to say to you. We will leave you two gentlemen to sail in company on board the *Warwick* and the *Vengeur*."

She rose to her feet and signed to Maxime to follow her, mirth and mischief in her whole attitude, and the two went in the direction of the boudoir. The *morganatic* couple (to use a convenient German expression which has no exact equivalent) had reached the door, when the Count interrupted himself in his talk with Eugène.

"Anastasie!" he cried pettishly, "just stay a moment, dear; you know very well that——"

"I am coming back in a minute," she interrupted; "I have a commission for Maxime to execute, and I want to tell him about it."

She came back almost immediately. She had noticed the inflection in her husband's voice, and knew that it would not be safe to retire to the boudoir; like all women who are compelled to study their husbands' characters in order to have their own way, and whose business it is to know exactly how far they can go without endangering a good understanding, she was very careful to avoid petty collisions in domestic life. It was Eugène who had brought about this unwonted incident; so the Countess looked at Maxime and indicated the law student with an air of exasperation. M. de Trailles addressed the Count, the Countess, and Eugène with the pointed remark, "You are busy, I do not want to interrupt you; good-day," and he went.

"Just wait a moment, Maxime!" the Count called after him.

"Come and dine with us," said the Countess, leaving Eugène and her husband together once more. She followed Maxime into the little drawing-room, where they sat together sufficiently long to feel sure that Rastignac had taken his leave.

The law student heard their laughter, and their voices, and the pauses in their talk; he grew malicious, exerting conversational powers for M. de Restaud, flattered him, and drew him into discussions, to the end that he might see the Countess again and discover the nature of her relations with old Goriot. This Countess with a husband and a lover, for Maxime clearly was her lover, was a mystery. What was the secret tie that bound her to the old tradesman? This mystery he meant to penetrate, hoping by its means to gain a sovereign ascendency over this fair typical Parisian.

"Anastasie!" the Count called again to his wife.

"Poor Maxime!" she said, addressing the young man. "Come, we must resign ourselves. This evening——"

"I hope, Nasie," he said in her ear, "that you will give orders not to admit that youngster, whose eyes light up like live coals when he looks at you. He will make you a declaration, and compromise you, and then you will compel me to kill him."

"Are you mad, Maxime?" she said. "A young lad of a student is, on the contrary, a capital lightning-conductor; is not that so? Of course, I mean to make Restaud furiously jealous of him."

Maxime burst out laughing, and went out, followed by the Countess, who stood at the window to watch him into his carriage; he shook his whip, and made his horse prance. She only returned when the great gate had been closed after him.

"What do you think, dear?" cried the Count, her husband, "this gentleman's family estate is not far from Verteuil, on the Charente; his great-uncle and my grandfather were acquainted."

"Delighted to find that we have acquaintances in common," said the Countess, with a preoccupied manner.

"More than you think," said Eugène, in a low voice.

"What do you mean?" she asked quickly.

"Why, only just now," said the student, "I saw a gentleman go out at that gate, old Goriot, my next door neighbor in the house where I am lodging."

At the sound of this name, and the prefix that embellished it, the Count, who was stirring the fire, let the tongs fall as though they had burned his fingers, and rose to his feet.

"Sir," he cried, "you might have called him 'Monsieur Goriot!'"

The Countess turned pale at first at the sight of her husband's vexation, then she reddened; clearly she was embarrassed, her answer was made in a tone that she tried to make natural, and with an air of assumed carelessness—

"You could not know anyone who is dearer to us both . . ."

She broke off, glanced at the piano as if some fancy had crossed her mind, and asked, "Are you fond of music, M. de Rastignac?"

"Exceedingly," answered Eugène, flushing, and disconcerted by a dim suspicion that he had somehow been guilty of a clumsy piece of folly.

"Do you sing?" she cried, going to the piano, and, sitting down before it, she swept her fingers over the keyboard from end to end. R-r-r-rah!

"No, Madame."

The Comte de Restaud walked to and fro.

"That is a pity; you are without one great means of success.—*Ca-ro, ca-a-ro, ca-a-a-ro, non du-bi-ta-re,*" sang the Countess.

Eugène had a second time waved a magic wand when he uttered Goriot's name, but the effect seemed to be entirely opposite to that produced by the formula "related to Mme. de Beauséant." His position was not unlike that of some visitor permitted as a favor to inspect a private collection of curiosities, when by inadvertence he comes into collision with a glass case full of sculptured figures, and three or four heads, imperfectly secured, fall at the shock. He wished the earth would open and swallow him. Mme. de Restaud's expression was reserved and chilly, her eyes had grown indifferent, and sedulously avoided meeting those of the unlucky student of law.

"Madame," he said, "you wish to talk with M. de Restaud; permit me to wish you good-day——"

The Countess interrupted him by a gesture, saying hastily, "Whenever you come to see us, both M. de Restaud and I shall be delighted to see you."

Eugène made a profound bow and took his leave, followed by M. de Restaud, who insisted, in spite of his remonstrances, on accompanying him into the hall.

"Neither your mistress nor I are at home to that gentleman when he calls," the Count said to Maurice.

As Eugène set foot on the steps, he saw that it was raining.

"Come," said he to himself, "somehow I have just made a mess of it, I do not know how. And now I am going to spoil my hat and coat into the bargain. I ought to stop in my corner, grind away at law, and never look to be anything but a boorish country magistrate. How can I go into society, when to manage properly you want a lot of cabs, varnished boots, gold watch chains, and all sorts of things; you have to wear white doeskin gloves that cost six francs in the morning, and primrose kid gloves every evening? A fig for that old humbug of a Goriot!"

When he reached the street door, the driver of a hackney coach, who had probably just deposited a wedding party at their door, and asked nothing better than a chance of making a little money for himself without his employer's knowledge, saw that Eugène had no umbrella, remarked his black coat, white waistcoat, yellow gloves, and varnished boots, and stopped and looked at him inquiringly. Eugène, in the blind desperation that drives a young man to plunge deeper and deeper into an abyss, as if he might hope to find a fortunate issue in its lowest depths, nodded in reply to the driver's signal, and stepped into the cab; a few stray petals of orange blossom and scraps of wire bore witness to its recent occupation by a wedding party.

"Where am I to drive, sir?" demanded the man, who, by this time, had taken off his white gloves.

"Confound it!" Eugène said to himself, "I am in for it now, and at least I will not spend cab-hire for nothing!—Drive to the Hôtel Beauséant," he said aloud.

"Which?" asked the man, a portentous word that reduced Eugène to confusion. This young man of fashion, *species incerta,* did not know that there were two Hôtels Beauséant; he was not aware how rich he was in relations who did not care about him.

"The Vicomte de Beauséant, Rue——"

"De Grenelle," interrupted the driver, with a jerk of his head. "You see, there are the hôtels of the Marquis and Comte de Beauséant in the Rue Saint-Dominique," he added, drawing up the step.

"I know all about that," said Eugène, severely.—"Everybody is laughing at me to-day, it seems!" he said to himself, as he deposited his hat on the opposite seat. "This escapade will cost me a king's ransom, but, at any rate, I shall call on my so-called cousin in a thoroughly aristocratic fashion. Goriot has cost me ten francs already, the old scoundrel! My word! I will tell Mme. de Beauséant about my adventure; perhaps it may amuse her. Doubtless she will know the secret of the criminal relation between that handsome woman and the old rat without a tail. It would be better to find favor in my cousin's eyes than to come in contact with that shameless woman, who seems to me to have very expensive tastes. Surely the beautiful Vicomtesse's personal interest would turn the scale for me, when the mere mention of her name produces such an effect. Let us look higher. If you set yourself to carry the heights of heaven, you must face God."

The innumerable thoughts that surged through his brain might be summed up in these phrases. He grew calmer, and recovered something of his assurance as he watched the falling rain. He told himself that though he was about to squander two of the precious five-franc pieces that remained to him, the money was well laid out in preserving his coat, boots, and hat; and his cabman's cry of "Gate, if you please," almost put him in spirits. A Swiss, in scarlet and gold, appeared, the great door groaned on its hinges, and

Rastignac, with sweet satisfaction, beheld his equipage pass under the archway and stop before the flight of steps beneath the awning. The driver, in a blue-and-red greatcoat, dismounted and let down the step. As Eugène stepped out of the cab he heard smothered laughter from the peristyle. Three or four lackeys were making merry over the festal appearance of the vehicle. In another moment the law student was enlightened as to the cause of their hilarity; he felt the full force of the contrast between his equipage and one of the smartest broughams in Paris; a coachman, with powdered hair, seemed to find it difficult to hold a pair of spirited horses, who stood chafing the bit. In Mme. de Restaud's courtyard, in the Chaussée d'Antin, he had seen the neat turn-out of a young man of six-and-twenty; in the Faubourg Saint-Germain he found the luxurious equipage of a man of rank; thirty thousand francs would not have purchased it.

"Who can be here?" said Eugène to himself. He began to understand, though somewhat tardily, that he must not expect to find many women in Paris who were not already appropriated, and that the capture of one of these queens would be likely to cost something more than bloodshed. "Confound it all! I expect my cousin also has her Maxime."

He went up the steps, feeling that he was a blighted being. The glass door was opened for him; the servants were as solemn as jackasses under the curry comb. So far, Eugène had only been in the ballroom on the ground floor of the Hôtel Beauséant; the fête had followed so closely on the invitation, that he had not had time to call on his cousin, and had therefore never seen Mme. de Beauséant's apartments; he was about to behold for the first time a great lady among the wonderful and elegant surroundings that reveal her character and reflect her daily life. He was the more curious, because Mme. de Restaud's drawing-room had provided him with a standard of comparison.

At half-past four the Vicomtesse de Beauséant was visible. Five minutes earlier she would not have received her cousin, but Eugène knew nothing of the recognized routine of various houses in Paris. He was conducted up the wide, white-painted, crimson-carpeted staircase, between the gilded balusters and masses of flowering plants, to Mme. de Beauséant's apartments. He did not know the rumor current about Mme. de Beauséant, one of the biographies told, with variations, in whispers, every evening in the salons of Paris.

For three years past her name had been spoken of in connection with that of one of the most wealthy and distinguished Portuguese nobles, the Marquis d'Ajuda-Pinto. It was one of those innocent *liaisons* which possess so much charm for the two thus attached to each other that they find the presence of a third person intolerable. The Vicomte de Beauséant, therefore, had himself set an example to the rest of the world by respecting, with as good a grace as might be, this morganatic union. Anyone who came to call on the Vicomtesse in the early days of this friendship was sure to find the Marquis d'Ajuda-Pinto there. As, under the circumstances, Mme. de Beauséant could not very well shut her door against these visitors, she gave them such a cold reception, and showed so much interest in the study of the ceiling, that no one could fail to understand how much he bored her; and when it became known in Paris that Mme. de Beauséant was bored by callers between two and four o'clock, she was left in perfect solitude during that interval. She went to the Bouffons or to the Opéra with M. de Beauséant and M. d'Ajuda-Pinto; and M. de Beauséant, like a well-bred man of the world, always left his wife and the Portuguese as soon as he had installed them. But M. d'Ajuda-Pinto must marry, and a Mlle. de Rochefide was the young lady. In the whole fashionable world there was but one person who as yet knew nothing of the arrangement, and that was Mme. de Beauséant. Some of her friends had hinted at the possibility, and she had laughed at them, believing that envy had prompted those ladies to try to make mischief. And now, though the banns were about to be published, and although the handsome Portuguese had come that day to break the news to the Vicomtesse, he had not found courage as yet to say one word about his treachery. How was it? Nothing is doubtless more difficult than the notification of an ultimatum of this kind. There are men who feel more at their ease when they stand up before another man who threatens their lives with sword or pistol than in the presence of a woman who, after two hours of lamentations and reproaches, falls into a dead swoon and requires salts. At this moment, therefore, M. d'Ajuda-Pinto was on thorns, and anxious to take his leave. He told himself that in some way or other the news would reach Mme. de Beauséant; he would write, it would be much better to do it by letter, and not to utter the words that should stab her to the heart.

So when the servant announced M. Eugène de Rastignac, the Marquis d'Ajuda-Pinto trembled with joy. To be sure, a loving woman shows even more ingenuity in inventing doubts of her lover than in varying the monotony of his happiness; and when she is about to be forsaken, she instinctively interprets every gesture as rapidly as Virgil's courser detected the presence of his companion by snuffing the breeze. It was impossible, therefore, that Mme. de Beauséant should not detect that involuntary thrill of satisfaction; slight though it was, it was appalling in its artlessness.

Eugène had yet to learn that no one in Paris should present himself in any house without first making himself acquainted with the whole history of its owner, and of its owner's wife and family, so that he may avoid making any of the terrible blunders which in Poland draw forth the picturesque exclamation, "Harness five bullocks to your cart!" probably because you will need them all to pull you out of the quagmire into which a false step has plunged you.

If, down to the present day, our language has no name for these conversational disasters, it is probably because they are believed to be impossible, the publicity given in Paris to every scandal is so prodigious. After the awkward incident at Mme. de Restaud's, no one but Eugène could have reappeared in his character of bullock-driver in Mme. de Beauséant's drawing-room. But if Mme. de Restaud and M. de Trailles had found him horribly in the way, M. d'Ajuda hailed his coming with relief.

"Good-by," said the Portuguese, hurrying to the door, as Eugène made his entrance into a dainty little pink-and-gray drawing-room, where luxury seemed nothing more than good taste.

"Until this evening," said Mme. de Beauséant, turning her head to give the Marquis a glance. "We are going to the Bouffons, are we not?"

"I cannot go," he said, with his fingers on the door handle.

Mme. de Beauséant rose and beckoned to him to return. She did not pay the slightest attention to Eugène, who stood there dazzled by the sparkling marvels around him; he began to think that this was some story out of the *Arabian Nights* made real, and did not know where to hide himself, when the woman before him seemed to be unconscious of his existence.

The Vicomtesse had raised the forefinger of her right hand, and gracefully signed to the Marquis to seat himself beside her. The Marquis felt the imperious sway of passion in her gesture; he came back towards her. Eugène watched him, not without a feeling of envy.

"That is the owner of the brougham!" he said to himself. "But is it necessary to have a pair of spirited horses, servants in livery, and torrents of gold to draw a glance from a woman here in Paris?"

The demon of luxury gnawed at his heart, greed burned in his veins, his throat was parched with the thirst of gold.

He had a hundred and thirty francs every quarter. His father, mother, brothers, sisters, and aunt did not spend two hundred francs a month among them. This swift comparison between his present condition and the aims he had in view helped to benumb his faculties.

"Why not?" the Vicomtesse was saying, as she smiled at the Portuguese. "Why cannot you come to the Italiens?"

"Affairs! I am to dine with the English Ambassador."

"Throw him over."

When a man once enters on a course of deception, he is compelled to add lie to lie. M. d'Ajuda therefore said, smiling, "Do you lay your commands on me?"

"Yes, certainly."

"That was what I wanted to have you say to me," he answered, dissembling his feelings in a glance which would have reassured any other woman.

He took the Vicomtesse's hand, kissed it, and went.

Eugène ran his fingers through his hair, and constrained himself to bow. He thought that now Mme. de Beauséant would give him her attention; but suddenly she sprang forward, rushed to a window in the gallery, and watched M. d'Ajuda step into his carriage; she listened to the order that he gave, and heard the Swiss repeat it to the coachman—

"To M. de Rochefide's house."

Those words, and the way in which M. d'Ajuda flung himself back in the carriage, were like a lightning flash and a thunderbolt for her; she walked back again with a deadly fear gnawing at her heart. The most terrible catastrophes only happen among the heights. The Vicomtesse went to her own room, sat down at a table, and took up a sheet of dainty notepaper.

"When, instead of dining with the English Ambassador," she wrote, "you go to the Rochefides, you owe me an explanation, which I am waiting to hear."

She retraced several of the letters, for her hand was trembling so that they were indistinct; then she signed the note with an initial C for "Claire de Bourgogne," and rang the bell.

"Jacques," she said to the servant, who appeared immediately, "take this note to M. de Rochefide's house at half-past seven, ask for the Marquis d'Ajuda. If M. d'Ajuda is there, leave the note without waiting for an answer; if he is not there, bring the note back to me."

"Madame la Vicomtesse, there is a visitor in the drawing-room."

"Ah! yes, of course," she said, opening the door.

Eugène was beginning to feel very uncomfortable, but at last the Vicomtesse appeared; she spoke to him, and the tremulous tones of her voice vibrated through his heart.

"Pardon me, Monsieur," she said; "I had a letter to write. Now I am quite at liberty."

She scarcely knew what she was saying, for even as she spoke she thought, "Ah! he means to marry Mlle. de Rochefide? But is he still free? This evening the marriage shall be broken off, or else. . . . But before to-morrow I shall know."

"Cousin . . ." the student replied.

"Eh?" said the Countess, with an insolent glance that sent a cold shudder through Eugène; he understood what that "Eh?" meant; he had learned a great deal in three hours, and his wits were on the alert. He reddened—

"Madame . . ." he began; he hesitated a moment, and then went on. "Pardon me; I am in such need of protection that the merest scrap of relationship could do me no harm."

Mme. de Beauséant smiled, but there was sadness in her smile; even now she felt forebodings of the coming pain, the air she breathed was heavy with the storm that was about to burst.

"If you knew how my family are situated," he went on, "you would love to play the part of a beneficent fairy godmother who graciously clears the obstacles from the path of her protégé."

"Well, cousin," she said, laughing, "and how I can be of service to you?"

"But do I know even that? I am distantly related to you, and this obscure and remote relationship is even now a perfect godsend to me. You have confused my ideas; I cannot remember the things that I meant to say to you. I know no one else here in Paris. . . . Ah! if I could only ask you to counsel me, ask you to look upon me as a poor child who would fain cling to the hem of your dress, who would lay down his life for you."

"Would you kill a man for me?"

"Two," said Eugène.

"You, child! Yes, you are a child," she said, keeping back the tears that came to her eyes; "you would love sincerely."

"Oh!" he cried, flinging up his head.

The audacity of the student's answer interested the Vicomtesse in him. The southern brain was beginning to scheme for the first time. Between Mme. de Restaud's blue boudoir and Mme. de Beauséant's rose-colored drawing-room he had made a three years' advance in a kind of law which is not a recognized study in Paris, although it is a sort of higher jurisprudence, and, when well understood, is a highroad to success of every kind.

"Ah! this is what I meant to say!" said Eugène. "I met Mme. de Restaud at your ball, and this morning I went to see her."

"You must have been very much in the way," said Mme. de Beauséant, smiling as she spoke.

"Yes, indeed. I am a novice, and my blunders will set everyone against me, if you do not give me your counsel. I believe that in Paris it is very difficult to meet with a young, beautiful, and wealthy woman of fashion who would be willing to teach me, what you women can explain so well—life. I shall find a M. de Trailles everywhere. So I have come to you to ask you to give me a key to a puzzle, to entreat you to tell me what sort of blunder I made this morning. I mentioned an old man——"

"Madame la Duchesse de Langeais," Jacques cut the student short; Eugène gave expression to his intense annoyance by a gesture.

"If you mean to succeed," said the Vicomtesse in a low voice, "in the first place you must not be so demonstrative."

"Ah! good-morning, dear," she continued, and rising and crossing the room, she grasped the Duchess's hand as affectionately as if they had been sisters; the Duchess responded in the prettiest and most gracious way.

"Two intimate friends!" said Rastignac to himself. "Henceforward I shall have two protectresses; those two women are great friends, no doubt, and this newcomer will doubtless interest herself in her friend's cousin."

"To what happy inspiration do I owe this piece of good fortune, dear Antoinette?" asked Mme. de Beauséant.

"Well, I saw M. d'Ajuda-Pinto at M. de Rochefide's door, so I thought that if I came I should find you alone."

Mme. de Beauséant's mouth did not tighten, her color did not rise, her expression did not alter, or rather, her brow seemed to clear as the Duchess uttered those deadly words—

"If I had known that you were engaged——" the speaker added, glancing at Eugène.

"This gentleman is M. Eugène de Rastignac, one of my cousins," said the Vicomtesse. "Have you any news of General de Montriveau?" she continued. "Sérizy told me yesterday that he never goes anywhere now; has he been to see you to-day?"

It was believed that the Duchess was desperately in love with M. de Montriveau, and that he was a faithless lover; she felt the question in her very heart, and her face flushed as she answered—

"He was at the Elysée yesterday."

"In attendance?"

"Claire," returned the Duchess, and hatred overflowed in the glance she threw at Mme. de Beauséant; "of course you know that M. d'Ajuda-Pinto is going to marry Mlle. de Rochefide; the banns will be published to-morrow."

This thrust was too cruel; the Vicomtesse's face grew white, but she answered, laughing, "One of those rumors that fools amuse themselves with. What should induce M. d'Ajuda to take one of the noblest names in Portugal to the Rochefides? The Rochefides were only ennobled yesterday."

"But Berthe will have two hundred thousand livres a year, they say."

"M. d'Ajuda is too wealthy to marry for money."

"But, my dear, Mlle. de Rochefide is a charming girl."

"Indeed?"

"And, as a matter of fact, he is dining with them to-day; the thing is settled. It is very surprising to me that you should know so little about it."

Mme. de Beauséant turned to Rastignac. "What was the blunder that you made, Monsieur?" she asked. "The poor boy is only just launched into the world, Antoinette, so that he understands nothing of all this that we are speaking of. Be merciful to him, and let us finish our talk to-morrow. Everything will be announced to-morrow, you know, and your kind informal communication can be accompanied by official confirmation."

The Duchess gave Eugène one of those insolent glances that measure a man from head to foot, and leave him crushed and annihilated.

"Madame, I have unwittingly plunged a dagger into Mme. de Restaud's heart; unwittingly—therein lies my offense," said the student of law, whose keen brain had served him sufficiently well, for he had detected the biting epigrams that lurked beneath this friendly talk. "You continue to receive, possibly you fear, those who know the amount of pain that they deliberately inflict; but a clumsy blunderer who has no idea how deeply he wounds is looked upon as a fool who does not know how to make use of his opportunities, and everyone despises him."

Mme. de Beauséant gave the student a glance, one of those glances in which a great soul can mingle dignity and gratitude. It was like balm to the law student, who was still smarting under the Duchess's insolent scrutiny; she had looked at him as an auctioneer might look at some article to appraise its value.

"Imagine, too, that I had just made some progress with the Comte de Restaud; for I should tell you, Madame," he went on turning to the Duchess with a mixture of humility and malice in his manner, "that as yet I am only a poor devil of a student, very much alone in the world, and very poor——"

"You should not tell us that, M. de Restignac. We women never care about anything that no one else will take."

"Bah!" said Eugène. "I am only two-and-twenty, and I must make up my mind to the drawbacks of my time of life. Besides, I am confessing my sins, and it would be impossible to kneel in a more charming confessional; you commit your sins in one drawing-room, and receive absolution for them in another."

The Duchess's expression grew colder; she did not like the flippant tone of these remarks, and showed that she considered them to be in bad taste by turning to the Vicomtesse with—"This gentleman has only just come——"

Mme. de Beauséant began to laugh outright at her cousin and at the Duchess both.

"He has only just come to Paris, dear, and is in search of someone who will give him lessons in good taste."

"Mme. la Duchesse," said Eugène, "is it not natural to wish to be initiated into the mysteries which charm us?" ("Come, now," he said to himself, "my language is superfinely elegant, I'm sure.")

"But Mme. de Restaud is herself, I believe, M. de Trailles' pupil," said the Duchess.

"Of that I had no idea, Madame," answered the law student, "so I rashly came between them. In fact, I got on very well with the lady's husband, and his wife tolerated me for a time until I took it into my head to tell them that I knew someone of whom I had just caught a glimpse as he went out by a back staircase, a man who had given the Countess a kiss at the end of a passage."

"Who was it?" both women asked together.

"An old man who lives at the rate of two louis a month in the Faubourg Saint-Marceau, where I, a poor student, lodge likewise. He is a truly unfortunate creature, everybody laughs at him—we call him 'Father Goriot.'"

"Why, child that you are," cried the Vicomtesse, "Mme. de Restaud was a Mlle. Goriot!"

"The daughter of a vermicelli manufacturer," the Duchess added; "and when the little creature went to Court, the daughter of a pastry-cook was presented on the same day. Do you remember, Claire? The King began to laugh, and made some joke in Latin about flour. People—what was it? —people——"

"Ejusdem farinæ," said Eugène.

"Yes, that was it," said the Duchess.

"Oh! is that her father?" the law student continued, aghast.

"Yes, certainly; the old man had two daughters; he dotes on them, so to speak, though they will scarcely acknowledge him."

"Didn't the second daughter marry a banker with a German name?" the Vicomtesse asked, turning to Mme. de Langeais, "a Baron de Nucingen? And her name is Delphine, is it not? Isn't she a fair-haired woman who has a side-box at the Opéra? She comes sometimes to the Bouffons, and laughs loudly to attract attention."

The Duchess smiled, and said—

"I wonder at you, dear. What do you take so much interest in people of that kind? One must have been as madly in love as Restaud was, to be infatuated with Mlle. Anastasie and her flour sacks. Oh! he will not find her a good bargain! She is in M. de Trailles' hands, and he will ruin her."

"And they do not acknowledge their father!" Eugène repeated.

"Oh! well, yes, their father, the father, a father," replied the Vicomtesse, "a kind father who gave them each five or six hundred thousand francs, it is said, to secure their happiness by marrying them well; while he only kept eight or ten thousand livres a year for himself, thinking that his daughters would always be his daughters, thinking that in them he would live his life twice over again, that in their houses he should find two homes, where he would be loved and looked up to, and made much of. And in two years' time both his sons-in-law have turned him out of their houses as if he were one of the lowest outcasts."

Tears came into Eugène's eyes. He was still under the spell of youthful beliefs, he had but just left home, pure and sacred feeling had been stirred within him, and this was his first day on the battlefield of civilization in Paris. Genuine feeling is so infectious that for a moment the three looked at each other in silence.

"*Eh, mon Dieu!*" said Mme. de Langeais; "yes, it seems very horrible, and yet we see such things every day. Is there not a reason for it? Tell me, dear, have you ever really thought what a son-in-law is? A son-in-law is the man for whom we bring up, you and I, a dear little one, bound to us very closely in innumerable ways; for seventeen years she will be the joy of her family, its 'white soul,' as Lamartine says, and suddenly she will become its scourge. When *he* comes and takes her from us, his love from the very beginning is like an ax laid to the root of all the old affection in our darling's heart, and all the ties that bound her to her family are severed. But yesterday our little daughter thought of no one but her mother and father, as we had no thought that was not for her; by to-morrow she will have become a hostile stranger. The tragedy is always going on under our eyes. On the one hand, you see a father who has sacrificed himself to his son, and his daughter-in-law shows him the last degree of insolence. On the other hand, it is the son-in-law who turns his wife's mother out of the house. I sometimes hear it said that there is nothing dramatic about society in these days; but the Drama of the Son-in-law is appalling, to say nothing of our marriages, which have come to be very poor farces. I can explain how it all came about in the old vermicelli maker's case. I think I recollect that Foriot——"

"Goriot, Madame."

"Yes, that Moriot was once President of his Section during the Revolution. He was in the secret of the famous scarcity of grain, and laid the foundation of his fortune in those days by selling flour for ten times its cost. He had as much flour as he wanted. My grandmother's steward sold him immense quantities. No doubt Noriot shared the plunder with the Committee of Public Salvation, as that sort of person always did. I recollect the steward telling my grandmother that she might live at Grandvilliers in complete security, because her corn was as good as a certificate of civism. Well, then, this Loriot, who sold corn to those butchers, has never had but one passion, they say—he idolizes his daughters. He settled one of them under Restaud's roof, and grafted the other into the Nucingen family tree, the Baron de Nucingen being a rich banker who had turned Royalist. You can quite understand so long as Bonaparte was Emperor, the two sons-in-law could manage to put up with the old Ninety-three; but after the restoration of the Bourbons, M. de Restaud felt bored by the old man's society, and the banker was still more tired of it. His daughters were still fond of him; they wanted 'to keep the goat and the cabbage,' so they used to see the Joriot whenever there was no one there, under pretense of affection. 'Come to-day, papa, we shall have you all to ourselves, and that will be much nicer!' and all that sort of thing. As for me, dear, I believe that love has second sight: poor Ninety-three, his heart must have bled! He saw that his daughters were ashamed of him, that if they loved their husbands his visits must make mischief. So he immolated himself. He made the sacrifice because he was a father; he went into voluntary exile. His daughters were satisfied, so he thought that he had done the best thing he could; but it was a family crime, and father and daughters were accomplices. You see this sort of thing everywhere. What could this old Doriot have been but a splash of mud in his daughters' drawing-rooms? He would only have been in the way, and bored other people, besides being bored himself. And this that happened between father and daughters may happen to the prettiest woman in Paris and the man she loves the best; if her love grows tiresome, he will go; he will descend to the basest trickery to leave her. It is the same with all love and friendship. Our heart is a treasury; if you pour out all its wealth at once, you are bankrupt. We show no more mercy to the affection that reveals its utmost extent than we do to another kind of prodigal who has not a penny left. Their father had given them all he had. For twenty years he had given his whole heart to them; then, one day, he gave them all his fortune too. The lemon was squeezed; the girls left the rest in the gutter."

"The world is very base," said the Vicomtesse, plucking at the threads of her shawl. She did not raise her eyes as she spoke; the words that Mme. de Langeais had meant for her in the course of the story had cut her to the quick.

"Base? Oh, no," answered the Duchess; "the world goes its own way, that is all. If I speak in this way, it is only to show that I am not duped by it. I think as you do," she said, pressing the Vicomtesse's hand. "The world is a slough; let us try to live on the heights above it."

She rose to her feet and kissed Mme. de Beauséant on the forehead as she said: "You look very charming to-day, dear. I have never seen such a lovely color in your cheeks before."

Then she went out with a slight inclination of the head to the cousin.

"Old Goriot is sublime!" said Eugène to himself, as he remembered how he had watched his neighbor work the silver vessel into a shapeless mass that night.

Mme. de Beauséant did not hear him; she was absorbed in her own thoughts. For several minutes the silence remained unbroken till the law student became almost paralyzed with embarrassment, and was equally afraid to go or stay or speak a word.

"The world is basely ungrateful and ill-natured," said the Vicomtesse at last. "No sooner does a trouble befall you than a friend is ready to bring the tidings and to probe your heart with the point of a dagger while calling on you to admire the handle. Epigrams and sarcasms already! Ah! I will defend myself!"

She raised her head like the great lady that she was, and lightnings flashed from her proud eyes.

"Ah!" she said, as she saw Eugène, "are you there?"

"Still," he said piteously.

"Well, then, M. de Rastignac, deal with the world as it deserves. You are determined to succeed? I will help you. You shall sound the depths of corruption in woman; you shall measure the extent of man's pitful vanity. Deeply as I am versed in such learning, there were pages in the book of life that I had not read. Now I know all. The more cold-blooded your calculations, the further you will go. Strike ruthlessly; you will be feared. Men and women for you must be nothing more than post-horses; take a fresh relay, and leave the last to drop by the roadside; in this way you will reach the goal of your ambition. You will be nothing here, you see, unless a woman interests herself in you; and she must be young and wealthy, and a woman of the world. Yet, if you have a heart, lock it carefully away like a treasure; do not let anyone suspect it, or you will be lost; you would cease to be the executioner, you would take the victim's place. And if ever you should love, never let your secret escape you! trust no one until you are very sure of the heart to which you open your heart. Learn to mistrust everyone; take every precaution for the sake of the love which does not exist as yet. Listen, Miguel"—the name slipped from her so naturally that she did not notice her mistake—"there is something still more appalling than the ingratitude of daughters who have cast off their old father and wish he were dead, and that is a rivalry between two sisters. Restaud comes of a good family; his wife has been received into their circle; she has been presented at court; and her sister, her wealthy sister, Mme. Delphine de Nucingen, the wife of a great capitalist, is consumed with envy, and ready to die of spleen. There is a gulf set between the sisters—indeed, they are sisters no longer—the two women who refuse to acknowledge their father do not acknowledge each other. So Mme. de Nucingen would lap all the mud that lies between the Rue Saint-Lazare and the Rue de Grenelle to gain admittance to my salon. She fancied that she should gain her end through de Marsay; she has made herself de Marsay's slave, and she bores him.

De Marsay cares very little about her. If you will introduce her to me, you will be her darling, her Benjamin; she will idolize you. If, after that, you can love her, do so; if not, make her useful. I will ask her to come once or twice to one of my great crushes, but I will never receive her here in the morning. I will bow to her when I see her, and that will be quite sufficient. You have shut the Comtesse de Restaud's door against you by mentioning old Goriot's name. Yes, my good friend, you may call at her house twenty times, and every time out of the twenty you will find that she is not at home. The servants have their orders, and will not admit you. Very well, then, now let old Goriot gain the right of entry into her sister's house for you. The beautiful Mme. de Nucingen will give the signal for a battle. As soon as she singles you out, other women will begin to lose their heads about you, and her enemies and rivals and intimate friends will all try to take you from her. There are women who will fall in love with a man because another woman has chosen him; like the city madams, poor things, who copy our millinery, and hope thereby to acquire our manners. You will have a success, and in Paris success is everything; it is the key of power. If the women credit you with wit and talent, the men will follow suit so long as you do not undeceive them yourself. There will be nothing you may not aspire to; you will go everywhere, and you will find out what the world is—an assemblage of fools and knaves. But you must be neither the one nor the other. I am giving you my name like Ariadne's clew of thread to take with you into this labyrinth; make no unworthy use of it," she said, with a queenly glance and curve of her throat; "give it back to me unsullied. And now, go; leave me. We women also have our battles to fight."

"And if you should ever need someone who would gladly set a match to a train for you—

"Well?" she asked.

He tapped his heart, smiled in answer to his cousin's smile, and went.

It was five o'clock, and Eugène was hungry; he was afraid lest he should not be in time for dinner, a misgiving which made him feel that it was pleasant to be borne so quickly across Paris. This sensation of physical comfort left his mind free to grapple with the thoughts that assailed him. A mortification usually sends a young man of his age into a furious rage; he shakes his fists at society, and vows vengeance when his belief in himself is shaken. Just then Rastignac was overwhelmed by the words, "You have shut the Countess's door against you."

"I shall call!" he said to himself, "and if Mme. de Beauséant is right, if I never find her at home—I . . . well, Mme. de Restaud shall meet me in every salon in Paris. I will learn to fence, and have some pistol practice, and kill that Maxime of hers!"

"And money?" cried an inward monitor. "How about money, where is that to come from?" And all at once the wealth displayed in the Comtesse de Restaud's drawing-room rose before his eyes. That was the luxury which Goriot's daughter had loved too well; the gilding, the ostentatious splendor, the unintelligent luxury of the parvenu, the riotous extravagance of a courtesan. Then the attractive vision suddenly went under an eclipse as he remembered the stately grandeur of the Hôtel de Beauséant. As his fancy wandered among these lofty regions in the great world of Paris, innumerable dark thoughts gathered in his heart; his ideas widened, and his conscience grew more elastic. He saw the world as it is; saw how the rich lived beyond the jurisdiction of law and public opinion, and found in success the *ultima ratio mundi.*

"Vautrin is right, success is virtue!" he said to himself.

Arrived in the Rue Neuve Sainte-Geneviève, he rushed up to his room for ten francs wherewith to satisfy the demands of the cabman, and went in to dinner. He glanced round the squalid room, saw the eighteen poverty-stricken creatures about to feed like cattle in their stalls, and the sight filled him with loathing. The transition was too sudden, and the contrast was so violent that it could not but act as a powerful stimulant; his ambition developed and grew beyond all bounds. On the one hand, he beheld a vision of social life in its most charming and refined forms, of quick-pulsed youth, of fair, impassioned faces invested with all the charm of poetry, framed in a marvelous setting of luxury or art; and, on the other hand, he saw a somber picture, the miry verge beyond these faces, in which passion was extinct and nothing was left of the drama but the cords and pulleys and bare mechanism. Mme. de Beauséant's counsels, the words uttered in anger by the forsaken lady, her petulant offer, came to his mind, and poverty was a ready expositor. Rastignac determined to open two parallel trenches, so as to insure success; he would be a learned doctor of law and a man of fashion. Clearly he was still a child! Those two lines are asymptotes, and will never meet.

"You are very dull, my lord Marquis," said Vautrin, with one of the shrewd glances that seem to read the innermost secrets of another mind.

"I am not in the humor to stand jokes from people who call me 'my lord Marquis,'" answered Eugène. "A marquis here in Paris, if he is not the veriest sham, ought to have a hundred thousand livres a year at least; and a lodger in the Maison Vauquer is not exactly Fortune's favorite."

Vautrin's glance at Rastignac was half-paternal, half-contemptuous. "Puppy!" it seemed to say; "I should make one mouthful of him!" Then he answered—

"You are in a bad humor; perhaps your visit to the beautiful Comtesse de Restaud was not a success."

"She has shut her door against me because I told her that her father dined at our table," cried Rastignac.

Glances were exchanged all round the room; old Goriot looked down.

"You have sent some snuff into my eye," he said to his neighbor, turning a little aside to rub his hand over his face.

"Anyone who molests Father Goriot will have henceforward to reckon with me," said Eugène, looking at the old man's neighbor; "he is worth all the rest of us put together. —I am not speaking of the ladies," he added, turning in the direction of Mlle. Taillefer.

Eugène's remarks produced a sensation, and his tone silenced the dinner-table. Vautrin alone spoke. "If you are going to champion Father Goriot, and set up for his responsible editor into the bargain, you have need be a crack shot and know how to handle the foils." he said, banteringly.

"So I intend," said Eugène.

"Then are you taking the field to-day?"

"Perhaps," Rastignac answered. "But I owe no account of myself to anyone, especially as I do not try to find out what other people do of a night."

Vautrin looked askance at Rastignac.

"If you do not mean to be deceived by the puppets, my boy, you must go behind and see the whole show, and not peep through holes in the curtain. That is enough," he added, seeing that Eugène was about to fly into a passion. "We can have a little talk whenever you like."

There was a general feeling of gloom and constraint. Old Goriot was so deeply dejected by the student's remark that he did not notice the change in the disposition of his fellow-lodgers, nor know that he had met with a champion capable of putting an end to the persecution.

"Then, M. Goriot sitting there is the father of a countess," said Mme. Vauquer in a low voice.

"And of a baroness," answered Rastignac.

"That is about all he is capable of," said Bianchon to Rastignac; "I have taken a look at his head; there is only one bump—the bump of Paternity; he must be an *eternal father*."

Eugène was too intent on his thoughts to laugh at Bianchon's joke. He determined to profit by Mme. de Beauséant's counsels, and was asking himself how he could obtain the necessary money. He grew grave. The wide savannahs of the world stretched before his eyes; all things lay before him, nothing was his. Dinner came to an end, the others went, and he was left in the dining-room.

"So you have seen my daughter?" Goriot spoke tremulously, and the sound of his voice broke in upon Eugène's dreams. The young man took the elder's hands, and looked at him with something like kindness in his eyes.

"You are a good and noble man," he said. "We will have some talk about your daughters by and by."

He rose without waiting for Goriot's answer, and went to his room. Then he wrote the following letter to his mother:

"My Dear Mother,—Can you nourish your child from your breast again? I am in a position to make a rapid fortune, but I want twelve hundred francs—I must have them at all costs. Say nothing about this to my father; perhaps he might make objections, and unless I have the money, I may be led to put an end to myself, and so escape the clutches of despair. I will tell you everything when I see you. I will not begin to try to describe my present situation; it would take volumes to put the whole story clearly and fully. I have not been gambling, my kind mother, I owe no one a penny; but if you would preserve the life that you gave me, you must send me the sum I mention. As a matter of fact, I go to see the Vicomtesse de Beauséant; she is using her influence for me; I am obliged to go into society, and I have not a penny to lay out on clean gloves. I can manage to exist on bread and water, or go without food, if need be, but I cannot do without the tools with which they cultivate the vineyards in this country. I must resolutely make up my mind at once to make my way, or stick in the mire for the rest of my days. I know that all your hopes are set on me, and I want to realize them quickly. Sell some of your old jewelry, my kind mother; I will give you other jewels very soon. I know enough of our affairs at home to know all that such a sacrifice means, and you must not think that I would lightly ask you to make it; I should be a monster if I could. You must think of my entreaty as a cry forced from me by imperative necessity. Our whole future lies in the subsidy with which I must begin my first campaign, for life in Paris is one continual battle. If you cannot otherwise procure the whole of the money, and are forced to sell our aunt's lace, tell her that I will send her some still handsomer," and so forth.

He wrote to ask each of his sisters for their savings—would they despoil themselves for him, and keep the sacrifice a secret from the family? To his request he knew that they would not fail to respond gladly, and he added to it an appeal to their delicacy by touching the chord of honor that vibrates so loudly in young and highly-strung natures.

Yet when he had written the letters, he could not help feeling misgivings in spite of his youthful ambition; his heart beat fast, and he trembled. He knew the spotless nobleness of the lives buried away in the lonely manor house; he knew what trouble and what joy his request would cause his sisters, and how happy they would be as they talked at the bottom of the orchard of that dear brother of theirs in Paris. Visions rose before his eyes; a sudden strong light revealed his sisters secretly counting over their little store, devising some girlish stratagem by which the money could be sent to him *incognito,* essaying, for the first time in their lives, a piece of deceit that reached the sublime in its unselfishness.

"A sister's heart is a diamond for purity, a deep sea of tenderness!" he said to himself. He felt ashamed of those letters.

What power there must be in the petitions put up by such hearts; how pure the fervor that bears their souls to Heaven in prayer! What exquisite joy they would find in self-sacrifice! What a pang for his mother's heart if she could not send him all that he asked for! And this noble affection, these sacrifices made at such terrible cost, were to serve as the ladder by which he meant to climb to Delphine de Nucingen. A few tears, like the last grains of incense flung upon the sacred altar fire of the hearth, fell from his eyes. He walked up and down, and despair mingled with his emotion. Old Goriot saw him through the half-open door.

"What is the matter, sir?" he asked from the threshold.

"Ah! my good neighbor, I am as much a son and brother as you are a father. You do well to fear for the Comtesse Anastasie; there is one M. Maxime de Trailles, who will be her ruin."

Old Goriot withdrew, stammering some words, but Eugène failed to catch their meaning.

The next morning Rastignac went out to post his letters. Up to the last moment he wavered and doubted, but he ended by flinging them into the box. "I shall succeed!" he said to himself. So says the gambler; so says the great captain; but the three words that have been the salvation of some few have been the ruin of many more.

A few days after this Eugène called at Mme. de Restaud's house; she was not at home. Three times he tried the experiment, and three times he found her doors closed against him, though he was careful to choose an hour when M. de Trailles was not there. The Vicomtesse was right.

The student studied no longer. He put in an appearance at lectures simply to answer to his name, and after thus attesting his presence, departed forthwith. He had been through a reasoning process familiar to most students. He had seen the advisibility of deferring his studies to the last moment before going up for his examinations; he made up his mind to cram his second and third year's work into the third year, when he meant to begin to work in earnest, and to complete his studies in law with one great effort. In the meantime he had fifteen months in which to navigate the ocean of Paris, to spread the nets and set the lines that should bring him a protectress and a fortune. Twice during that week he saw Mme. de Beauséant; he did not go to her house until he had seen the Marquis d'Ajuda drive away.

Victory for yet a few days was with the great lady, the most poetic figure in the Faubourg Saint-Germain; and the marriage of the Marquis d'Ajuda-Pinto with Mlle. de Rochefide was postponed. The dread of losing her happiness filled those days with a fever of joy unknown before, but the end was only so much the nearer. The Marquis d'Ajuda and the Rochefides agreed that this quarrel and reconciliation was a very fortunate thing; Mme. de Beauséant (so they hoped) would gradually become reconciled to the idea of the marriage, and in the end would be brought to sacrifice d'Ajuda's morning visits to the exigencies of a man's career, exigencies which she must have foreseen. In spite of the most solemn promises, daily renewed, M. d'Ajuda was playing a part, and the Vicomtesse was eager to be deceived. "Instead of taking the leap heroically from the window, she is falling headlong down the staircase," said her most intimate friend, the Duchesse de Langeais. Yet this after-glow of happiness lasted long enough for the Vicomtesse to be of service to her young cousin. She had a half-superstitious affection for him. Eugène had shown her sympathy and devotion at a crisis when a woman sees no pity, no real comfort in any eyes; when if a man is ready with soothing flatteries, it is because he has an interested motive.

Rastignac made up his mind that he must learn the whole of Goriot's previous history; he would come to his bearings before attempting to board the Maison de Nucingen. The results of his inquiries may be given briefly as follows:—

In the days before the Revolution, Jean-Joachim Goriot was simply a workman in the employ of a vermicelli maker. He was a skillful, thrifty workman, sufficiently enterprising to buy his master's business when the latter fell a chance victim to the disturbances of 1789. Goriot established himself in the Rue de la Jussienne, close to the Corn Exchange. His plain good sense led him to accept the position of President of the Section, so as to secure for his business the protection of those in power at that dangerous epoch. This prudent step had led to success; the foundations of his fortune were laid in the time of the Scarcity (real or artificial), when the price of grain of all kinds rose enormously in Paris. People used to fight for bread at the bakers' doors; while other persons went to the grocers' shops and bought Italian paste foods without brawling over it. It was during this year that Goriot made the money, which, at a later time, was to give him all the advantage of the great capitalist over the small buyer; he had, moreover, the usual luck of average ability; his mediocrity was the salvation of him. He excited no one's envy; it was not even suspected that he was rich till the peril of being rich was over, and all his intelligence was concentrated, not on political, but on commercial speculations. Goriot was an authority second to none on all questions relating to corn, flour, and "middlings"; and the production, storage, and quality of grain. He could estimate the yield of the harvest, and foresee market prices; he bought his cereals in Sicily, and imported Russian wheat. Anyone who had heard him hold forth on the regulations that control the importation and exportation of grain, who had seen his grasp of the subject, his clear insight into the principles involved, his appreciation of weak points in the way that the system worked, would have thought that here was the stuff of which a minister is made. Patient, active, and persevering, energetic and prompt in action, he surveyed his business horizon with an eagle's eye. Nothing there took him by surprise; he foresaw all things, knew all that was happening, and kept his own counsel; he was a diplomatist in his quick comprehension of a situation; and in the routine of business he was as patient and plodding as a soldier on the march. Beyond this business horizon he could not see. He used to spend his hours of leisure on the threshold of his shop, leaning against the framework of the door. Take him from his dark little counting-house, and he became once more the rough, slow-witted workman, a man who cannot understand a piece of reasoning, who is indifferent to all intellectual pleasures, and falls asleep at the play, a Parisian Dolibom in short, against whose stupidity other minds are powerless.

Natures of this kind are nearly all alike; in almost all of them you will find some hidden depth of sublime affection. Two all-absorbing affections filled the vermicelli maker's heart to the exclusion of every other feeling; into them he seemed to put all the forces of his nature, as he put the whole power of his brain into the corn trade. He had regarded his wife, the only daughter of a rich farmer of La Brie, with a devout admiration; his love for her had been boundless. Goriot had felt the charm of a lovely sensitive nature, which, in its delicate strength, was the very opposite of his own. Is there any instinct more deeply implanted in the heart of man than the pride of protection, a protection which is constantly exerted for a fragile and defenseless creature? Join love thereto, the warmth of gratitude that all generous souls feel for the source of their pleasures, and you have the explanation of many strange incongruities in human nature.

After seven years of unclouded happiness, Goriot lost his wife. It was very unfortunate for him. She was beginning to gain an ascendency over him in other ways; possibly she might have brought that barren soil under cultivation, she might have widened his ideas and given other directions to his thoughts. But when she was dead, the instinct of fatherhood developed in him till it almost became a mania. All the affection balked by death seemed to turn to his daughters, and he found full satisfaction for his heart in loving them. More or less brilliant proposals were made to him from time to time; wealthy merchants or farmers with daughters vied with each other in offering inducements to him to marry again; but he determined to remain a widower. His father-in-law, the only man for whom he felt a decided friendship, gave out that Goriot had made a vow to be faithful to his wife's memory. The frequenters of the Corn Exchange, who could not comprehend this sublime piece of folly, joked about it among themselves, and found a ridiculous nickname for him. One of them ventured (after a glass over a bargain) to call him by it, and a blow from the vermicelli maker's fist sent him headlong into a gutter in the Rue Oblin. He could think of nothing else when his children were concerned; his love for them made him fidgety and anxious; and this was so well known, that one day, a competitor, who wished to get rid of him to secure the field to himself, told Goriot that Delphine had just been knocked down by a cab. The vermicelli maker turned ghastly pale, left the Exchange at once, and did not return for several days afterwards; he was ill in consequence of the shock and the subsequent relief on discovering that it was a false alarm. This time, however, the offender did not escape with a bruised shoulder; at a critical moment in the man's affairs, Goriot drove him into bankruptcy, and forced him to disappear from the Corn Exchange.

As might have been expected, the two girls were spoiled. With an income of sixty thousand francs, Goriot scarcely spent twelve hundred on himself, and found all his happiness in satisfying the whims of the two girls. The best masters were engaged, that Anastasie and Delphine might be endowed with all the accomplishments which distinguish a good education. They had a chaperon—luckily for them, she was a woman who had sense and good taste;—they learned to ride; they had a carriage for their use; they lived as the mistress of a rich old lord might live; they had only to express a wish, their father would hasten to give them their most extravagant desires, and asked nothing of them in return but a kiss. Goriot had raised the two girls to the level of the angels; and, quite naturally, he himself was left beneath them. Poor man! he loved them even for the pain that they gave him.

When the girls were old enough to be married, they were left free to choose for themselves. Each had half her father's fortune as her dowry; and when the Comte de Restaud came to woo Anastasie for her beauty, her social aspirations led her to leave her father's house for a more exalted sphere. Delphine wished for money; she married Nucingen, a banker of German extraction, who became a Baron of the Holy Roman Empire. Goriot remained a vermicelli maker as before. His daughters and his sons-in-law began to demur; they did not like to see him still engaged in trade, though his whole life was bound up with his business. For five years he stood out against their entreaties, then he yielded, and consented to retire on the amount realized by the sale of his business and the savings of the last few years. It was this capital that Mme. Vauquer, in the early days of his residence with her, had calculated would bring in eight or ten thousand livres in a year. He had taken refuge in her lodging-house, driven there by despair when he knew that his daughters were compelled by their husbands not only to refuse to receive him as an inmate in their houses, but even to see him no more except in private.

This was all the information which Rastignac gained from a M. Muret, who had purchased Goriot's business, information which confirmed the Duchesse de Langeais's suppositions, and herewith the preliminary explanation of this obscure but terrible Parisian tragedy comes to an end.

Towards the end of the first week in December Rastignac received two letters—one from his mother, and one from his eldest sister. His heart beat fast, half with happiness, half with fear, at the sight of the familiar handwriting. Those two little scraps of paper contained life or death for his hopes. But while he felt a shiver of dread as he remembered their dire poverty at home, he knew their love for him so well that he could not help fearing that he was draining their very life-blood. His mother's letter ran as follows:—

"My Dear Child,—I am sending you the money that you asked for. Make a good use of it. Even to save your life I could not raise so large a sum a second time without your father's knowledge, and there would be trouble about it. We should be obliged to mortgage the land. It is impossible to judge of the merits of schemes of which I am ignorant; but what sort of schemes can they be, that you should fear to tell me about them? Volumes of explanation would not have been needed; we mothers can understand at a word, and that word would have spared me the anguish of uncertainty. I do not know how to hide the painful impression that your letter has made upon me, my dear son. What can you have felt when you were moved to send this chill of dread through my heart? It must have been very painful to you to write the letter that gave me so much pain as I read it. To what courses are you committed? You are going to appear to be something that you are not, and your whole life and success depends upon this? You are about to see a society into which you cannot enter without rushing into expense that you cannot afford, without losing precious time that is needed for your studies? Ah! my dear Eugène, believe your mother, crooked ways cannot lead to great ends. Patience and endurance are the two qualities most needed in your position. I am not scolding you; I do not want any tinge of bitterness to spoil our offering. I am only talking like a mother whose trust in you is as great as her foresight for you. You know the steps that you must take, and I, for my part, know your purity of heart, and how good your intentions are; so I can say to you without a doubt, 'Go forward, beloved!' If I tremble, it is because I am a mother, but my prayers and blessings will be with you at every step. Be very careful, dear boy. You must have a man's prudence, for it lies with you to shape the destinies of five others who are dear to you, and must look to you. Yes, our fortunes depend upon you, and your success is ours. We all pray to God to be with you in all that you do. Your aunt Marcillac has been most generous beyond words in this matter; she saw at once how it was, even down to your gloves. 'But I have a weakness for the eldest!' she said gayly. You must love your aunt very much, dear Eugène. I shall wait till you have succeeded before telling you all that she has done for you, or her money would burn your fingers. You, who are young, do not know what it is to part with something that is a piece of your past! But what would we not sacrifice for your sake? Your aunt says that I am to send you a kiss on the forehead for her, and that kiss is to bring you luck again and again, she says. She would have written to you herself, the dear kind-hearted woman, but she is troubled with the gout in her fingers just now. Your father is very well. The vintage of 1819 has turned out better than we expected. Good-by, dear boy; I will say nothing about your sisters, because Laure is writing to you, and I must let her have the pleasure of giving you all the home news. Heaven send that you may succeed! Oh! yes, dear Eugène, you must succeed. I have come, through you, to a knowledge of a pain so sharp that I do not think I could endure it a second time. I have come to know what it is to be poor, and to long for money for my children's sake. There, good-by! Do not leave us for long without news of you; and here, at the last, take a kiss from your mother."

By the time Eugène had finished the letter he was in tears. He thought of Father Goriot crushing his silver keepsake into a shapeless mass before he sold it to meet his daughter's bill of exchange.

"Your mother has broken up her jewels for you," he said to himself; "your aunt shed tears over those relics of hers before she sold them for your sake. What right have you to heap execrations on Anastasie? You have followed her example; you have selfishly sacrificed others to your own future, and she sacrifices her father to her lover; and of you two, which is the worse?"

He was ready to renounce his attempts; he could not bear to take that money. The fires of remorse burned in his heart, and gave him intolerable pain, the generous secret remorse which men seldom take into account when they sit in judgment upon their fellow-men; but perhaps the angels in heaven, beholding it, pardon the criminal whom our justice condemns. Rastignac opened his sister's letter; its simplicity and kindness revived his heart.

"Your letter came just at the right time, dear brother. Agathe and I had thought of so many different ways of spending our money, that we did not know what to buy with it; and now you have come in, and, like the servant who upset all the watches that belonged to the King of Spain, you have restored harmony; for, really and truly, we did not know which of all the things we wanted we wanted most, and we were always quarreling about it, never thinking, dear Eugène, of a way of spending our money which would satisfy us completely. Agathe jumped for joy. Indeed, we have been like two mad things all day, 'to such a prodigious degree' (as aunt would say), that mother said, with her severe expression, 'Whatever can be the matter with you, mesdemoiselles?' I think if we had been scolded a little, we should have been still better pleased. A woman ought to be very glad to suffer for one she loves! I, however, in my inmost soul, was doleful and cross in the midst of all my joy. I shall make a bad wife, I am afraid, I am too fond of spending. I had bought two sashes and a nice little stiletto for piercing eyelet-holes in my stays, trifles that I really did not want, so that I have less than that slow-coach Agathe, who is so economical, and hoards her money like a magpie. She had two hundred francs! And I have only one hundred and fifty! I am nicely punished; I could throw my sash down the well; it will be painful to me to wear it now. Poor dear, I have robbed you. And Agathe was so nice about it. She said, 'Let us send the three hundred and fifty francs in our two names!' But I could not help telling you everything just as it happened.

"Do you know how we managed to keep your commandments? We took our glittering hoard, we went out for a walk, and when once fairly on the highway we ran all the way to Ruffec, where we handed over the coin, without more ado, to M. Grimbert of the Messageries Royales. We came back again like swallows on the wing. 'Don't you think that happiness has made us lighter?' Agathe said. We said all sorts of things, which I shall not tell you, Monsieur le Parisien, because they were all about you. Oh, we love you dearly, dear brother; it was all summed up in those few words. As for keeping the secret, little masqueraders like us are capable of anything (according to our aunt), even of holding our tongues. Our mother has been on a mysterious journey to Angoulême, and the aunt went with her, not without solemn councils, from which we were shut out, and M. le Baron likewise. They are silent as to the weighty political considerations that prompted their mission, and conjectures are rife in the State of Rastignac. The Infantas are embroidering a muslin robe with open-work sprigs for her Majesty the Queen; the work progresses in the most profound secrecy. There be but two more breadths to finish. A decree has gone forth that no wall shall be built on the side of Verteuil, but that a hedge shall be planted instead thereof. Our subjects may sustain some disappointment of fruit and espaliers, but strangers will enjoy a fair prospect. Should the heir-presumptive lack pocket-handkerchiefs, be it known unto him that the dowager Lady of Marcillac, exploring the recesses of her drawers and boxes (known respectively as Pompeii and Herculaneum), having brought to light a fair piece of cambric whereof she wotted not, the Princesses Agathe and Laure place at their brother's disposal their thread, their needles, and hands somewhat of the reddest. The two young Princes, Don Henri and Don Gabriel, retain their fatal habits of stuffing themselves with grape-jelly, of teasing their sisters, of taking their pleasure by going a-birdnesting, and of cutting switches for themselves from the osier-beds, mauger the laws of the realm. Moreover, they list not to learn aught, wherefore the Papal Nuncio (called of the commonalty, M. le Curé) threateneth them with excommunication, since that they neglect the sacred canons of grammatical construction for the construction of other cannon, deadly engines made of the stems of elder.

"Farewell, dear brother, never did letter carry so many wishes for your success, so much love fully satisfied. You will have a great deal to tell us when you come home! You will tell me everything, won't you? I am the oldest. From something the aunt let fall, we think you must have had some success.

" 'Something was said of a lady, but nothing more was said . . .'

"Of course not, in our family! Oh, by-the-by, Eugène, would you rather that we made that piece of cambric into shirts for you instead of pocket-handkerchiefs? If you want some really nice shirts at once, we ought to lose no time in beginning upon them; and if the fashion is different now in Paris, send us one for a pattern; we want more particularly to know about the cuffs. Good-by! good-by! Take my kiss on the left side of your forehead, on the temple that belongs to me, and to no one else in the world. I am leaving the other side of the sheet for Agathe, who has solemnly promised not to read a word that I have written; but, all the same, I mean to sit by her while she writes, so as to be quite sure that she keeps her word.—Your loving sister.

"LAURE DE RASTIGNAC."

"Yes!" said Eugène to himself. "Yes! Success at all costs now! Riches could not repay such devotion as this. I wish I could give them every sort of happiness Fifteen hundred and fifty francs," he went on, after a pause. "Every shot must go to the mark! Laure is right. Trust a woman! I have only calico shirts. Where someone else's welfare is concerned, a young girl becomes as ingenious as a thief. Guileless where she herself is in question, and full of foresight for me,—she is like a heavenly angel forgiving the strange incomprehensible sins of earth."

The world lay before him. His tailor had been summoned and sounded, and had finally surrendered. When Rastignac met M. de Trailles, he had seen at once how great a part the tailor plays in a young man's career; a tailor is either a deadly enemy of a stanch friend, with an invoice for a bond of friendship; between these two extremes there is, alack! no middle term. In this representative of his craft Eugène discovered a man who understood that his was a sort of paternal function for young men at their entrance into life, who regarded himself as a stepping-stone between a young man's present and future. And Rastignac in gratitude made the man's fortune by an epigram of a kind in which he excelled at a later period of his life.

"I have twice known a pair of trousers turned out by him make a match of twenty thousand livres a year!"

Fifteen hundred francs, and as many suits of clothes as he chose to order! At that moment the poor child of the South felt no more doubts of any kind. The young man went down to breakfast with the indefinable air which the consciousness of the possession of money gives to youth. No sooner are the coins slipped into a student's pocket than his wealth, in imagination at least, is piled into a fantastic column, which affords him a moral support. He begins to hold up his head as he walks; he is conscious that he has a means of bringing his powers to bear on a given point; he looks you straight in the face; his gestures are quick and decided; only yesterday he was diffident and shy, anyone might have pushed him aside; to-morrow, he will take the wall of a prime minister. A miracle has been wrought in him. Nothing is beyond the reach of his ambition, and his ambition soars at random; he is light-hearted, generous, and enthusiastic; in short, the fledging bird has discovered that he has wings. A poor student snatches at every chance pleasure much as a dog runs all sorts of risks to steal a bone, cracking it and sucking the marrow as he flies from pursuit; but a young man who can rattle a few runaway gold coins in his pocket can take his pleasure deliberately, can taste the whole of the sweets of secure possession; he soars far above earth; he has forgotten what the word *poverty* means; all Paris is his. Those are days when the whole world shines radiant with light, when everything glows and sparkles before the eyes of youth, days that bring joyous energy that is never brought into harness, days of debts and of painful fears that go hand in hand with every delight. Those who do not know the left bank of the Seine between the Rue Saint-Jacques and the Rue des Saints-Pères know nothing of life.

"Ah! if the women of Paris but knew," said Rastignac, as he devoured Mme. Vauquer's stewed pears (at five for a penny), "they would come here in search of a lover."

Just then a porter from the Messageries Royales appeared at the door of the room; they had previously heard the bell ring as the wicket opened to admit him. The man asked for M. Eugène de Rastignac, holding out two bags for him to take, and a form of receipt for his signature. Vautrin's keen glance cut Eugène like a lash.

"Now you will be able to pay for those fencing lessons and go to the shooting gallery," he said.

"Your ship has come in," said Mme. Vauquer, eying the bags.

Mlle. Michonneau did not dare to look at the money, for fear her eyes should betray her cupidity.

"You have a kind mother," said Mme. Couture.

"You have a kind mother, sir," echoed Poiret.

"Yes, mamma has been drained dry," said Vautrin, "and now you can have your fling, go into society, and fish for heiresses and dance with countesses who have peach blossom in their hair. But take my advice, young man, and don't neglect your pistol practice."

Vautrin struck an attitude, as if he were facing an antagonist. Rastignac, meaning to give the porter a tip, felt in his pockets and found nothing. Vautrin flung down a franc piece on the table.

"Your credit is good," he remarked, eying the student, and Rastignac was forced to thank him, though, since the sharp encounter of wits at dinner that day, after Eugène came in from calling on Mme. de Beauséant, he had made up his mind that Vautrin was insufferable. For a week, in fact, they had both kept silence in each other's presence, and watched each other. The student tried in vain to account to himself for this attitude.

An idea, of course, gains in force by the energy with which it is expressed; it strikes where the brain sends it, by a law as mathematically exact as the law that determines the course of a shell from a mortar. The amount of impression it makes is not to be determined so exactly. Sometimes, in an impressible nature, the idea works havoc, but there are, no less, natures so robustly protected, that this sort of projectile falls flat and harmless on skulls of triple brass, as cannon-shot against solid masonry; then there are flaccid and spongy-fibered natures into which ideas from without sink like spent bullets into the earthworks of a redoubt. Rastignac's head was something of the powder-magazine order; the least shock sufficed to bring about an explosion. He was too quick, too young, not to be readily accessible to ideas; and open to that subtle influence of thought and feeling in others which causes so many strange phenomena that make an impression upon us of which we are all unconscious at the time. Nothing escaped his mental vision; he was lynx-eyed; in him the mental powers of perception, which seem like duplicates of the senses, had the mysterious power of swift projection that astonishes us in intellects of a high order—slingers who are quick to detect the weak spot in any armor.

In the past month Eugène's good qualities and defects had rapidly developed with his character. Intercourse with the world and the endeavor to satisfy his growing desires had brought out his defects. But Rastignac came from the South side of the Loire, and had the good qualities of his countrymen. He had the impetuous courage of the South, that rushes to the attack of a difficulty, as well as the southern impatience of delay or suspense. The traits are held to be defects in the North; they made the fortune of Murat, but they likewise cut short his career. The moral would appear to be that when the dash and boldness of the South side of the Loire meets, in a southern temperament, with the guile of the North, the character is complete, and such a man will gain (and keep) the crown of Sweden.

Rastignac, therefore, could not stand the fire from Vautrin's batteries for long without discovering whether this was a friend or a foe. He felt as if this strange being was reading his inmost soul, and dissecting his feelings, while Vautrin himself was so close and secretive that he seemed to have something of the profound and unmoved serenity of a sphinx, seeing and hearing all things and saying nothing. Eugène, conscious of that money in his pocket, grew rebellious.

"Be so good as to wait a moment," he said to Vautrin, as the latter rose, after slowly emptying his coffee-cup, sip by sip.

"What for?" inquired the older man, as he put on his large-brimmed hat and took up the sword-cane that he was wont to twirl like a man who will face three or four footpads without flinching.

"I will repay you in a minute," returned Eugène. He unsealed one of the bags as he spoke, counted out a hundred and forty francs, and pushed them towards Mme. Vauquer. "Short reckonings make good friends," he added, turning to the widow; "that clears our accounts till the end of the year. Can you give me change for a five-franc piece?"

"Good friends make short reckonings," echoed Poiret, with a glance at Vautrin.

"Here is your franc," said Rastignac, holding out the coin to the sphinx in the black wig.

"Anyone might think that you were afraid to owe me a trifle," exclaimed this latter, with a searching glance that seemed to read the young man's inmost thoughts; there was a satirical and cynical smile on Vautrin's face such as Eugène had seen scores of times already; every time he saw it, it exasperated him almost beyond endurance.

"Well . . . so I am," he answered. He held both the bags in his hand, and had risen to go up to his room.

Vautrin made as if he were going out through the sitting-room, and the student turned to go through the second door that opened into the square lobby at the foot of the staircase.

"Do you know, Monsieur le Marquis de Rastignacorama, that what you were saying just now was not exactly polite?" Vautrin remarked, as he rattled his sword-cane across the panels of the sitting-room door, and came up to the student.

Rastignac looked coolly at Vautrin, drew him to the foot of the staircase, and shut the dining-room door. They were standing in the little square lobby between the kitchen and the dining-room; the place was lighted by an iron-barred fanlight above a door that gave access into the garden. Sylvie came out of her kitchen, and Eugène chose that moment to say—

"*Monsieur* Vautrin, I am not a marquis, and my name is not Rastignacorama."

"They will fight," said Mlle. Michonneau, in an indifferent tone.

"Fight!" echoed Poiret.

"Not they," replied Mme. Vauquer, lovingly fingering her pile of coins.

"But there they are under the lime-trees," cried Mlle. Victorine, who had risen so that she might see out into the garden. "Poor young man! he was in the right, after all."

"We must go upstairs, my pet," said Mme. Couture; "it is no business of ours."

At the door, however, Mme. Couture and Victorine found their progress barred by the portly form of Sylvie the cook.

"Whatever can have happened?" she said. "M. Vautrin said to M. Eugène, 'Let us have an explanation!' then he took him by the arm, and there they are, out among the artichokes."

Vautrin came in while she was speaking. "Mamma Vauquer," he said, smiling, "don't frighten yourself at all. I am only going to try my pistols under the lime-trees."

"Oh! Monsieur," cried Victorine, clasping her hands as she spoke, "why do you want to kill M. Eugène?"

Vautrin stepped back a pace or two, and gazed at Victorine.

"Oh! this is something fresh!" he exclaimed in a bantering tone, that brought the color into the poor girl's face. "That young fellow yonder is very nice, isn't he?" he went on. "You have given me a notion, my pretty child; I will make you both happy."

Mme. Couture laid her hand on the arm of her ward, and drew the girl away, as she said in her ear—

"Why, Victorine, I cannot imagine what has come over you this morning."

"I don't want any shots fired in my garden," said Mme. Vauquer. "You will frighten the neighborhood and bring the police up here all in a moment."

"Come, keep cool, Mamma Vauquer," answered Vautrin. "There, there; it's all right; we will go to the shooting-gallery."

He went back to Rastignac, laying his hand familiarly on the young man's arm.

"When I have given you ocular demonstration of the fact that I can put a bullet through the ace on a card five times running at thirty-five paces," he said, "that won't take away your appetite, I suppose? You look to me to be inclined to be a trifle quarrelsome this morning, and as if you would rush on your death like a blockhead."

"Do you draw back?" asked Eugène.

"Don't try to raise my temperature," answered Vautrin; "it is not cold this morning. Let us go and sit over there," he added, pointing to the green-painted garden seats; "no one can overhear us. I want a little talk with you. You are not a bad sort of youngster, and I have no quarrel with you. I like you, take Tromp—(confound it!)—take Vautrin's word for it. What makes me like you? I will tell you by-and-by. Meantime, I can tell you that I know you as well as if I had made you myself, as I will prove to you in a minute. Put down your bags," he continued, pointing to the round table.

Rastignac deposited his money on the table, and sat down. He was consumed with curiosity, which the sudden change in the manner of the man before him had excited to the highest pitch. Here was a strange being who, a moment ago, had talked of killing him, and now posed as his protector.

"You would like to know who I really am, what I was, and what I do now," Vautrin went on. "You want to know too much, youngster. Come! come! keep cool! You will hear more astonishing things than that. I have had my misfortunes. Just hear me out first, and you shall have your turn afterwards. Here is my past in three words. Who am I? Vautrin. What do I do? Just what I please. Let us change the subject. You want to know my character. I am good-natured to those who do me a good turn, or to those whose hearts speak to mine. These last may do anything they like with me; they may bruise my shins, and I shall not tell them to 'mind what they are about'; but, *nom d'une pipe,* the Devil himself is not an uglier customer than I can be if people annoy me, or if I don't happen to take to them; and you may just as well know at once that I think no more of killing a man than of that," and he spat before him as he spoke. "Only when it is absolutely necessary to do so, I do my best to kill him properly. I am what you call an artist. I have read Benvenuto Cellini's *Memoirs,* such as you see me; and, what is more, in Italian! A fine-spirited fellow he was! From him I learned to follow the example set us by Providence, who strikes us down at random, and to admire the beautiful whenever and wherever it is found. And, setting other questions aside, is it not a glorious part to play, when you pit yourself against mankind, and the luck is on your side? I have thought a good deal about the constitution of your present social Dis-order. A duel is downright childish, my boy! utter nonsense and folly! When one of two living men must be got out of the way, none but an idiot would leave chance to decide which it is to be; and in a duel it is a toss-up—heads or tails—and there you are! Now I, for instance, can hit the ace in the middle of a card five times running, send one bullet after another through the same hole, and at thirty-five paces, moreover! With that little accomplishment you might think yourself certain of killing your man, mightn't you? Well, I have fired, at twenty paces, and missed, and the rogue who had never handled a pistol in his life—look here!"—(he unbuttoned his waistcoat and exposed his chest, covered, like a bear's back, with a shaggy fell; the student gave a startled shudder)—"he was a raw lad, but he made his mark on me," the extraordinary man went on, drawing Rastignac's fingers over a deep scar on his breast. "But that happened when I myself was a mere boy; I was one-and-twenty then (your age), and I had some beliefs left —in a woman's love, and in a pack of rubbish that you will be over head and ears in directly. You and I were to have fought just now, weren't we? You might have killed me. Suppose that I were put under the earth, where would you be? You would have to clear out of this, go to Switzerland, draw on papa's purse—and he has none too much in it as it is. I mean to open your eyes to your real position, that is what I am going to do; but I shall do it from the point of view of a man who, after studying the world very closely, sees that there are but two alternatives—stupid obedience or revolt. I obey nobody; is that clear? Now, do you know how much you will want at the pace you are going? A million; and promptly, too, or that little head of yours will be swaying to and fro in the drag-nets at Saint-Cloud, while we are gone to find out whether or no there is a Supreme Being. I will put you in the way of that million."

He stopped a moment and looked at Eugène.

"Aha! you do not look so sourly at Papa Vautrin now! At the mention of the million you look like a young girl when somebody has said, 'I will come for you this evening!' and she betakes herself to her toilet as a cat licks its whiskers over a saucer of milk. All right. Come, now, let us go into the question, young man; all between ourselves, you know. We have a papa and mamma down yonder, a great-aunt, two sisters (aged eighteen and seventeen), two young brothers (one fifteen, and the other ten), that is about the roll-call of the crew. The aunt brings up the two sisters; the curé comes and teaches the boys Latin. Boiled chestnuts are oftener on the table than white bread. Papa make a suit of clothes last a long while; if mamma has a different dress winter and summer, it is about as much as she has; the sisters manage as best they can. I know all about it; I have lived in the South.

"That is how things are at home. They send you twelve hundred francs a year, and the whole property only brings in three thousand francs all told. We have a cook and a man-servant; papa is a baron, and we must keep up appearances. Then we have our ambitions; we are connected with the Beauséants, and we go afoot through the streets; we want to be rich, and we have not a penny; we eat Mme. Vauquer's messes, and we like grand dinners in the Faubourg Saint-Germain; we sleep on a truckle-bed, and dream of a mansion! I do not blame you for wanting these things. It is not given to everyone to have ambition, my little tramp. What sort of men do the women run after? Men of ambition. Men of ambition have stronger frames, their blood is richer in iron, their hearts are warmer than those of ordinary men. Women feel that when their power is greatest they look their best, and that those are their happiest hours; they like power in men, and prefer the strongest even if it is a power that may be their own destruction. I am going to make an inventory of your desires in order to put the question at issue before you. Here it is—

"We are hungry as a wolf, and those newly-cut teeth of ours are sharp; what are we to do to keep the pot boiling? In the first place, we have the Code to browse upon; it is not amusing, and we are none the wiser for it, but that cannot be helped. So far so good. We mean to make an advocate of ourselves with a prospect of one day being made President of a Court of Assize, when we shall send poor devils, our betters, to the galleys with a T. F.[1] on their shoulders, so that the rich may be convinced that they can sleep in peace. There is no fun in that; and you are a long while coming to it; for, to begin with, there are two years of nauseous drudgery in Paris, we see all the lollipops that we long for out of our reach. It is tiresome to want things and never to have them. If you were a pallid creature of the mollusk order, you would have nothing to fear, but it is different when you have the hot blood of a lion and are ready to get into a score of scrapes everyday of your life. This is the ghastliest form of torture known in this inferno of God's making, and you will give in to it. Or suppose that you are a good boy, drink nothing stronger than milk, and bemoan your hard lot; you, with your generous nature, will endure hardships that would drive a dog mad, and make a start, after

[1] Travaux forcés.

long waiting, as deputy to some rascal or other in a hole of a place where the Government will fling you a thousand francs a year like the scraps that are thrown to the butcher's dog. Bark at thieves, plead the cause of the rich, send men of heart to the guillotine, that is your work! Many thanks! If you have no influence, you may rot in your provincial tribunal. At thirty you will be a Justice with twelve hundred francs a year (if you have not flung off the gown for good before then). By the time you are forty you may look to marry a miller's daughter, an heiress with some six thousand livres a year. Much obliged! If you have influence, you may possibly be Public Prosecutor by the time you are thirty; with a salary of a thousand crowns, you could look to marry the mayor's daughter. Some petty piece of political trickery, such as mistaking Villèle for Manuel in a bulletin (the names rhyme, and that quiets your conscience), and you will probably be Procureur-Général by the time you are forty, with a chance of becoming a deputy. Please to observe, my dear boy, that our conscience will have been a little damaged in the process, and that we shall endure twenty years of drudgery and hidden poverty, and that our sisters are wearing Dian's livery. I have the honor to call your attention to another fact: to wit, that there are but twenty Procureurs-Généraux at a time in all France, while there are some twenty thousand of you young men who aspire to that elevated position; that there are some mountebanks among you who would sell their family to screw their fortunes a peg higher. If this sort of thing sickens you, try another course. The Baron de Rastignac thinks of becoming an advocate, does he? There's a nice prospect for you! Ten years of drudgery straight away. You are obliged to live at the rate of a thousand francs a month; you must have a library of law books, live in chambers, go into society, go down on your knees to ask a solicitor for briefs, lick the dust off the floor of the Palais de Justice. If this kind of business led to anything, I should not say no; but just give me the names of five advocates here in Paris who by the time that they are fifty are making fifty thousand francs a year! Bah! I would sooner turn pirate on the high seas than have my soul shrivel up inside me like that. How will you find the capital? There is but one way, marry a woman who has money. There is no fun in it. Have you a mind to marry? You hang a stone round your neck; for if you marry for money, what becomes of our exalted notions of honor and so forth? You might as well fly in the face of social conventions at once. Is it nothing to crawl like a serpent before your wife, to lick her mother's feet, to descend to dirty actions that would sicken swine—faugh!—never mind if you at least make your fortune. But you will be as doleful as a dripstone if you marry for money. It is better to wrestle with men than to wrangle at home with your wife. You are at the crossway of the roads of life, my boy; choose your way.

"But you have chosen already. You have gone to see your cousin of Beauséant, and you have had an inkling of luxury; you have been to Mme. de Restaud's house, and in Father Goriot's daughter you have seen a glimpse of the Parisienne for the first time. That day you came back with a word written upon your forehead. I knew it, I could read it—'*Success!*' Yes, success at any price. 'Bravo,' said I to myself, 'here is the sort of fellow for me.' You wanted money. Where was it to come from? You have drained your sisters' little hoards (all brothers sponge more or less on their sisters). Those fifteen hundred francs of yours (got together, God knows how! in a country where there are more chestnuts than five-franc pieces) will slip away like soldiers after pillage. And, then, what will you do? Shall you begin to work? Work, or what you understand by work at this moment, means, for a man of Poiret's caliber, an old age in Mamma Vauquer's lodging-house. There are fifty thousand young men in your position at this moment, all bent as you are on solving one and the same problem—how to acquire a fortune rapidly. You are but a unit in that aggregate. You can guess, therefore, what efforts you must make, how desperate the struggle is. There are not fifty thousand good positions for you; you must fight and devour one another like spiders in a pot. Do you know how a man makes his way here? By brilliant genius or by skillful corruption. You must neither cut your way through these masses of men like a cannon ball, or steal among them like a plague. Honesty is nothing to the purpose. Men bow before the power of genius; they hate it, and try to slander it, because genius does not divide the spoil; but if genius persists, they bow before it. To sum it all up in a phrase, if they fail to smother genius in the mud, they fall on their knees and worship it. Corruption is a great power in the world, and talent is scarce. So corruption is the weapon of superfluous mediocrity; you will be made to feel the point of it everywhere. You will see women who spend more than ten thousand francs a year on dress, while their husband's salary (his whole income) is six thousand francs. You will see officials buying estates on twelve hundred francs a year. You will see women who sell themselves body and soul to drive in a carriage belonging to the son of a peer of France, who has a right to drive in the middle rank at Longchamp. You have seen that poor simpleton of a Goriot obliged to meet a bill with his daughter's name at the back of it, though her husband has fifty thousand francs a year. I defy you to walk a couple of yards anywhere in Paris without stumbling on some infernal complication. I'll bet my head to a head of that salad that you will stir up a hornet's nest by taking a fancy to the first young, rich, and pretty woman you meet. They are all dodging the law, all at logger-heads with their husbands. If I were to begin to tell you all that vanity or necessity (virtue is not often mixed up in it, you may be sure), all that vanity and necessity drive them to do for lovers, finery, housekeeping, or children, I should never come to an end. So an honest man is the common enemy.

"But do you know what an honest man is? Here, in Paris, an honest man is the man who keeps his own counsel, and will not divide the plunder. I am not speaking now of those poor bond-slaves who do the work of the world without a reward for their toil—God Almighty's outcast, I call them. Among them, I grant you, is virtue in all the flower of its stupidity, but poverty is no less their portion. At this moment, I think I see the long faces those good folk would pull if God played a practical joke on them and stayed away at the Last Judgment.

"Well, then, if you mean to make a fortune quickly, you must either be rich to begin with, or make people believe that you are rich. It is no use playing here except for high stakes; once take to low play, it is all up with you. If in the scores of professions that are open to you, there are ten men who rise very rapidly, people are sure to call them thieves. You can draw your own conclusions. Such is life. It is no cleaner than a kitchen; it reeks like a kitchen; and if you mean to cook your dinner, you must expect to soil your hands; the real art is in getting them clean again, and therein lies the whole morality of our epoch. If I take this tone in speaking of the world to you, I have the right to do so; I know it well. Do you think that I am blaming it? Far from it; the world has always been as it is now. Moralists' strictures will never change it. Mankind are not perfect, but one age is more or less hypocritical than another, and then simpletons say that its morality is high or low. I do not think that the rich are any worse than the poor; man is much the same, high or low, or wherever he is. In a million of these human cattle there may be half a score of bold spirits who rise above the rest, above the laws; I am one of them. And you, if you are cleverer than your fellows, make straight to your end, and hold your head high. But you must lay your account with envy and slander and mediocrity, and every man's hand will be against you. Napoleon met with a Minister of War, Aubry by name, who all but sent him to the colonies.

"Feel your pulse. Think whether you can get up morning after morning, strengthened in yesterday's purpose. In that case I will make you an offer that no one would decline. Listen attentively. You see, I have an idea of my own. My idea is to live a patriarchal life on a vast estate, say a hundred thousand acres, somewhere in the Southern States of America. I mean to be a planter, to have slaves, to make a few snug millions by selling my cattle, timber, and tobacco; I want to live an absolute monarch, and to do just as I please; to lead such a life as no one here in these squalid dens of lath and plaster ever imagines. I am a great poet; I do not write my poems, I feel them, and act them. At this moment I have fifty thousand francs, which might possibly buy forty negroes. I want two hundred thousand francs, because I want to have two hundred negroes to carry out my notions of the patriarchal life properly. Negroes, you see, are like a sort of family ready grown, and there are no inquisitive public prosecutors out there to interfere with you. That investment in ebony ought to mean three or four million francs in ten years' time. If I am successful, no one will ask me who I am. I shall be Mr. Four Millions, an American citizen. I shall be fifty years old by then, and sound and hearty still; I shall enjoy life after my own fashion. In two words, if I find you an heiress with a million, will you give me two hundred thousand francs? Twenty per cent. commission, eh? Is that too much? Your little wife will be very much in love with you. Once married, you will show signs of uneasiness and remorse; for a couple of weeks you will be depressed. Then, some night after sundry grimacings, comes the confession, between two kisses, 'Two hundred thousand francs of debts, my darling!' This sort of farce is played every day in Paris, and by young men of the highest fashion. When a young wife has given her heart, she will not refuse her purse. Perhaps you are thinking that you will lose the money for good? Not you. You will make two hundred thousand francs again by some stroke of business. With your capital and your brains you should be able to accumulate as large a fortune as you could wish. *Ergo,* in six months you will have made your own fortune, and your old friend Vautrin's, and made an amiable woman very happy, to say nothing of your people at home, who must blow on their fingers to warm them, in the winter, for lack of firewood. You need not be surprised at my proposal, nor at the demand I make. Forty-seven out of every sixty great matches here in Paris are made after just such a bargain as this. The Chamber of Notaries compels my gentleman to——"

"What must I do?" said Rastignac, eagerly interrupting Vautrin's speech.

"Next to nothing," returned the other, with a slight involuntary movement, the suppressed exultation of the angler when he feels a bite at the end of his line. "Follow me carefully! The heart of a girl whose life is wretched and unhappy is a sponge that will thirstily absorb love; a dry sponge that swells at the first drop of sentiment. If you pay court to a young girl whose existence is a compound of loneliness, despair, and poverty, and who has no suspicion that she will come into fortune, good Lord! it is quint and quatorze at piquet; it is knowing the numbers of the lottery beforehand; it is speculating in the Funds when you have news from a sure source; it is building up a marriage on an indestructible foundation. The girl may come in for millions, and she will fling them, as if they were so many pebbles, at your feet. 'Take it, my beloved! Take it, Alfred, Adolphe, Eugène!' or whoever it was that showed his sense by sacrificing himself for her. And as for sacrificing himself, this is how I understand it. You sell a coat that is getting shabby, so that you can take her to the *Cadran bleu,* treat her to mushrooms on toast, and then go to the Ambigu-Comique in the evening; you pawn your watch to buy her a shawl. I need not remind you of the fiddle-faddle sentimentality that goes down so well with all women; you spill a few drops of water on your stationery, for instance; those are the tears you shed while far away from her. You look to me as if you were perfectly acquainted with the argot of the heart. Paris, you see, is like a forest in the New World, where you have to deal with a score of varieties of savages—Illinois and Hurons, who live on the proceeds of their social hunting. You are a hunter of millions; you set your snares; you use lures and nets; there are many ways of hunting. Some hunt heiresses, others a legacy; some fish for souls, yet others sell their clients, bound hand and foot. Everyone who comes back from the chase with his game-bag well filled meets with a warm welcome in good society. In justice to this hospitable part of the world, it must be said that you have to do with the most easy and good-natured of great cities. If the proud aristocracies of the rest of Europe refuse admittance among their ranks to a disreputable millionaire, Paris stretches out a hand to him, goes to his banquets, eats his dinners, and hobnobs with his infamy."

"But where is such a girl to be found?" asked Eugène.

"Under your eyes; she is yours already."

"Mlle. Victorine?"

"Precisely."

"And what was that you said?"

"She is in love with you already, your little Baronne de Rastignac!"

"She has not a penny," Eugène continued, much mystified.

"Ah! now we are coming to it! Just another word or two, and it will all be clear enough. Her father, Taillefer, is an old scoundrel; it is said that he murdered one of his friends at the time of the Revolution. He is one of your comedians that sets up to have opinions of his own. He is a banker—senior partner in the house of Frédéric Taillefer and Company. He has one son, and means to leave all he has to the boy, to the prejudice of Victorine. For my part, I don't like to see injustice of this sort. I am like Don Quixote, I have a fancy for defending the weak against the strong. If it should please God to take that youth away from him, Taillefer would have only his daughter left; he would want to leave his money to someone or other; an absurd notion, but it is only human nature, and he is not likely to have any more children, as I know. Victorine is gentle and amiable; she will soon twist her father round her fingers, and set his head spinning like a German top by plying him with sentiment! She will be too much touched by your devotion to forget you; you will marry her. I mean to play Providence for you, and Providence is to do my will. I have a friend whom I have attached closely to myself, a colonel in the Army of the Loire, who has just been transferred into the *garde royale*. He has taken my advice and turned ultra-royalist; he is not one of those fools who never change their opinions. Of all pieces of advice, my cherub, I would give you this—don't stick to your opinions any more than to your words. If anyone asks you for them, let him have them—at a price. A man who prides himself on going in a straight line through life is an idiot who believes in infallibility. There are no such things as principles; there are only events, and there are no laws but those of expediency: a man of talent accepts events and the circumstances in which he finds himself, and turns everything to his own ends. If laws and principles were fixed and invariable, nations would not change them as readily as we change our shirts. The individual is not obliged to be more particular than the nation. A man whose services to France have been of the very slightest is a fetish looked on with superstitious awe because he has always seen everything in red; but he is good, at the most, to be put into the Museum of Arts and Crafts, among the automatic machines, and labeled La Fayette; while the prince at whom everybody flings a stone, the man who despises humanity so much that he spits as many oaths as he is asked for in the face of humanity, saved France from being torn in pieces at the Congress of Vienna; and they who should have given him laurels fling mud at him. Oh! I know something of affairs, I can tell you; I have the secrets of many men! Enough. When I find three minds in agreement as to the application of a principle, I shall have a fixed and immovable opinion—I shall have to wait a long while first. In the Tribunals you will not find three judges of the same opinion on a single point of law. To return to the man I was telling you of. He would crucify Jesus Christ again, if I bade him. At a word from his old chum Vautrin he will pick a quarrel with a scamp that will not send so much as five francs to his sister, poor girl, and"—(here Vautrin rose to his feet and stood like a fencing-master about to lunge)—"turn him off into the dark!" he added.

"How frightful!" said Eugène. "You do not really mean it? Mr. Vautrin, you are joking!"

"There! there! Keep cool!" said the other. "Don't behave like a baby. But if you find any amusement in it, be indignant, flare up! Say that I am a scoundrel, a rascal, a rogue, a bandit; but do not call me a blackleg nor a spy! There, out with it, fire away! I forgive you; it is quite natural at your age. I was like that myself once. Only remember this, you will do worse things yourself some day. You will flirt with some pretty woman and take her money. You have thought of that, of course," said Vautrin, "for how are you to succeed unless love is laid under contribution? There are no two ways about virtue, my dear student; it either is, or it is not. Talk of doing penance for your sins! It is a nice system of business, when you pay for your crime by an act of contrition! You seduce a woman that you may set your foot on such and such a rung of the social ladder; you sow dissension among the children of a family; you descend, in short, to every base action that can be committed at home or abroad, to gain your own ends for your own pleasure or your profit; and can you imagine that these are acts of faith, hope, or charity? How is it that a dandy, who in a night has robbed a boy of half his fortune, gets only a couple of months in prison; while a poor devil who steals a banknote for a thousand francs, with aggravating circumstances, is condemned to penal servitude? Those are your laws. Not a single provision but lands you in some absurdity. That man with yellow gloves and a golden tongue commits many a murder; he sheds no blood, but he drains his victim's veins as surely; a desperado forces open a door with a crowbar, dark deeds both of them! You yourself will do every one of the things that I suggest to you to-day, bar the bloodshed. Do you believe that there is any absolute standard in this world? Despise mankind and find out the meshes that you can slip through in the net of the Code. The secret of a great success for which you are at a loss to account is a crime that has never been found out, because it was properly executed."

"Silence, sir! I will not hear any more; you make me doubt myself. At this moment my sentiments are all my science."

"Just as you please, my fine fellow; I did not think you were so weak-minded," said Vautrin; "I shall say no more about it. One last word, however," and he looked hard at the student—"you have my secret," he said.

"A young man who refuses your offer knows that he must forget it.'

"Quite right, quite right; I am glad to hear you say so. Somebody else might not be so scrupulous, you see. Keep in mind what I want to do for you. I will give you a fortnight. The offer is still open."

"What a head of iron the man has!" said Eugène to himself as he watched Vautrin walk unconcernedly away with his cane under his arm. "Yet Mme. de Beauséant said as much more gracefully; he has only stated the case in cruder language. He would tear my heart with claws of steel. What made me think of going to Mme. de Nucingen? He guessed my motives before I knew them myself. To sum it up, that outlaw has told me more about virtue than all I have learned from men and books. If virtue admits of no compromises, I have certainly robbed my sisters," he said, throwing down the bags on the table.

He sat down again and fell, unconscious of his surroundings, into deep thought.

"To be faithful to an ideal of virtue! A heroic martyrdom! Pshaw! everyone believes in virtue, but who is virtuous? Nations have made an idol of Liberty, but what nation on the face of the earth is free? My youth is still like a blue and cloudless sky. If I set myself to obtain wealth or power, does it not mean that I must make up my mind to lie, and fawn, and cringe, and swagger, and flatter, and dissemble? To consent to be the servant of others who have likewise fawned, and lied, and flattered? Must I cringe to them before I can hope to be their accomplice? Well, then, I decline. I mean to work nobly and with a single heart. I will work day and night; I will owe my fortune to nothing but my own exertions. It may be the slowest of all roads to success, but I shall lay my head on the pillow at night untroubled by evil thoughts. Is there a greater or a better thing than this—to look back over your life and know that it is stainless as a lily? I and my life are like a young man and his betrothed. Vautrin has put before me all that comes after ten years of marriage. The devil! my head is swimming. I do not want to think at all; the heart is a sure guide."

Eugène was roused from his musings by the voice of the stout Sylvie, who announced that the tailor had come, and Eugène therefore made his appearance before the man with the two money bags, and was not ill pleased that it should be so. When he had tried on his dress suit, he put on his new morning costume, which completely metamorphosed him.

"I am quite equal to M. de Trailles," he said to himself. "In short, I look like a gentleman."

"You asked me, sir, if I knew the houses where Mme. de Nucingen goes," old Goriot's voice spoke from the doorway of Eugène's room.

"Yes."

"Very well then, she is going to the Maréchale Carigliano's ball on Monday. If you can manage to be there, I shall hear from you whether my two girls enjoyed themselves, and how they were dressed, and all about it in fact."

"How did you find that out, my good Goriot?" said Eugène, putting a chair by the fire for his visitor.

"Her maid told me. I hear all about their doings from Thérèse and Constance," he added gleefully.

The old man looked like a lover who is still young enough to be made happy by the discovery of some little stratagem which brings him information of his lady-love without her knowledge.

"*You* will see them both!" he said, giving artless expression to a pang of jealousy.

"I do not know," answered Eugène. "I will go to Mme. de Beauséant and ask her for an introduction to the Maréchale."

Eugène felt a thrill of pleasure at the thought of appearing before the Vicomtesse, dressed as henceforward he always meant to be. The "abysses of the human heart," in the moralists' phrase, are only insidious thoughts, involuntary promptings of personal interest. The instinct of enjoyment turns the scale; those rapid changes of purpose which have furnished the text for so much rhetoric are calculations prompted by the hope of pleasure. Rastignac, beholding himself well dressed and impeccable as to gloves and boots, forgot his virtuous resolutions. Youth, moreover, when bent upon wrongdoing, does not dare to behold itself in the mirror of consciousness; mature age has seen itself; and therein lies the whole difference between these two phases of life.

A friendship between Eugène and his neighbor, old Goriot, had been growing up for several days past. This secret friendship and the antipathy that the student had begun to entertain for Vautrin arose from the same psychological causes. The bold philosopher who shall investigate the effects of mental action upon the physical world will doubtless find more than one proof of the material nature of our sentiments in the relations which they create between human beings and other animals. What physiognomist is as quick to discern character as a dog is to discover from a stranger's face whether this is a friend or no? Those by-words—"atoms," "affinities"—are facts surviving in modern languages for the confusion of philosophic wiseacres who amuse themselves by winnowing the chaff of language to find its grammatical roots. We *feel* that we are loved. Our sentiments make themselves felt in everything, even at a great distance. A letter is a living soul, and so faithful an echo of the voice that speaks in it, that finer natures look upon a letter as one of love's most precious treasures. Old Goriot's affection was of the instinctive order, a canine affection raised to a sublime pitch; he had scented compassion in the air, and the kindly respect and youthful sympathy in the student's heart. This friendship had, however, scarcely reached the stage at which confidences are made. Though Eugène had spoken of his wish to meet Mme. de Nucingen, it was not because he counted on the old man to introduce him to her house, for he hoped that his own audacity might stand him in good stead. All that old Goriot had said as yet about his daughters had referred to the remarks that the student had made so freely in public on that day of the two visits.

"How could you think that Mme. de Restaud bore you a grudge for mentioning my name?" he had said on the day following that scene at dinner. "My daughters are very fond of me; I am a happy father; but my sons-in-law have behaved badly to me, and rather than make trouble between my darlings and their husbands, I choose to see my daughters secretly. Fathers who can see their daughters at any time have no idea of all the pleasure that this mystery gives me; I cannot always see mine when I wish, do you understand? So when it is fine I walk out in the Champs-Elysées, after finding out from their waiting-maids whether my daughters mean to go out. I wait near the entrance; my heart beats fast when the carriages begin to come; I admire them in their dresses, and as they pass they give me a little smile, and it seems as if everything was lighted up for me by a ray of bright sunlight. I wait, for they always go back the same way, and then I see them again; the fresh air has done them good and brought color into their cheeks; all about me people say, 'What a beautiful woman that is!' and it does my heart good to hear them.

"Are they not my own flesh and blood? I love the very horses that draw them; I envy the little lap-dog on their knees. Their happiness is my life. Everyone loves after his own fashion, and mine does no one any harm; why should people trouble their heads about me? I am happy in my own way. Is there any law against my going to see my girls in the evening when they are going out to a ball? And what a disappointment it is when I get there too late, and am told that 'Madame has gone out!' Once I waited till three o'clock in the morning for Nasie; I had not seen her for two whole days. I was so pleased, that it was almost too much for me! Please do not speak of me unless it is to say how good my daughters are to me. They are always wanting to heap presents upon me, but I will not have it. 'Just keep your money,' I tell them. 'What should I do with it? I want nothing.' And what am I, sir, after all? An old carcase, whose soul is always where my daughters are. When you have seen Mme. de Nucingen, tell me which you like the most," said the old man after a moment's pause, while Eugène put the last touches to his toilet. The student was about to go out to walk in the Garden of the Tuileries until the hour when he could venture to appear in Mme. de Beauséant's drawing-room.

That walk was a turning-point in Eugène's career. Several women noticed him; he looked so handsome, so young, and so well dressed. This almost admiring attention gave a new turn to his thoughts. He forgot his sisters and the aunt who had robbed herself for him; he no longer remembered his own virtuous scruples. He had seen hovering above his head the fiend so easy to mistake for an angel, the Devil with rainbow wings, who scatters rubies, and aims his golden shafts at palace fronts, who invests women with purple, and thrones with a glory that dazzles the eyes of fools till they forget the simple origins of royal dominion; he had heard the rustle of that Vanity whose tinsel seems to us to be the symbol of power. However cynical Vautrin's words had been, they had made an impression on his mind, as the sordid features of the old crone who whispers, "A lover, and gold in torrents," remain engraven on a young girl's memory.

Eugène lounged about the walks till it was nearly five o'clock, then he went to Mme. de Beauséant, and received one of the terrible blows against which young hearts are defenseless. Hitherto the Vicomtesse had received him with the kindly urbanity, the bland grace of manner that is the result of fine breeding, but is only complete when it comes from the heart.

To-day Mme. de Beauséant bowed constrainedly, and spoke curtly—

"M. de Rastignac, I cannot possibly see you, at least not at this moment. I am engaged . . ."

An observer, and Rastignac instantly became an observer, could read the whole history, the character and customs of caste, in the phrase, in the tones of her voice, in her glance and bearing. He caught a glimpse of the iron hand beneath the velvet glove—the personality, the egoism beneath the manner, the wood beneath the varnish. In short, he heard that unmistakable I THE KING that issues from the plumed canopy of the throne, and finds its last echo under the crest of the simplest gentleman.

Eugène had trusted too implicitly to the generosity of a woman; he could not believe in her haughtiness. Like all the unfortunate, he had subscribed, in all good faith, the generous compact which should bind the benefactor to the recipient, and the first article in that bond, between two large-hearted natures, is a perfect equality. The kindness which knits two souls together is as rare, as divine, and as little understood as the passion of love, for both love and kindness are the lavish generosity of noble natures. Rastignac was set upon going to the Duchesse de Carigliano's ball, so he swallowed down this rebuff.

"Madame," he faltered out, "I would not have come to trouble you about a trifling matter; be so kind as to permit me to see you later, I can wait."

"Very well, come and dine with me," she said, a little confused by the harsh way in which she had spoken, for this lady was as genuinely kind-hearted as she was highborn.

Eugène was touched by this sudden relenting, but none the less he said to himself as he went away, "Crawl in the dust, put up with every kind of treatment. What must the rest of the world be like when one of the kindest of women forgets all her promises of befriending me in a moment, and tosses me aside like an old shoe? So it is everyone for himself? It is true that her house is not a shop, and I have put myself in the wrong by needing her help. You should cut your way through the world like a cannon ball, as Vautrin said."

But the student's bitter thoughts were soon dissipated by the pleasure which he promised himself in this dinner with the Vicomtesse. Fate seemed to determine that the smallest accidents in his life should combine to urge him into a career, which the terrible sphinx of the Maison Vauquer had described as a field of battle where you must either slay or be slain, and cheat to avoid being cheated. You leave your conscience and your heart at the barriers, and wear a mask on entering into this game of grim earnest, where, as in ancient Sparta, you must snatch your prize without being detected if you would deserve the crown.

On his return he found the Vicomtesse gracious and kindly, as she had always been to him. They went together to the dining-room, where the Vicomte was waiting for his wife. In the time of the Restoration the luxury of the table was carried, as is well known, to the highest degree, and M. de Beauséant, like many jaded men of the world, had few pleasures left but those of good cheer; in this matter, in fact, he was a gourmand of the schools of Louis XVIII. and of the Duc d'Escars, and luxury was supplemented by splendor. Eugène, dining for the first time in a house where the traditions of grandeur had descended through many generations, had never seen any spectacle like this that now met his eyes. In the time of the Empire, balls had always ended with a supper, because the officers who took part in them must be fortified for immediate service, and even in Paris might be called upon to leave the ballroom for the battlefield. This arrangement had gone out of fashion under the Monarchy, and Eugène had so far only been asked to dances. The self-possession which pre-eminently distinguished him in later life already stood him in good stead, and he did not betray his amazement. Yet as he saw for the first time the finely wrought silverplate, the completeness of every detail, the sumptuous dinner, noiselessly served, it was difficult for such an ardent imagination not to prefer this life of studied and refined luxury to the hardships of the life which he had chosen only that morning.

His thoughts went back for a moment to the lodging-house, and with a feeling of profound loathing, he vowed to himself that at New Year he would go; prompted at least as much by a desire to live among cleaner surroundings as by a wish to shake off Vautrin, whose huge hand he seemed to feel on his shoulder at that moment. When you consider the numberless forms, clamorous or mute, that corruption takes in Paris, common sense begins to wonder what mental aberration prompted the State to establish great colleges and schools there, and assemble young men in the capital; how it is that pretty women are respected, or that the gold coin displayed in the money-changer's wooden saucers does not take to itself wings in the twinkling of an eye; and when you come to think further, how comparatively few cases of crime there are, and to count up the misdemeanors committed by youth, is there not a certain amount of respect due to these patient Tantaluses who wrestle with themselves and nearly always come off victorious? The struggles of the poor student in Paris, if skillfully drawn, would furnish a most dramatic picture of modern civilization.

In vain Mme. de Beauséant looked at Eugène as if asking him to speak; the student was tongue-tied in the Vicomte's presence.

"Are you going to take me to the Italiens this evening?" the Vicomtesse asked her husband.

"You cannot doubt that I should obey you with pleasure," he answered, and there was a sarcastic tinge in his politeness which Eugène did not detect, "but I ought to go to meet someone at the Variétés."

"His mistress," said she to herself.

"Then, is not Ajuda coming for you this evening?" inquired the Vicomte.

"No," she answered, petulantly.

"Very well, then, if you really must have an arm, take that of M. de Rastignac."

The Vicomtesse turned to Eugène with a smile. "That would be a very compromising step for you," she said.

"'A Frenchman loves danger, because in danger there is glory,' to quote M. de Chateaubriand," said Rastignac, with a bow.

A few moments later he was sitting beside Mme. de Beauséant in a brougham, that whirled them through the streets of Paris to a fashionable theater. It seemed to him that some fairy magic had suddenly transported him into a box facing the stage. All the lorgnettes of the house were pointed at him as he entered, and at the Vicomtesse in her charming toilet. He went from enchantment to enchantment.

"You must talk to me, you know," said Mme. de Beauséant. "Ah! look. There is Mme. de Nucingen in the third box from ours. Her sister and M. de Trailles are on the other side."

The Vicomtesse glanced as she spoke at the box where Mlle. de Rochefide should have been; M. d'Ajuda was not there, and Mme. de Beauséant's face lighted up in a marvelous way.

"She is charming," said Eugène, after looking at Mme. de Nucingen.

"She has white eyelashes."

"Yes, but she has such a pretty slender figure!"

"Her hands are large."

"Such beautiful eyes!"

"Her face is long."

"Yes, but length gives distinction."

"It is lucky for her that she has some distinction in her face. Just see how she fidgets with her opera-glass! The Goriot blood shows itself in every movement," said the Vicomtesse, much to Eugène's astonishment.

Indeed, Mme. de Beauséant seemed to be engaged in making a survey of the house, and to be unconscious of Mme. Nucingen's existence; but no movement made by the latter was lost upon the Vicomtesse. The house was full of the loveliest women in Paris, so that Delphine de Nucingen was not a little flattered to receive the undivided attention of Mme. de Beauséant's young, handsome, and well-dressed cousin, who seemed to have no eyes for anyone else.

"If you look at her so persistently, you will make people talk, M. de Rastignac. You will never succeed if you fling yourself at anyone's head like that."

"My dear cousin," said Eugène, "you have protected me indeed so far, and now if you would complete your work, I only ask of you a favor which will cost you but little, and be of very great service to me. I have lost my heart."

"Already!"

"Yes."

"And to that woman!"

"How could I aspire to find anyone else to listen to me?" he asked, with a keen glance at his cousin. "Her Grace the Duchesse de Carigliano is a friend of the Duchesse de Berri," he went on, after a pause; "you are sure to see her. Will you be so kind as to present me to her, and to take me with you to her ball on Monday? I shall meet Mme. de Nucingen there, and enter upon my first skirmish."

"Willingly," she said. "If you have a liking for her already, your affairs of the heart are like to prosper. That is de Marsay over there in the Princesse Galathionne's box. Mme. de Nucingen is racked with jealousy. There is no better time for approaching a woman, especially if she happens to be a banker's wife. All those ladies of the Chaussée-d'Antin love revenge."

"Then, what would you do yourself in such a case?"

"I should suffer in silence."

At this point the Marquis d'Ajuda appeared in Mme. de Beauséant's box.

"I have made a muddle of my affairs to come to you," he said, "and I am telling you about it, so that it may not be a sacrifice."

Eugène saw the glow of joy on the Vicomtesse's face, and knew that this was love, and learned the difference between love and the affectations of Parisian coquetry. He admired his cousin, grew mute, and yielded his place to M. d'Ajuda with a sigh.

"How noble, how sublime a woman is when she loves like that!" he said to himself. "And *he* could forsake her for a doll! Oh! how could anyone forsake her?"

There was a boy's passionate indignation in his heart. He could have flung himself at Mme. de Beauséant's feet; he longed for the power of the Devil if he could snatch her away and hide her in his heart, as an eagle snatches up some white yearling from the plains and bears it to his eyrie. It was humiliating to him to think that in all this gallery of fair pictures he had not one picture of his own. "To have a mistress and an almost royal position is a sign of power," he said to himself. And he looked at Mme. de Nucingen as a man measures another who has insulted him.

The Vicomtesse turned to him, and the expression of her eyes thanked him a thousand times for his discretion. The first act came to an end just then.

"Do you know Mme. de Nucingen well enough to present M. de Rastignac to her?" she asked of the Marquis d'Ajuda.

"She will be delighted," said the Marquis. The handsome Portuguese rose as he spoke and took the student's arm, and in another moment Eugène found himself in Mme. de Nucingen's box.

"Madame," said the Marquis, "I have the honor of presenting to you the Chevalier Eugène de Rastignac; he is a cousin of Mme. de Beauséant's. You have made so deep an impression upon him, that I thought I would fill up the measure of his happiness by bringing him nearer to his divinity."

Words spoken half jestingly to cover their somewhat disrespectful import; but such an implication, if carefully disguised, never gives offense to a woman. Mme. de Nucingen smiled, and offered Eugène the place which her husband had just left.

"I do not venture to suggest that you should stay with me, Monsieur," she said. "Those who are so fortunate as to be in Mme. de Beauséant's company do not desire to leave it."

"Madame," Eugène said, lowering his voice, "I think that to please my cousin I should remain with you.—Before my lord Marquis came we were speaking of you and of your exceedingly distinguished appearance," he added aloud.

M. d'Ajuda turned and left them.

"Are you really going to stay with me, Monsieur?" asked the Baroness. "Then we shall make each other's acquaintance. Mme. de Restaud told me about you, and has made me anxious to meet you."

"She must be very insincere, then, for she has shut her door on me."

"What?"

"Madame, I will tell you honestly the reason why; but I must crave your indulgence before confiding such a secret to you. I am your father's neighbor; I had no idea that Mme. de Restaud was his daughter. I was rash enough to mention his name; I meant no harm, but I annoyed your sister and her husband very much. You cannot think how severely the Duchesse de Langeais and my cousin blamed this apostasy on a daughter's part, as a piece of bad taste. I told them all about it, and they both burst out laughing. Then Mme. de Beauséant made some comparison between you and your sister, speaking in high terms of you, and saying how very fond you were of my neighbor, M. Goriot. And, indeed, how could you help loving him? He adores you so passionately that I am jealous already. We talked about you this morning for two hours. So this evening I was quite full of all that your father had told me, and while I was dining with my cousin I said that you could not be as beautiful as affectionate. Mme. de Beauséant meant to gratify such warm admiration, I think, when she brought me here, telling me, in her gracious way, that I should see you."

"Then, even now, I owe you a debt of gratitude, Monsieur," said the banker's wife. "We shall be quite old friends in a little while."

"Although a friendship with you could not be like an ordinary friendship," said Rastignac; "I should never wish to be your friend."

Such stereotyped phrases as these, in the mouths of beginners, possess an unfailing charm for women, and are insipid only when read coldly; for a young man's tone, glance, and attitude give a surpassing eloquence to the banal phrases. Mme. de Nucingen thought that Rastignac was adorable. Then, woman-like, being at a loss how to reply to the student's outspoken admiration, she answered a previous remark.

"Yes, it is very wrong of my sister to treat our poor father as she does," she said; "he has been a Providence to us. It was not until M. de Nucingen positively ordered me only to receive him in the mornings that I yielded the point. But I have been unhappy about it for a long while; I have shed many tears over it. This violence to my feelings, with my husband's brutal treatment, have been the two causes of my unhappy married life. There is certainly no woman in Paris whose lot seems more enviable than mine, and yet, in reality, there is not one so much to be pitied. You will think I must be out of my senses to talk to you like this; but you know my father, and I cannot regard you as a stranger."

"You will find no one," said Eugène, "who longs as eagerly as I do to be yours. What do all women seek? Happiness." (He answered his own question in low, vibrating tones.) "And if happiness for a woman means that she is to be loved and adored, to have a friend to whom she can pour out her wishes, her fancies, her sorrows and joys; to whom she can lay bare her heart and soul, and all her fair defects and her gracious virtues, without fear of a betrayal; believe me, the devotion and the warmth that never fails can only be found in the heart of a young man who, at a bare sign from you, would go to his death, who neither knows nor cares to know anything as yet of the world, because you will be all the world to him. I myself, you see (you will laugh at my simplicity), have just come from a remote country district; I am quite new to this world of Paris; I have only known true and loving hearts; and I made up my mind that here I should find no love. Then I chanced to meet my cousin, and to see my cousin's heart from very near; I have divined the inexhaustible treasures of passion, and, like Cherubino, I am the lover of all women, until the day comes when I find *the* woman to whom I may devote myself. As soon as I saw you, as soon as I came into the theater this evening, I felt myself borne towards you as if by the current of a stream. I had so often thought of you already, but I had never dreamed that you would be so beautiful! Mme. de Beauséant told me that I must not look so much at you. She does not know the charm of your red lips, your fair face, nor see how soft your eyes are. . . . I also am beginning to talk nonsense; but let me talk."

Nothing pleases women better than to listen to such whispered words as these; the most puritanical among them listens even when she ought not to reply to them; and Rastignac, having once begun, continued to pour out his story, dropping his voice, that she might lean and listen; and Mme. de Nucingen, smiling, glanced from time to time at de Marsay, who still sat in the Princesse Galathionne's box.

Rastignac did not leave Mme. de Nucingen till her husband came to take her home.

"Madame," Eugène said, "I shall have the pleasure of calling upon you before the Duchesse de Carigliano's ball."

"If Matame infites you to come," said the Baron, a thickset Alsatian, with indications of a sinister cunning in his full-moon countenance, "you are quide sure of being well receifed."

"My affairs seem to be in a promising way," said Eugène to himself.—"'Can you love me?' I asked her, and she did not resent it. The bit is in the horse's mouth, and I have only to mount and ride;" and with that he went to pay his respects to Mme. de Beauséant, who was leaving the theater on d'Ajuda's arm.

The student did not know that the Baroness's thoughts had been wandering; that she was even then expecting a letter from de Marsay, one of those letters that brings about a rupture that rends the soul; so, happy in his delusion, Eugène went with the Vicomtesse to the peristyle, where people were waiting till their carriages were announced.

"That cousin of yours is hardly rcognizable for the same man," said the Portuguese laughingly to the Vicomtesse, when Eugène had taken leave of them. "He will break the bank. He is as supple as an eel; he will go a long way, of that I am sure. Who else could have picked out a woman for him, as you did, just when she needed consolation?"

"But it is not certain that she does not still love the faithless lover," said Mme. de Beauséant.

The student meanwhile walked back from the Théâtre-Italien to the Rue Neuve-Sainte-Geneviève, making the most delightful plans as he went. He had noticed how closely Mme. de Restaud had scrutinized him when he appeared in the Vicomtesse's box, and again when he sat beside Mme. de Nucingen, and inferred that the Countess's doors would not be closed in future. Four important houses were now open to him—for he meant to stand well with the Maréchale; he had four supporters in the inmost circle of society in Paris. Even now it was clear to him that, once involved in this intricate social machinery, he must attach himself to a spoke of the wheel that was to turn and raise his fortunes; he would not examine himself too curiously as to the methods, but he was certain of the end, and conscious of the power to gain and keep his hold.

"If Mme. de Nucingen takes an interest in me, I will teach her how to manage her husband. That husband of hers is a great speculator; he might put me in the way of making a fortune by a single stroke."

He did not say this bluntly in so many words; as yet, indeed, he was not sufficient of a diplomatist to sum up a situation, to see its possibilities at a glance, and calculate the chances in his favor. These were nothing but hazy ideas that floated over his mental horizon; they were less cynical than Vautrin's notions; but if they had been tried in the crucible of conscience, no very pure result would have issued from the test. It is by a succession of such like transactions that men sink at last to the level of the relaxed morality of this epoch, when there have never been so few of those who square their courses with their theories, so few of those noble characters who do not yield to temptation, for whom the slightest deviation from the line of rectitude is a crime. To these magnificent types of uncompromising Right we owe two masterpieces—the Alceste of Molière, and, in our own day, the characters of Jeanie Deans and her father in Sir Walter Scott's novel. Perhaps a work which should chronicle the opposite course, which should trace out all the devious courses through which a man of the world, a man of ambition, drags his conscience, just steering clear of crime that he may gain his end and yet save appearances, such a chronicle would be no less edifying and no less dramatic.

Rastignac went home. He was fascinated by Mme. de Nucingen; he seemed to see her before him, slender and graceful as a swallow. He recalled the intoxicating sweetness of her eyes, her fair hair, the delicate silken tissue of the skin, beneath which it almost seemed to him that he could see the blood coursing; the tones of her voice still exerted a spell over him; he had forgotten nothing; his walk perhaps heated his imagination by sending a glow of warmth through his veins. He knocked unceremoniously at Goriot's door.

"I have seen Mme. Delphine, neighbor," said he.

"Where?"

"At the Italiens."

"Did she enjoy it? . . . Just come inside," and the old man left his bed, unlocked the door, and promptly returned again.

It was the first time that Eugène had been in old Goriot's room, and he could not control his feeling of amazement at the contrast between the den in which the father lived and the costume of the daughter whom he had just beheld. The window was curtainless, the walls were damp, in places the varnished wall-paper had come away and gave glimpses of the grimy yellow plaster beneath. The wretched bed on which the old man lay boasted but one thin blanket, and a wadded quilt made out of large pieces of Mme. Vauquer's old dresses. The floor was damp and gritty. Opposite the window stood a chest of drawers made of rosewood, one of the old-fashioned kind with a curving front and brass handles, shaped like rings of twisted vine stems covered with flowers and leaves. On a venerable piece of furniture with wooden shelf stood a ewer and basin and shaving apparatus. A pair of shoes stood in one corner; a night-table by the bed had neither a door nor marble slab. There was not a trace of a fire in the empty grate; the square walnut table with the cross-bar against which old Goriot had crushed and twisted his posset-dish stood near the hearth. The old man's hat was lying on a broken-down bureau. An arm-chair stuffed with straw and a couple of chairs completed the list of ramshackle furniture. From the tester of the bed, tied to the ceiling by a piece of rag, hung a strip of some cheap material in large red and black checks. No poor drudge in a garret could be worse lodged than old Goriot in Mme. Vauquer's lodging-house. The mere sight of the room sent a chill through you and a sense of oppression; it was like the worst cell in a prison. Luckily, Goriot could not see the effect that his surroundings produced on Eugène as the latter deposited his candle on the night-table. The old man turned round, keeping the bed-clothes huddled up to his chin.

"Well," he said, "and which do you like the best, Mme. de Restaud or Mme. de Nucingen?"

"I like Mme. Delphine the best," said the law student, "because she loves you the best."

At the words so heartily spoken the old man's hand slipped out from under the bedclothes and grasped Eugène's.

"Thank you, thank you," he said, gratefully. "Then what did she say about me?"

The student repeated the Baroness's remarks with some embellishments of his own, the old man listening the while as though he heard a voice from Heaven.

"Dear child!" he said. "Yes, yes, she is very fond of me. But you must not believe all that she tells you about Anastasie. The two sisters are jealous of each other, you see, another proof of their affection. Mme. de Restaud is very fond of me too. I know she is. A father sees his children as God sees all of us; he looks into the very depths of their hearts; he knows their intentions; and both of them are so loving. Oh! if I only had good sons-in-law, I should be too happy, and I dare say there is no perfect happiness here below. If I might live with them—simply hear their voices, know that they are there, see them go and come as I used to do at home when they were still with me; why, my heart bounds at the thought. . . . Were they nicely dressed?"

"Yes," said Eugène. "But, M. Goriot, how is it that your daughters have such fine houses, while you live in such a den as this?"

"Dear me, why should I want anything better?" he replied, with seeming carelessness. "I can't quite explain to you how it is; I am not used to stringing words together properly, but it all lies there——" he said, tapping his heart. "My real life is in my two girls, you see; and so long as they are happy and smartly dressed, and have soft carpets under their feet, what does it matter what clothes I wear or where I lie down of a night? I shall never feel cold so long as they are warm; I shall never feel dull if they are laughing. I have no troubles but theirs. When you, too, are a father, and you hear your children's little voices, you will say to yourself, 'That has all come from me.' You will feel that those little ones are akin to every drop in your veins, that they are the very flower of your life (and what else are they?); you will cleave so closely to them that you seem to feel every movement that they make. Everywhere I hear their voices sounding in my ears. If they are sad, the look in their eyes freezes my blood. Some day you will find out that there is far more happiness in another's happiness than in your own. It is something that I cannot explain, something within that sends a glow of warmth all through you. In short, I live my life three times over. Shall I tell you something funny? Well, then, since I have been a father, I have come to understand God. He is everywhere in the world, because the whole world comes from Him. And it is just the same with my children, Monsieur. Only, I love my daughters better than God loves the world, for the world is not so beautiful as God Himself is, but my children are more beautiful than I am. Their lives are so bound up with mine that I felt somehow that you would see them this evening. Great Heavens! If any man would make my little Delphine as happy as a wife is when she is loved, I would black his boots and run on his errands. That miserable M. de Marsay is a cur; I know all about him from her maid. A longing to wring his neck comes over me now and then. He does not love her! does not love a pearl of a woman, with a voice like a nightingale and shaped like a model. Where can her eyes have been when she married that great lump of an Alsatian? They ought both of them to have married young men, good-looking and good-tempered—but, after all, they had their own way."

Father Goriot was sublime. Eugène had never yet seen his face light up as it did now with the passionate fervor of a father's love. It is worthy of remark that strong feeling has a very subtle and pervasive power; the roughest nature, in the endeavor to express a deep and sincere affection, communicates to others the influence that has put resonance into the voice and eloquence into every gesture, wrought a change in the very features of the speaker; for under the inspiration of passion the stupidest human being attains to the highest eloquence of ideas, if not of language, and seems to move in some sphere of light. In the old man's tones and gesture there was something just then of the same spell that a great actor exerts over his audience. But does not the poet in us find expression in our affections?

"Well," said Eugène, "perhaps you will not be sorry to hear that she is pretty sure to break with de Marsay before long. That sprig of fashion has left her for the Princesse Galathionne. For my own part, I fell in love with Mme. Delphine this evening."

"Stuff!" said old Goriot.

"I did indeed, and she did not regard me with aversion. For a whole hour we talked of love, and I am to go to call on her on Saturday, the day after to-morrow."

"Oh! how I should love you, if she should like you. You are kind-hearted; you would never make her miserable. If you were to forsake her, I would cut your throat at once. A woman does not love twice, you see! Good Heavens! what nonsense I am talking, M. Eugène! It is cold; you ought not to stay here. *Mon Dieu!* so you have heard her speak? What message did she give you for me?"

"None at all," said Eugène to himself; aloud he answered, "She told me to tell you that your daughter sends you a good kiss."

"Good-night, neighbor! Sleep well, and pleasant dreams to you! I have mine already made for me by that message from her. May God grant you all your desires! You have come in like a good angel on me to-night, and brought with you the air that my daughter breathes."

"Poor old fellow!" said Eugène as he lay down. "It is enough to melt a heart of stone. His daughter no more thought of him than of the Grand Turk."

Ever after this conference Goriot looked upon his neighbor as a friend, a confidant such as he had never hoped to find; and there was established between the two the only relationship that could attach this old man to another man. The passions never miscalculate. Old Goriot felt that this friendship brought him closer to his daughter Delphine; he thought that he should find a warmer welcome for himself if the Baroness should care for Eugène. Moreover, he had confided one of his troubles to the younger man. Mme. de Nucingen, for whose happiness he prayed a thousand times daily, had never known the joys of love. Eugène was certainly (to make use of his own expression) one of the nicest young men that he had ever seen, and some prophetic instinct seemed to tell him that Eugène was to give her the happiness which had not been hers. These were the beginnings of a friendship that grew up between the old man and his neighbor; but for this friendship the catastrophe of the drama must have remained a mystery.

The affection with which old Goriot regarded Eugène, by whom he seated himself at breakfast, the change in Goriot's face, which, as a rule, looked as expressionless as a plaster cast, and a few words that passed between the two, surprised the other lodgers. Vautrin, who saw Eugène for the first time since their interview, seemed as if he would fain read the student's very soul. During the night Eugène had had some time in which to scan the vast field which lay before him; and now, as he remembered yesterday's proposal, the thought of Mlle. Taillefer's dowry came, of course, to his mind, and he could not help thinking of Victorine as the most exemplary youth may think of an heiress. It chanced that their eyes met. The poor girl did not fail to see that Eugène looked very handsome in his new clothes. So much was said in the glance thus exchanged, that Eugène could not doubt but that he was associated in her mind with the vague hopes that lie dormant in a girl's heart and gather round the first attractive newcomer. "Eight hundred thousand francs!" a voice cried in his ears, but suddenly he took refuge in the memories of yesterday evening, thinking that his extemporized passion for Mme. de Nucingen was a talisman that would preserve him from this temptation.

"They gave Rossini's *Barber of Seville* at the Italiens yesterday evening," he remarked. "I never heard such delicious music. Good gracious! how lucky people are to have a box at the Italiens!"

Old Goriot drank in every word that Eugène let fall, and watched him as a dog watches his master's slightest movement.

"You men are like fighting cocks," said Mme. Vauquer; "you do what you like."

"How did you get back?" inquired Vautrin.

"I walked," answered Eugène.

"For my own part," remarked the tempter, "I do not care about doing things by halves. If I want to enjoy myself that way, I should prefer to go in my carriage, sit in my own box, and do the thing comfortably. Everything or nothing; that is my motto."

"And a good one, too," commented Mme. Vauquer.

"Perhaps you will see Mme. de Nucingen to-day," said Eugène, addressing Goriot in an undertone. "She will welcome you with open arms, I am sure; she would want to ask you for all sorts of little details about me. I have found out that she would do anything in the world to be known by my cousin Mme. de Beauséant; don't forget to tell her that I love her too well not to think of trying to arrange this."

Rastignac went at once to the École de Droit. He had no mind to stay a moment longer than was necessary in that odious house. He wasted his time that day; he had fallen a victim to that fever of the brain that accompanies the too vivid hopes of youth. Vautrin's arguments had set him meditating on social life, and he was deep in these reflections when he happened on his friend Bianchon in the Jardin du Luxembourg.

"What makes you look so solemn?" said the medical student, putting an arm through Eugène's they went towards the Palais.

"I'm tormented by temptations."

"What kind? There is a cure for temptation."

"What?"

"Yielding to it."

"You laugh, but you don't know what it is all about. Have you read Rousseau?"

"Yes."

"Do you remember that he asks the reader somewhere what he would do if he could make a fortune by killing an old mandarin somewhere in China by mere force of wishing it, and without stirring from Paris?"

"Yes,"

"Well, then?"

"Pshaw! I am at my thirty-third mandarin."

"Seriously, though. Look here, suppose you were sure that you could do it, and had only to give a nod. Would you do it?"

"Is he well stricken in years, this mandarin of yours? Pshaw! after all, young or old, paralytic, or well and sound, my word for it. . . . Well, then. Hang it, no!"

"You are a good fellow, Bianchon. But suppose you loved a woman well enough to lose your soul in hell for her, and that she wanted money, lots of money for dresses and a carriage, and all her whims, in fact?"

"Why, here you are taking away my reason, and want me to reason!"

"Well, then, Bianchon, I am mad; bring me to my senses. I have two sisters as beautiful and innocent as angels, and I want them to be happy. How am I to find two hundred thousand francs apiece for them in the next five years? Now and then in life, you see, you must play for heavy stakes, and it is no use wasting your luck on low play."

"But you are only stating the problem that lies before everyone at the outset of his life, and you want to cut the Gordian knot with a sword. If that is the way of it, dear boy, you must be an Alexander, or to the hulks you go. For my own part, I am quite contented with the little lot I mean to make for myself somewhere in the country, when I mean to step into my father's shoes and plod along. A man's affections are just as fully satisfied by the smallest circle as they can be by a vast circumference. Napoleon himself could only dine once, and he could not have more mistresses than a house student at the Capucins. Happiness, old man, depends on what lies between the sole of your foot and the crown of your head; and whether it costs a million or a hundred louis, the actual amount of pleasure that you receive rests entirely with you, and is just exactly the same in any case. I am for letting that Chinaman live."

"Thank you, Bianchon; you have done me good. We will always be friends."

"I say," remarked the medical student, as they came to the end of a broad walk in the Jardin des Plantes, "I saw the Michonneau and Poiret a few minutes ago on a bench chatting with a gentleman whom I used to see in last year's troubles hanging about the Chamber of Deputies; he seems to me, in fact, to be a detective dressed up like a decent retired tradesman. Let us keep an eye on that couple; I will tell you why some time. Good-bye; it is nearly four o'clock, and I must be in to answer to my name."

When Eugène reached the lodging-house, he found old Goriot waiting for him.

"Here!" cried the old man, "here is a letter from her. Pretty handwriting, eh?"

Eugéne broke the seal and read—

> "SIR,—I have heard from my father that you are fond of Italian music. I shall be delighted if you will do me the pleasure of accepting a seat in my box. La Fodor and Pellegrini will sing on Saturday, so I am sure that you will not refuse me. M. de Nucingen and I shall be pleased if you will dine with us; we shall be quite by ourselves. If you will come and be my escort, my husband will be glad to be relieved from his conjugal duties. Do not answer, but simply come. —Yours sincerely,
>
> "D. DE N."

"Let me see it," said old Goriot, when Eugène had read the letter. "You are going, aren't you?" he added, when he had smelt the writing-paper. "How nice it smells! Her fingers have touched it, that is certain."

"A woman does not fling herself at a man's head in this way," the student was thinking. "She wants to use me to bring back de Marsay; nothing but pique makes a woman do a thing like this."

"Well," said old Goriot, "what are you thinking about?"

Eugène did not know the fever of vanity that possessed some women in those days; how should he imagine that to open a door in the Faubourg Saint-Germain a banker's wife would go to almost any length? For the coterie of the Faubourg Saint-Germain was a charmed circle, and the women who moved in it were at that time the queens of society; and among the greatest of these *Dames du Petit-Château* as they were called, were Mme. de Beauséant and her friends the Duchesse de Langeais and the Duchesse de Maufrigneuse. Rastignac was alone in his ignorance of the frantic efforts made by women who lived in the Chaussée-d'Antin to enter this seventh heaven and shine among the brightest constellations of their sex. But his cautious disposition stood him in good stead, and kept his judgment cool, and the not altogether enviable power of imposing instead of accepting conditions.

"Yes, I am going," he replied.

So it was curiosity that drew him to Mme. de Nucingen; while, if she had treated him disdainfully, passion perhaps might have brought him to her feet. Still he waited almost impatiently for to-morrow, and the hour when he could go to her. There is almost as much charm for a young man in a first flirtation as there is in first love. The certainty of success is a source of happiness to which men do not confess, and all the charm of certain women lies in this. The desire of conquest springs no less from the easiness than from the difficulty of triumph, and every passion is excited or sustained by one or other of these two motives which divide the empire of love. Perhaps this division is one result of the great question of temperaments; which, after all, dominates social life. The melancholic temperament may stand in need of the tonic of coquetry, while those of nervous or sanguine complexion withdraw if they meet with a too stubborn resistance. In other words, the lymphatic temperament is essentially despondent, and the rhapsodic is bilious.

Eugène lingered over his toilet with an enjoyment of all its little details that is grateful to a young man's self-love, though he will not own to it for fear of being laughed at. He thought, as he arranged his hair, that a pretty woman's glances would wander through the dark curls. He indulged in childish tricks like any young girl dressing for a dance, and gazed complacently at his graceful figure while he smoothed out the creases of his coat.

"There are worse figures, that is certain," he said to himself.

Then he went downstairs, just as the rest of the household were sitting down to dinner, and took with good humor the boisterous applause excited by his elegant appearance. The amazement with which any attention to dress is regarded in a lodging-house is a very characteristic trait. No one can put on a new coat but everyone else must say his say about it.

"Clk! clk! clk!" cried Bianchon, making the sound with his tongue against the roof of his mouth, like a driver urging on a horse.

"He holds himself like a duke and a peer of France," said Mme. Vauquer.

"Are you going a-courting?" inquired Mlle. Michonneau.

"Cock-a-doodle-doo!" cried the artist.

"My compliments to my lady your wife," from the employé at the Muséum.

"Your wife; have you a wife?" asked Poiret.

"Yes, in compartments, water-tight and floats, guaranteed fast color, all prices from twenty-five to forty sous, neat check patterns in the latest fashion and best taste, will wash, half-linen, half-cotton, half-wool; a certain cure for toothache and other complaints under the patronage of the Royal College of Physicians! children like it! a remedy for headache, indigestion, and all other diseases affecting the throat, eyes, and ears!" cried Vautrin, with a comical imitation of the volubility of a quack at a fair. "And how much shall we say for this marvel, gentlemen? Twopence? No. Nothing of the sort. All that is left is stock after supplying the Great Mogul. All the crowned heads of Europe, including the Gr-r-r-rand Duke of Baden, have been anxious to get a sight of it. Walk up! walk up! gentlemen! Pay at the desk as you go in! Strike up the music there! Brooum, la, la, trinn! la, la, boum! boum! Mister Clarinette, there you are out of tune!" he added gruffly; "I will rap your knuckles for you!"

"Goodness! what an amusing man!" said Mme. Vauquer to Mme. Couture; "I should never feel dull with him in the house."

This burlesque of Vautrin's was the signal for an outburst of merriment, and under cover of jokes and laughter Eugène caught a glance from Mlle. Taillefer; she had leaned over to say a few words in Mme. Couture's ear.

"The cab is at the door," announced Sylvie.

"But where is he going to dine?" asked Bianchon.

"With Madame la Baronne de Nucingen."

"M. Goriot's daughter," said the law student.

At this, all eyes turned to the old vermicelli maker; he

was gazing at Eugène with something like envy in his eyes.

Rastignac reached the house in the Rue Saint-Lazare, one of those many-windowed houses with a mean-looking portico and slender columns, which are considered the thing in Paris; a typical banker's house, decorated in the most ostentatious fashion; the walls lined with stucco, the landings of marble mosaic. Mme. de Nucingen was sitting in a little drawing-room; the room was painted in the Italian fashion, and decorated like a restaurant. The Baroness seemed depressed. The effort that she made to hide her feelings aroused Eugène's interest; it was plain that she was not playing a part. He had expected a little flutter of excitement at his coming, and he found her dispirited and sad. The disappointment piqued his vanity.

"My claim to your confidence is very small, Madame," he said, after rallying her on her abstracted mood; "but if I am in the way, please tell me so frankly; I count on your good faith."

"No, stay with me," she said; "I shall be all alone if you go. Nucingen is dining in town, and I do not want to be alone; I want to be taken out of myself."

"But what is the matter?"

"You are the very last person whom I should tell," she exclaimed.

"Then I am connected in some way with this secret. I wonder what it is."

"Perhaps. Yet, no," she went on; "it is a domestic quarrel, which ought to be buried in the depths of the heart. I am very unhappy; did I not tell you so the day before yesterday? Golden chains are the heaviest of all fetters."

When a woman tells a young man that she is very unhappy, and when the young man is clever, and well dressed, and has fifteen hundred francs lying idle in his pocket, he is sure to think as Eugène said, and he becomes a coxcomb.

"What can you have left to wish for?" he answered. "You are young, beautiful, beloved, and rich."

"Do not let us talk of my affairs," she said, shaking her head mournfully. "We will dine together *tête-à-tête,* and afterwards we will go to hear the most exquisite music. Am

I to your taste?" she went on, rising and displaying her gown of white cashmere, covered with Persian designs in the most superb taste.

"I wish that you were altogether mine," said Eugène; "you are charming."

"You would have a forlorn piece of property," she said, smiling bitterly. "There is nothing about me that betrays my wretchedness; and yet, in spite of appearances, I am in despair. I cannot sleep; my troubles have broken my night's rest; I shall grow ugly."

"Oh! that is impossible," cried the law student; "but I am curious to know what these troubles can be that a devoted love cannot efface."

"Ah! if I were to tell you about them, you would shun me," she said. "Your love for me as yet is only the conventional gallantry that men use to masquerade in; and, if you really loved me, you would be driven to despair. I must keep silence, you see. Let us talk of something else for pity's sake," she added. "Let me show you my rooms."

"No, let us stay here," answered Eugène; he sat down on the sofa before the fire, and boldly took Mme. de Nucingen's hand in his. She surrendered it to him; he even felt the pressure of her fingers in one of the spasmodic clutches that betray terrible agitation.

"Listen," said Rastignac; "if you are in trouble, you ought to tell me about it. I want to prove to you that I love you for yourself alone. You must speak to me frankly about your troubles, so that I can put an end to them, even if I have to kill half-a-dozen men; or I shall go, never to return."

"Very well," she cried, putting her hand to her forehead in an agony of despair, "I will put you to the proof, and this very moment. Yes," she said to herself, "I have no other resource left."

She rang the bell.

"Are the horses put in for the master?" she asked of the servant.

"Yes, Madame."

"I shall take his carriage myself. He can have mine and my horses. Serve dinner at seven o'clock."

"Now, come with me," she said to Eugène, who thought as he sat in the banker's carriage beside Mme. de Nucingen that he must surely be dreaming.

"To the Palais-Royal," she said to the coachman; "stop near the Théâtre-Français."

She seemed to be too troubled and excited to answer the innumerable questions that Eugène put to her. He was at a loss what to think of her mute resistance, her obstinate silence.

"Another moment and she will escape me," he said to himself.

When the carriage stopped at last, the Baroness gave the law student a glance that silenced his wild words, for he was almost beside himself.

"Is it true that you love me?" she asked.

"Yes," he answered, and in his manner and tone there was no trace of the uneasiness that he felt.

"You will not think ill of me, will you, whatever I may ask of you?"

"No."

"Are you ready to do my bidding?"

"Blindly."

"Have you ever been to a gaming-house?" she asked in a tremulous voice.

"Never."

"Ah! now I can breathe. You will have luck. Here is my purse," she said. "Take it! there are a hundred francs in it, all that such a fortunate woman as I can call her own. Go up into one of the gaming-houses—I do not know where they are, but there are some near the Palais-Royal. Try your luck with the hundred francs at a game they call roulette; lose it all, or bring me back six thousand francs. I will tell you about my troubles when you come back."

"Devil take me, I'm sure, if I have a glimmer of a notion of what I am about, but I will obey you," he added, with inward exultation, as he thought, "She has gone too far to draw back—she can refuse me nothing now!"

Eugène took the dainty little purse, inquired the way of a secondhand clothes-dealer, and hurried to No. 9, which happened to be the nearest gaming-house. He mounted the staircase, surrendered his hat, and asked the way to the roulette-table, whither the attendant took him, not a little to the astonishment of the regular comers. All eyes were fixed on Eugène as he asked, without bashfulness, where he was to deposit his stakes.

"If you put a louis on one only of those thirty-six numbers, and it turns up, you will win thirty-six louis," said a respectable-looking, white-haired old man in answer to his inquiry.

Eugène staked the whole of his money on the number 21 (his own age). There was a cry of surprise; before he knew what he had done, he had won.

"Take your money off, sir," said the old gentleman; "you don't often win twice running by that system."

Eugène took the rake that the old man handed to him, and drew in his three thousand six hundred francs, and, still perfectly ignorant of what he was about, staked again on the red. The bystanders watched him enviously as they saw him continue to play. The disc turned, and again he won; the banker threw him three thousand six hundred francs once more.

"You have seven thousand two hundred francs of your own," the old gentleman said in his ear. "Take my advice and go away with your winnings; red has turned up eight times already. If you are charitable, you will show your gratitude for sound counsel by giving a trifle to an old prefect of Napoleon's who is down on his luck."

Rastignac's head was swimming; he saw ten of his louis pass into the white-haired man's possession, and went downstairs with his seven thousand francs; he was still ignorant of the game, and stupefied by his luck.

"So that is over; and now where will you take me?" he asked, as soon as the door was closed, and he showed the seven thousand francs to Mme. de Nucingen.

Delphine flung her arms about him, but there was no passion in that wild embrace.

"You have saved me!" she cried, and tears of joy flowed fast.

"I will tell you everything, my friend. For you will be my friend, will you not? I am rich, you think, very rich; I have everything I want, or I seem as if I had everything. Very well, you must know that M. de Nucingen does not allow me the control of a single penny; he pays all the bills for the house expenses; he pays for my carriages and opera box; he does not give me enough to pay for my dress, and he reduces me to poverty in secret on purpose. I am too proud to beg from him. I should be the vilest of women if I could take his money at the price at which he offers it. Do you ask how I, with seven hundred thousand francs of my own, could let myself be robbed? It is because I was proud, and scorned to speak. We are so young, so artless when our married life begins! I never could bring myself to ask my husband for money; the words would have made my lips bleed, I did not dare to ask; I spent my savings first, and then the money that my poor father gave me, then I ran into debt. Marriage for me is a hideous farce; I cannot talk about it; let it suffice to say that Nucingen and I have separate rooms, and that I would fling myself out of the window sooner than consent to any other manner of life. I suffered agonies when I had to confess to my girlish extravagance, my debts for jewelry and trifles (for our poor father had never refused us anything, and spoiled us), but at last I found courage to tell him about them. After all, I had a fortune of my own.

"Nucingen flew into a rage; he said that I should be the ruin of him, and used frightful language! I wished myself a hundred feet down in the earth. He had my dowry, so he paid my debts, but he stipulated at the same time that my expenses in future must not exceed a certain fixed sum, and I gave way for the sake of peace. And then," she went on, "I wanted to gratify the self-love of someone whom you know. He may have deceived me, but I should do him the justice to say that there was nothing petty in his character. But, after all, he threw me over disgracefully. If, at a woman's utmost need, *somebody* heaps gold upon her, he ought never to forsake her; that love should last forever! But you, at one-and-twenty, you, the soul of honor, with the unsullied conscience of youth, will ask me how a woman can bring herself to accept money in such a way? *Mon Dieu!* is it not natural to share everything with the one to whom we owe our happiness? When all has been given, why should we pause and hesitate over a part? Money is as nothing between us until the moment when the sentiment that bound us together ceases to exist. Were we not bound to each other for life? Who that believes in love foresees such an end of love? You swear to love us eternally; how, then, can our interests be separate?

"You do not know how I suffered to-day when Nucingen refused to give me six thousand francs; he spends as much as that every month on his mistress, an opera dancer! I thought of killing myself. The wildest thoughts came into my head. There have been moments in my life when I have envied my servants, and would have changed places with my maid. It was madness to think of going to our father, Anastasie and I have bled him dry; our poor father would have sold himself if he could have raised six thousand francs that way. I should have driven him frantic to no purpose. You have saved me from shame and death; I was beside myself with anguish. Ah! Monsieur, I owed you this explanation after my mad ravings. When you left me just now, as soon as you were out of sight, I longed to escape, to run away . . . where, I did not know. Half the women in Paris lead such lives as mine; they live in apparent luxury, and in their souls are tormented by anxiety. I know of poor creatures even more miserable than I; there are women who are driven to ask their tradespeople to make out false bills, women who rob their husbands. Some men believe that an Indian shawl worth a hundred louis only cost five hundred francs, others that a shawl costing five hundred francs is worth a hundred louis. There are women, too, with narrow incomes, who scrape and save and starve their children to pay for a dress. I am innocent of these base meannesses. But this is the last extremity of my torture. Some women will sell themselves to their husbands, and so obtain their way, but I, at any rate, am free. If I chose, Nucingen would cover me with gold, but I would rather weep on the breast of a man whom I can respect. Ah! to-night, M. de Marsay will no longer have a right to think of me as a woman whom he has paid." She tried to conceal her tears from him, hiding her face in her hands; Eugène drew them away and looked at her; she seemed to him sublime at that moment.

"It is hideous, is it not," she cried, "to speak in a breath of money and affection? You cannot love me after this," she added.

The incongruity between the ideas of honor which make women so great, and the errors in conduct which are forced upon them by the constitution of society, had thrown Eugène's thoughts into confusion; he uttered soothing and consoling words, and wondered at the beautiful woman before him, and at the artless imprudence of her cry of pain.

"You will not remember this against me?" she asked; "promise me that you will not."

"Ah! Madame, I am incapable of doing so," he said. She took his hand and held it to her heart, a movement full of grace that expressed her deep gratitude.

"I am free and happy once more, thanks to you," she said. "Oh! I have felt lately as if I were in the grasp of an iron hand. But after this I mean to live simply and to spend nothing. You will think me just as pretty, will you not, my friend? Keep this," she went on, as she took only six of the bank-notes. "In conscience I owe you a thousand crowns, for I really ought to go halves with you."

Eugène's maiden conscience resisted; but when the Baroness said, "I am bound to look on you as an accomplice or as an enemy," he took the money.

"It shall be a last stake in reserve," he said, "in case of misfortune."

"That was what I was dreading to hear," she cried, turning pale. "Oh, if you would that I should be anything to you, swear to me that you will never re-enter a gaming-house. Great Heaven! that I should corrupt you! I should die of sorrow!"

They had reached the Rue Saint-Lazare by this time. The contrast between the ostentation of wealth in the house, and the wretched condition of its mistress, dazed the student; and Vautrin's cynical words began to ring in his ears.

"Seat yourself there," said the Baroness, pointing to a low chair beside the fire. "I have a difficult letter to write," she added. "Tell me what to say."

"Say nothing," Eugène answered her. "Put the bills in an envelope, direct it, and send it by your maid."

"Why, you are a love of a man," she said. "Ah! see what it is to have been well brought up. That is the Beauséant through and through," she went on, smiling at him.

"She is charming," thought Eugène, more and more in love. He looked round him at the room; there was an ostentatious character about the luxury, a meretricious taste in the splendor.

"Do you like it?" she asked, as she rang for her maid. "Thérèse, take this to M. de Marsay, and give it into his hands yourself. If he is not at home, bring the letter back to me."

Thérèse went, but not before she had given Eugène a spiteful glance.

Dinner was announced. Rastignac gave his arm to Mme. de Nucingen, she led the way into a pretty dining-room, and again he saw the luxury of the table which he had admired in his cousin's house.

"Come and dine with me on opera evenings, and we will go to the Italiens afterwards," she said.

"I should soon grow used to the pleasant life if it could last, but I am a poor student, and I have my way to make."

"Oh! you will succeed," she said, laughing. "You will see. All that you wish will come to pass. *I* did not expect to be so happy."

It is the wont of women to prove the impossible by the possible, and to annihilate facts by presentiments. When Mme. de Nucingen and Rastignac took their places in her box at the Bouffons, her face wore a look of happiness that made her so lovely that everyone indulged in those small slanders against which women are defenseless; for the scandal that is uttered lightly is often seriously believed. Those who know Paris believe nothing that is said, and say nothing of what is done there.

Eugène took the Baroness's hand in his, and by some light pressure of the fingers, or a closer grasp of the hand, they found a language in which to express the sensations which the music gave them. It was an evening of intoxicating delight for both; and when it ended, and they went out together, Mme. de Nucingen insisted on taking Eugène with her as far as the Pont Neuf, he disputing with her the whole of the way for a single kiss after all those that she had showered upon him so passionately at the Palais-Royal; Eugène reproached her with inconsistency.

"That was gratitude," she said, "for devotion that I did not dare to hope for, but now it would be a promise."

"And will you give me no promise, ingrate?"

He grew vexed. Then, with one of those impatient gestures that fill a lover with ecstasy, she gave him her hand to kiss, and he took it with a discontented air that delighted her.

"I shall see you at the ball on Monday," she said.

As Eugène went home in the moonlight, he fell to serious reflections. He was satisfied, and yet dissatisfied. He was pleased with an adventure which would probably give him his desire, for in the end one of the prettiest and best-dressed women in Paris would be his; but, as a set-off, he saw his hopes of fortune brought to nothing; and as soon as he realized this fact, the vague thoughts of yesterday evening began to take a more decided shape in his mind. A check is sure to reveal to us the strength of our hopes. The more Eugène learned of the pleasures of life in Paris, the more impatient he felt of poverty and obscurity. He crumpled the bank-note in his pocket, and found any quantity of plausible excuses for appropriating it.

He reached the Rue Neuve-Sainte-Geneviève at last, and from the stairhead he saw a light in Goriot's room; the old man had lighted a candle, and set the door ajar, lest the student should pass him by, and go to his room without "telling him all about his daughter," to use his own expression. Eugène, accordingly, told him everything without reserve.

"Then they think that I am ruined!" cried old Goriot, in an agony of jealousy and desperation. "Why, I have still thirteen hundred livres a year! *Mon Dieu!* Poor little girl! why did she not come to me? I would have sold my *rentes;* she should have had some of the principal, and I would have bought a life-annuity with the rest. My good neighbor, why did not *you* come to tell me of her difficulty? How had you the heart to go and risk her poor little hundred francs at play? This is heartbreaking work. You see what it is to have sons-in-law. Oh! if I had hold of them, I would wring their necks. *Mon Dieu! crying!* Did you say she was crying?"

"With her head on my waistcoat," said Eugène.

"Oh! give it to me," said old Goriot. "What! my daughter's tears have fallen there—my darling Delphine, who never used to cry when she was a little girl! Oh! I will buy you another; do not wear it again; let me have it. By the terms of her marriage-contract, she ought to have the use of her property. To-morrow morning I will go and see Derville; he is an attorney. I will demand that her money should be invested in her own name. I know the law. I am an old wolf; I will show my teeth."

"Here, father; this is a bank-note for a thousand francs that she wanted me to keep out of our winnings. Keep them for her, in the pocket of the waistcoat."

Goriot looked hard at Eugène, reached out and took the law student's hand, and Eugène felt a tear fall on it.

"You will succeed," the old man said. "God is just, you see. I know an honest man when I see him, and I can tell you, there are not many men like you. I am to have another dear child in you, am I? There, go to sleep; you can sleep, you are not yet a father. She was crying! and I have to be told about it!—and I was quietly eating my dinner, like an idiot, all the time—I, who would sell the Father, Son, and Holy Ghost to save one tear to either of them."

"An honest man!" said Eugène to himself as he lay down. "Upon my word, I think I will be an honest man all my life; it is so pleasant to obey the voice of conscience." Perhaps none but believers in God do good in secret; and Eugène believed in a God.

The next day Rastignac went at the appointed time to Mme. de Beauséant, who took him with her to the Duchesse de Carigliano's ball. The Maréchale received Eugène most graciously. Mme. de Nucingen was there. Delphine's dress seemed to suggest that she wished for the admiration of others, so that she might shine the more in Eugène's eyes; she was eagerly expecting a glance from him, hiding, as she thought, this eagerness from all beholders. This moment is full of charm for the one who can guess all that passes in a woman's mind. Who has not refrained from giving his opinion, to prolong her suspense, concealing his pleasure from a desire to tantalize, seeking a confession of love in her uneasiness, enjoying the fears that he can dissipate by a smile? In the course of the evening the law student suddenly comprehended his position; he saw that, as the cousin of Mme. de Beauséant, he was a personage in this world. He was already credited with the conquest of Mme. de Nucingen, and for this reason was a conspicuous figure; he caught the envious glances of other young men, and experienced the earliest pleasures of coxcombry. People wondered at his luck, and scraps of these conversations came to his ears as he went from room to room; all the women prophesied his success; and Delphine, in her dread of losing him, promised that this evening she would not refuse the kiss that all his entreaties could scarcely win yesterday.

Rastignac received several invitations. His cousin presented him to other women who were present; women who could claim to be of the highest fashion; whose houses were looked upon as pleasant; and this was the loftiest and most fashionable society in Paris into which he was launched. So this evening had all the charm of a brilliant début; it was an evening that he was to remember even in old age, as a woman looks back on her first ball and the memories of her girlish triumphs.

The next morning, at breakfast, he related the story of his success for the benefit of old Goriot and the lodgers. Vautrin began to smile in a diabolical fashion.

"And do you suppose," cried that cold-blooded logician, "that a young man of fashion can live here in the Rue

Neuve-Sainte-Geneviève, in the Maison Vauquer—an exceedingly respectable boarding-house in every way, I grant you, but an establishment that, none the less, falls short of being fashionable? The house is comfortable, it is lordly in its abundance; it is proud to be the temporary abode of a Rastignac; but, after all, it is in the Rue Neuve-Sainte-Geneviève, and luxury would be out of place here, where we only aim at the purely *patriarchalorama.* If you mean to cut a figure in Paris, my young friend," Vautrin continued, with half-paternal jocularity, "you must have three horses, a tilbury for the mornings, and a closed carriage for the evening; you should spend altogether about nine thousand francs on your stables. You would show yourself unworthy of your destiny if you spent no more than three thousand francs with your tailor, six hundred in perfumery, a hundred crowns to your shoemaker, and a hundred more to your hatter. As for your laundress, there goes another thousand francs; a young man of fashion must of necessity make a great point of his linen; if your linen comes up to the required standard, people often do not look any further. Love and the Church demand a fair altar-cloth. That is fourteen thousand francs. I am saying nothing of losses at play, bets, and presents; it is impossible to allow less than two thousand francs for pocket-money. I have led that sort of life, and I know all about these expenses. Add the cost of necessaries next; three hundred louis for provender, a thousand francs for a place to roost in. Well, my boy, for all these little wants of ours we had need to have twenty-five thousand francs every year in our purse, or we shall find ourselves in the kennel, and people laughing at us, and our career is cut short, good-by to success, and good-by to your mistress! I am forgetting your valet and your groom! Is Christophe going to carry your *billets-doux* for you? And do you mean to employ the stationery you use at present? Suicidal policy! Hearken to the wisdom of your elders!" he went on, his bass voice growing louder at each syllable. "Either take up your quarters in a garret, live virtuously, and wed your work, or set about the thing in a different way."

Vautrin winked and leered in the direction of Mlle. Taillefer to inforce his remarks by a look which recalled the late tempting proposals by which he had sought to corrupt the student's mind.

Several days went by, and Rastignac lived in a whirl of gayety. He dined almost every day with Mme. de Nucingen, and went wherever she went, only returning to the Rue Neuve-Sainte-Geneviève in the small hours. He rose at mid-day, and dressed to go into the Bois with Delphine if the day was fine, squandering in this way time that was worth far more than he knew. He turned as eagerly to learn the lessons of luxury, and was as quick to feel its fascination, as the flowers of the date palm to receive the fertilizing pollen. He played high, lost and won large sums of money, and at last became accustomed to the extravagant life that young men lead in Paris. He sent fifteen hundred francs out of his first winnings to his mother and sisters, sending handsome presents as well as the money. He had given out that he meant to leave the Maison Vauquer; but January came and went, and he was still there, still unprepared to go.

One rule holds good of most young men—whether rich or poor. They never have money for the necessaries of life, but they have always money to spare for their caprices—an anomaly which finds its explanation in their youth and in the almost frantic eagerness with which youth grasps at pleasure. They are reckless with anything obtained on credit, while everything for which they must pay in ready money is made to last as long as possible; if they cannot have all that they want, they make up for it, it would seem, by squandering what they have. To state the matter simply—a student is far more careful of his hat than of his coat, because the latter being a comparatively costly article of dress, it is in the nature of things that a tailor should be a creditor; but it is otherwise with the hatter; the sums of money spent with him are so modest, that he is the most independent and unmanageable of his tribe, and it is almost impossible to bring him to terms. The young man in the balcony of a theater who displays a gorgeous waistcoat for the benefit of the fair owners of opera glasses, has very probably no socks in his wardrobe, for the hosier is another of the genus of weevils that nibble at the purse. This was Rastignac's condition. His purse was always empty for Mme. Vauquer, always full at the demand of vanity; there was a periodical ebb and flow in his fortunes, which was seldom favorable to the payment of just debts. If he was to leave that unsavory and mean abode, where from time to time his pretensions met with humiliation, the first step was to pay his hostess for a month's board and lodging, and the second to purchase furniture worthy of the new lodgings he must take in his quality of dandy, a course that remained impossible. Rastignac, out of his winnings at cards, would pay his jeweler exorbitant prices for gold watches and chains, and then, to meet the exigencies of play, would carry them to the pawnbroker, that discreet and forbidding-looking friend of youth; but when it was a question of paying for board or lodging, or for the necessary implements for the cultivation of his Elysian fields, his imagination and pluck alike deserted him. There was no inspiration to be found in vulgar necessity, in debts contracted for past requirements. Like most of those who trust to their luck, he put off till the last moment the payment of debts that among the bourgeoisie are regarded as sacred engagements, acting on the plan of Mirabeau, who never settled his baker's bill until it underwent a formidable transformation into a bill of exchange.

It was about this time when Rastignac was down on his luck and fell into debt, that it became clear to the law student's mind that he must have some more certain source of income if he meant to live as he had been doing. But while he groaned over the thorny problems of his precarious situation, he felt that he could not bring himself to renounce the pleasures of this extravagant life, and decided that he must continue it at all costs. His dreams of obtaining a fortune appeared more and more chimerical, and the real obstacles grew more formidable. His initiation into the secrets of the Nucingen household had revealed to him that if he were to attempt to use this love affair as a means of mending his fortunes, he must swallow down all sense of decency, and renounce all the generous ideas which redeem the sins of youth. He had chosen this life of apparent splendor, but secretly gnawed by the canker worm of remorse, a life of fleeting pleasure dearly paid for by persistent pain; like *Le Distrait* of La Bruyère, he had descended so far as to make his bed in a ditch; but (also like *Le Distrait*) he himself was uncontaminated as yet by the mire that stained his garments.

"So we have killed our mandarin, have we?" said Bianchon one day as they left the dinner table.

"Not yet," he answered, "but he is at the last gasp."

The medical student took this for a joke, but it was not a jest. Eugène had dined in the house that night for the first time for a long while, and had looked thoughtful during the meal. He had taken his place beside Mlle. Taillefer, and stayed through the dessert, giving his neighbor an expressive glance from time to time. A few of the boarders discussed the walnuts at the table, and others walked about the room, still taking part in a conversation which had begun among them. People usually went when they chose; the amount of time that they lingered being determined by the amount of interest that the conversation possessed for them, or by the difficulty of the process of digestion. In winter-time the room was seldom empty before eight o'clock, when the four women had it all to themselves, and made up for the silence previously imposed upon them by the preponderating masculine element. This evening Vautrin had noticed Eugène's abstractedness, and stayed in the room, though he had seemed to be in a hurry to finish his dinner and go. All through the talk afterwards he had kept out of sight of the law student, who quite believed that Vautrin had left the room. He now took up his position cunningly in the sitting-room instead of going when the last boarders went. He had fathomed the young man's thoughts, and felt that a crisis was at hand. Rastignac was, in fact, in a dilemma, which many another young man must have known.

Mme. de Nucingen might love him, or might merely be playing with him, but in either case Rastignac had been made to experience all the alternations of hope and despair of genuine passion, and all the diplomatic arts of a Parisienne had been employed on him. After compromising herself by continually appearing in public with Mme. de Beauséant's cousin she still hesitated, and would not give him the lover's privileges which he appeared to enjoy. For a whole month she had so wrought on his senses, that at last she had made an impression on his heart. If in the earliest days the student had fancied himself to be the master, Mme. de Nucingen had since become the stronger of the two, for she had skillfully roused and played upon every instinct, good or bad, in the two or three men comprised in a young student in Paris. This was not the result of deep design on her part, nor was she playing a part, for women are in a manner true to themselves even through their grossest deceit, because their actions are prompted by a natural impulse.

It may have been that Delphine, who had allowed this young man to gain such an ascendency over her, conscious that she had been too demonstrative, was obeying a sentiment of dignity, and either repented of her concessions, or it pleased her to suspend them. It is so natural to a Parisienne, even when passion has almost mastered her, to hesitate and pause before taking the plunge; to probe the heart of him to whom she intrusts her future. And once already Mme. de Nucingen's hopes had been betrayed, and her loyalty to a selfish young lover had been despised. She had good reason to be suspicious. Or it may have been that something in Eugène's manner (for his rapid success was making a coxcomb of him) had warned her that the grotesque nature of their position had lowered her somewhat in his eyes. She doubtless wished to assert her dignity; he was young, and she would be great in his eyes; for the lover who had forsaken her had held her so cheap that she was determined that Eugène should not think her an easy conquest, and for this very reason—he knew that de Marsay had been his predecessor. Finally, after the degradation of submission to the pleasure of a heartless young rake, it was so sweet to her to wander in the flower-strewn realms of love, that it was not wonderful that she should wish to dwell a while on the prospect, to tremble with the vibrations of love, to feel the freshness of the breath of its dawn. The true lover was suffering for the sins of the false. This inconsistency is unfortunately only to be expected so long as men do not know how many flowers are mown down in a young woman's soul by the first stroke of treachery.

Whatever her reasons may have been, Delphine was playing with Rastignac, and took pleasure in playing with him, doubtless because she felt sure of his love, and confident that she could put an end to the torture as soon as it was her royal pleasure to do so. Eugène's self-love was engaged; he could not suffer his first passage of love to end in a defeat, and persisted in his suit, like a sportsman determined to bring down at least one partridge to celebrate his first Feast of Saint Hubert. The pressure of anxiety, his wounded self-love, his despair, real or feigned, drew him nearer and nearer to this woman. All Paris credited him with this conquest, and yet he was conscious that he had made no progress since the day when he saw Mme. de Nucingen for the first time. He did not know as yet that a woman's coquetry is sometimes more delightful than the pleasure of secure possession of her love, and was possessed with helpless rage. If, at this time, while she denied herself to love, Eugène gathered the springtide spoils of his life, the fruit, somewhat sharp and green, and dearly bought, was no less delicious to the taste. There were moments when he had not a sou in his pockets, and at such times he thought in spite of his conscience of Vautrin's offer and the possibility of fortune by a marriage with Mlle. Taillefer. Poverty would clamor so loudly that more than once he was on the point of yielding to the cunning temptations of the terrible sphinx, whose glance had so often exerted a strange spell over him.

Poiret and Mlle. Michonneau went up to their rooms; and Rastignac, thinking that he was alone with the women in the dining-room, sat between Mme. Vauquer and Mme. Couture, who was nodding over the woolen cuffs that she was knitting by the stove, and looked at Mlle. Taillefer so tenderly that she lowered her eyes.

"Can you be in trouble, M. Eugène?" Victorine said after a pause.

"Who has not his troubles?" answered Rastignac. "If we men were sure of being loved, sure of a devotion which would be our reward for the sacrifices which we are always ready to make, then perhaps we should have no troubles."

For answer Mlle. Taillefer only gave him a glance, but it was impossible to mistake its meaning.

"You, for instance, Mademoiselle; you feel sure of your heart to-day, but are you sure that it will never change?"

A smile flitted over the poor girl's lips; it seemed as if a ray of light from her soul had lighted up her face. Eugène was dismayed at the sudden explosion of feeling caused by his words.

"Ah! but suppose," he said, "that you should be rich and happy to-morrow, suppose that a vast fortune dropped down from the clouds for you, would you still love the man whom you loved in your days of poverty?"

A charming movement of the head was her only answer.

"Even if he were very poor?"

Again the same mute answer.

"What nonsense are you talking, you two?" exclaimed Mme. Vauquer.

"Never mind," answered Eugène; "we understand each other."

"So there is to be an engagement of marriage between M. le Chevalier Eugène de Rastignac and Mlle. Victorine Taillefer, is there?" The words were uttered in Vautrin's deep voice, and Vautrin appeared at the door as he spoke.

"Oh! how you startled me!" Mme. Couture and Mme. Vauquer exclaimed together.

"I might make a worse choice," said Rastignac, laughing. Vautrin's voice had thrown him into the most painful agitation that he had yet known.

"No bad jokes, gentlemen!" said Mme. Couture. "My dear, let us go upstairs."

Mme. Vauquer followed the two ladies. meaning to pass the evening in their room, an arrangement that economized fire and candlelight. Eugène and Vautrin were left alone.

"I felt sure you would come round to it," said the elder man with the coolness that nothing seemed to shake. "But stay a moment! I have as much delicacy as anybody else.

Don't make up your mind on the spur of the moment; you are a little thrown off your balance just now. You are in debt, and I want you to come over to my way of thinking after sober reflection, and not in a fit of passion or desperation. Perhaps you want a thousand crowns. There, you can have them if you like."

The tempter took out a pocket-book, and drew thence three bank-notes, which he fluttered before the student's eyes. Eugène was in a most painful dilemma. He had debts, debts of honor. He owed a hundred louis to the Marquis d'Ajuda and to the Comte de Trailles; he had not the money, and for this reason had not dared to go to Mme. de Restaud's house, where he was expected that evening. It was one of those informal gatherings where tea and little cakes are handed round, but where it is possible to lose six thousand francs at whist in the course of a night.

"You must see," said Eugène, struggling to hide a convulsive tremor, "that after what has passed between us, I cannot possibly lay myself under any obligation to you."

"Quite right; I should be sorry to hear you speak otherwise," answered the tempter. "You are a fine young fellow, honorable, brave as a lion, and as gentle as a young girl. You would be a fine haul for the Devil! I like youngsters of your sort. Get rid of one or two more prejudices, and you will see the world as it is. Make a little scene now and then, and act a virtuous part in it, and a man with a head on his shoulders can do exactly as he likes amid deafening applause from the fools in the gallery. Ah! a few days yet, and you will be with us; and if you would only be tutored by me, I would put you in the way of achieving all your ambitions. You should no sooner form a wish than it should be realized to the full; you should have all your desires—honors, wealth, or women. Civilization should flow with milk and honey for you. You should be our pet and favorite, our Benjamin. We would all work ourselves to death for you with pleasure; every obstacle should be removed from your path. You have a few prejudices left; so you think that I am a scoundrel, do you? Well, M. de Turenne, quite as honorable a man as you take yourself to be, had some little private transactions with bandits, and did not feel that his honor was tarnished. You would rather not lie under any obligation to me, eh? You need not draw back on that account," Vautrin went on, and a smile stole over his lips. "Take those bits of paper and write across this," he added, producing a piece of stamped paper, "*Accepted the sum of three thousand five hundred francs due this day twelvemonth,* and fill in the date. The rate of interest is stiff enough to silence any scruples on your part; it gives you the right to call me a Jew. You can call quits with me on the score of gratitude. I am quite willing that you should despise me to-day, because I am sure that you will have a kindlier feeling towards me later on. You will find out fathomless depths in my nature, enormous and concentrated forces that weaklings call vices, but you will never find me base or ungrateful. In short, I am neither a pawn nor a bishop, but a castle, a tower of strength, my boy."

"What manner of man are you?" cried Eugène. "Were you created to torment me?"

"Why, no; I am a good-natured fellow, who is willing to do a dirty piece of work to put you high and dry above the mire for the rest of your days. Do you ask the reason of this devotion? All right; I will tell you that some of these days. A word or two in your ear will explain it. I have begun by shocking you, by showing you the way to ring the changes, and giving you a sight of the mechanism of the social machine; but your first fright will go off like a conscript's terror on the battlefield. You will grow used to regarding men as common soldiers who have made up their minds to lose their lives for some self-constituted king. Times have altered strangely. Once you could say to a bravo, 'Here are a hundred crowns; go and kill Monsieur So-and-so for me,' and you could sup quietly after turning someone off into the dark for the least thing in the world. But nowadays I propose to put you in the way of a handsome fortune; you have only to nod your head, it won't compromise you in any way, and you hesitate. 'Tis an effeminate age."

Eugène accepted the draft, and received the bank-notes in exchange for it.

"Well, well. Come, now, let us talk rationally," Vautrin continued. "I mean to leave this country in a few months time for America, and set about planting tobacco. I will send you the cigars of friendship. If I make money at it, I will help you in your career. If I have no children—which will probably be the case, for I have no anxiety to raise slips of myself here—you shall inherit my fortune. That is what you may call standing by a man; but I myself have a liking for you. I have a mania, too, for devoting myself to someone else. I have done it before. You see, my boy, I live in a loftier sphere than other men do; I look on all actions as means to an end, and the end is all that I look at. What is a man's life to me? Not *that*," he said, and he snapped his thumb-nail against his teeth. "A man, in short, is everything to me, or just nothing at all. Less than nothing if his name happens to be Poiret: you can crush him like a bug, he is flat and he is offensive. But a man is a god when he is like you; he is not a machine covered with a skin, but a theater in which the greatest sentiments are displayed—great thoughts and feelings—and for these, and these only, I live. A sentiment—what is that but the whole world in a thought? Look at old Goriot. For him, his two girls are the whole universe; they are the clew by which he finds his way through creation. Well, for my own part, and I have fathomed the depths of life, there is only one real sentiment—comradeship between man and man. Pierre and Jaffier, that is my passion. I know *Venice Preserved* by heart. Have you met many men plucky enough when a comrade says, 'Let us bury a dead body!' to go and do it without a word or plaguing him by taking a high moral tone? I have done it myself. I should not talk like this to just everybody, but you are not like an ordinary man; one can talk to you, you can understand things. You will not dabble about much longer among the tadpoles in these swamps. Well, then, it is all settled. You will marry. Both of us carry our point. Mine is made of iron, and will never soften, he! he!"

Vautrin went out. He would not wait to hear the student's repudiation, he wished to put Eugène at his ease. He seemed to understand the secret springs of the faint resistance still made by the younger man; the struggles in which men seek to preserve their self-respect by justifying their blameworthy actions to themselves.

"He may do as he likes; I shall not marry Mlle. Taillefer, that is certain," said Eugène to himself.

He regarded this man with abhorrence, and yet the very cynicism of Vautrin's ideas, and the audacious way in which he used other men for his own ends, raised him in the student's eyes; but the thought of a compact threw Eugène into a fever of apprehension, and not until he had recovered somewhat did he dress, call for a cab, and go to Mme. de Restaud's.

For some days the Countess had paid more and more attention to a young man whose every step seemed a triumphal progress in the great world; it seemed to her that he might be a formidable power before long. He paid Messieurs de Trailles and d'Ajuda, played at whist for part of the evening, and made good his losses. Most men who have their way to make are more or less of fatalists, and Eugène was superstitious; he chose to consider that his luck was Heaven's reward for his perseverance in the right way. As soon as possible on the following morning he asked Vautrin whether the bill that he had given was still in the other's possession; and on receiving a reply in the affirmative, he repaid the three thousand francs with a not unnatural relief.

"Everything is going on well," said Vautrin.

"But I am not your accomplice," said Eugène.

"I know, I know," Vautrin broke in. "You are still acting like a child. You are making mountains out of molehills at the outset."

Two days later, Poiret and Mlle. Michonneau were sitting together on a bench in the sun. They had chosen a little frequented alley in the Jardin des Plantes, and a gentleman was chatting with them, the same person, as a matter of fact, about whom the medical student had, not without good reason, his own suspicions.

"Mademoiselle," this M. Gondureau was saying, "I do not see any cause for your scruples. His Excellency Monseigneur the Minister of Police——"

"Ah!" echoed Poiret, "his Excellency Monseigneur the Minister of Police!"

"Yes, his Excellency is taking a personal interest in the matter," said Gondureau.

Who would think it probable that Poiret, a retired clerk, doubtless possessed of some notions of civic virtue, though there might be nothing else in his head—who would think it likely that such a man would continue to lend an ear to the supposed independent gentleman of the Rue de Buffon, when the latter dropped the mask of a decent citizen by that word "police," and gave a glimpse of the features of a detective from the Rue de Jérusalem? And yet nothing was more natural. Perhaps the following remarks from the hitherto unpublished records made by certain observers will throw a light on the particular species to which Poiret belonged in the great family of fools. There is a race of quill-drivers, confined in the columns of the budget between the first degree of latitude (a kind of administrative Greenland where the salaries begin at twelve hundred francs) to the third degree, a more temperate zone, where incomes grow from three to six thousand francs, a climate where the *bonus* flourishes like a half-hardy annual in spite of some difficulties of culture. A characteristic trait that best reveals the feeble narrow-mindedness of these inhabitants of petty officialdom is a kind of involuntary, mechanical, and instinctive reverence for the Grand Lama of every Ministry, known to the rank and file only by his signature (an illegible scrawl) and by his title—"His Excellency Monseigneur le Ministre," five words which produce as much effect as the *il Bondo Cani* of the *Calife de Bagdad,* five words which in the eyes of this low order of intelligence represent a sacred power from which there is no appeal. The Minister is administratively infallible for the clerks in the employ of the Government, as the Pope is infallible for good Catholics. Something of his peculiar radiance invests everything he does or says, or that is said or done in his name; the robe of office covers everything and legalizes everything done by his orders; does not his very title—His Excellency—vouch for the purity of his intentions and the righteousness of his will, and serve as a sort of passport and introduction to ideas that otherwise would not be entertained for a moment? Pronounce the words "his Excellency," and these poor folk will forthwith proceed to do what they would not do for their own interests. Passive obedience is as well known in a Government department as in the army itself; and the administrative system silences consciences, annihilates the individual, and ends (give it time enough) by fashioning a man into a vice or a thumbscrew, and he becomes part of the machinery of Government. Wherefore, M. Gondureau, who seemed to know something of human nature, recognized Poiret at once as one of these dupes of officialdom, and brought out for his benefit, at the proper moment, the *deux ex machinâ,* the magical words "his Excellency," so as to dazzle Poiret just as he himself unmasked his batteries, for he took Poiret and the Michonneau for the male and female of the same species.

"If his Excellency himself, his Excellency the Minister . . . Ah! that is quite another thing," said Poiret.

"You seem to be guided by this gentleman's opinion, and you hear what he says," said the man of independent means, addressing Mlle. Michonneau. "Very well, his Excellency is at this moment absolutely certain that the so-called Vautrin, who lodges at the Maison Vauquer, is a convict who escaped from penal servitude at Toulon, where he is known by the nickname *Trompe-la-Mort.*"

"Trompe-la-Mort?" said Poiret. "Dear me, he is very lucky if he deserves that nickname."

"Well, yes," said the detective. "They call him so because he has been so lucky as not to lose his life in the very risky business that he has carried through. He is a dangerous man, you see! He has qualities that are out of the common; the thing he is wanted for, in fact, was a matter which gained him no end of credit with his own set——"

"Then is he a man of honor?" asked Poiret.

"Yes, according to his notions. He agreed to take another man's crime upon himself—a forgery committed by a very handsome young fellow that he had taken a great fancy to, a young Italian, a bit of a gambler, who has since gone into the army, where his conduct has been unexceptionable."

"But if his Excellency the Minister of Police is certain that M. Vautrin is this Trompe-la-Mort, why should he want me?" asked Mlle. Michonneau.

"Oh, yes," said Poiret, "if the Minister, as you have been so obliging as to tell us, really knows for a certainty——"

"Certainty is not the word; he only suspects. You will soon understand how things are. Jacques Collin, nicknamed Trompe-la-Mort, is in the confidence of every convict in the three prisons; he is their man of business and their banker. He makes a very good thing out of managing their affairs, which want a *man of mark* to see about them."

"Ha! ha! do you see the pun, Mademoiselle?" asked Poiret. "This gentleman calls him a *man of mark* because he is a *marked man*—branded, you know.

"This so-called Vautrin," said the detective, "receives the money belonging to my lords the convicts, invests it for them, and holds it at the disposal of those who escape, or hands it over to their families if they leave a will, or to their mistresses when they draw upon him for their benefit."

"Their mistresses! You mean their wives," remarked Poiret.

"No, sir. A convict's wife is usually an illegitimate connection. We call them concubines."

"Then they all live in a state of concubinage."

"Naturally."

"Why, these are abominations that his Excellency ought not to allow. Since you have the honor of seeing his Excellency, you, who seem to have philanthropic ideas, ought really to enlighten him as to their immoral conduct—they are setting a shocking example to the rest of society."

"But the Government does not hold them up as models of all the virtues, my dear sir."

"Of course not, sir; but still——"

"Just let the gentleman say what he has to say, dearie," said Mlle. Michonneau.

'You see how it is, Mademoiselle," Gondureau continued. "The Government may have the strongest reasons for getting this illicit hoard into its hands; it mounts up to something considerable, by all that we can make out. Trompe-la-Mort not only holds very large sums for his friends the convicts, but he has other amounts which are paid over to him by the Society of the Ten Thousand——"

"Ten Thousand Thieves!" cried Poiret in alarm.

"No. The Society of the Ten Thousand is not an association of petty offenders, but of people who set about their work on a large scale—they won't touch a matter unless there are ten thousand francs in it. It is composed of the most distinguished of the men who are sent straight to the Assize Courts when they come up for trial. They know the Code too well to risk their necks when they are nabbed. Collin is their confidential agent and legal adviser. By means of the large sums of money at his disposal he has established a sort of detective system of his own; it is widespread, and mysterious in its workings. We have had spies all about him for a twelve-month, and yet we could not manage to fathom his games. His capital and his cleverness are at the service of vice and crime; this money furnishes the necessary funds for a regular army of blackguards in his pay who wage incessant war against society. If we can catch Trompe-la-Mort, and take possession of his funds, we should strike at the root of this evil. So this job is a kind of Government affair—a State secret—and likely to redound to the honor of those who bring the thing to a successful conclusion. You, sir, for instance, might very well be taken into a Government department again; they might make you secretary to a Commissary of Police; you could accept that post without prejudice to your retiring pension."

Mlle. Michonneau interposed at this point with, "What is there to hinder Trompe-la-Mort from making off with the money?"

"Oh!" said the detective, "a man is told off to follow him everywhere he goes, with orders to kill him if he were to rob the convicts. Then it is not quite as easy to make off with a lot of money as it is to run away with a young lady of family. Besides, Collin is not the sort of fellow to play such a trick; he would be disgraced, according to his notions."

"You are quite right, sir," said Poiret, "utterly disgraced he would be."

"But none of all this explains why you do not come and take him without more ado," remarked Mlle. Michonneau.

"Very well, Mademoiselle, I will explain—but," he added in her ear, "keep your companion quiet, or I shall never have done. The old boy ought to pay people handsomely for listening to him.—Trompe-la-Mort, when he came back here," he went on aloud, "slipped into the skin of an honest man; he turned up disguised as a decent Parisian citizen, and took up his quarters in an unpretending lodging-house. He is cunning, that he is! You won't catch him napping. Then M. Vautrin is a man of consequence, who transacts a good deal of business."

"Naturally," said Poiret to himself.

"And suppose that the Minister were to make a mistake and get hold of the real Vautrin, he would put every one's back up among the business men in Paris, and public opinion would be against him. M. le Prefet de Police is on slippery ground; he has enemies. They would take advantage of any mistake. There would be a fine outcry and fuss made by the Opposition, and he would be sent packing. We must set about this just as we did about the Cogniard affair, the sham Comte de Sainte-Hélène; if he had been the real Comte de Sainte-Hélène, we should have been in the wrong box. We want to be quite sure what we are about."

"Yes, but what you want is a pretty woman," said Mlle. Michonneau briskly.

"Trompe-la-Mort would not let a woman come near him," said the detective. "I will tell you a secret—he does not like them."

"Still, I do not see what I can do, supposing that I did agree to identify him for two thousand francs."

"Nothing simpler," said the stranger. "I will send you a little bottle containing a dose that will send a rush of blood to the head; it will do him no harm whatever, but he will fall down as if he were in a fit. The drug can be put into wine or coffee; either will do equally well. You carry your man to bed at once, and undress him to see that he is not dying. As soon are you are alone, you give him a slap on the shoulder, and, *presto!* the letters will appear."

"Why, that is just nothing at all," said Poiret.

"Well, do you agree?" said Gondureau, addressing the old maid.

"But, my dear sir, suppose there are no letters at all," said Mlle. Michonneau; "am I to have the two thousand francs all the same?"

"No."

"What will you give me, then?"

"Five hundred francs."

"It is such a thing to do for so little! It lies on your conscience just the same, and I must quiet my conscience, sir."

"I assure you," said Poiret, "that Mademoiselle has a great deal of conscience, and not only so, she is a very amiable person, and very intelligent."

"Well, now," Mlle. Michonneau went on, "make it three thousand francs if he is Trompe-la-Mort, and nothing at all if he is an ordinary man."

"Done!" said Gondureau, "but on condition that the thing is settled to-morrow."

"Not quite so soon, my dear sir; I must consult my confessor first."

"You are a sly one," said the detective as he rose to his feet. "Good-by till to-morrow, then. And if you should want to see me in a hurry, go to the Petite Rue Sainte-Anne at the bottom of the Cour de la Sainte Chapelle. There is only one door under the archway. Ask there for M. Gondureau."

Bianchon, on his way back from Cuvier's lecture, overheard the sufficiently striking nickname of Trompe-la-Mort, and caught the celebrated chief detective's *"Done!"*

"Why didn't you close with him? It would be three hundred francs a year," said Poiret to Mlle. Michonneau.

"Why didn't I?" she asked. "Why, it wants thinking over. Suppose that M. Vautrin is this Trompe-la-Mort, perhaps we might do better for ourselves with him. Still, on the other hand, if you ask him for money, it would put him on his guard, and he is just the man to clear out without paying, and that would be an abominable sell."

"And suppose you did warn him," Poiret went on, "didn't that gentleman say that he was closely watched? You would spoil everything."

"Anyhow," thought Mlle. Michonneau, "I can't abide him. He says nothing but disagreeable things to me."

"But you can do better than that," Poiret resumed. "As that gentleman said (and he seemed to me to be a very good sort of man, besides being very well got up), it is an act of obedience to the laws to rid society of a criminal, however virtuous he may be. Once a thief, always a thief. Suppose he were to take it into his head to murder us all? The deuce! We should be guilty of manslaughter, and be the first to fall victims in the bargain!"

Mlle. Michonneau's musings did not permit her to listen very closely to the remarks that fell one by one from Poiret's lips like water dripping from a leaky tap. When once this elderly babbler began to talk, he would go on like clockwork unless Mlle. Michonneau stopped him. He started on some subject or other, and wandered on through parenthesis after parenthesis till he came to regions as remote as possible from his premises without coming to any conclusions by the way.

By the time they reached the Maison Vauquer he had tacked together a whole string of examples and quotations more or less irrelevant to the subject in hand, which led him to give a full account of his own deposition in the case of the Sieur Ragoulleau *versus* Dame Morin, when he had been summoned as a witness for the defense.

As they entered the dining-room, Eugène de Rastignac was talking apart with Mlle. Taillefer; the conversation appeared to be of such thrilling interest that the pair never noticed the two older lodgers as they passed through the room. None of this was thrown away on Mlle. Michonneau.

"I knew how it would end," remarked that lady, addressing Poiret. "They have been making eyes at each other in a heartrending way for a week past."

"Yes," he answered. "So she was found guilty."

"Who?"

"Mme. Morin."

"I am talking about Mlle. Victorine," said Mlle. Michonneau, as she entered Poiret's room with an absent air, "and you answer, 'Mme. Morin.' Who may Mme. Morin be?"

"What can Mlle Victorine be guilty of?" demanded Poiret.

"Guilty of falling in love with M. Eugène de Rastignac, and going further and further without knowing exactly where she is going, poor innocent!"

That morning Mme. de Nucingen had driven Eugène to despair. In his own mind he had completely surrendered himself to Vautrin, and deliberately shut his eyes to the motive for the friendship which that extraordinary man professed for him, nor would he look to the consequences of such an alliance. Nothing short of a miracle could extricate him now out of the gulf into which he had walked an hour ago, when he exchanged vows in the softest of whispers with Mlle. Taillefer. To Victorine it seemed as if she heard an angel's voice that heaven was opening above her; the Maison Vauquer took strange and wonderful hues, like a stage fairy-palace. She loved and she was beloved; at any rate, she believed that she was loved; and what woman would not likewise have believed after seeing Rastignac's face and listening to the tones of his voice during that hour snatched under the argus eyes of the Maison Vauquer? He had trampled on his conscience; he knew that he was doing wrong, and did it deliberately; he had said to himself that a woman's happiness should atone for this venial sin. The energy of desperation had lent new beauty to his face; the lurid fire that burned in his heart shone from his eyes. Luckily for him, the miracle took place. Vautrin came in in high spirits, and at once read the hearts of these two young creatures whom he had brought together by the combinations of his infernal genius, but his deep voice broke in upon their bliss.

"A charming girl is my Fanchette
In her simplicity,"

he sang mockingly.

Victorine fled. Her heart was more full than it had ever been, but it was full of joy, and not of sorrow. Poor child! A pressure of the hand, the light touch of Rastignac's hair against her cheek, a word whispered in her ear so closely that she felt the student's warm breath on her, the pressure of a trembling arm about her waist, a kiss upon her throat—such had been her betrothal. The near neighborhood of the stout Sylvie, who might invade that glorified room at any moment, only made these first tokens of love more ardent, more eloquent, more entrancing than the noblest deeds done for love's sake in the most famous romances.

This *plain-song* of love, to use the pretty expression of our forefathers, seemed almost criminal to the devout young girl who went to confession every fortnight. In that one hour she had poured out more of the treasures of her soul than she could give in later days of wealth and happiness, when her whole self followed the gift.

"The thing is arranged," Vautrin said to Eugène, who remained. "Our two dandies have fallen out. Everything was done in proper form. It is a matter of opinion. Our pigeon has insulted my hawk. They will meet to-morrow in the redoubt at Clignancourt. By half-past eight in the morning Mlle. Taillefer, calmly dipping her bread and butter in her coffee cup, will be sole heiress of her father's fortune and affections. A funny way of putting it, isn't it? Taillefer's youngster is an expert swordsman, and quite cocksure about it, but he will be bled; I have just invented a thrust for his benefit, a way of raising your sword point and driving it at the forehead. I must show you that thrust; it is an uncommonly handy thing to know."

Rastignac heard him in dazed bewilderment; he could not find a word in reply. Just then Goriot came in, and Bianchon and a few of the boarders likewise appeared.

"That is just as I intended," Vautrin said. "You know quite well what you are about. Good, my little eaglet! You are born to command, you are strong, you stand firm on your feet, you are game! I respect you."

He made as though he would take Eugène's hand, but Rastignac hastily withdrew it, sank into a chair, and turned ghastly pale; it seemed to him that there was a sea of blood before his eyes.

"Oh! so we have still a few dubious tatters of the swaddling clothes of virtue about us!" murmured Vautrin. "But Papa Doliban has three millions; I know the amount of his fortune. Once have her dowry in your hands, and your character will be as white as the bride's white dress, even in your own eyes."

Rastignac hesitated no longer. He made up his mind that he would go that evening to warn the Taillefers, father and son. But just as Vautrin left him, old Goriot came up and said in his ear, "You look melancholy, my boy; I will cheer you up. Come with me."

The old vermicelli dealer lighted his dip at one of the lamps as he spoke. Eugène went with him, his curiosity had been aroused.

"Let us go up to your room," the worthy soul remarked, when he had asked Sylvie for the law student's key. "This morning," he resumed, "you thought that *she* did not care about you, did you not? Eh? She would have nothing to say to you, and you went away out of humor and out of heart. Stuff and rubbish! She wanted you to go because she was expecting *me!* Now do you understand? We were to complete the arrangements for taking some chambers for you, a jewel of a place, you are to move into it in three days' time. Don't split upon me. She wants it to be a surprise; but I couldn't bear to keep the secret from you. You will be in the Rue d'Artois, only a step or two from the Rue Saint-Lazare, and you are to be housed like a prince! Anyone might have thought we were furnishing the house for a bride. Oh! we have done a lot of things in the last month, and you knew nothing about it. My attorney has appeared on the scene, and my daughter is to have thirty-six thousand francs a year, the interest on her money, and I shall insist on having her eight hundred thousand francs invested in sound securities, landed property that won't run away."

Eugène was dumb. He folded his arms and paced up and down his cheerless, untidy room. Old Goriot waited till the student's back was turned, and seized the opportunity to go to the chimney-piece and set upon it a little red morocco case with Rastignac's arms stamped in gold on the leather.

"My dear boy," said the kind soul, "I have been up to the eyes in this business. You see, there was plenty of selfishness on my part; I have an interested motive in helping you to change lodgings. You will not refuse me if I ask you something; will you, eh?"

"What is it?"

"There is a room on the fifth floor, up above your rooms, that is to let along with them; that is where I am going to live, isn't that so? I am getting old; I am too far from my girls. I shall not be in the way, but I shall be there, that is all. You will come and talk to me about her every evening. It will not put you about, will it? I shall have gone to bed before you come in, but I shall hear you come up, and I shall say to myself, 'He has just seen my little Delphine. He has been to a dance with her, and she is happy, thanks to him.' If I were ill, it would do my heart good to hear you moving about below, to know when you leave the house and when you come in. It is only a step to the Champs-Élysées, where they go every day, so I shall be sure of seeing them, whereas now I am sometimes too late. And then —perhaps she may come to see you! I shall hear her, I shall see her in her soft quilted pelisse tripping about as daintily as a kitten. In this one month she has become my little girl again, so light-hearted and gay. Her soul is recovering, and her happiness is owing to you! Oh! I would do impossibilities for you. Only just now she said to me, 'I am very happy, papa!' When they say 'father' stiffly, it sends a chill through me; but when they call me 'papa,' it is as if they were little girls again, and it brings all the old memories back. I feel most their father then; I even believe that they belong to me, and to no one else."

The good old man wiped his eyes, he was crying.

"It is a long while since I have heard them talk like that, a long, long time since she took my arm as she did to-day. Yes, indeed, it must be quite ten years since I walked side by side with one of my girls. How pleasant it was to keep step with her, to feel the touch of her gown, the warmth of her arm! Well, I took Delphine everywhere this morning; I went shopping with her, and I brought her home again. Oh! you must let me live near you. You may want someone to do you a service some of these days, and I shall be on the spot to do it. Oh! if only that great dolt of an Alsatian would die, if his gout would have the sense to attack his stomach, how happy my poor child would be! You would be my son-in-law; you would be her husband in the eyes of the world. Bah! she has known no happiness, that excuses everything. Our Father in heaven is surely on the side of fathers on earth who love their children. How fond of you she is!" he said, raising his head after a pause. "All the time we were going about together she chatted away about you. 'He is nice-looking, papa; isn't he? He is kind-hearted! Does he talk to you about me?' Pshaw! she said enough about you to fill whole volumes; between the Rue d'Artois and the Passage des Panoramas she poured her heart out into mine. I did not feel old once during that delightful morning; I felt as light as a feather. I told her how you had given that bank-note to me; it moved my darling to tears. But what can this be on your chimney-piece?" said old Goriot at last. Rastignac had showed no sign, and he was dying of impatience.

Eugène stared at his neighbor in dumb and dazed bewilderment. He thought of Vautrin, of that duel to be fought to-morrow morning, and of this realization of his dearest hopes, and the violent contrast between the two sets of ideas gave him all the sensations of nightmare. He went to the chimney-piece, saw the little square case, opened it, and found a watch of Bréguet's make wrapped in paper, on which these words were written:—

> "I want you to think of me every hour, *because* . . .
>
> "DELPHINE."

That last word doubtless contained an allusion to some scene that had taken place between them. Eugène felt touched. Inside the gold watch-case his arms had been wrought in enamel. The chain, the key, the workmanship, and design of the trinket were all such as he had imagined, for he had long coveted such a possession. Old Goriot was radiant. Of course he had promised to tell his daughter every little detail of the scene and of the effect produced upon Eugène by her present; he shared in the pleasure and excitement of the young people, and seemed to be not the least happy of the three. He loved Rastignac already for his own as well as for his daughter's sake.

"You must go and see her; she is expecting you this evening. That great lout of an Alsatian is going to have supper with his opera-dancer. Aha! he looked very foolish when my attorney let him know where he was. He says he idolizes my daughter, does he? He had better let her alone, or I will kill him. To think that my Delphine is his"—he heaved a sigh—"it is enough to make me murder him, but it would not be manslaughter to kill that animal; he is a pig with calf's brains.—You will take me with you, will you not?"

"Yes, dear Father Goriot; you know very well how fond I am of you——"

"Yes, I do know very well. You are not ashamed of me, are you? Not you! Let me embrace you," and he flung his arms round the student's neck.

"You will make her very happy; promise me that you will! You will go to her this evening, will you not?"

"Oh! yes. I must go out; I have some urgent business on hand."

"Can I be of any use?"

"My word, yes! Will you go to old Taillefer's while I go to Mme. Nucingen? Ask him to make an appointment with me some time this evening; it is a matter of life and death."

"Really, young man!" cried old Goriot, with a change of countenance; "are you really paying court to his daughter, as those simpletons were saying down below? . . . *Tonnerre de Dieu!* you have no notion what a tap *à la Goriot* is like, and if you are playing a double game, I shall put a stop to it by one blow of the fist. . . . Oh! the thing is impossible!"

"I swear to you that I love but one woman in the world," said the student. "I only knew it a moment ago."

"Oh! what happiness!" cried Goriot.

"But young Taillefer has been called out; the duel comes off to-morrow morning, and I have heard it said that he may lose his life in it."

"But what business is it of yours?" said Goriot.

"Why, I ought to tell him so, that he may prevent his son from putting in an appearance——"

Just at that moment Vautrin's voice broke in upon them; he was standing at the threshold of his door and singing—

> "Oh! Richard, oh my king!
> All the world abandons thee!
> Broum! broum! broum! broum! broum!
>
> The same old story everywhere,
> A roving heart and a . . . tra la la."

"Gentlemen!" shouted Christophe, "the soup is ready, and everyone is waiting for you."

"Here," Vautrin called down to him, "come and take a bottle of my Bordeaux."

"Do you think your watch is pretty?" asked Goriot. "She has good taste, hasn't she? Eh?"

Vautrin, old Goriot, and Rastignac came downstairs in company, and, all three of them being late, were obliged to sit together.

Eugène was as distant as possible in his manner to Vautrin during dinner; but the other, so charming in Mme. Vauquer's opinion, had never been so witty. His lively sallies and sparkling talk put the whole table in good humor. His assurance and coolness filled Eugène with consternation.

"Why, what has come to you to-day?" inquired Mme. Vauquer. "You are as merry as a skylark."

"I am always in spirits after I have made a good bargain."

"Bargain?" said Eugène.

"Well, yes, bargain. I have just delivered a lot of goods, and I shall be paid a handsome commission on them.—Mlle. Michonneau," he went on, seeing that the elderly spinster was scrutinizing him intently, "have you any objection to some feature in my face, that you are making those lynx eyes at me? Just let me know, and I will have it changed to oblige. . . . We shall not fall out about it, Poiret, I daresay?" he added, winking at the superannuated clerk.

"Bless my soul, you ought to stand as model for a burlesque Hercules," said the young painter.

"I will, upon my word! if Mlle. Michonneau will consent to sit as the Venus of Père-Lachaise," replied Vautrin.

"There's Poiret," suggested Bianchon.

"Oh! Poiret shall pose as Poiret. He can be a garden god!" cried Vautrin; "his name means a pear——"

"A sleepy pear!" Bianchon put in. "You will come in between the pear and the cheese."

"What stuff you are all talking!" said Mme. Vauquer; "you would do better to treat us to your Bordeaux; I see a glimpse of a bottle there. It would keep us all in a good humor, and it is good for the stomach besides."

"Gentleman," said Vautrin, "the Lady President calls us to order. Mme. Couture and Mlle. Victorine will take your jokes in good part, but respect the innocence of the aged Goriot. I propose a glass or two of Bordeauxrama, rendered twice illustrious by the name of Laffitte, no political allusions intended.—Come, you Turk!" he added, looking at Christophe, who did not offer to stir. "Christophe! Here! What, you don't answer to your own name? Bring us some liquor, Turk!"

"Here it is, sir," said Christophe, holding out the bottle.

Vautrin filled Eugène's glass and Goriot's likewise, then he deliberately poured out a few drops into his own glass, and sipped it while his two neighbors drank their wine. All at once he made a grimace.

"Corked!" he cried. "The devil! You can drink the rest of this, Christophe, and go and find another bottle; take from the right-hand side, you know. There are sixteen of us; take down eight bottles."

"If you are going to stand treat," said the painter, "I will pay for a hundred chestnuts."

"Oh! oh!"

"Booououh!"

"Prrrr!"

These exclamations came from all parts of the table like squibs from a set firework.

"Come, now, Mamma Vauquer, a couple of bottles of champagne," called Vautrin.

"*Quien!* just like you! Why not ask for the whole house at once? A couple of bottles of champagne; that means twelve francs! I shall never see the money back again, I know! But if M. Eugène has a mind to pay for it, I have some currant cordial."

"That currant cordial of hers is as bad as a black draught," muttered the medical student.

"Shut up, Bianchon," exclaimed Rastignac; "the very mention of black draught makes me feel—— Yes, champagne, by all means; I will pay for it," he added.

"Sylvie," called Mme. Vauquer, "bring in some biscuits, and the little cakes."

"Those little cakes are moldy graybeards," said Vautrin. "But trot out the biscuits."

The Bordeaux wine circulated; the dinner table became a livelier scene than ever, and the fun grew fast and furious. Imitations of the cries of various animals mingled with the loud laughter; the Museum official having taken it into his head to mimic a cat-call rather like the caterwauling of the animal in question, eight voices simultaneously struck up with the following variations:—

"Scissors to grind!"

"Chick-weed for singing bir-ds!"

"Brandy-snaps, ladies!"

"China to mend!"

"Boat ahoy!"

"Sticks to beat your wives or your clothes!"

"Old clo'!"

"Cherries all ripe!"

But the palm was awarded to Bianchon for the nasal accent with which he rendered the cry of "Umbrellas to me-end!"

A few seconds later, and there was a head-splitting racket in the room, a storm of tomfoolery, a sort of cats' concert, with Vautrin as conductor of the orchestra, the latter keeping an eye the while on Eugène and old Goriot. The wine seemed to have gone to their heads already. They leaned back in their chairs, looking at the general confusion with an air of gravity, and drank but little; both of them were absorbed in the thought of what lay before them to do that evening, and yet neither of them felt able to rise and go. Vautrin gave a side glance at them from time to time, and watched the change that came over their faces, choosing the moment when their eyes drooped and seemed about to close, to bend over Rastignac and to say in his ear—

"My little lad, you are not quite shrewd enough to outwit Papa Vautrin yet, and he is too fond of you to let you make a mess of your affairs. When I have made up my mind to do a thing, no one short of Providence can put me off. Aha! we were for going round to warn old Taillefer, telling tales out of school! The oven is hot, the dough is kneaded, the bread is ready for the oven; to-morrow we will eat it up and whisk away the crumbs; and we are not going to spoil the baking? . . . No, no, it is all as good as done! We may suffer from a few conscientious scruples, but they will be digested along with the bread. While we are having our forty winks, Colonel Count Franchessini will clear the way to Michel Taillefer's inheritance with the point of his sword. Victorine will come in for her brother's money, a snug fifteen thousand francs a year. I have made inquiries already, and I know that her late mother's property amounts to more than three hundred thousand——"

Eugène heard all this, and could not answer a word; his tongue seemed to be glued to the roof of his mouth, an irresistible drowsiness was creeping over him. He still saw the table and the faces round it, but it was through a bright mist. Soon the noise began to subside, one by one the boarders went. At last, when their numbers had so dwindled that the party consisted of Mme. Vauquer, Mme. Couture, Mlle. Victorine, Vautrin, and old Goriot, Rastignac watched as though in a dream how Mme. Vauquer busied herself by collecting the bottles, and drained the remainder of the wine out of each to fill others.

"Oh! how uproarious they are! what a thing it is to be young!" said the widow.

These were the last words that Eugène heard and understood.

"There is no one like M. Vautrin for a bit of fun like this," said Sylvie. "There, just hark at Christophe, he is snoring like a top."

"Good-bye, mamma," said Vautrin; "I am going to a theater on the boulevard to see M. Marty in *Le Mont Sauv-*

age, a fine play taken from *Le Solitaire*. . . . If you like, I will take you and these two ladies——"

'Thank you; I must decline," said Mme. Couture.

"What! my good lady!" cried Mme. Vauquer, "decline to see a play founded on *Le Solitaire*, a work by Atala de Chateaubriand. We were so fond of that book that we cried over it like Magdalens under the *line-trees* last summer, and then it is an improving work that might edify your young lady."

"We are forbidden to go to the play," answered Victorine.

"Just look, those two yonder have dropped off where they sit," said Vautrin, shaking the heads of the two sleepers in a comical way.

He altered the sleeping student's position, settled his head more comfortably on the back of his chair, kissed him warmly on the forehead, and began to sing—

> "Sleep, little darlings;
> I watch while you slumber."

"I am afraid he may be ill," said Victorine.

"Then stop and take care of him," returned Vautrin. "'Tis your duty as a meek and obedient wife," he whispered in her ear. "The young fellow worships you, and you will be his little wife—there's your fortune for you. In short," he added aloud, "they lived happily ever afterwards, were much looked up to in all the country side, and had a numerous family. That is how all the romances end.—Now, mamma," he went on, as he turned to Mme. Vauquer and put his arm round her waist, "put on your bonnet, your best flowered silk, and the countess's scarf, while I go out to call a cab—all my own self."

And he started out, singing as he went—

> "Oh! sun! divine sun!
> Ripening the pumpkins every one."

"My goodness! Well, I'm sure, Mme. Couture, I could live happily in a garret with a man like that.—There, now," she added, looking round for the old vermicelli maker, "there is that old Goriot half seas over. *He* never thought of taking me anywhere, the old skinflint. But he will measure his length somewhere. My word! it is disgraceful to lose his senses like that, at his age! You will be telling me that he couldn't lose what he hadn't got—Sylvie! just take him up to his room!"

Sylvie took him by the arm, supporting him upstairs, and flung him just as he was, like a package, across the bed.

"Poor young fellow!" said Mme. Couture, putting back Eugène's hair that had fallen over his eyes; "he is like a young girl, he does not know what dissipation is."

"Well, I can tell you this, I know," said Mme. Vauquer, "I have taken lodgers these thirty years, and a good many have passed through my hands as the saying is, but I have never seen a nicer nor a more aristocratic looking young man than M. Eugène. How handsome he looks sleeping! Just let his head rest on your shoulder, Mme. Couture. Pshaw! he falls over towards Mlle. Victorine. There's a special providence for young things. A little more, and he would have broken his head against the knob of the chair. They'd make a pretty pair, those two would!"

"Hush, my good neighbor," cried Mme. Couture, "you are saying such things——"

"Pooh!" put in Mme. Vauquer, "he does not hear.—Here, Sylvie! come and help me to dress. I shall put on my best stays."

"What! your best stays just after dinner, Madame?" said Sylvie. "No, you can get someone else to lace you. I am not going to be your murderer. It's a rash thing to do, and might cost you your life.."

"I don't care, I must do honor to M. Vautrin."

"Are you so fond of your heirs as all that?"

"Come, Sylvie, don't argue," said the widow, as she left the room.

"At her age, too!" said the cook to Victorine, pointing to her mistress as she spoke.

Mme. Couture and her ward were left in the dining-room, and Eugène slept on, on Victorine's shoulder. The sound of Christophe's snoring echoed through the silent house; Eugène's quiet breathing seemed all the quieter by force of contrast, he was sleeping as peacefully as a child. Victorine was very happy; she was free to perform one of those acts of charity which form an innocent outlet for all the overflowing sentiments of a woman's nature; he was so close to her that she could feel the throbbing of his heart; there was a look of almost maternal protection and a conscious pride in Victorine's face. Among the countless thoughts that crowded up in her young innocent heart, there was a wild flutter of joy at this close contact.

"Poor, dear child!" said Mme. Couture, squeezing her hand.

The old lady looked at the girl. Victorine's innocent, pathetic face, so radiant with the new happiness that had befallen her, called to mind some naïve work of mediæval art, when the painter neglected the accessories, reserving all the magic of his brush for the quiet, austere outlines and ivory tints of the face, which seems to have caught something of the golden glory of heaven.

"After all, he only took two glasses, mamma," said Victorine, passing her fingers through Eugène's hair.

"Indeed, if he had been a dissipated young man, child, he would have carried the wine like the rest of them. His drowsiness does him credit."

There was a sound of wheels outside in the street.

"There is M. Vautrin, mamma," said the girl. "Just take M. Eugène. I would rather not have that man see me like this; there are some ways of looking at you that seem to sully your soul and make you feel as though you had nothing on."

"Oh, no, you are wrong!" said Mme. Couture. "M. Vautrin is a worthy man; he reminds me a little of my late husband, poor dear M. Couture, rough but kind-hearted; his bark is worse than his bite."

Vautrin came in while she was speaking; he did not make a sound, but looked for a while at the picture of the two young faces—the lamplight, falling full upon them, seemed to caress them.

"Well," he remarked, folding his arms, "here is a picture! It would have suggested some pleasing pages to Bernardin de Saint-Pierre (good soul), who wrote *Paul et Virginie*. Youth is very charming, Mme. Couture!—Sleep on, poor boy," he added, looking at Eugène, "luck sometimes comes while we are sleeping.—There is something touching and attractive to me about this young man, Madame," he continued; "I know that his nature is in harmony with his face. Just look, the head of a cherub on an angel's shoulder! He deserves to be loved. If I were a woman, I would die (no—not such a fool), I would live for him." He bent lower and spoke in the widow's ear. "When I see those two together, Madame, I cannot help think that Providence meant them for each other; He works by secret ways, and tries the reins and the heart," he said in a loud voice. "And when I see you, my children, thus united by a like purity and by all human affections, I say to myself that it is quite impossible that the future should separate you. God is just."—He turned to Victorine. "It seems to me," he said, "that I have seen the line of success in your hand. Let me look at it, Mlle. Victorine; I am well up in palmistry, and I have told fortunes many a time. Come, now, don't be frightened. Ah! what do I see? Upon my word, you will be one of the richest heiresses in Paris before very long. You will heap riches on the man who loves you. Your father will want you to go and live with him. You will marry a young and handsome man with a title, and he will idolize you."

The heavy footsteps of the coquettish widow, who was coming down the stairs, interrupted Vautrin's fortune-telling. "Here is Mamma Vauquerre, fair as a starr-r-r, dressed within an inch of her life.—Aren't we a trifle pinched for room?" he inquired, with his arm round the lady; "we are screwed up very tightly about the bust, mamma! If we are much agitated, there may be an explosion; but I will pick up the fragments with all the care of an antiquary."

"There is a man who can talk the language of French gallantry!" said the widow, bending to speak in Mme. Couture's ear.

"Good-bye, little ones!" said Vautrin, turning to Eugène and Victorine. "Bless you both!" and he laid a hand on either head. "Take my word for it, young lady, an honest man's prayers are worth something; they should bring you happiness, for God hears them."

"Good-by, dear," said Madame Vauquer to her lodger. "Do you think that M. Vautrin means to run away with me?" she added, lowering her voice.

"Lack-a-day!" said the widow.

"Oh! mamma dear, suppose it should really happen as that kind M. Vautrin said!" said Victorine with a sigh, as she looked at her hands. The two women were alone together.

"Why, it wouldn't take much to bring it to pass," said the elder lady; "just a fall from his horse, and your monster of a brother——"

"Oh, mamma!"

"Good Lord! Well, perhaps it is a sin to wish bad luck to an enemy," the widow remarked. "I will do penance for it. Still, I would strew flowers on his grave with the greatest pleasure, and that is the truth. Black-hearted, that he is! The coward couldn't speak up for his own mother, and cheats you out of your share by deceit and trickery. My cousin had a pretty fortune of her own, but, unluckily for you, nothing was said in the marriage contract about anything that she might come in for."

"It would be very hard if my good fortune is to cost someone else his life," said Victorine. "If I cannot be happy unless my brother is to be taken out of the world, I would rather stay here all my life."

"*Mon Dieu!* it is just as that good M. Vautrin says, and he is full of piety, you see," Mme. Couture remarked. "I am very glad to find that he is not an unbeliever like the rest of them that talk of the Almighty with less respect than they do of the Devil. Well, as he was saying, who can know the ways by which it may please Providence to lead us?"

With Sylvie's help the two women at last succeeded in getting Eugène up to his room; they laid him on the bed, and the cook unfastened his clothes to make him more comfortable. Before they left the room, Victorine snatched an opportunity when her guardian's back was turned, and pressed a kiss on Eugène's forehead, feeling all the joy that this stolen pleasure could give her. Then she looked round the room, and gathering up, as it were, into one single thought all the untold bliss of that day, she made a picture of her memories, and dwelt upon it until she slept, the happiest creature in Paris.

That evening's merrymaking, in the course of which Vautrin had given the drugged wine to Eugène and old Goriot, was his own ruin. Bianchon, flustered with wine, forgot to open the subject of Trompe-la-Mort with Mlle. Michonneau. The mere mention of the name would have set Vautrin on his guard; for Vautrin, or, to give him his real name, Jacques Collin, was in fact the notorious escaped convict.

But it was the joke about the Venus of Père-Lachaise that finally decided his fate. Mlle. Michonneau had very nearly made up her mind to warn the convict and to throw herself on his generosity, with the idea of making a better bargain for herself by helping him to escape that night; but as it was, she went out escorted by Poiret in search of the famous chief of detectives in the Petite Rue Sainte-Anne, still thinking that it was the district superintendent—one Gondureau—with whom she had to do. The head of the department received his visitors courteously. There was a little talk, and the details were definitely arranged. Mlle. Michonneau asked for the draught that she was to administer in order to set about her investigation. But the great man's evident satisfaction set Mlle. Michonneau thinking; and she began to see that this business involved something more than the mere capture of a runaway convict. She racked her brains while he looked in a drawer in his desk for the little phial, and it dawned upon her that in consequence of treacherous revelations made by the prisoners the police were hoping to lay their hands on a considerable sum of money. But on hinting her suspicions to the old fox of the Petite Rue Sainte-Anne, that officer began to smile, and tried to put her off the scent.

"A delusion," he said. "Collin's *sorbonne* is the most dangerous that has yet been found among the dangerous classes. That is all, and the rascals are quite aware of it. They rally round him; he is the backbone of the federation, its Bonaparte, in short; he is very popular with them all. The rogue will never leave his *chump* in the Place de Grève."

As Mlle. Michonneau seemed mystified, Gondureau explained the two slang words for her benefit. *Sorbonne* and *chump* are two forcible expressions borrowed from thieves' Latin, thieves, of all people, being compelled to consider the human head in its two aspects. A *sorbonne* is the head of a living man, his faculty of thinking—his council; a *chump* is a contemptuous epithet that implies how little a human head is worth after the axe has done its work.

"Collin is playing us off," he continued. "When we come across a man like a bar of steel tempered in the English fashion, there is always one resource left—we can kill him if he takes it into his head to make the least resistance. We are reckoning on several methods of killing Collin to-morrow morning. It saves a trial, and society is rid of him without all the expense of guarding and feeding him. What with getting up the case, summoning witnesses, paying their expenses, and carrying out the sentence, it costs a lot to go through all the proper formalities before you can get quit of one of these good-for-nothings, over and above the three thousand francs that you are going to have. There is a saving in time as well. One good thrust of the bayonet into Trompe-la-Mort's paunch will prevent scores of crimes, and save fifty scoundrels from following his example; they will be very careful to keep themselves out of the police courts. That is doing the work of the police thoroughly, and true philanthropists will tell you that it is better to prevent crime than to punish it."

"And you do a service to our country," said Poiret.

"Really, you are talking in a very sensible manner to-night, that you are," said the head of the department. "Yes, of course, we are serving our country, and we are very hardly used too. We do society very great services that are not recognized. In fact, a superior man must rise above vulgar prejudices, and a Christian must resign himself to the mishaps that doing right entails, when right is done in an out-of-the-way style. Paris is Paris, you see! That is the explanation of my life.—I have the honor to wish you a good-evening, Mademoiselle. I shall bring my men to the Jardin du Roi in the morning. Send Christophe to the Rue du Buffon, tell him to ask for M. Gondureau in the house where you saw me before.—Your servant, sir. If you should ever have anything stolen from you, come to me, and I will do my best to get it back for you."

"Well, now," Poiret remarked to Mlle. Michonneau, "there are idiots who are scared out of their wits by the word police.

That was a very pleasant-spoken gentleman, and what he wants you to do is as easy as saying 'Good-day.'"

The next day was destined to be one of the most extraordinary in the annals of the Maison Vauquer. Hitherto the most startling occurrence in its tranquil existence had been the portentous, meteor-like apparition of the sham Comtesse de l'Ambermesnil. But the catastrophes of this great day were to cast all previous events into the shade, and supply an inexhaustible topic of conversation for Mme. Vauquer and her boarders so long as she lived.

In the first place, Goriot and Eugène de Rastignac both slept till close upon eleven o'clock. Mme. Vauquer, who came home about midnight from the Gaîté, lay abed till half-past ten. Christophe, after a prolonged slumber (he had finished Vautrin's first bottle of wine), was behindhand with his work, but Poiret and Mlle. Michonneau uttered no complaint, though breakfast was delayed. As for Victorine and Mme. Couture, they also lay late. Vautrin went out before eight o'clock and only came back just as breakfast was ready. Nobody protested, therefore, when Sylvie and Christophe went up at a quarter-past eleven, knocked at all doors, and announced that breakfast was waiting. While Sylvie and the man were upstairs, Mlle. Michonneau, who came down first, poured the contents of the phial into the silver cup belonging to Vautrin—it was standing with the others in the bain-marie that kept the cream hot for the morning coffee. The spinster had reckoned on this custom of the house to do her stroke of business. The seven lodgers were at last collected together, not without some difficulty. Just as Eugène came downstairs, stretching himself and yawning, a commissionaire handed him a letter from Mme. de Nucingen. It ran thus:—

"I feel neither false vanity nor anger where you are concerned, my friend. Till two o'clock this morning I waited for you. Oh, that waiting for one whom you love! No one that had passed through that torture could inflict it on another. I know now that you have never loved before. What can have happened? Anxiety has taken hold of me. I would have come myself to find out what had happened, if I had not feared to betray the secrets of my heart. How can I walk out or drive out at this time of day? Would it not be ruin? I have felt to the full how wretched it is to be a woman. Send a word to reassure me, and explain how it is that you have not come after what my father told you. I shall be angry, but I will forgive you. One word, for pity's sake. You will come to me very soon, will you not? If you are busy, a word will be enough. Say, 'I will hasten to you,' or else, 'I am ill.' But if you were ill my father would have come to tell me so. What can have happened? . . ."

"Yes, indeed, what has happened?" exclaimed Eugène, and, hurrying down to the dining-room, he crumpled up the letter without reading any more. "What time is it?"

"Half-past eleven," said Vautrin, dropping a lump of sugar into his coffee.

The escaped convict cast a glance at Eugène, a cold and fascinating glance; men gifted with this magnetic power can quell furious lunatics in a madhouse by such a glance, it is said. Eugène shook in every limb. There was the sound of wheels in the street, and in another moment a man with a scared face rushed into the room. It was one of M. Taillefer's servants; Mme. Couture recognized the livery at once.

"Mademoiselle," he cried, "your father is asking for you—something terrible has happened! M. Frédéric has had a sword thrust in the forehead in a duel, and the doctors have given him up. You will scarcely be in time to say good-by to him! he is unconscious."

"Poor young fellow!" exclaimed Vautrin. "How can people brawl when they have a certain income of thirty thousand livres? Young people have bad manners, and that is a fact."

"Sir!" cried Eugène.

"Well, what then, you big baby!" said Vautrin, swallowing down his coffee imperturbably, an operation which Mlle. Michonneau watched with such close attention that she had no emotion to spare for the amazing news that had struck the others dumb with amazement. "Are there not duels every morning in Paris?" added Vautrin.

"I will go with you, Victorine," said Mme. Couture, and the two women hurried away at once without either hats or shawls. But before she went, Victorine, with her eyes full of tears, gave Eugène a glance that said—"How little I thought that our happiness should cost me tears!"

"Dear me, you are a prophet, M. Vautrin," said Mme. Vauquer.

"I am all sorts of things," said Vautrin.

"Queer, isn't it?" said Mme. Vauquer, stringing together a succession of commonplaces suited to the occasion. "Death takes us off without asking us about it. The young often go before the old. It is a lucky thing for us women that we are not liable to fight duels, but we have other complaints that men don't suffer from. We bear children, and it takes a long time to get over it. What a windfall for Victorine! Her father will have to acknowledge her now!"

"There!' said Vautrin, looking at Eugène, "yesterday she had not a penny; this morning she has several millions to her fortune."

"I say, M. Eugène!" cried Mme. Vauquer, "you have landed on your feet!"

At this exclamation, old Goriot looked at the student, and saw the crumpled letter still in his hand.

"You have not read it through! What does this mean? Are you going to be like the rest of them?" he asked.

"Madame, I shall never marry Mlle. Victorine," said Eugène, turning to Mme. Vauquer with an expression of terror and loathing that surprised the onlookers at this scene.

Old Goriot caught the student's hand and grasped it warmly. He could have kissed it.

"Oh, ho!" said Vautrin, "the Italians have a good proverb—*Col tempo.*"

"Is there any answer?" said Mme. de Nucingen's messenger, addressing Eugène.

"Say that I will come directly."

The man went. Eugène was in a state of such violent excitement that he could not be prudent.

"What is to be done?" he exclaimed aloud. "There are no proofs!"

Vautrin began to smile. Though the drug he had taken was doing its work, the convict was so vigorous that he rose to his feet, gave Rastignac a look, and said in hollow tones, "Luck comes to us while we sleep, young man," and fell stiff and stark, as if he were struck dead.

"So there is a Divine Justice!" said Eugène.

"Well, if ever! What has come to that poor dear M. Vautrin?"

"A stroke!" cried Mlle. Michonneau.

"Here, Sylvie! girl, run for the doctor," called the widow. "Oh, M. Rastignac, just go for M. Bianchon, and be as quick as you can; Sylvie might not be in time to catch our doctor, M. Grimprel."

Rastignac was glad of an excuse to leave that den of horrors, his hurry for the doctor was nothing but a flight.

"Here, Christophe, go round to the chemist's and ask for something that's good for the apoplexy."

Christophe likewise went.

"Father Goriot, just help us to get him upstairs."

Vautrin was taken up among them, carried carefully up the narrow staircase, and laid upon his bed.

"I can do no good here, so I shall go to see my daughter," said M. Goriot.

"Selfish old thing!" cried Mme. Vauquer. "Yes, go; I wish you may die like a dog."

"Just go and see if you can find some ether," said Mlle. Michonneau to Mme. Vauquer; the former, with some help from Poiret, had unfastened the sick man's clothes.

Mme. Vauquer went down to her room, and left Mlle. Michonneau mistress of the situation.

"Now! just pull down his shirt and turn him over, quick! You might be of some use in sparing my modesty," she said to Poiret, "instead of standing there like a stock."

Vautrin was turned over; Mlle. Michonneau gave his shoulder a sharp slap, and the two portentous letters appeared, white against the red.

"There, you have earned your three thousand francs very easily," exclaimed Poiret, supporting Vautrin while Mlle. Michonneau slipped on the shirt again. "Ouf! how heavy he is," he added, as he laid the convict down.

"Hush! Suppose there is a strong box here!" said the old maid briskly; her glances seemed to pierce the walls, she scrutinized every article of the furniture with greedy eyes. "Could we find some excuse for opening that desk?"

"It mightn't be right," responded Poiret to this.

"Where is the harm? It is money stolen from all sorts of people, so it doesn't belong to anyone now. But we haven't time, there is the Vauquer."

"Here is the ether," said that lady. "I must say that this is an eventful day. Lord! that man can't have had a stroke; he is as white as curds."

"White as curds?" echoed Poiret.

"And his pulse is steady," said the widow, laying her hand on his breast.

"Steady?" said the astonished Poiret.

"He is all right."

"Do you think so?" asked Poiret.

"Lord! Yes, he looks as if he were sleeping. Sylvie has gone for a doctor. I say, Mlle. Michonneau, he is sniffing the ether. Pooh! it is only a spasm. His pulse is good. He is as strong as a Turk. Just look, Mademoiselle, what a fur tippet he has on his chest; that is the sort of man to live till he is a hundred. His wig holds on tightly, however. Dear me! it is glued on, and his own hair is red; that is why he wears a wig. They always say that red-haired people are either the worst or the best. Is he one of the good ones, I wonder?"

"Good to hang," said Poiret.

"Round a pretty woman's neck, you mean," said Mlle. Michonneau, hastily. "Just go away, M. Poiret. It is a woman's duty to nurse you men when you are ill. Besides, for all the good you are doing, you may as well take yourself off," she added. "Mme. Vauquer and I will take great care of dear M. Vautrin."

Poiret went out on tiptoe without a murmur, like a dog kicked out of the room by his master.

Rastignac had gone out for the sake of physical exertion; he wanted to breathe the air, he felt stifled. Yesterday evening he had meant to prevent the murder arranged for half-past eight that morning. What had happened? What ought he to do now? He trembled to think that he himself might be implicated. Vautrin's coolness still further dismayed him.

"Yet, how if Vautrin should die without saying a word?" Rastignac asked himself.

He hurried along the alleys of the Luxembourg Gardens as if the hounds of justice were after him, and he already heard the baying of the pack.

"Well," shouted Bianchon, "have you seen the *Pilote?*"

The *Pilote* was a Radical sheet, edited by M. Tissot. It came out several hours later than the morning papers, and was meant for the benefit of the country subscribers; for it brought the morning's news into provincial districts twenty-four hours sooner than the ordinary local journals.

"There is a wonderful history in it," said the house student of the Hôpital Cochin. "Young Taillefer called out Count Franchessini, of the Old Guard, and the Count put a couple of inches of steel into his forehead. And here is little Victorine one of the richest heiresses in Paris! If we had known that, eh? What a game of chance death is! They said Victorine was sweet on you; was there any truth in it?"

"Shut up, Bianchon; I shall never marry her. I am in love with a charming woman, and she is in love with me, so——"

"You said that as if you were screwing yourself up to be faithful to her. I should like to see the woman worth the sacrifice of Master Taillefer's money!"

"Are all the devils of hell at my heels?" cried Rastignac.

"What is the matter with you? Are you mad? Give us your hand," said Bianchon, "and let me feel your pulse. You are feverish."

"Just go to Mother Vauquer's," said Rastignac; "that scoundrel Vautrin has dropped down like one dead."

"Aha!" said Bianchon, leaving Rastignac to his reflections, "you confirm my suspicions, and now I mean to make sure for myself."

The law student's long walk was a memorable one for him. He made in some sort a survey of his conscience. After a close scrutiny, after hesitation and self-examination, his honor at any rate came out scathless from this sharp and terrible ordeal, like a bar of iron tested in the English fashion. He remembered old Goriot's confidences of the evening before; he recollected the rooms taken for him in the Rue d'Artois, so that he might be near Delphine; and then he thought of his letter, and read it again and kissed it.

"Such a love is my anchor of safety," he said to himself. "How the old man's heart must have been wrung! He says nothing about all that he has been through; but who could not guess? Well, then, I will be like a son to him; his life shall be made happy. If she cares for me, she will often come to spend the day with him. That grand Comtesse de Restaud is a heartless thing; she would make her father into her hall porter. Dear Delphine! she is kinder to the old man; she is worthy to be loved. Ah! this evening I shall be very happy!"

He took out his watch and admired it.

"I have had nothing but success! If two people mean to love each other forever, they may help each other, and I can take this. Besides, I shall succeed, and I will repay her a hundredfold. There is nothing criminal in this *liaison;* nothing that could cause the most austere moralist to frown. How many respectable people contract similar unions! We deceive nobody; it is deception that makes a position humiliating. If you lie, you lower yourself at once. She and her husband have lived apart for a long while. Besides, how if I called upon that Alsatian to resign a wife whom he cannot make happy?"

Rastignac's battle with himself went on for a long while; and though the scruples of youth inevitably gained the day, an irresistible curiosity led him, about half-past four, to return to the Maison Vauquer through the gathering dusk.

Bianchon had given Vautrin an emetic, reserving the contents of the stomach for chemical analysis at the hospital. Mlle. Michonneau's officious alacrity had still further strengthened his suspicions of her. Vautrin, moreover, had recovered so quickly, that it was impossible not to suspect some plot against the leader of all frolics at the lodging-house. Vautrin was standing in front of the stove in the dining-room when Rastignac came in. All the lodgers were assembled sooner than usual by the news of young Taillefer's duel. They were anxious to hear any detail about the affair, and to talk over the probable change in Victorine's prospects. Old Goriot alone was absent, but the rest were chatting. No sooner did Eugène come into the room, than his eyes met the inscrutable gaze of Vautrin. It was the same look that had read his thoughts before—the look that had such power to waken evil thoughts in his heart. He shuddered.

"Well, dear boy," said the escaped convict, "I am likely to cheat death for a good while yet. According to these ladies, I have had a stroke that would have felled an ox, and come off with flying colors."

"A bull, you might say," cried the widow.

"You really might be sorry to see me still alive," said Vautrin in Rastignac's car, thinking that he guessed the student's thoughts. "You must be mighty sure of yourself."

"Mlle. Michonneau was talking the day before yesterday about a gentleman nicknamed Trompe-la-Mort," said Bianchon; "and, upon my word, that name would do very well for you."

Vautrin seemed thunderstruck. He turned pale, and staggered back. He turned his magnetic glance, like a ray of vivid light, on Mlle. Michonneau; the old maid shrank and trembled under the influence of that strong will, and collapsed into a chair. The mask of good-nature had dropped from the convict's face; from the unmistakable ferocity of that sinister look, Poiret felt that the old maid was in danger, and hastily stepped between them. None of the lodgers understood this scene in the least. They looked on in mute amazement. There was a pause. Just then there was a sound of tramping feet outside; there were soldiers there, it seemed, for there was a ring of several rifles on the pavement of the street. Collin was mechanically looking round the walls for a way of escape, when four men entered by way of the sitting-room.

"In the name of the King and the Law!" said an officer, but the words were almost lost in a murmur of astonishment.

Silence fell on the room. The lodgers made way for three of the men, who had each a hand on a cocked pistol in a side pocket. Two policemen, who followed the detectives, kept the entrance to the sitting-room, and two more appeared in the doorway that gave access to the staircase. A sound of footsteps came from the garden, and again the rifles of several soldiers rang on the cobble-stones under the window. All chance of salvation by flight was cut off for Trompe-la-

Mort, to whom all eyes instinctively turned. The chief walked straight up to him, and commenced operations by giving him a sharp blow on the head, so that the wig fell off, and Collin's face was revealed in all its ugliness. There was a terrible suggestion of strength mingled with cunning in the short, brick-red crop of hair, the whole head was in harmony with his powerful frame, and at that moment the fires of hell seemed to gleam from his eyes. In that flash the real Vautrin shone forth, revealed at once before them all; they understood his past, his present and future, his pitiless doctrines, his actions, the religion of his own good pleasure, the majesty with which his cynicism and contempt for mankind invested him, the physical strength of an organism proof against all trials. The blood flew to his face, and his eyes glared like the eyes of a wildcat. He started back with savage energy and a fierce growl that drew exclamations of alarm from the lodgers. At that leonine start the police caught at their pistols under cover of the general clamor. Collin saw the gleaming muzzles of the weapons, saw his danger, and instantly gave proof of a power of the highest order. There was something horrible and majestic in the spectacle of the sudden transformation in his face; he could only be compared to a caldron full of the steam that can send mountains flying, a terrific force dispelled in a moment by a drop of cold water. The drop of water that cooled his wrathful fury was a reflection that flashed across his brain like lightning. He began to smile, and looked down at his wig.

"You are not in the politest of humors to-day," he remarked to the chief, and he held out his hands to the policemen with a jerk of his head.

"Gentlemen," he said, "put on the bracelets or the handcuffs. I call on those present to witness that I make no resistance."

A murmur of admiration ran through the room at the sudden outpouring like fire and lava flood from this human volcano, and its equally sudden cessation.

"There's a sell for you, master crusher," the convict added, looking at the famous director of police.

"Come, strip!" said he of the Petite Rue Sainte-Anne, contemptuously.

"Why?" asked Collin. "There are ladies present; I deny nothing, and surrender."

He paused and looked round the room like an orator who is about to overwhelm his audience.

"Take this down, Daddy Lachapelle," he went on, addressing a little, white-haired old man who had seated himself at the end of the table; and after drawing a printed form from a portfolio, was proceeding to draw up a document. "I acknowledge myself to be Jacques Collin, otherwise known as Trompe-la-Mort, condemned to twenty years' penal servitude, and I have just proved that I have come fairly by my nickname.—If I had as much as raised my hand," he went on, addressing the other lodgers, "those three sneaking wretches yonder would have drawn claret on Mamma Vauquer's domestic hearth. The rogues have laid their heads together to set a trap for me."

Mme. Vauquer felt sick and faint at these words.

"Good Lord!" she cried, "this does give one a turn; and me at the Gaité with him only last night!" she said to Sylvie.

"Summon your philosophy, mamma," Collin resumed. "Is it a misfortune to have sat in my box at the Gaité yesterday evening? After all, are you better than we are? The brand upon our shoulders is less shameful than the brand set on your hearts, you flabby members of a society rotten to the core. Not the best man among you could stand up to me." His eyes rested upon Rastignac, to whom he spoke with a pleasant smile that seemed strangely at variance with the savage expression in his eyes.—"Our little bargain still holds good, dear boy; you can accept any time you like! Do you understand?" And he sang—

> "A charming girl is my Fanchette
> In her simplicity."

"Don't you trouble yourself," he went on; "I can get in my money. They are too much afraid of me to swindle me."

The convicts' prison, its language and customs, its sudden sharp transitions from the humorous to the horrible, its appalling grandeur, its triviality and its dark depths, were all revealed in turn by the speaker's discourse; he seemed to be no longer a man, but the type and mouthpiece of a degenerate race, a brutal, supple, clear-headed race of savages. In one moment Collin became the poet of an inferno, wherein all thoughts and passions that move human nature (save repentance) find a place. He looked about him like a fallen archangel who is for war to the end. Rastignac lowered his eyes, and acknowledged this kinship claimed by crime as an expiation of his own evil thoughts.

"Who betrayed me?" said Collin, and his terrible eyes traveled round the room. Suddenly they rested on Mlle. Michonneau.

"It was you, old cat!" he said. "That sham stroke of apoplexy was your doing, lynx eyes! . . . Two words from me, and your throat would be cut in less than a week; but I forgive you, I am a Christian. You did not sell me either. But who did?—— Aha! you may rummage upstairs," he shouted, hearing the police officers opening his cupboards and taking possession of his effects. "The nest is empty, the birds flew away yesterday, and you will be none the wiser. My ledgers are here," he said, tapping his forehead. "Now I know who sold me! It could only be that blackguard Fil-de-Soie. That is who it was, old catchpoll, eh?" he said, turning to the chief. "It was timed so neatly to get the bank-notes up above there. There is nothing left for you—spies! As for Fil-de-Soie, he will be under the daisies in less than a fortnight, even if you were to tell off the whole force to protect him. How much did you give the Michonnette?" he asked of the police officers. "A thousand crowns? Oh you Ninon in decay, Pompadour in tatters, Venus of the graveyard, I was worth more than that! If you had given me warning, you should have had six thousand francs. Ah! you had no suspicion of that, old trafficker in flesh and blood, or I should have had the preference. Yes, I would have given six thousand francs to save myself an inconvenient journey and some loss of money," he said, as they fastened the handcuffs on his wrists. "These folks will amuse themselves by dragging out this business till the end of time to keep me idle! If they were to send me straight to jail, I should soon be back at my old tricks in spite of the duffers at the Quai des Orfèvres. Down yonder they would all turn themselves inside out to help their general—their good

Trompe-la-Mort—to get clear away. Is there a single one among you that can say, as I can, that he has ten thousand brothers ready to do anything for him?" he asked proudly. "There is some good there," he said, tapping his heart; "I have never betrayed anyone!—Look you here, you slut," he said to the old maid, "they are all afraid of me, do you see? but the sight of you turns them sick. Rake in your gains."

He was silent for a moment, and looked round at the lodgers' faces.

"What dolts you are, all of you! Have you never seen a convict before? A convict of Collin's stamp, whom you see before you, is a man less weak-kneed than others; he lifts up his voice against the colossal fraud of the Social Contract, as Jean Jacques did, whose pupil he is proud to declare himself. In short, I stand here single-handed against a Government and a whole subsidized machinery of tribunals and police, and I am a match for them all."

"Ye Gods!" cried the painter, "what a magnificent sketch one might make of him!"

"Look here, you gentleman-in-waiting to his highness the gibbet, master of ceremonies to the widow" (a nickname full of somber poetry, given by prisoners to the guillotine), "be a good fellow, and tell me if it really was Fil-de-Soie who sold me. I don't want him to suffer for someone else, that would not be fair."

But before the chief had time to answer, the rest of the party returned from making their investigations upstairs. Everything had been opened and inventoried. A few words passed between them and the chief, and the official preliminaries were complete.

"Gentlemen," said Collin, addressing the lodgers, "they will take me away directly. You have all made my stay among you very agreeable, and I shall look back upon it with gratitude. Receive my adieux, and permit me to send you figs from Provence."

He advanced a step or two, and then turned to look once more at Rastignac.

"Good-by, Eugène," he said, in a sad and gentle tone, a strange transition from his previous rough and stern manner. "If you should be hard up, I have left you a devoted friend," and, in spite of his shackles, he managed to assume a posture of defense, called, "One! two!" like a fencing master, and lunged. "If anything goes wrong, apply in that quarter. Man and money, all at your service."

The strange speaker's manner was sufficiently burlesque, so that no one but Rastignac knew that there was a serious meaning underlying the pantomime.

As soon as the police, soldiers, and detectives had left the house, Sylvie, who was rubbing her mistress's temples with vinegar, looked round at the bewildered lodgers.

"Well," said she, "he was a man, he was, for all that."

Her words broke the spell. Everyone had been too much excited, too much moved by very various feelings, to speak. But now the lodgers began to look at each other, and then all eyes were turned at once on Mlle. Michonneau, a thin, shriveled, dead-alive, mummy-like figure crouching by the stove; her eyes were downcast, as if she feared that the green eye-shade could not shut out the expression of those faces from her. This figure and the feeling of repulsion she had so long excited were explained all at once. A smothered murmur filled the room; it was so unanimous, that it seemed as if the same feeling of loathing had pitched all the voices in one key. Mlle. Michonneau heard it, and did not stir. It was Bianchon who was the first to move; he bent over his neighbor, and said in a low voice, "If that creature is going to stop here, and have dinner with us, I shall clear out."

In the twinkling of an eye it was clear that everyone in the room, save Poiret, was of the medical student's opinion, so that the latter, strong in the support of the majority, went up to that elderly person.

"You are more intimate with Mlle. Michonneau than the rest of us," he said; "speak to her, make her understand that she must go, and go at once."

"At once!" echoed Poiret in amazement.

Then he went across to the crouching figure, and spoke a few words in her ear.

"I have paid beforehand for the quarter; I have as much right to be here as anyone else," she said, with a viperous look at the boarders.

"Never mind that! we will club together and pay you the money back," said Rastignac.

"Monsieur is taking Collin's part," she said, with a questioning, malignant glance at the law student; "it is not difficult to guess why." Eugène started forward at the words, as if he meant to spring upon her and wring her neck. That glance, and the depths of treachery that it revealed, had been a hideous enlightment.

"Let her alone!" cried the boarders.

Rastignac folded his arms, and was silent.

"Let us have no more of Mlle. Judas," said the painter, turning to Mme. Vauquer. "If you don't show the Michonneau to the door, Madame, we shall all leave your shop, and wherever we go we shall say that there are only convicts and spies left there. If you do the other thing, we shall hold our tongues about the business; for when all is said and done, it might happen in the best society until they brand them on the forehead, when they send them to the hulks. They ought not to let convicts go about Paris disguised like decent citizens, so as to carry on their antics like a set of rascally humbugs, which they are."

At this Mme. Vauquer recovered miraculously. She sat up and folded her arms; her eyes were wide open now, and there was no sign of tears in them.

"Why, do you really mean to be the ruin of my establishment, my dear sir? There is M. Vautrin—— Goodness," she cried, interrupting herself, "I can't help calling him by the name he passed himself off by for an honest man! There is one room to let already, and you want me to turn out two more lodgers in the middle of the season, when no one is moving——"

"Gentlemen, let us take our hats and go and dine at Flicoteaux's in the Place Sorbonne," cried Bianchon.

Mme. Vauquer glanced round, and saw in a moment on which side her interest lay. She waddled across to Mlle. Michonneau.

"Come now," she said; "you would not be the ruin of my establishment, would you, eh? There's a dear, kind soul. You see what a pass these gentlemen have brought me to; just go up to your room for this evening."

"Never a bit of it!" cried the boarders. "She must go, and go this minute!"

"But the poor lady has had no dinner," said Poiret, with piteous entreaty.

"She can go and dine where she likes," shouted several voices.

"Turn her out, the spy!"

"Turn them both out! Spies!"

"Gentlemen," cried Poiret, his heart swelling with the courage that love gives to the ovine male, "respect the weaker sex."

"Spies are of no sex," said the painter.

"A precious sexorama!"

"Turn her into the streetorama!"

"Gentlemen, this is not manners! If you turn people out of the house, it ought not to be done so unceremoniously and with no notice at all. We have paid our money, and we are not going," said Poiret, putting on his cap, and taking a chair beside Mlle. Michonneau, with whom Mme. Vauquer was remonstrating.

"Naughty boy," said the painter, with a comical look; "run away, naughty little boy!"

"Look here," said Bianchon; "if you do not go, all the rest of us will," and the boarders, to a man, made for the sitting-room door.

"Oh, Mademoiselle, what is to be done?" cried Mme. Vauquer. "I am a ruined woman. You can't stay here; they will go further, do something violent."

Mlle. Michonneau rose to her feet.

"She is going!—She is not going!—She is going!—No, she isn't."

These alternate exclamations, and a suggestion of hostile intentions, borne out by the behavior of the insurgents, compelled Mlle. Michonneau to take her departure. She made some stipulations, speaking in a low voice in her hostess's ear, and then—"I shall go to Mme. Buneaud's," she said, with a threatening look.

"Go where you please, Mademoiselle," said Mme. Vauquer, who regarded this choice of an opposition establishment as an atrocious insult. "Go and lodge with the Buneaud; the wine would give the cat the colic, and the food is cheap and nasty."

The boarders stood aside in two rows to let her pass; not a word was spoken. Poiret looked so wistfully after Mlle. Michonneau, and so artlessly revealed that he was in two minds whether to go or stay, that the boarders, in their joy at being quit of Mlle. Michonneau, burst out laughing at the sight of him.

"Hist!—st!—st! Poiret," shouted the painter. "Hallo! I say, Poiret, hallo!" The employé from the Muséum began to sing—

> "Partant pour la Syrie,
> Le jeune et beau Dunois . . ."

"Get along with you; you must be dying to go, *trahit sua quemque voluptas!*" said Bianchon.

"Everyone to his taste—free rendering from Virgil," said the tutor.

Mlle. Michonneau made a movement as if to take Poiret's arm, with an appealing glance that he could not resist. The two went out together, the old maid leaning upon him, and there was a burst of applause, followed by peals of laughter.

"Bravo, Poiret!"

"Who would have thought it of old Poiret!"

"Apollo Poiret!"

"Mars Poiret!"

"Intrepid Poiret!"

A messenger came in at that moment with a letter for Mme. Vauquer, who read it through, and collapsed in her chair.

"The house might as well be burned down at once," cried she, "if there are to be any more of these thunderbolts! Young Taillefer died at three o'clock this afternoon. It serves me right for wishing well to those ladies at that poor young man's expense. Mme. Couture and Victorine want me to send their things, because they are going to live with her father. M. Taillefer allows his daughter to keep old Mme. Couture with her as lady companion. Four rooms to let! and five lodgers gone! . . ."

She sat up, and seemed about to burst into tears.

"Bad luck has come to lodge here, I think," she cried.

Once more there came a sound of wheels from the street outside.

"What! another windfall for somebody!" was Sylvie's comment.

But it was Goriot who came in, looking so radiant, so flushed with happiness, that he seemed to have grown young again.

"Goriot in a cab!" cried the boarders; "the world is coming to an end."

The good soul made straight for Eugène, who was standing rapt in thought in a corner, and laid a hand on the young man's arm.

"Come," he said, with gladness in his eyes.

"Then you haven't heard the news?" said Eugène. "Vautrin was an escaped convict; they have just arrested him; and young Taillefer is dead."

"Very well, but what business is it of ours?" replied old Goriot. "I am going to dine with my daughter *in your house,* do you understand? She is expecting you. Come!"

He carried off Rastignac with him by main force, and they departed in as great a hurry as a pair of eloping lovers.

"Now, let us have dinner," cried the painter, and everyone drew his chair to the table.

"Well, I never!" said the portly Sylvie. "Nothing goes right to-day! The haricot mutton has caught! Bah! you will have to eat it, burnt as it is, more's the pity!"

Mme. Vauquer was so dispirited that she could not say a word as she looked round the table and saw only ten people where eighteen should be; but everyone tried to comfort and cheer her. At first the dinner contingent, as was natural, talked about Vautrin and the day's events; but the conversation wound round to such topics of interest as duels, jails, justice, prison life, and alterations that ought to be made in the laws. They soon wandered miles away from Jacques Collin and Victorine and her brother. There might be only ten of them, but they made noise enough for twenty; indeed, there seemed to be more of them than usual; that was the only difference between yesterday and to-day. Indifference to the fate of others is a matter of course in this selfish world, which, on the morrow of a tragedy, seeks among the events of Paris for a fresh sensation for its daily renewed appetite, and this indifference soon gained the upper hand. Mme. Vauquer herself grew calmer under the soothing influence of hope, and the mouthpiece of hope was the portly Sylvie.

That day had gone by like a dream for Eugène, and the sense of unreality lasted into the evening; so that, in spite of his energetic character and clear-headedness, his ideas were a chaos as he sat beside Goriot in the cab. The old man's voice was full of unwonted happiness, but Eugène had been shaken by so many emotions that the words sounded in his ears like words spoken in a dream.

"It was finished this morning! All three of us are going to dine there together, together! Do you understand? I have not dined with my Delphine, my little Delphine, these four years, and I shall have her for a whole evening! We have been at your lodging the whole time since morning. I have been working like a porter in my shirt-sleeves, helping to carry in the furniture. Aha! you don't know what pretty ways she has; at table she will look after me, 'Here, papa, just try this, it is nice.' And I shall not be able to eat. Oh, it is a long while since I have been with her in quiet everyday life as we shall have her."

"It really seems as if the world had been turned upside down."

"Upside down?" repeated old Goriot. "Why, the world has never been so right-side up. I see none but smiling faces in the streets, people who shake hands cordially and embrace each other, people who all look as happy as if they were going to dine with their daughter, and gobble down a nice little dinner that she went with me to order of the chef at the Café des Anglais. But, pshaw! with her beside you gall and wormwood would be as sweet as honey."

"I feel as if I were coming back to life again," said Eugène.

"Why, hurry up there!" cried old Goriot, letting down the window in front. "Get on faster; I will give you five francs if you get to the place I told you of in ten minutes' time."

With this prospect before him the cabman crossed Paris with miraculous celerity.

"How that fellow crawls!" said the old Goriot.

"But where are you taking me?" Eugène asked him.

"To your own house," said Goriot.

The cab stopped in the Rue d'Artois. Old Goriot stepped out first and flung ten francs to the man with the recklessness of a widower returning to bachelor ways.

"Come along upstairs," he said to Rastignac. They crossed a courtyard, and climbed up to the third floor of a new and handsome house. Here they stopped before a door; but before Goriot could ring, it was opened by Thérèse, Mme. du Nucingen's maid. Eugène found himself in a charming set of chambers; an anteroom, a little drawing-room, a bedroom, and a study, looking out upon a garden. The furniture and the decoration of the little drawing-room were of the most daintily charming description, the room was full of soft light, and Delphine rose up from a low chair by the fire and stood before him. She set her fire-screen down on the chimney-piece, and spoke with tenderness in every tone of her voice.

"So we had to go in search of you, sir, you who were so slow to understand!"

Thérèse left the room. The student took Delphine in his arms and held her in a tight clasp, his eyes filled with tears of joy. This last contrast between his present surroundings and the scenes he had just witnessed was too much for Rastignac's overwrought nerves, after the day's strain and excitement that had wearied heart and brain; he was almost overcome by it.

"I felt sure myself that he loved you," murmured old Goriot, while Eugène lay back bewildered on the sofa utterly unable to speak a word or to reason out how and why the magic wand had been waved to bring about this final transformation scene.

"But you must see your rooms," said Mme. de Nucingen. She took his hand and led him into a room carpeted and furnished like her own; indeed, down to the smallest details, it was a reproduction in miniature of Delphine's apartment.

"There is no bed," said Rastignac.

"No, Monsieur," she answered, reddening, and pressing his hand. Eugène, looking at her, understood, young though he was, how deeply modesty is implanted in the heart of a woman who loves.

"You are one of those beings whom we cannot choose but to adore forever," he said in her ear. "Yes, the deeper and truer love is, the more mysterious and closely veiled it should be; I can dare to say so, since we understand each other so well. No one shall learn our secret."

"Oh! so I am nobody, I suppose," growled the father.

"You know quite well that 'we' means you."

"Ah! that is what I wanted. You will not mind me, will you? I shall go and come like a good fairy who makes himself felt everywhere without being seen, shall I not? Eh, Delphinette, Ninette, Dedel—was it not a good idea of mine to say to you, 'There are some nice rooms to let in the Rue d'Artois; let us furnish them for him'? And she would not hear of it! Ah! your happiness has been all my doing. I am the author of your happiness and of your existence. Fathers must always be giving if they would be happy themselves; always giving—they would not be fathers else."

"Was that how it happened?" asked Eugène.

"Yes. She would not listen to me. She was afraid that people would talk, as if the rubbish that they say about you were to be compared with happiness! Why, all women dream of doing what she has done——"

Father Goriot found himself without an audience, for Mme. de Nucingen had led Rastignac into the study; he heard a kiss given and taken, low though the sound was.

The study was furnished as elegantly as the other rooms, and nothing was wanting there.

"Have we guessed your wishes rightly?" she asked, as they returned to the drawing-room for dinner.

"Yes," he said, "only too well, alas! For all this luxury so well carried out, this realization of pleasant dreams, the elegance that satisfies all the romantic fancies of youth, appeals to me so strongly that I cannot but feel that it is my rightful possession; but I cannot accept it from you, and I am too poor as yet to——"

"Ah! ah! you say me nay already," she said with arch imperiousness, and a charming little pout of the lips, a woman's way of laughing away scruples.

But Eugène had submitted so lately to that solemn self-questioning, and Vautrin's arrest had so plainly shown him the depths of the pit that lay ready to his feet, that the instincts of generosity and honor had been strengthened in him, and he could not allow himself to be coaxed into abandoning his high-minded determinations. Profound melancholy filled his mind.

"Do you really mean to refuse?" said Mme. de Nucingen. "And do you know what such a refusal means? That you are not sure of yourself, that you do not dare to bind yourself to me. Are you really afraid of betraying my affection? If you love me, if I—love you, why should you shrink back from such a slight obligation? If you but knew what a pleasure it has been to see after all the arrangements of this bachelor establishment, you would not hesitate any longer, you would ask me to forgive you for your hesitation. I had some money that belonged to you, and I have made good use of it, that is all. You mean this for magnanimity, but it is very little of you. You are asking me for far more than this. . . . " ("Ah!" she cried, as Eugène's passionate glance was turned on her), "and you are making difficulties about the merest trifles. Oh, if you feel no love whatever for me, refuse, by all means. My fate hangs on a word from you. Speak!—Father," she said after a pause, "make him listen to reason. Can he imagine that I am less nice than he is on the point of honor?"

Old Goriot was looking on and listening to this pretty quarrel with a placid smile, as if he had found some balm for all the sorrows of life.

"Child that you are!" she cried again, catching Eugène's hand. "You are just beginning life; you find barriers at the outset that many a man finds insurmountable; a woman's hand opens the way, and you shrink back! Why, you are sure to succeed! You will have a brilliant future. Success is written on that broad forehead of yours, and will you not be able to repay me my loan of to-day? Did not a lady in olden times arm her knight with sword and helmet and coat of mail, and find him a charger, so that he might fight for her in the tournament? Well, then, Eugène, these things that I offer you are the weapons of this age; everyone who means to be something must have such tools as these. A pretty place your garret must be if it is like papa's room! See, dinner is waiting all this time. Do you want to make me unhappy?—Why don't you answer?" she said, shaking his hand. *"Mon Dieu!* papa, make up his mind for him, or I will go away and never see him any more."

"I will make up your mind," said Goriot, coming down from the clouds. "Now, my dear M. Eugène, the next thing is to borrow money of the Jews, isn't it?"

"There is positively no help for it," said Eugène.

"All right, I will give you credit," said the other, drawing out a cheap leather pocket-book, much the worse for wear. "I have turned Jew myself; I paid for everything; here are the invoices. You do not owe a penny for anything here. It did not come to very much—five thousand francs at most, and I am going to lend you the money myself. I am not a woman—you cannot refuse me. You shall give me a receipt on a scrap of paper, and you can return it some time or other."

Delphine and Eugène looked at each other in amazement, tears sprang to their eyes. Rastignac held out his hand and grasped Goriot's warmly.

"Well, what is all this about? Are you not my children?"

"Oh my poor father," said Mme. de Nucingen, "how did you do it?"

"Ah! now you ask me. When I made up my mind to move him nearer to you, and saw you buying things as if they were wedding presents, I said to myself, 'She will never be able to pay for them.' The attorney says that those law proceedings will last quite six months before your husband can be made to disgorge your fortune. Well and good. I sold out my property in the Funds that brought in thirteen hundred and fifty livres a year, and bought a safe annuity of twelve hundred francs a year for fifteen thousand francs. Then I paid your tradesmen out of the rest of the capital. As for me, children, I have a room upstairs for which I pay fifty crowns a year; I can live like a prince on two francs a day, and still have something left over. I shall not have to spend anything much on clothes, for I never wear anything out. This fortnight past I have been laughing in my sleeve, thinking to myself, 'How happy they are going to be!' and—well, now, are you not happy?"

"Oh papa! papa!" cried Mme. de Nucingen, springing to her father, who took her on his knee. She covered him with kisses, her fair hair brushed his cheek, her tears fell on the withered face that had grown so bright and radiant.

"Dear father, what a father you are! No, there is not another father like you under the sun. If Eugène loved you before, what must he feel for you now?"

"Why, children! why, Delphinette!" cried Goriot, who had not felt his daughter's heart beat against his breast for ten years, "do you want me to die of joy? My poor heart will break! Come, M. Eugène, we are quits already." And the old man strained her to his breast with such fierce and passionate force that she cried out.

"Oh! you are hurting me!" she said.

"I am hurting you!" He grew pale at the words. The pain expressed in his face seemed greater than it is given to humanity to know. The agony of this Christ of paternity can only be compared with the masterpieces of those princes of the palette who have left for us the record of their visions of an agony suffered for a whole world by the Saviour of men. Old Goriot pressed his lips very gently against the waist that his fingers had grasped too roughly.

"Oh! no, no," he cried. "I have not hurt you, have I?" and his smile seemed to repeat the question. "*You* have hurt me with that cry just now.—The things cost rather more than that," he said in her ear, with another gentle kiss, "but I had to deceive him about it, or he would have been angry."

Eugène sat dumb with amazement in the presence of this inexhaustible love; he gazed at Goriot, and his face betrayed the artless admiration which shapes the beliefs of youth.

"I will be worthy of all this," he cried.

"Oh! my Eugène, that is nobly said," and Mme. de Nucingen kissed the law student on the forehead.

"He gave up Mlle. Taillefer and her millions for you," said old Goriot. "Yes, the little thing was in love with you, and now that her brother is dead she is as rich as Crœsus."

"Oh! why did you tell her?" cried Rastignac.

"Eugène," Delphine said in his ear, "I have one regret now this evening. Ah! how I will love you! and forever!"

"This is the happiest day I have had since you two were married!" cried Goriot. "God may send me any suffering, so long as I do not suffer through you, and I can still say, 'In this short month of February I had more happiness than other men have in their whole lives.'—Look at me, Fifine!" he said to his daughter. "She is very beautiful, is she not? Tell me, now, have you seen many women with that pretty soft color—that little dimple of hers? No, I thought not. Ah, well, and but for me this lovely woman would never have been. And very soon happiness will make her a thousand times lovelier, happiness through you. I could give up my place in heaven to you, neighbor, if needs be, and go down to hell instead. Come, let us have dinner," he added, scarcely knowing what he said, "everything is ours."

"Poor dear father!"

He rose and went over to her, and took her face in his hands, and set a kiss on the plaits of hair. "If you only knew, little one, how happy you can make me—how little it takes to make me happy! Will you come and see me sometimes? I shall be just above, so it is only a step. Promise me, say that you will!"

"Yes, dear father."

"Say it again."

"Yes, I will, my kind father."

"Hush, hush! I should make you say it a hundred times over if I followed my own wishes: Let us have dinner."

The three behaved like children that evening, and old Goriot's spirits were certainly not the least wild. He lay at his daughter's feet, kissed them, gazed into her eyes, rubbed his head against her dress; in short, no young lover could have been more extravagant or more tender.

"You see!" Delphine said with a look at Eugène, "so long as my father is with us, he monopolizes me. He will be rather in the way sometimes."

Eugène had himself already felt certain twinges of jealousy, and could not blame this speech that contained the germ of all ingratitude.

"And when will the rooms be ready?" asked Eugène, looking round. "We must all leave them this evening, I suppose."

"Yes, but to-morrow you must come and dine with me," she answered, with an eloquent glance. "It is our night at the Italiens."

"I shall go to the pit," said her father.

It was midnight. Mme. de Nucingen's carriage was waiting for her, and old Goriot and the student walked back to the Maison Vauquer, talking of Delphine, and warming over their talk till there grew up a curious rivalry between the two violent passions. Eugène could not help seeing that the father's selfless love was deeper and more steadfast than his own.

For this worshiper Delphine was always pure and fair, and her father's adoration drew its fervor from a whole past as well as a future of love.

They found Mme. Vauquer by the stove, with Sylvie and Christophe to keep her company; the old landlady, sitting like Marius among the ruins of Carthage, was waiting for the two lodgers that yet remained to her, and bemoaning her lot with the sympathetic Sylvie. Tasso's lamentations as recorded in Byron's poem are undoubtedly eloquent, but for sheer force of truth they fall far short of the widow's cry from the depths.

"Only three cups of coffee in the morning, Sylvie! Oh dear! to have your house emptied in this way is enough to break your heart. What is life, now my lodgers are gone? Nothing at all. Just think of it! It is just as if all the furniture had been taken out of the house, and your furniture is your life. How have I offended Heaven to draw down all this trouble upon me? And haricot beans and potatoes laid in for twenty people! The police in my house, too! We shall have to live on potatoes now, and Christophe will have to go!"

The Savoyard, who was fast asleep, suddenly woke up at this, and said, "Madame?" questioningly.

"Poor fellow!" said Sylvie, "he is like a dog."

"In the dead season, too! Nobody is moving now. I would like to know where the lodgers are to drop down from. It drives me distracted. And that old witch of a Michonneau goes and takes Poiret with her! What can she have done to him to make him so fond of her? He runs about after her like a little dog."

"Lord," said Sylvie, flinging up her head, "those old maids are up to all sorts of tricks."

"There's that poor M. Vautrin that they made out to be a convict," the widow went on. "Well, you know that is too much for me, Sylvie; I can't bring myself to believe it. Such a lively man as he was, and paid fifteen francs a month for his coffee of an evening, and paid you every penny on the nail, too."

"And open-handed he was!" said Christophe.

"There is some mistake," said Sylvie.

"Why, no there isn't! he said so himself!" said Mme. Vauquer. "And to think that all these things have happened in my house, and in a quarter where you never see a cat go by. On my word as an honest woman, it's like a dream. For, look here, we saw Louis XVI. meet with his mishap; we saw the fall of the Emperor; and we saw him come back and fall again; there was nothing out of the way in all that, but lodging-houses are not liable to revolutions. You can do without a king, but you must eat all the same; and so long as a decent woman, a de Conflans born and bred, will give you all sorts of good things for dinner, nothing short of the end of the world ought to—but there, it is the end of the world, that is just what it is!"

"And to think that Mlle. Michonneau, who made all this mischief, is to have a thousand crowns a year for it, so I hear," cried Sylvie.

"Don't speak of her, she is a wicked woman!' said Mme. Vauquer. "She is going to the Buneaud, who charges less than cost. But the Buneaud is capable of anything; she must have done frightful things, robbed and murdered people in her time. *She* ought to be put in jail for life instead of that poor dear——"

Eugène and Goriot rang the door-bell at that moment.

now I may seem to you to be frivolous, petty, shallow, like a Parisienne, but remember, my friend, that I am ready to give up all for you; and that if I long more than ever for an entrance into the Faubourg Saint-Germain, it is because I shall meet you there."

"Mme. de Beauséant's note seems to say very plainly that she does not expect to see the *Baron* de Nucingen at her ball; don't you think so?" said Eugène.

"Why, yes," said the Baroness as she returned the letter. "Those women have a talent for insolence. But it is of no consequence, I shall go. My sister is sure to be there, and sure to be very beautifully dressed.—Eugène," she went on, lowering her voice, "she will go to dispel ugly suspicions. You do not know the things that people are saying about her! Only this morning Nucingen came to tell me that they had been discussing her at the club. Great Heavens! on what does a woman's character and the honor of a whole family depend! I feel that I am nearly touched and wounded in my poor sister. According to some people, M. de Trailles must have put his name to bills for a hundred thousand francs; nearly all of them are overdue, and proceedings are threatened. In this predicament, it seems that my sister sold her diamonds to a Jew—the beautiful diamonds that belonged to her husband's mother, Mme. de Restaud the elder,—you have seen her wearing them. In fact, nothing else has been talked about for the last two days. So I can see that Anastasie is sure to come to Mme. de Beauséant's ball in tissue of gold, and ablaze with diamonds, to draw all eyes upon her; and I will not be outshone. She has tried to eclipse me all her life; she has never been kind to me, and I have helped her so often, and always had money for her when she had none.—But never mind other people now, to-day I mean to be perfectly happy."

At one o'clock that morning Eugène was still with Mme. de Nucingen. In the midst of their lovers' farewell, a farewell full of hope of bliss to come, she said in a troubled voice, "I am very fearful, superstitious. Give what name you like to my presentiments, but I am afraid that my happiness will be paid for by some horrible catastrophe."

"Child!" said Eugène.

"Ah! have we changed places, and am I the child to-night?" she asked laughingly.

Eugène went back to the Maison Vauquer, never doubting but that he should leave it for good on the morrow; and on the way he fell to dreaming the bright dreams of youth, when the cup of happiness has left its sweetness on the lips.

"Well?" cried Goriot, as Rastignac passed by his door.

"Yes," said Eugène; "I will tell you everything to-morrow."

"Everything, will you not?" cried the old man. "Go to bed. To-morrow our happy life will begin."

Next day, Goriot and Rastignac were ready to leave the lodging-house, and only awaited the good pleasure of a porter to move out of it; but towards noon there was a sound of wheels in the Rue Neuve-Sainte-Geneviève, and a carriage stopped before the door of the Maison Vauquer. Mme. de Nucingen alighted, and asked if her father was still in the house, and, receiving an affirmative reply from Sylvie, ran lightly upstairs.

It so happened that Eugène was at home all unknown to his neighbor. At breakfast time he had asked Goriot to superintend the removal of his goods, saying that he would meet him in the Rue d'Artois at four o'clock; but Rastignac's name had been called early on the list at the École de Droit, and he had gone back at once to the Rue Neuve-Sainte-Geneviève. No one had seen him come in, for Goriot had gone to find a porter, and the mistress of the house was likewise out. Eugène had thought to pay her himself, for it struck him that if he left this, Goriot in his zeal would probably pay for him. As it was, Eugène went up to his room to see that nothing had been forgotten, and blessed his foresight when he saw the blank bill bearing Vautrin's signature lying in the drawer where he had carelessly thrown it on the day when he had repaid the amount. There was no fire in the grate, so he was about to tear it into little pieces, when he heard a voice speaking in Goriot's room, and the speaker was Delphine! He made no more noise, and stood still to listen, thinking that she should have no secrets from him; but after the first few words, the conversation between the father and daughter was so strange and interesting that it absorbed all his attention.

"Ah! thank Heaven that you thought of asking him to give an account of the money settled on me before I was utterly ruined, father. Is it safe to talk?" she added.

"Yes, there is no one in the house," said her father faintly.

"What is the matter with you?" asked Mme. de Nucingen.

"God forgive you! you have just dealt me a staggering blow, child!" said the old man. "You cannot know how much I love you, or you would not have burst in upon me like this, with such news, especially if all is not lost. Has something so important happened that you must come here about it? In a few minutes we should have been in the Rue d'Artois."

"Eh! does one think what one is doing after a catastrophe? It has turned my head. Your attorney has found out the state of things now, but it was bound to come out sooner or later. We shall want your long business experience; and I came to you like a drowning man who catches at a branch. When M. Derville found that Nucingen was throwing all sorts of difficulties in his way, he threatened him with proceedings, and told him plainly that he would soon obtain an order from the President of the Tribunal. So Nucingen came to my room this morning, and asked if I meant to ruin us both. I told him that I knew nothing whatever about it, that I had a fortune, and ought to be put into possession of my fortune, and that my attorney was acting for me in the matter; I said again that I knew absolutely nothing about it, and could not possibly go into the subject with him. Wasn't that what you told me to tell him?"

"Yes, quite right," answered Goriot.

"Well, then," Delphine continued, "he told me all about his affairs. He had just invested all his capital and mine in business speculations; they have only just been started, and very large sums of money are locked up. If I were to compel him to refund my dowry now, he would be forced to file his petition; but if I will wait a year, he undertakes, on his honor, to double or treble my fortune, by investing it in building land, and I shall be mistress at last of the whole of my property. He was speaking the truth, father dear; he frightened me! He asked my pardon for his conduct; he has given me my liberty; I am free to act as I please on condition that I leave him to carry on my business in my name. To prove his sincerity, he promised that M. Derville might inspect the accounts as often I pleased, so that I might be assured that everything was being conducted properly. In short, he put himself into my power, bound hand and foot. He wishes the present arrangements as to the expenses of housekeeping to continue for two more years, and entreated me not to exceed my allowance. He showed me plainly that it was all that he could do to keep up appearances; he has broken with his opera dancer; he will be compelled to practice the most strict economy (in secret) if he is to bide his time with unshaken credit. I scolded, I did all I could to drive him to desperation, so as to find out more. He showed me his ledgers—he broke down and cried at last. I never saw a man in such a state. He lost his head completely, talked of killing himself, and raved till I felt quite sorry for him."

"Do you really believe that silly rubbish?" . . . cried her father. "It was all got up for your benefit! I have had to do with Germans in the way of business; honest and straightforward they are pretty sure to be, but when with their simplicity and frankness they are sharpers and humbugs as well, they are the worst rogues of all. Your husband is taking advantage of you. As soon as pressure is brought to bear on him he shams dead; he means to be more the master under your name than in his own. He will take advantage of the position to secure himself against the risks of business. He is as sharp as he is treacherous; he is a bad lot! No, no; I am not going to leave my girls behind me without a penny when I go to Père-Lachaise. I know something about business still. He has sunk his money in speculation, he says; very well then, there is something to show for it—bills, receipts, papers of some sort. Let him produce them, and come to an arrangement with you. We will choose the most promising of his speculations, take them over at our own risk, and have the securities transferred into your name; they shall represent the separate estate of Delphine Goriot, wife of the Baron de Nucingen. Does that fellow really take us for idiots? Does he imagine that I could stand the idea of your being without fortune, without bread, for forty-eight hours? I would not stand it a day—no, not a night, not a couple of hours! If there had been any foundation for the idea, I should never get over it. What! I have worked hard for forty years, carried sacks on my back, and sweated and pinched and saved all my life for you, my darlings, for you who made the toil and every burden borne for you seem light; and now, my fortune, my whole life, is to vanish in smoke! I should die raving mad if I believed a word of it. By all that's holiest in heaven and earth, we will have this cleared up at once; go through the books, have the whole business looked thoroughly into! I will not sleep, nor rest, nor eat, until I have satisfied myself that all your fortune is in existence. Your money is settled upon you, God be thanked! and, luckily, your attorney, Maître Derville, is an honest man. Good Lord! you shall have your snug little million, your fifty thousand francs a year, as long as you live, or I will raise a racket in Paris, I will so! If the Tribunals put upon us, I will appeal to the Chambers. If I knew that you were well and comfortably off as far as money is concerned, that thought would keep me easy in spite of bad health and troubles. Money? why, it is life! Money does everything. That great dolt of an Alsatian shall sing to another tune! Look here, Delphine, don't give way, don't make a concession of half a quarter of a farthing to that fathead, who has ground you down and made you miserable. If he can't do without you, we will give him a good cudgeling, and keep him in order. Great Heavens! my brain is on fire; it is as if there were something red-hot inside my head. My Delphine lying on straw! You! my Fifine! Good gracious! Where are my gloves? Come, let us go at once; I mean to see everything with my own eyes—books, cash, and correspondence, the whole business. I shall have no peace until I know for certain that your fortune is secure."

"Oh! father dear, be careful how you set about it! If there is the least hint of vengeance in the business, if you show yourself openly hostile, it will be all over with me. He knows whom he has to deal with; he thinks it quite natural that if you put the idea into my head, I should be uneasy about my money; but I swear to you that he has it in his own hands, and that he had meant to keep it. He is just the man to abscond with all the money and leave us in the lurch, the scoundrel! He knows quite well that I will not dishonor the name I bear by bringing him into a court of law. His position is strong and weak at the same time. If we drive him to despair, I am lost."

"Why, then, the man is a rogue?"

"Well, yes, father," she said, flinging herself into a chair. "I wanted to keep it from you to spare your feelings," and she burst into tears; "I did not want you to know that you had married me to such a man as he is. He is just the same in private life—body and soul and conscience—the same through and through—hideous! I hate him; I despise him! Yes, after all that that despicable Nucingen has told me, I cannot respect him any longer. A man capable of mixing himself up in such affairs, and of talking about them to me as he did, without the slightest scruple,—it is because I have read him through and through that I am afraid of him. He, my husband, frankly proposed to give me my liberty, and do you know what that means? It means that if things turn out badly for him, I am to play into his hands, and be his stalking-horse."

"But there is law to be had! There is a Place de Grève for sons-in-law of that sort," cried her father; "why, I would guillotine him myself if there was no headsman to do it."

"No, father, the law cannot touch him. Listen, this is what he says, stripped of all his circumlocutions—'Take your choice, you and no one else can be my accomplice; either everything is lost, you are ruined and have not a farthing, or you will let me carry this business through myself.' Is that plain speaking? He *must* have my assistance. He is assured that his wife will deal fairly by him; he knows that I shall leave his money to him and be content with my own. It is an unholy and dishonest compact, and he holds out threats of ruin to compel me to consent to it. He is buying my conscience, and the price is liberty to be Eugène's wife in all but name. 'I connive at your errors, and you allow me to commit crimes and ruin poor families!' Is that sufficiently explicit? Do you know what he means by speculations? He buys up land in his own name, then he finds men of straw to run up houses upon it. These men make a bargain with a contractor to build the houses, paying them by bills at long dates; then in consideration of a small sum they leave my husband in possession of the houses, and finally slip through the fingers of the deluded contractors by going into bankruptcy. The name of the firm of Nucingen has been used to dazzle the poor contractors. I saw that. I noticed, too, that Nucingen had sent bills for large amounts to Amsterdam, London, Naples, and Vienna, in order to prove, if necessary, that large sums had been paid away by the firm. How could we get possession of those bills?"

Eugène heard a dull thud on the floor; old Goriot must have fallen to his knees.

"Great Heavens! what have I done to you? Bound my daughter to this scoundrel who does as he likes with her!—Oh! my child, my child! forgive me!" cried the old man.

"Yes, if I am in the depths of despair, perhaps you are to blame," said Delphine. "We have so little sense when we marry! What do we know of the world, of business, or men, or life? Our fathers should think for us! Father dear, I am not blaming you in the least, forgive me for what I said. This is all my own fault. Nay, do not cry, papa," she said, kissing him.

"Do not you cry either, my little Delphine. Look up and let me kiss away the tears. There! I shall find my wits and unravel this skein of your husband's winding."

"No, let me do that; I shall be able to manage him. He is fond of me, well and good; I shall use my influence to make him invest my money as soon as possible in landed property in my own name. Very likely I could get him to buy back Nucingen in Alsace in my name; that has always been a pet idea of his. Still, come to-morrow and go through the books, and look into the business. M. Derville knows little of mercantile matters. No, not to-morrow though. I do not want to be upset. Mme. de Beauséant's ball will be the day after to-morrow, and I must keep quiet, so as to look my best and freshest, and do honor to my dear Eugène! . . . Come, let us see his room."

But as she spoke a carriage stopped in the Rue Neuve-Sainte-Geneviève, and the sound of Mme. de Restaud's voice came from the staircase. "Is my father in?" she asked of Sylvie.

This accident was luckily timed for Eugène, whose one idea had been to throw himself down on the bed and pretend to be asleep.

"Oh, father, have you heard about Anastasie?" said Delphine, when she heard her sister speak. "It looks as though some strange things had happened in that family."

"What sort of things?" asked Goriot. "This is like to be the death of me. My poor head will not stand a double misfortune."

"Good-morning, father," said the Countess from the threshold. "Oh! Delphine, are you here?"

Mme. de Restaud seemed taken aback by her sister's presence.

"Good-morning, Nasie," said the Baroness. "What is there so extraordinary in my being here? *I* see our father every day."

"Since when?"

"If you came yourself, you would know."

"Don't tease, Delphine," said the Countess fretfully. "I am very miserable, I am lost. Oh! my poor father, it is hopeless this time!"

"What is it, Nasie?" cried Goriot. "Tell us all about it, child! How white she is! Quick, do something, Delphine; be kind to her, and I will love you even better, if that were possible."

"Poor Nasie!" said Mme. de Nucingen, drawing her sister to a chair. "We are the only two people in the world whose love is always sufficient to forgive you everything. Family affection is the surest, you see."

The Countess inhaled the salts and revived.

"This will kill me!" said their father. "There," he went on, stirring the smoldering fire, "come nearer, both of you. It is cold. What is it, Nasie? Be quick and tell me, this is enough to——"

"Well, then, my husband knows everything," said the Countess. "Just imagine it; do you remember, father, that bill of Maxime's some time ago? Well, that was not the first. I had paid ever so many before that. About the beginning of January M. de Trailles seemed very much troubled. He said nothing to me; but it is so easy to read the hearts of those you love, a mere trifle is enough; and then you feel things instinctively. Indeed, he was more tender and affectionate than ever, and I was happier than I had ever been before. Poor Maxime! in himself he was really saying good-by to me, so he has told me since; he meant to blow his brains out! At last I worried him so, and begged and implored so hard; for two hours I knelt at his knees and prayed and entreated, and at last he told me—that he owed a hundred thousand francs. Oh! papa! a hundred thousand francs! I was beside myself! You had not the money, I knew; I had eaten up all that you had——"

"No," said Goriot; "I could not have got it for you unless I had stolen it. But I would have done that for you, Nasie! I will do it yet."

The words came from him like a sob, a hoarse sound like the death rattle of a dying man; it seemed indeed like the agony of death when the father's love was powerless. There was a pause, and neither of the sisters spoke. It must have been selfishness indeed that could hear unmoved that cry of anguish that, like a pebble thrown over a precipice, revealed the depths of his despair.

"I found the money, father, by selling what was not mine to sell," and the Countess burst into tears.

Delphine was touched; she laid her head on her sister's shoulder, and cried too.

"Then it is all true," she said.

Anastasie bowed her head, Mme. de Nucingen flung her arms about her, kissed her tenderly, and held her sister to her heart.

"I shall always love you and never judge you, Nasie," she said.

"My angels!" murmured Goriot faintly. "Oh, why should it be trouble that draws you together?"

This warm and palpitating affection seemed to give the Countess courage.

"To save Maxime's life," she said, "to save all my own happiness, I went to the money-lender you know of, a man of iron forged in hell-fire; nothing can melt him; I took all the family diamonds that M. de Restaud is so proud of—his and mine too—and sold them to that M. Gosbeck. *Sold them!* Do you understand? I saved Maxime, but I am lost. Restaud found it all out."

"How? Who told him? I will kill him," cried Goriot.

"Yesterday he sent to tell me to come to his room. I went. . . . 'Anastasie,' he said in a voice—oh! such a voice; that was enough, it told me everything—'where are your diamonds?'—'In my room——'—'No,' he said, looking straight at me, 'there they are on that chest of drawers——' and he lifted his handkerchief and showed me the casket. 'Do you know where they come from?' he said. I fell at his feet. . . . I cried; I besought him to tell me the death he wished to see me die."

"You said that!" cried Goriot. "By God in heaven, whoever lays a hand on either of you as long as I am alive may reckon on being roasted by slow fires! Yes, I will cut him in pieces like . . ."

Goriot stopped; the words died away in his threat.

"And then, dear, he asked something worse than death of me. Oh! Heaven preserve all other women from hearing such words as I heard then!"

"I will murder that man," said Goriot quietly. "But he has only one life, and he deserves to die twice.—And then, what next?" he added, looking at Anastasie.

"Then," the Countess resumed, "there was a pause, and he looked at me. 'Anastasie,' he said, 'I will bury this in silence; there shall be no separation; there are the children. I will not kill M. de Trailles. I might miss him if we fought, and as for other ways of getting rid of him, I should come into collision with the law. If I killed him in your arms, it would bring dishonor on *those* children. But if you do not want to see your children perish, nor their father nor me, you must first of all submit to two conditions. Answer me. Have I a child of my own?' I answered, 'Yes.'—'Which?'—'Ernest, our eldest boy.'—'Very well,' he said, 'and now swear to obey me in this particular from this time forward.' I swore. 'You will make over your property to me when I require you to do so.' "

"Do nothing of the kind!" cried Goriot. "Aha! M. de Restaud, you could not make your wife happy; she has looked for happiness and found it elsewhere, and you make her suffer for your own ineptitude? He will have to reckon with me. Make yourself easy, Nasie. Aha! he cares about his heir! Good, very good. I will get hold of the boy; isn't he my grandson? What the blazes! I can surely go to see the brat! I will stow him away somewhere; I will take care of him, you may be quite easy. I will bring Restaud to terms, the monster! I shall say to him, 'A word or two with you! If you want your son back again, give my daughter her property, and leave her to do as she pleases.' "

"Father!"

"Yes. I am your father, Nasie, a father indeed! That rogue of a great lord had better not ill-treat my daughter. *Tonnerre!* What is it in my veins? There is the blood of a tiger in me; I could tear those two men to pieces! Oh! children, children! so this is what your lives are! Why, it is death! . . . What will become of you when I shall be here no longer? Fathers ought to live as long as their children. Ah! Lord God in heaven! how ill Thy world is ordered! Thou hast a Son, if what they tell us is true, and yet Thou leavest us to suffer so through our children. My darlings, my darlings! to think that trouble only should bring you to me, that I should only see you with tears on your faces! Ah! yes, yes, you love me, I see that you love me. Come to me and pour out your griefs to me; my heart is large enough to hold them all. Oh; you might rend my heart in pieces, and every fragment would make a father's heart. If only I could bear all your sorrows for you! . . . Ah! you were so happy when you were little and still with me. . . ."

"We have never been happy since," said Delphine. "Where are the old days when we slid down the sacks in the great granary?"

"That is not all, father," said Anastasie in Goriot's ear. The old man gave a startled shudder. "The diamonds only sold for a hundred thousand francs. Maxime is hard pressed. There are twelve thousand francs still to pay. He has given me his word that he will be steady and give up play in future. His love is all that I have left in the world. I have paid such a fearful price for it that I shall die if I lose him now. I have sacrificed my fortune, my honor, my peace of mind, and my children for him. Oh! do something, so that at the least Maxime may be at large and live undisgraced in the world, where he will assuredly make a career for himself. Something more than my happiness is at stake; the children have nothing, and if he is sent to Sainte-Pélagie all his prospects will be ruined."

"I haven't the money, Nasie. I have *nothing*—nothing left. This is the end of everything. Yes, the world is crumbling into ruin, I am sure. Fly! Save yourselves! Ah!—I have still my silver buckles left, and half a dozen silver spoons and forks, the first I ever had in my life. But I have nothing else except my life annuity, twelve hundred francs . . ."

"Then what has become of your money in the Funds?"

"I sold out, and only kept a trifle for my wants. I wanted twelve thousand francs to furnish some rooms for Delphine."

"In your own house?" asked Mme. de Restaud, looking at her sister.

"What does it matter where they were?" asked Goriot. "The money is spent now."

"I see how it is," said the Countess. "Rooms for M. de Rastignac. Poor Delphine, take warning by me!"

"M. de Rastignac is incapable of ruining the woman he loves, dear."

"Thanks! Delphine. I thought you would have been kinder to me in my troubles, but you never did love me."

"Yes, yes, she loves you, Nasie!" cried Goriot; "she was saying so only just now. We were talking about you, and she insisted that you were beautiful, and that she herself was only pretty!"

"Pretty!" said the Countess. "She is as hard as a marble statue."

"And if I am?" cried Delphine, flushing up, "how have you treated me? You would not recognize me; you closed the doors of every house against me; you have never let an opportunity of mortifying me slip by. And when did I come, as you were always doing, to drain our poor father, a thousand francs at a time, till he is left as you see him now? That is all your doing, sister! I myself have seen my father as often as I could. I have not turned him out of the house, and then come and fawned upon him when I wanted money. I did not so much as know that he had spent those twelve thousand francs on me. I am economical, as you know; and when papa has made me presents, it has never been because I came and begged for them."

"You were better off than I. M. de Marsay was rich, as you have reason to know. You always were as slippery as gold. Good-by; I have neither sister nor——"

"Oh! hush, hush! Nasie!" cried her father.

"Nobody else would repeat what everybody has ceased to believe. You are an unnatural sister!" cried Delphine.

"Oh, children, children! hush! hush! or I will kill myself before your eyes."

"There, Nasie, I forgive you," said Mme. de Nucingen; "you are very unhappy. But I am kinder than you are. How could you say *that* just when I was ready to do anything in the world to help you, even to be reconciled with my husband, which for my own sake I—— Oh! it is just like you; you have behaved cruelly to me all through these nine years."

"Children, children, kiss each other!" cried the father. "You are angels, both of you."

"No. Let me alone," cried the Countess, shaking off the hand that her father had laid on her arm. "She is more merciless than my husband. Anyone might think she was a model of all the virtues herself!"

"I would rather have people think that I owed money to M. de Marsay than own that M. de Trailles had cost me more than two hundred thousand francs," retorted Mme. de Nucingen.

"Delphine!" cried the Countess, stepping towards her sister.

"I shall tell you the truth about yourself if you begin to slander me," said the Baroness coldly.

"Delphine! you are a——"

Old Goriot sprang between them, grasped the Countess's hand, and laid his own over her mouth.

"Good Heavens, father! What have you been handling this morning?" said Anastasie.

"Ah, well, yes, I ought not to have touched you," said the poor father, wiping his hands on his trousers, "but I have been packing up my things; I did not know that you were coming to see me."

He was glad that he had drawn down her wrath upon himself.

"Ah!" he sighed, as he sat down, "you children have broken my heart between you. This is killing me. My head feels as if it were on fire. Be good to each other and love each other! This will be the death of me! Delphine! Nasie! come, be sensible; you are both in the wrong. Come, Dedel," he added, looking through his tears at the Baroness, "she must have twelve thousand francs, you see; let us see if we can find them for her. Oh, my girls, do not look at each other like that!" and he sank on his knees beside Delphine. "Ask her to forgive you—just to please me," he said in her ear. "She is more miserable than you are. Come now, Dedel."

"Poor Nasie!" said Delphine, alarmed at the wild extravagant grief in her father's face, "I was in the wrong, kiss me——"

"Ah! that is like balm to my heart," cried Father Goriot. "But how are we to find twelve thousand francs? I might offer myself as a substitute in the army——"

"Oh! father dear!" they both cried, flinging their arms about him. "No, no!"

"God reward you for the thought. We are not worth it, are we, Nasie?" asked Delphine.

"And besides, father dear, it would only be a drop in the bucket," observed the Countess.

"But is flesh and blood worth nothing?" cried the old man in his despair. "I would give body and soul to save you, Nasie. I would do a murder for the man who would rescue you. I would do, as Vautrin did, go to the hulks, go——" He stopped as if struck by a thunderbolt, and put both hands to his head. "Nothing left!" he cried, tearing his hair.

"If I only knew of a way to steal money, but it is so hard to do it, and then you can't set to work by yourself, and it takes time to rob a bank. Yes, it is time I was dead; there is nothing left me to do but to die. I am no good in the world; I am no longer a father! No. She has come to me in her extremity, and, wretch that I am, I have nothing to give her. Ah! you put your money into a life annuity, old scoundrel; and had you not daughters? You did not love them. Die, die in a ditch, like the dog that you are! Yes, I am worse than a dog; a beast would not have done as I have done! Oh! my head . . . it throbs as if it would burst."

"Papa!" cried both the young women at once, "do, pray, be reasonable!" and they clung to him to prevent him from dashing his head against the wall. There was a sound of sobbing.

Eugène, greatly alarmed, took the bill that bore Vautrin's signature, saw that the stamp would suffice for a larger sum, altered the figures, made it into a regular bill for twelve thousand francs, payable to Goriot's order, and went to his neighbor's room.

"Here is the money, Madame," he said, handing the piece of paper to her. "I was asleep; your conversation awoke me, and by this means I learned all that I owed to M. Goriot. This bill can be discounted, and I shall meet it punctually at the due date."

The Countess stood motionless and speechless, but she held the bill in her fingers.

"Delphine," she said, with a white face, and her whole frame quivering with indignation, anger, and rage, "I forgave you everything; God is my witness that I forgave you, but I cannot forgive this! So this gentleman was there all the time, and you knew it! Your petty spite has led you to wreak your vengeance on me by betraying my secrets, my life, my children's lives, my shame, my honor! There, you are nothing to me any longer. I hate you. I will do all that I can to injure you, I will . . ."

Anger paralyzed her; the words died in her dry parched throat.

"Why, he is my son, my child; he is your brother, your preserver!" cried Goriot. "Kiss his hand, Nasie! Stay,

I will embrace him myself," he said, straining Eugène to his breast in a frenzied clasp. "Oh my boy! I will be more than a father to you; I would be everything in the world to you; if I had God's power, I would fling worlds at your feet. Why don't you kiss him, Nasie? He is not a man, but an angel, an angel out of heaven."

"Never mind her, father; she is mad just now."

"Mad! am I? And what are you?" cried Mme. de Restaud.

"Children, children, I shall die if you go on like this," cried the old man, and he staggered and fell on the bed as if a bullet had struck him.—"They are killing me between them," he said to himself.

The Countess fixed her eyes on Eugène, who stood stock-still; all his faculties were numbed by this violent scene.

"Sir? . . ." she said, doubt and inquiry in her face, tone, and bearing; she took no notice now of her father nor of Delphine, who was hastily unfastening his waistcoat.

"Madame," said Eugène, answering the question before it was asked, "I will meet the bill, and keep silence about it."

"You have killed our father, Nasie!" said Delphine, pointing to Goriot, who lay unconscious on the bed. The Countess fled.

"I freely forgive her," said the old man, opening his eyes; "her position is horrible; it would turn an older head than hers. Comfort Nasie, and be nice to her, Delphine; promise it to your poor father before he dies," he asked, holding Delphine's hands in a convulsive clasp.

"Oh! what ails you, father?" she cried in real alarm.

"Nothing, nothing," said Goriot; "it will go off. There is something heavy pressing on my forehead, a little headache. . . . Ah! poor Nasie, what a life lies before her!"

Just as he spoke, the Countess came back again and flung herself on her knees before him. "Forgive me!" she cried.

"Come," said her father, "you are hurting me still more."

"Monsieur," the Countess said, turning to Rastignac, "misery made me unjust to you. You will be a brother to me, will you not?" and she held out her hand. Her eyes were full of tears as she spoke.

"Nasie," cried Delphine, flinging her arms round her sister, "my little Nasie, let us forget and forgive."

"No, no," cried Nasie; "I shall never forget!"

"Dear angels," cried Goriot, "it is as if a dark curtain over my eyes had been raised; your voices have called me back to life. Kiss each other once more. Well, now, Nasie, that bill will save you, won't it?"

"I hope so. I say, papa, will you write your name on it?"

"There! how stupid of me to forget that! But I am not feeling at all well, Nasie, so you must not remember it against me. Send and let me know as soon as you are out of your strait. No, I will go to you. No, after all, I will not go; I might meet your husband, and I should kill him on the spot. And as for signing away your property, I shall have a word to say about that. Quick, my child, and keep Maxime in order in future."

Eugène was too bewildered to speak.

"Poor Anastasie, she always had a violent temper," said Mme. de Nucingen, "but she has a good heart."

"She came back for the indorsement," said Eugène in Delphine's ear.

"Do you think so?"

"I only wish I could think otherwise. Do not trust her," he answered, raising his eyes as if he confided to Heaven the thoughts that he did not venture to express.

"Yes. She is always acting a part to some extent."

"How do you feel now, dear Father Goriot?" asked Rastignac.

"I should like to go to sleep," he replied.

Eugène helped him to bed, and Delphine sat by the bedside, holding his hand until he fell asleep. Then she went.

"This evening at the Italiens," she said to Eugène, "and you can let me know how he is. To-morrow you will leave this place, Monsieur. Let us go into your room.—Oh, how frightful!" she cried on the threshold. "Why, you are even worse lodged than our father. Eugène, you have behaved well. I would love you more if that were possible; but, dear boy, if you are to succeed in life. you must not begin by flinging twelve thousand francs out of the windows like that. The Comte de Trailles is a confirmed gambler. My sister shuts her eyes to it. He would have made the twelve thousand francs in the same way that he wins and loses heaps of gold."

A groan from the next room brought them back to Goriot's bedside; to all appearance he was asleep, but the two lovers caught the words, "They are not happy!" Whether he was awake or sleeping, the tone in which they were spoken went to his daughter's heart. She stole up to the pallet-bed on which her father lay, and kissed his forehead. He opened his eyes.

"Ah! Delphine!" he said.

"How are you now?" she asked.

"Quite comfortable. Do not worry about me; I shall get up presently. Don't stay with me, children; go, go and be happy."

Eugène went back with Delphine as far as her door; but he was not easy about Goriot, and would not stay to dinner, as she proposed. He wanted to be back at the Maison Vauquer. Old Goriot had left his room, and was just sitting down to dinner as he came in. Bianchon had placed himself where he could watch the old man carefully; and when the old vermicelli maker took up his square of bread and smelt it to find out the quality of the flour, the medical student, studying him closely, saw that the action was purely mechanical, and shook his head.

"Just come and sit over here, hospitaler of Cochin," said Eugène.

Bianchon went the more willingly because his change of place brought him next to the old lodger.

"What is wrong with him?" asked Rastignac.

"It is all up with him, or I am much mistaken! Something very extraordinary must have taken place; he looks to me as if he were in imminent danger of serous apoplexy. The lower part of his face is composed enough, but the upper part is drawn and distorted. Then there is that peculiar look about the eyes that indicates an effusion of serum in the brain; they look as though they were covered with a film of fine dust, do you notice? I shall know more about it by to-morrow morning."

"Is there any cure for it?"

"None. It might be possible to stave death off for a time if a way could be found of setting up a reaction in the lower extremities; but if the symptoms do not abate by to-morrow evening, it will be all over with him, poor old fellow! Do you know what has happened to bring this on? There must have been some violent shock, and his mind has given away."

"Yes, there was," said Rastignac, remembering how the two daughters had struck blow on blow at their father's heart.

"But Delphine at any rate loves her father," he said to himself.

That evening at the opera Rastignac chose his words carefully, lest he should give Mme. de Nucingen needless alarm.

"Do not be anxious about him," she said, however, as soon as Eugène began, "our, father has really a strong constitution, but this morning we gave him a shock. Our whole fortunes were in peril, so the thing was serious, you see. I could not live if your affection did not make me insensible to troubles that I should once have thought too hard to bear. At this moment I have but one fear left but one misery to dread—to lose the love that has made me feel so glad to live. Everything else is as nothing to me compared with your love; I care for nothing else, for you are all the world to me. If I feel glad to be rich, it is for your sake. To my shame be it said, I think of my lover before my father. Do you ask why? I cannot tell you, but all my life is in you. My father gave me a heart, but you have taught it to beat. The whole world may condemn me; what does it matter if I stand acquitted in your eyes, for you have no right to think ill of me for the faults which a tyrannous love has forced me to commit for you! Do you think me an unnatural daughter? Oh, no! no one could help loving such a dear kind father as ours. But how could I hide the inevitable consequences of our miserable marriages from him? Why did he allow us to marry when he did? Was it not his duty to think for us and foresee for us? To-day I know he suffers as much as we do, but how can it be helped? And as for comforting him we could not comfort him in the least. Our resignation would give him more pain and hurt him far more than complaints and upbraidings. There are times in life when everything turns to bitterness."

Eugène was silent; the artless and sincere outpouring made an impression on him.

Parisian women are often false, intoxicated with vanity, selfish and self-absorbed, frivolous and shallow; yet of all women, when they love, they sacrifice their personal feelings to their passion; they rise but so much the higher for all the pettiness overcome in their nature, and become sublime. Then Eugène was struck by the profound discernment and insight displayed by this woman in judging of natural affection, when a privileged affection has separated and set her at a distance apart. Mme. de Nucingen was piqued by the silence.

"What are you thinking about?" she asked.

"I am thinking about what you said just now. Hitherto I have always felt sure that I cared far more for you than you did for me."

She smiled, and would not give way to the happiness she felt, lest their talk should exceed the conventional limits of propriety. She had never heard the vibrating tones of a sincere and youthful love; a few more words and she feared for her self-control.

"Eugène," she said, changing the conversation, "I wonder whether you know what has been happening? All Paris will go to Mme. de Beauséant's to-morrow. The Rochefides and the Marquis d'Ajuda have agreed to keep the matter a profound secret, but to-morrow the King will sign the marriage-contract, and your poor cousin the Vicomtesse knows nothing of it as yet. She cannot put off her ball, and the Marquis will not be there. People are wondering what will happen?"

"The world laughs at baseness and connives at it. But this will kill Mme. de Beauséant."

"Oh, no," said Delphine, smiling, "you do not know that kind of woman. Why, all Paris will be there, and so shall I; I ought to go there for your sake."

"Perhaps, after all, it is one of those absurd reports that people set in circulation here."

"We shall know the truth to-morrow."

Eugène did not return to the Maison Vauquer. He could not forego the pleasure of occupying his new rooms in the Rue d'Artois. Yesterday evening he had been obliged to leave Delphine soon after midnight, but that night it was Delphine who stayed with him until two o'clock in the morning. He rose late, and waited for Mme. de Nucingen, who came about noon to breakfast with him. Youth snatches eagerly at these rosy moments of happiness, and Eugène had almost forgotten Goriot's existence. The pretty things that surrounded him were growing familiar; this domestication in itself was one long festival for him, and Mme. de Nucingen was there to glorify it all by her presence. It was four o'clock before they thought of Goriot, and of how he had looked forward to the new life in that house. Eugène said that the old man ought to be moved at once, lest he should grow too ill to move. He left Delphine, and hurried back to the lodging-house. Neither old Goriot nor young Bianchon was in the dining-room with the others.

"Aha!" said the painter as Eugène came in, "Father Goriot has broken down at last. Bianchon is upstairs with him. One of his daughters—the Comtesse de Restaurama—came to see the old gentleman, and he would get up and go out, and made himself worse. Society is about to lose one of its brightest ornaments."

Rastignac sprang to the staircase.

"Hey! M. Eugène!"

"M. Eugène, the mistress is calling you," shouted Sylvie.

"It is this, sir," said the widow. "You and M. Goriot should by rights have moved out on the 15th of February. That was three days ago; to-day is the 18th, I ought really to be paid a month in advance; but if you will engage to pay for both, I shall be quite satisfied."

"Why can't you trust him?"

"Trust him, indeed! If the old gentleman went off his head and died, those daughters of his would not pay me a farthing, and his things won't fetch ten francs. This morning he went out with all the spoons and forks he has left, I don't know why. He had got himself up to look quite young, and—Lord, forgive me—but I thought he had rouge on his cheeks; he looked quite young again."

"I will be responsible," said Eugène, shuddering with horror, for he foresaw the end.

He climbed the stairs and reached old Goriot's room. The old man was tossing on his bed. Bianchon was with him.

"Good-evening, father," said Eugène.

The old man turned his glassy eyes on him, smiled gently, and said—

"How is *she?*"

"She is quite well. But how are you?"

"There is nothing much the matter."

"Don't tire him," said Bianchon, drawing Eugène into a corner of the room.

"Well?" said Rastignac.

"Nothing but a miracle can save him now. Serious congestion has set in; I have put on mustard plasters, and luckily he can feel them, they are acting."

"Is it possible to move him?"

"Quite out of the question. He must stay where he is, and be kept as quiet as possible——"

"Dear Bianchon," said Eugène, "we will nurse him between us."

"I have had the head physician round from my hospital to see him."

"And what did he say?"

"He will give no opinion till to-morrow evening. He promised to look in again at the end of the day. Unluckily, the preposterous creature must needs go and do something foolish this morning; he will not say what it was. He is as obstinate as a mule. As soon as I begin to talk to him he pretends not to hear, and lies as if he were asleep instead of answering, or if he opens his eyes he begins to groan. Some time this morning he went out on foot in the streets, nobody knows where he went, and he took everything that he had of any value with him. He has been driving some confounded bargain, and it has been too much for his strength. One of his daughters has been here."

"Was it the Countess?" asked Eugène. "A tall, dark-haired woman, with large bright eyes, slender figure, and little feet?"

"Yes."

"Leave him to me for a bit," said Rastignac. "I will make him confess; he will tell me all about it."

"And meanwhile I will get my dinner. But try not to excite him; there is still some hope left."

"All right."

"How they will enjoy themselves to-morrow," said old Goriot when they were alone. "They are going to a grand ball."

"What were you doing this morning, papa, to make yourself so poorly this evening that you have to stop in bed?"

"Nothing."

"Did not Anastasie come to see you?" demanded Rastignac.

"Yes," said old Goriot.

"Well, then, don't keep anything from me. What more did she want of you?"

"Oh, she was very miserable," he answered, gathering up all his strength to speak. "It was this way, my boy. Since that affair of the diamonds, Nasie has not had a penny of her own. For this ball she had ordered a golden gown like a setting for a jewel! Her mantua maker, a woman without a conscience, would not give her credit, so Nasie's waiting-woman advanced a thousand francs on account. Poor Nasie! reduced to such shifts! It cut me to the heart to think of it! But when Nasie's maid saw how things were between her master and mistress, she was afraid of losing her money, and came to an understanding with the dressmaker, and the woman refuses to send the ball-dress until the money is paid. The gown is ready, and the ball is to-morrow night; Nasie was in despair. She wanted to borrow my forks and spoons to pawn them. Her husband is determined that she shall go and wear the diamonds, so as to contradict the stories that are told all over Paris. How can she go to that heartless scoundrel and say, 'I owe a thousand francs to my dress-maker; pay her for me'? She cannot. I saw that myself. Delphine will be there too in a superb toilet, and Anatasie ought not to be outshone by her youngest sister. And then—she was drowned in tears, poor girl! I felt so humbled yesterday when I had not the twelve thousand francs, that I would have given the rest of my miserable life to wipe out that wrong. You see, I could have borne anything once, but latterly this want of money has broken my heart. Oh! I did not do it by halves; I titivated myself up a bit, and went out and sold my spoons and forks and buckles for six hundred francs; then I went to old Daddy Gobseck, and sold a year's interest in my annuity for four hundred francs down. Pshaw! I can live on dry bread, as I did when I was a young man; if I have done it before, I can do it again. My Nasie shall have one happy evening, at any rate. She shall be smart. The bank-note for a thousand francs is here under my pillow; it warms me to have it lying there under my head, for it is going to make my poor Nasie happy. She can turn that bad girl Victorie out of the house. A servant that cannot trust her mistress, did anyone ever hear the like! I shall be quite well to-morrow. Nasie is coming at ten o'clock. They must not think that I am ill, or they will not go to the ball; they will stop and take care of me. To-morrow Nasie will come and hold me in her arms as if I were one of her children; her kisses will make me well again. After all, I might have spent the thousand francs on physic; I would far rather give them to my little Nasie, who can charm all the pain away. At any rate, I am some comfort to her in her misery; and that makes up for my unkindness in buying an annuity. She is in the depths, and I cannot draw her out of them now. Oh! I will go into business again, I will buy wheat in Odessa; out there, wheat fetches a quarter of the price it sells for here. There is a law against the importation of grain, but the good folk who made the law forgot to prohibit the introduction of wheat products and food stuffs made from corn. Hey! hey! . . . That struck me this morning. There is a fine trade to be done in starch."

Eugène, watching the old man's face, thought that his friend was light-headed.

"Come," he said, "do not talk any more, you must rest——" Just then Bianchon came up, and Eugène went down to dinner.

The two students sat up with him that night, relieving each other in turn. Bianchon brought up his medical books and studied; Eugène wrote letters home to his mother and sisters. Next morning Bianchon thought the symptoms more hopeful, but the patient's condition demanded continual attention, which the two students alone were willing to give—a task impossible to describe in the squeamish phraseology of the epoch. Leeches must be applied to the wasted body; the poultices and hot foot-baths, and other details of the treatment, required the physical strength and devotion of the two young men. Mme. de Restaud did not come; but she sent a messenger for the money.

"I expected she would come herself, but it would have been a pity for her to come, she would have been anxious about me," said the father, and to all appearance he was well content.

At seven o'clock that evening Thérèse came with a letter from Delphine.

"What are you doing, dear friend? I have been loved for a very little while, and am I neglected already? In the confidences of heart and heart, I have learned to know your soul—you are too noble not to be faithful forever, for you know that love with all its infinite subtle changes of feeling is never the same. Once you said, as we were listening to the Prayer in *Mosè in Egitto*, 'For some it is the monotony of a single note; for others, it is the infinite of sound.' Remember that I am expecting you this evening to take me to Mme. de Beauséant's ball. Everyone knows now that the King signed M. d'Ajuda's marriage-contract this morning, and the poor Vicomtesse knew nothing of it until two o'clock this afternoon. All Paris will flock to her house, of course, just as a crowd fills the Place de Grève to see an execution. It is horrible, is it not, to go out of curiosity to see if she will hide her anguish, and whether she will die courageously? I certainly should not go, my friend, if I had been at her house before; but, of course, she will not receive society any more after this, and all my efforts would be in vain. My position is a very unusual one, and besides, I am going there partly on your account. I am waiting for you. If you are not beside me in less than two hours, I do not know whether I could forgive such treason."

Rastignac took up a pen and wrote—

"I am waiting till the doctor comes to know if there is any hope of your father's life. He is lying dangerously ill. I will come and bring you the news, but I am afraid it may be a sentence of death. When I come you can decide whether you can go to the ball.—Yours a thousand times."

At half-past eight the doctor arrived. He did not take a very hopeful view of the case, but thought that there was no immediate danger. Improvements and relapses might be expected, and the good man's life and reason hung in the balance.

"It would be better for him to die at once," the doctor said as he took leave.

Eugène left Goriot to Bianchon's care, and went to carry the sad news to Mme. de Nucingen. Family feeling lingered in her, and this must put an end for the present to her plans of amusement.

"Tell her to enjoy her evening as if nothing had happened," cried Goriot. He had been lying in a sort of stupor, but he suddenly sat upright as Eugène went out.

Eugène, half heartbroken, entered Delphine's room. Her hair had been dressed; she wore her dancing slippers; she had only to put on her ball-dress; but when the artist is giving the finishing stroke to his creation, the last touches require more time than the whole groundwork of the picture.

"Why! you are not dressed!" she cried.

"Madame, your father——"

"My father again!" she exclaimed, breaking in upon him. "You need not teach me what is due to my father. I have known my father this long while. Not a word, Eugène. I will hear what you have to say when you are dressed. My carriage is waiting, take it, go round to your rooms and dress. Thérèse has put out everything in readiness for you. Come back as soon as you can; we will talk about my father on the way to Mme. de Beauséant's. We must go early; if we have to wait our turn in a row of carriages, we shall be lucky if we get there by eleven o'clock."

"Madame——"

"Quick! not a word!" she cried, darting into her dressing-room for a necklace.

"Do go, M. Eugène, or you will vex Madame," said Thérèse, hurrying him away; and Eugène was too horror-stricken by this elegant parricide to resist.

He went to his rooms and dressed, sad, thoughtful, and dispirited. The world of Paris was like an ocean of mud for him just then; and it seemed that whoever set foot in that black mire must needs sink into it up to the chin.

"Their crimes are paltry," said Eugène to himself. "Vautrin was greater."

He had seen society in its three great phases—Obedience, Struggle, and Revolt; the Family, the World, and Vautrin; and he hesitated in his choice. Obedience was dull, Revolt impossible, Struggle hazardous. His thoughts wandered back to the home circle. He thought of the quiet uneventful life, the pure happiness of the days spent among those who loved him there. Those loving and beloved beings passed their lives in obedience to the natural laws of the hearth, and in that obedience found a deep and constant serenity, unvexed by torments such as these. Yet, for all his good impulses, he could not bring himself to make profession of the religion of pure souls to Delphine, nor to prescribe the duties of piety to her in the name of love. His education had begun to bear its fruits; he loved selfishly already. Besides, his tact had discovered to him the real nature of Delphine; he divined instinctively that she was capable of stepping over her father's corpse to go to the ball; and within himself he felt that he had neither the strength of mind to play the part of mentor, nor the strength of character to vex her, nor the courage to leave her to go alone.

"She would never forgive me for putting her in the wrong over it," he said to himself. Then he turned the doctor's dictum over in his mind; he tried to believe that Goriot was not so dangerously ill as he had imagined, and ended by collecting together a sufficient quantity of traitorous excuses for Delphine's conduct. She did not know how ill her father was; the kind old man himself would have made her go to the ball if she had gone to see him. So often it happens that this one or that stands condemned by the social laws that govern family relations; and yet there are peculiar circumstances in the case, differences of temperament, divergent interests, innumerable complications of family life that excuse the apparent offense.

Eugène did not wish to see too clearly; he was ready to sacrifice his conscience to his mistress. Within the last few days his whole life had undergone a change. Woman had entered into his world and thrown it into chaos, family claims dwindled away before her; she had appropriated all his being to her uses. Rastignac and Delphine found each other at a crisis in their lives when their union gave them the most poignant bliss. Their passion, so long proved, had only gained in strength by the gratified desire that often extinguishes passion. This woman was his, and Eugène recognized that not until then had he loved her; perhaps love is only gratitude for pleasure. This woman, vile or sublime, he adored for the pleasures she had brought as her dower; and Delphine loved Rastignac as Tantalus would have loved some angel who had satisfied his hunger and quenched the burning thirst in his parched throat.

"Well," said Mme. de Nucingen when he came back in evening dress, "how is my father?"

"Very dangerously ill," he answered; "if you will grant me a proof of your affection, we will just go in to see him on the way."

"Very well," she said. "Yes, but afterwards. Dear Eugène, do be nice, and don't preach to me. Come."

They set out. Eugène said nothing for a while.

"What is it now?" she asked.

"I can hear the death-rattle in your father's throat," he said, almost angrily. And with the hot indignation of youth, he told the story of Mme. de Restaud's vanity and cruelty, of her father's final act of self-sacrifice, that had brought about this struggle between life and death, of the price that had been paid for Anastasie's golden embroideries. Delphine cried.

"I shall look frightful," she thought. She dried her tears.

"I will nurse my father; I will not leave his bedside," she said aloud.

"Ah! now you are as I would have you," exclaimed Rastignac.

The lamps of five hundred carriages lit up the darkness about the Hôtel de Beauséant. A gendarme in all the glory of his uniform stood on either side of the brightly lighted gateway. The great world was flocking thither that night in its eager curiosity to see the great lady at the moment of her fall, and the rooms on the ground floor were already full to overflowing, when Mme. de Nucingen and Rastignac appeared. Never since Louis XIV. tore her lover away from

La grande Mademoiselle, and the whole Court hastened to visit that unfortunate princess, had a disastrous love affair made such a sensation in Paris. But the youngest daughter of the almost royal house of Burgundy had risen proudly above her pain, and moved till the last moment like a queen in this world—its vanities had always been valueless for her, save in so far as they contributed to the triumph of her passion. The salons were filled with the most beautiful women in Paris, resplendent in their toilets, and radiant with smiles. Ministers and ambassadors, the most distinguished men at Court, men bedizened with decorations, stars, and ribbons, men who bore the most illustrious names in France, had gathered about the Vicomtesse.

The music of the orchestra vibrated in wave after wave of sound from the golden ceiling of the palace, now made desolate for its queen.

Mme. de Beauséant stood at the door of the first salon to receive the guests who were styled her friends. She was dressed in white, and wore no ornament in the plaits of hair braided about her head; her face was calm; there was no sign there of pride, nor of pain, nor of joy that she did not feel. No one could read her soul; she stood there like some Niobe carved in marble. For a few intimate friends there was a tinge of satire in her smile; but no scrutiny saw any change in her, nor had she looked otherwise in the days of the glory of her happiness. The most callous of her guests admired her as young Rome applauded some gladiator who could die smiling. It seemed as if society had adorned itself for a last audience of one of its sovereigns.

"I was afraid that you would not come," she said to Rastignac.

"Madame," he said, in an unsteady voice, taking her speech as a reproach, "I shall be the last to go, that is why I am here."

"Good," she said, and she took his hand. "You are perhaps the only one that I can trust here among all these. Oh, my friend, when you love, love a woman whom you are sure that you can love always. Never forsake a woman."

She took Rastignac's arm, and went towards a sofa in the card-room.

"I want you to go to the Marquis," she said. "Jacques, my footman, will go with you; he has a letter that you will take. I am asking the Marquis to give my letters back to me. He will give them all up, I like to think that. When you have my letters, go up to my room with them. Someone shall bring me word."

She rose to go to meet the Duchesse de Langeais, her most intimate friend, who had come like the rest of the world.

Rastignac went. He asked for the Marquis d'Ajuda at the Hôtel Rochefide, feeling certain that the latter would be spending his evening there, and so it proved. The Marquis went to his own house with Rastignac, and gave a casket to the student, saying as he did so, "They are all there."

He seemed as if he was about to say something to Eugène, to ask about the ball, or the Vicomtesse; perhaps he was on the brink of the confession that, even then, he was in despair, and knew that his marriage had been a fatal mistake; but a proud gleam shone in his eyes, and with deplorable courage he kept his noblest feelings a secret.

"Do not even mention my name to her, my dear Eugène." He grasped Rastignac's hand sadly and affectionately, and turned away from him. Eugène went back to the Hôtel Beauséant, the servant took him to the Vicomtesse's room. There were signs there of preparations for a journey. He sat down by the fire, fixed his eyes on the cedar wood casket, and fell into deep mournful musings. Mme. de Beauséant loomed large in these imaginations, like a goddess in the Iliad.

"Ah! my friend! . . ." said the Vicomtesse; she crossed the room and laid her hand on Rastignac's shoulder. He saw the tears in his cousin's uplifted eyes, saw that one hand was raised to take the casket, and that the fingers of the other trembled. Suddenly she took the casket, put it in the fire, and watched it burn.

"They are dancing," she said. "They all came very early; but death will be long in coming. Hush! my friend," and she laid a finger on Rastignac's lips, seeing that he was about to speak. "I shall never see Paris again. I am taking my leave of this world. At five o'clock this morning I shall set out on my journey; I mean to bury myself in the remotest part of Normandy. I have had very little time to make my arrangements; since three o'clock this afternoon I have been busy signing documents, setting my affairs in order; there was no one whom I could send to . . ."

She broke off.

"He was sure to be . . ."

Again she broke off; the weight of her sorrow was more than she could bear. In such moments as these everything is agony, and some words are impossible to utter.

"And so I counted upon you to do me this last piece of service this evening," she said. "I should like to give you some pledge of friendship. I shall often think of you. You have seemed to me to be kind and noble, fresh-hearted and true, in this world where such qualities are seldom found. I should like you to think sometimes of me. Stay," she said, glancing about her, "there is this box that has held my gloves. Every time I opened it before going to a ball or to the theater, I used to feel that I must be beautiful, because I was so happy; and I never touched it except to lay some gracious memory in it: there is so much of my old self in it, of a Mme. de Beauséant who now lives no longer. Will you take it? I will leave directions that it is to be sent to you in the Rue d'Artois.—Mme. de Nucingen looked very charming this evening. Eugène, you must love her. Perhaps we may never see each other again, my friend; but be sure of this, that I shall pray for you who have been kind to me.—Now let us go downstairs. People shall not think that I am weeping. I have all time and eternity before me, and where I am going I shall be alone, and no one will ask me the reason of my tears. One last look round first."

She stood for a moment. Then she covered her eyes with her hands for an instant, dashed away the tears, bathed her face with cold water, and took the student's arm.

"Let us go!" she said.

This suffering, endured with such noble fortitude, shook Eugène with a more violent emotion than he had felt before. They went back to the ballroom, and Mme. de Beauséant went through the rooms on Eugène's arm—the last delicately gracious act of a gracious woman. In another moment he saw the sisters, Mme. de Restaud and Mme. de Nucingen.

The Countess shone in all the glory of her magnificent diamonds; every stone must have scorched like fire, she was never to wear them again. Strong as love and pride might be in her, she found it difficult to meet her husband's eyes. The sight of her was scarcely calculated to lighten Rastignac's sad thoughts; through the blaze of those diamonds he seemed to see the wretched pallet-bed on which old Goriot was lying. The Vicomtesse misread his melancholy; she withdrew her hand from his arm.

"Come," she said, "I must not deprive you of a pleasure."

Eugène was soon claimed by Delphine. She was delighted with the impression that she had made, and eager to lay at her lover's feet the homage she had received in this new world in which she hoped to live and move henceforth.

"What do you think of Nasie?" she asked him.

"She has discounted everything, even her own father's death," said Rastignac.

Towards four o'clock in the morning the rooms began to empty. A little later the music ceased, and the Duchesse de Langeais and Rastignac were left in the great ballroom. The Vicomtesse, who thought to find the student there alone, came back there at the last. She had taken leave of M. de Beauséant, who had gone off to bed, saying again as he went, "It is a great pity, my dear, to shut yourself up at your age! Pray stay among us."

Mme. de Beauséant saw the Duchess, and, in spite of herself, an exclamation broke from her.

"I saw how it was, Clara," said Mme. de Langeais. "You are going from among us, and you will never come back. But you must not go until you have heard me, until we have understood each other."

She took her friend's arm, and they went together into the next room. There the Duchess looked at her with tears in her eyes; she held her friend in a close embrace, and kissed her cheek.

"I could not let you go without a word, dearest; the remorse would have been too hard to bear. You can count upon me as surely as upon yourself. You have shown yourself great this evening; I feel that I am worthy of our friendship, and I mean to prove myself worthy of it. I have not always been kind; I was in the wrong; forgive me, dearest; I wish I could unsay anything that may have hurt you; I take back those words. One common sorrow has brought us together again, for I do not know which of us is the more miserable. M. de Montriveau was not here to-night; do you understand what that means?—None of those who saw you to-night, Clara, will ever forget you. I mean to make one last effort. If I fail, I shall go into a convent. Clara, where are you going?"

"Into Normandy, to Courcelles. I shall love and pray there until the day when God shall take me from this world.—M. de Rastignac!" called the Vicomtesse, in a tremulous voice, remembering that the young man was waiting there.

The student knelt to kiss his cousin's hand.

"Good-by, Antoinette!" said Mme. de Beauséant. "May you be happy."—She turned to the student. "You are young," she said; "you have some beliefs still left. I have been privileged, like some dying people, to find sincere and reverent feeling in those about me as I take my leave of this world."

It was nearly five o'clock that morning when Rastignac came away. He had put Mme. de Beauséant into her traveling carriage, and received her last farewells, spoken amid fast-falling tears; for no greatness is so great that it can rise above the laws of human affection, or live beyond the jurisdiction of pain, as certain demagogues would have the people believe. Eugène returned on foot to the Maison Vauquer through the cold and darkness. His education was nearly complete.

"There is no hope for poor old Goriot," said Bianchon, as Rastignac came into the room. Eugene looked for a while at the sleeping man, then he turned to his friend. "Dear fellow, you are content with the modest career you have marked out for yourself; keep to it. I am in hell, and I must stay there. Believe everything that you hear said of the world, nothing is too impossibly bad. No Juvenal could paint the horrors hidden away under the covering of gems and gold."

At two o'clock in the afternoon Bianchon came to wake Rastignac, and begged him to take charge of Goriot, who

M—9

had grown worse as the day wore on. The medical student was obliged to go out.

"Poor old man, he has not two days to live, maybe not many hours," he said; "but we must do our utmost, all the same, to fight the disease. It will be a very troublesome case, and we shall want money. We can nurse him between us, of course, but, for my own part, I have not a penny. I have turned out his pockets, and rummaged through his drawers—result, *nix*. I asked him about it while his mind was clear, and he told me had not a farthing of his own. What have you?"

"I have twenty francs left," said Rastignac; "but I will take them to the roulette table, I shall be sure to win."

"And if you lose?"

"Then I shall go to his sons-in-law and his daughters and ask them for money."

"And suppose they refuse?" Bianchon retorted. "The most pressing thing just now is not really money; we must put mustard poultices, as hot as they can be made, on his feet and legs. If he calls out, there is still some hope for him. You know how to set about doing it, and besides, Christophe will help you. I am going round to the dispensary to persuade them to let us have the things we want on credit. It is a pity that we could not move him to the hospital; poor fellow, he would be better there. Well, come along, I leave you in charge; you must stay with him till I come back."

The two young men went back to the room where the old man was lying. Eugène was startled at the change in Goriot's face, so livid, distorted, and feeble.

"How are you, papa?" he said, bending over the pallet-bed. Goriot turned his dull eyes upon Eugène, looked at him attentively, and did not recognize him. It was more than the student could bear; the tears came into his eyes.

"Bianchon, ought we to have curtains put up in the windows?"

"No, the temperature and the light do not affect him now. It would be a good thing for him if he felt heat or cold; but we must have a fire in any case to make tisanes and heat the other things. I will send round a few sticks; they will last till we can have in some firewood. I burned all the bark fuel you had left, as well as his, poor man, yesterday and during the night. The place was so damp that the water stood in drops on the walls; I could hardly get the room dry. Christophe came in and swept the floor, but the place is like a stable; I had to burn juniper, the smell was something horrible."

"*Mon Dieu!*" said Rastignac. "To think of those daughters of his."

"One moment, if he asks for something to drink, give him this," said the house student, pointing to a large white jar. "If he begins to groan, and the belly feels hot and hard to the touch, you know what to do; get Christophe to help you. If he should happen to grow much excited, and begin to talk a good deal, and even to ramble in his talk, do not be alarmed. It would not be a bad symptom. But send Christophe to the Hospice Cochin. Our doctor, my chum, or I will come and apply moxas. We had a great consultation this morning while you were asleep. A surgeon, a pupil of Gall's came, and our house surgeon, and the head physician from the Hôtel-Dieu. Those gentlemen considered that the symptoms were very unusual and interesting; the case must be carefully watched, for it throws a light on several obscure and rather important scientific problems. One of the authorities says that if there is more pressure of serum on one or other portions of the brain, it should affect his mental capacities in such and such directions. So if he should talk, notice very carefully what kind of ideas his mind seems to run on; whether memory, or penetration, or the reasoning faculties are exercised; whether sentiments or practical questions fill his thoughts; whether he makes forecasts or dwells on the past; in fact, you must be prepared to give an accurate report of him. It is quite likely that the extravasation fills the whole brain, in which case he will die in the imbecile state in which he is lying now. You cannot tell anything about these mysterious nervous diseases. Suppose the crash came here," said Bianchon, touching the back of the head, "very strange things have been known to happen; the brain sometimes partially recovers, and death is delayed. Or the congested matter may pass out of the brain altogether through channels which can only be determined by a post-mortem examination. There is an old man at the Hospital for Incurables, an imbecile patient, in his case the effusion has followed the direction of the spinal cord; he suffers horrid agonies, but he lives."

"Did they enjoy themselves?" It was old Goriot who spoke. He had recognized Eugène.

"Oh! he thinks of nothing but his daughters," said Bianchon. "Scores of times last night he said to me, 'They are dancing now! She has her dress.' He called them by their names. He made me cry, the Devil take it, calling with that tone in his voice, for 'Delphine! my little Delphine! and Nasie!' Upon my word," said the medical student, "it was enough to make anyone burst out crying."

"Delphine," said the old man, "she is there, isn't she? I knew she was there," and his eyes sought the door.

"I am going down now to tell Sylvie to get the poultices ready," said Bianchon. "They ought to go on at once."

Rastignac was left alone with the old man. He sat at the foot of the bed, and gazed at the face before him, so horribly changed that it was shocking to see.

"Noble natures cannot dwell in this world," he said; "Mme. de Beauséant has fled from it, and there he lies dying. What place indeed is there in the shallow petty frivolous thing called society for noble thoughts and feelings?"

Pictures of yesterday's ball rose up in his memory, in strange contrast to the deathbed before him. Bianchon suddenly appeared.

"I say, Eugène, I have just seen our head surgeon at the hospital, and I ran all the way back here. If the old man shows any signs of reason, if he begins to talk, cover him with a mustard poultice from the neck to the base of the spine, and send round for us."

"Dear Bianchon," exclaimed Eugène.

"Oh! it is an interesting case from a scientific point of view," said the medical student, with all the enthusiasm of a neophyte.

"So!" said Eugène. "Am I really the only one who cares for the poor old man for his own sake?"

"You would not have said so if you had seen me this morning," returned Bianchon, who did not take offense at this speech. "Doctors who have seen a good deal of practice never see anything but the disease, but, my dear fellow, I can see the patient still."

He went. Eugène was left alone with the old man, and with an apprehension of a crisis that set in, in fact, before very long.

"Ah! dear boy, is that you?" said old Goriot, recognizing Eugène.

"Do you feel better?" asked the law student, taking his hand.

"Yes. My head felt as if it were being screwed in a vice, but now it is set free again. Did you see my girls? They will be here directly; as soon as they know that I am ill they will hurry here at once; they used to take such care of me in the Rue de la Jussienne! Great Heavens! if only my room was fit for them to come into! There has been a young man here, who has burned up all my bark fuel."

"I can hear Christophe coming upstairs," Eugène answered. "He is bringing up some firewood that that young man has sent you."

"Good, but how am I to pay for the wood? I have not a penny left, dear boy. I have given everything, everything. I am a pauper now. Well, at least the golden gown was grand, was it not? (Ah! what pain this is!) Thanks, Christophe! God will reward you, my boy; I have nothing left now."

Eugène went over to Christophe and whispered in the man's ear, "I will pay you well, and Sylvie too, for your trouble."

"My daughters told you that they were coming, didn't they, Christophe? Go again to them, and I will give you five francs. Tell them that I am not feeling well, that I should like to kiss them both and see them once again before I die. Tell them that, but don't alarm them more than you can help."

Rastignac signed to Christophe to go, and the man went.

"They will come before long," the old man went on. "I know them so well. My tender-hearted Delphine! If I am going to die, she will feel it so much! And so will Nasie. I do not want to die; they will cry if I die; and if I die, dear Eugène, I shall not see them any more. It will be very dreary there where I am going. For a father it is hell to be without your children; I have served my apprenticeship already since they married. My heaven was in the Rue de la Jussienne. Eugène, do you think that if I go to heaven I could come back to earth, and be near them in spirit? I have heard some such things said. Is it true? It is as if I could see them at this moment as they used to be when we all lived in the Rue de la Jussienne. They used to come downstairs of a morning. 'Good-morning, papa!' they used to say, and I would take them on my knees; we had all sorts of little games of play together, and they had such pretty coaxing ways.

"We always had breakfast together, too, every morning, and they had dinner with me—in fact, I was a father then. I enjoyed my children. They did not think for themselves so long as they lived in the Rue de la Jussienne; they knew nothing of the world; they loved me with all their hearts. *Mon Dieu!* why could they not always be little girls? (Oh! my head! this racking pain in my head!) Ah! ah! forgive me, children; this pain is fearful; it must be agony indeed, for you have used me to endure pain. *Mon Dieu!* if only I held their hands in mine, I should not feel it at all.—Do you think that they are on the way? Christophe is so stupid; I ought to have gone myself. *He* will see them. But you went to the ball yesterday; just tell me how they looked. They did not know that I was ill, did they, or they would not have been dancing, poor little things? Oh! I must not be ill any longer. They stand too much in need of me; their fortunes are in danger. And such husbands as they are bound to! I must get well! (Oh! what pain this is! what pain this is! . . . ah! ah!)—I must get well, you see; for they *must* have money, and I know how to set about making some. I will go to Odessa and manufacture starch there. I am an old hand, I will make millions. (Oh! this is agony!)"

Goriot was silent for a moment; it seemed to require his whole strength to endure the pain.

"If they were here, I should not complain," he said. "So why should I complain now?"

He seemed to grow drowsy with exhaustion, and lay quietly for a long time. Christophe came back; and Rastignac, thinking that Goriot was asleep, allowed the man to give his story aloud.

"First of all, sir, I went to Mme. la Comtesse," he said; "but she and her husband were so busy that I couldn't get to speak to her. When I insisted that I must see her, M. de Restaud came out to me himself, and went on like this—'M. Goriot is dying, is he? Very well, it is the best thing he can do. I want Mme. de Restaud to transact some important business, when it is all finished she can go.' The gentleman looked angry, I thought. I was just going away when Mme. de Restaud came out into an antechamber through a door that I did not notice, and said, 'Christophe, tell my father that my husband wants me to discuss some matters with him, and I cannot leave the house, the life or death of my children is at stake; but as soon as it is over, I will come.' As for Mme. la Baronne, that is another story! I could not speak to her either, and I did not even see her. Her waiting-woman said, 'Ah yes, but Madame only came back from a ball at a quarter to five this morning; she is asleep now, and if I wake her before mid-day she will be cross. As soon as she rings, I will go and tell her that her father is worse. It will be time enough then to tell her bad news!' I begged and prayed, but, there! it was no good. Then I asked for M. le Baron, but he was out."

"To think that neither of his daughters should come!" exclaimed Rastignac. "I will write to them both."

"Neither of them!" cried the old man, sitting upright in bed. "They are busy, they are asleep, they will not come! I knew that they would not. Not until you are dying do you know your children. . . . Oh! my friend, do not marry, do not have children! You give them life; they give you your deathblow. You bring them into the world, and they send you out of it. No, they will not come. I have known that these ten years. Sometimes I have told myself so, but I did not dare to believe it."

The tears gathered and stood without overflowing the red sockets.

"Ah! if I were rich still, if I had kept my money, if I had not given all to them, they would be with me now; they would fawn on me and cover my cheeks with their kisses! I should be living in a great mansion; I should have grand apartments and servants and a fire in my room; and *they* would be about me all in tears, and their husbands and their children. I should have had all that; now—I have nothing. Money brings everything to you; even your daughters. My money. Oh! where is my money? If I had plenty of money to leave behind me, they would nurse me and tend me; I should hear their voices, I should see their faces. Ah, God! who knows? They both of them have hearts of stone. I loved them too much; it was not likely that they should love me. A father ought always to be rich; he ought to keep his children well in hand, like unruly horses. I have gone down on my knees to them. Wretches! this is the crowning act that brings the last ten years to a proper close. If you but knew how much they made of me just after they were married. (Oh! this is cruel torture!) I had just given them each eight hundred thousand francs; they were bound to be civil to me after that, and their husbands too were civil. I used to go to their houses: it was, 'My kind father' here, 'My dear father' there. There was always a place for me at their tables. I used to dine with their husbands now and then, and they were very respectful to me. I was still worth something, they thought. How should they know? I had not said anything about my affairs. It is worth while to be civil to a man who has given his daughters eight hundred thousand francs apiece; and they showed me every attention then—but it was all for my money. Grand people are not great. I found that out by experience! I went to the theater with them in their carriage; I might stay as long as I cared to stay at their evening parties. In fact, they acknowledged me their father; publicly they owned that they were my daughters. But I was always a shrewd one, you see, and nothing was lost upon me. Everything went straight to the mark and pierced my heart. I saw quite well that it was all sham and pretense, but there is no help for such things as these. I felt less at my ease at their dinner-table than I did downstairs here. I had nothing to say for myself. So these grand folks would ask in my son-in-law's ear, 'Who may that gentleman be?'—'The father-in-law with the dollars; he is very rich.'—'The devil, he is!' they would say, and look again at me with the respect due to my money. Well, if I was in the way sometimes, I paid dearly for my mistakes. And besides, who is perfect? (My head is one sore!) Dear M. Eugène, I am suffering so now, that a man might die of the pain; but it is nothing, nothing to be compared with the pain I endured when Anastasie made me feel, for the first time, that I had said something stupid. She looked at me, and that glance of hers opened all my veins. I used to want to know everything, to be learned; and one thing I did learn thoroughly—I knew that I was not wanted here on earth.

"The next day I went to Delphine for comfort, and what should I do there but make some stupid blunder that made her angry with me. I was like one driven out of his senses. For a week I did not know what to do; I did not dare to go to see them for fear they should reproach me. And that was how they both turned me out of the house.

"Oh God! Thou knowest all the misery and anguish that I have endured; Thou hast counted all the wounds that have been dealt to me in these years that have aged and changed me and whitened my hair and drained my life; why dost Thou make me to suffer so to-day? Have I not more than expiated the sin of loving them too much? They themselves have been the instruments of vengeance; they have tortured me for my sin of affection.

"Ah, well! fathers know no better; I loved them so; I went back to them as a gambler goes to the gaming table. This love was my vice, you see, my mistress—they were everything in the world to me. They were always wanting something or other, dresses and ornaments, and what not; their maids used to tell me what they wanted, and I used to give them the things for the sake of the welcome that they bought for me. But, at the same time, they used to give me little lectures on my behavior in society; they began about it at once. Then they began to feel ashamed of me. That is what comes of having your children well brought up. I could not go to school again at my time of life. (This pain is fearful! *Mon Dieu!* These doctors! these doctors! If they would open my head, it would give me some relief!) Oh, my daughters, my daughters! Anastasie! Delphine! If I could only see them! Send for the police, and make them come to me! Justice is on my side, the whole world is on my side, I have natural rights, and the law with me. I protest! The country will go to ruin if a father's rights are trampled under foot. That is easy to see. The whole world turns on fatherly love; fatherly love is the foundation of society; it will crumble into ruin when children do not love their fathers. Oh! if I could only see them, and hear them, no matter what they said; if I could simply hear their voices, it would soothe the pain. Delphine! Delphine most of all. But tell them when they come not to look so coldly at me as they do. Oh! my friend, my good M. Eugène, you do not know what it is when all the golden light in a glance suddenly turns to a leaden gray. It has been one long winter here since the light in their eyes shone no more for me. I have had nothing but disappointments to devour. Disappointment has been my daily bread; I have lived on humiliation and insults. I have swallowed down all the affronts for which they sold me my poor stealthy little moments of joy; for I love them so! Think of it! a father hiding himself to get a glimpse of his children! I have given all my life to them, and to-day they will not give me one hour! I am hungering and thirsting for them, my heart is burning in me, but they will not come to bring me relief in the agony, for I am dying now, I feel that this is death. Do they not know what it means to trample on a father's corpse? There is a God in heaven who avenges us fathers whether we will or no.

"Oh! they will come! Come to me, darlings, and give me one more kiss; one last kiss, the Viaticum for your father who will pray God for you in heaven. I will tell Him that you have been good children to your father, and plead your cause with God! After all, it is not their fault. I tell you they are innocent, my friend. Tell everyone that it is not their fault, and no one need be distressed on my account. It is all my own fault, I taught them to trample upon me. I loved to have it so. It is no one's affair but mine; man's justice and God's justice have nothing to do in it. God would be unjust if He condemned them for anything they may have done to me. I did not behave to them properly; I was stupid enough to resign my rights. I would have humbled myself in the dust for them. What could you expect? The most beautiful nature, the noblest soul, would have been spoiled by such indulgence. I am a wretch, I am justly punished. I, and I only, am to blame for all their sins; I spoiled them. To-day they are as eager for pleasure as they used to be for sugar-plums. When they were little girls I indulged them in every whim. They had a carriage of their own when they were fifteen. They have never been crossed. I am guilty, and not they—but I sinned through love.

"My heart would open at the sound of their voices. I can hear them; they are coming. Yes! yes! they are coming. The law demands that they should be present at their father's deathbed; the law is on my side. It would only cost them the hire of a cab. I would pay that. Write to them, tell them that I have millions to leave to them! On my word of honor, yes. I am going to manufacture Italian paste foods at Odessa. I understand the trade. There are millions to be made in it. Nobody has thought of the scheme as yet. You see, there will be no waste, no damage in transit, as there always is with wheat and flour. Hey! hey! and starch too; there are millions to be made in the starch trade! You will not be telling a lie. Millions, tell them; and even if they really come because they covet the money, I would rather let them deceive me; and I shall see them in any case. I want my children! I gave them life; they are mine, mine!" and he sat upright. The head thus raised, with its scanty white hair, seemed to Eugène like a threat; every line that could still speak spoke of menace.

"There, there, dear father," said Eugène, "lie down again; I will write to them at once. As soon as Bianchon comes back I will go for them myself, if they do not come before."

"If they do not come?" repeated the old man, sobbing. "Why, I shall be dead before then; I shall die in a fit of rage, of rage! Anger is getting the better of me. I can see my whole life at this minute. I have been cheated! They do not love me—they have never loved me all their lives! It is all clear to me. They have not come, and they will not come. The longer they put off their coming, the less they are likely to give me this joy. I know them. They have never cared to guess my disappointments, my sorrows, my wants; they never cared to know my life; they will have no presentiment of my death; they do not even know the secret of my tenderness for them. Yes, I see it all now. I have laid my heart open so often, that they take everything I do for them as a matter of course. They might have asked me for the very eyes out of my head, and I would have bidden them to pluck them out. They think that all fathers are like theirs. You should always make your value felt. Their own children will avenge me. Why, for their own sakes they should come to me! Make them understand that they are laying up retribution for their own deathbeds. All crimes are summed up in this one. . . . Go to them; just tell them that if they stay away it will be parricide! There is enough laid to their charge already without adding that to the list. Cry aloud as I do now, 'Nasie! Delphine! here! Come to your father; the father who has been so kind to you is lying ill!'—Not a sound; no one comes! Then am I to die like a dog? This is to be my reward—I am forsaken at the last. They are wicked, heartless women; curses on them, I loathe them. I shall rise at night from my grave to curse them again; for, after all, my friends, have I done wrong? They are behaving very badly to me, eh? . . . What am I saying? Did you not tell me just now that Delphine was in the room? She is more tender-hearted than her sister. . . . Eugène, you are my son, you know. You will love her; be a father to her! Her sister is very unhappy. And there are their fortunes! Ah, God! I am dying, this anguish is almost more than I can bear! Cut off my head; leave me nothing but my heart."

"Christophe!" shouted Eugène, alarmed by the way in which the old man moaned, and by his cries, "go for M. Bianchon, and send a cab here for me.—I am going to fetch them, dear father; I will bring them back to you."

"Make them come! Compel them to come! Call out the Guard, the military, anything and everything, but make them come!" He looked at Eugène, and a last gleam of intelligence shone in his eyes. "Go to the authorities, to the Public Prosecutor, let them bring them here; come they shall!"

"But you have cursed them."

"Who said that!" said the old man in dull amazement. "You know quite well that I love them, I adore them! I shall be quite well again if I can see them. . . . Go for them, my good neighbor, my dear boy, you are kind-hearted; I wish I could repay you for your kindness, but I have nothing to give you now, save the blessing of a dying man. Ah! if I could only see Delphine, to tell her to pay my debt to you. If the other cannot come, bring Delphine to me at any rate. Tell her that unless she comes, you will not love her any more. She is so fond of you that she will come to me then. Give me something to drink! There is a fire in my bowels. Press something against my forehead! If my daughters would lay their hands there, I think I should get better. . . . *Mon Dieu!* who will recover their money for them when I am gone? . . . I will manufacture vermicelli out in Odessa; I will go to Odessa for their sakes."

"Here is something to drink," said Eugène, supporting the dying man on his left arm, while he held a cup of tisane to Goriot's lips.

"How you must love your own father and mother!" said the old man, and grasped the student's hand in both of his. It was a feeble, trembling grasp. "I am going to die; I shall die without seeing my daughters; do you understand? To be always thirsting, and never to drink; that has been my life for the last ten years. . . . I have no daughters, my sons-in-law killed them. No, since their marriages they have been dead to me. Fathers should petition the Chambers to pass a law against marriage. If you love your daughters, do not let them marry. A son-in-law is a rascal who poisons a girl's mind and contaminates her whole nature. Let us have no more marriages. It robs us of our daughters; we are left alone upon our deathbeds, and they are not with us then. They ought to pass a law for dying fathers. This is awful! It cries for vengeance! They cannot come, because my sons-in-law forbid them! . . . Kill them! . . . Restaud and the Alsatian, kill them both! They have murdered me between them! . . . Death or my daughters! . . . Ah! it is too late, I am dying, and they are not here! . . . Dying without them! . . . Nasie! Fifine! Why do you not come to me? your papa is going——"

"Dear Father Goriot, calm yourself. There, there, lie quietly and rest; don't worry yourself, don't think."

"I shall not see them. Oh! the agony of it!"

"You *shall* see them."

"Really?" cried the old man, still wandering. "Oh! shall I see them; I shall see them and hear their voices. I shall die happy. Ah! well, after all, I do not wish to live; I cannot stand this much longer; this pain that grows worse and worse. But, oh! to see them, to touch their dresses—ah! nothing but their dresses, that is very little; still, to feel something that belongs to them. Let me touch their hair with my fingers . . . their hair . . ."

His head fell back on the pillow, as if a sudden heavy blow had struck him down, but his hands groped feebly over the quilt, as if to find his daughters' hair.

"My blessing on them . . ." he said, making an effort, "my blessing . . ."

His voice died away. Just at that moment Bianchon came into the room.

"I met Christophe," he said; "he is gone for your cab."

Then he looked at the patient, and raised the closed eyelids with his fingers. The two students saw how dead and lusterless the eyes beneath had grown.

"He will not get over this, I am sure," said Bianchon. He felt the old man's pulse, and laid a hand over his heart.

"The machinery works still, more is the pity; in his state it would be better for him to die.

"Ah! my word, it would!"

"What is the matter with you? You are as pale as death."

"Dear fellow, the moans and cries that I have just heard. . . . There is a God! Ah! yes, yes, there is a God, and He has made a better world for us, or this world of ours would be a nightmare. I could have cried like a child; but this is too tragical, and I am sick at heart."

"We want a lot of things, you know; and where is the money to come from?"

Rastignac took out his watch.

"There, be quick and pawn it. I do not want to stop on the way to the Rue du Helder; there is not a moment to lose, I am afraid, and I must wait here till Christophe comes back. I have not a farthing; I shall have to pay the cabman when I get home again."

Rastignac rushed down the stairs, and drove off to the Rue du Helder. The awful scene through which he had just passed quickened his imagination, and he grew fiercely indignant. He reached Mme. de Restaud's house only to be told by the servant that his mistress could see no one.

"But I have brought a message from her father, who is dying," Rastignac told the man.

"The Count has given us the strictest orders, sir——"

"If it is M. de Restaud who has given the orders, tell him that his father-in-law is dying, and that I am here, and must speak with him at once."

The man went.

Eugène waited for a long while. "Perhaps her father is dying at this moment," he thought.

Then the man came back, and Eugène followed him to the little drawing-room. M. de Restaud was standing before the fireless grate, and did not ask his visitor to seat himself.

"M. le Comte," said Rastignac, "M. Goriot, your father-in-law, is lying at the point of death in a squalid den in the Latin Quarter. He has not a penny to pay for firewood; he is expected to die at any moment, and keeps calling for his daughter——"

"I feel very little affection for M. Goriot, sir, as you probably are aware," the Count answered coolly. "His character has been compromised in connection with Mme. de Restaud; he is the author of the misfortunes that have embittered my life and troubled my peace of mind. It is a matter of perfect indifference to me if he lives or dies. Now you know my feelings with regard to him. Public opinion may blame me, but I care nothing for public opinion. Just now I have other and much more important matters to think about than the things that fools and chatterers may say about me. As for Mme. de Restaud, she cannot leave the house; she is no condition to do so. And, besides, I shall not allow her to leave it. Tell her father that as soon as she has done her duty by her husband and child she shall go to see him. If she has any love for her father, she can be free to go to him, if she chooses, in a few seconds; it lies entirely with her——"

"M. le Comte, it is no business of mine to criticize your conduct; you can do as you please with your wife, but may I count upon your keeping your word with me? Well, then, promise me to tell her that her father has not twenty-four hours to live; that he looks in vain for her, and has cursed her already as he lies on his deathbed,—that is all I ask."

"You can tell her yourself," the Count answered, impressed by the thrill of indignation in Eugène's voice.

The Count led the way to the room where his wife usually sat. She was drowned in tears, and lay crouching in the depths of an arm-chair, as if she were tired of life and longed to die. It was piteous to see her. Before venturing to look at Rastignac, she glanced at her husband in evident and abject terror that spoke of complete prostration of body and mind; she seemed crushed by a tyranny both mental and physical. The Count jerked his head towards her; she construed this as a permission to speak.

"I heard all that you said, Monsieur. Tell my father that if he knew all he would forgive me. . . . I did not think there was such torture in the world as this; it is more than I can endure, Monsieur!—But I will not give way as long as I live," she said, turning to her husband. "I am a mother.—Tell my father that I have never sinned against him in spite of appearances!" she cried aloud in her despair.

Eugène bowed to the husband and wife; he guessed the meaning of the scene, and that this was a terrible crisis in the Countess's life. M. de Restaud's manner had told him that his errand was a fruitless one; he saw that Anastasie had no longer any liberty of action. He came away mazed and bewildered, and hurried to Mme. de Nucingen. Delphine was in bed.

"Poor dear Eugène, I am ill," she said. "I caught cold after the ball, and I am afraid of pneumonia. I am waiting for the doctor to come."

"If you were at death's door," Eugène broke in, "you must be carried somehow to your father. He is calling for you. If you could hear the faintest of those cries, you would not feel ill any longer."

"Eugène, I dare say my father is not quite so ill as you say; but I cannot bear to do anything that you do not approve, so I will do just as you wish. As for *him*, he would die of grief I know if I went out to see him and brought on a dangerous illness. Well, I will go as soon as I have seen the doctor.—Ah!" she cried out, "you are not wearing your watch, how is that?"

Eugène reddened.

"Eugène, Eugène! if you have sold it already or lost it. . . . Oh! it would be very wrong of you!"

The student bent over Delphine and said in her ear, "Do you want to know? Very well, then, you shall know. Your father has nothing left to pay for the shroud that they will lay him in this evening. Your watch has been pawned, for I had nothing either."

Delphine sprang out of bed, ran to her desk, and took out her purse. She gave it to Eugène, and rang the bell, crying—

"I will go, I will go at once, Eugène. Leave me, I will dress. Why, I should be an unnatural daughter! Go back; I will be there before you.—Thérèse," she called to the waiting-woman, "ask M. de Nucingen to come upstairs at once and speak to me."

Eugène was almost happy when he reached the Rue Neuve-Sainte-Geneviève; he was so glad to bring the news to the dying man that one of his daughters was coming. He fumbled in Delphine's purse for money, so as to dismiss the cab at once; and discovered that the young, beautiful, and wealthy woman of fashion had only seventy francs in her private purse.

He climbed the stairs and found Bianchon supporting Goriot, while the house surgeon from the hospital was applying moxas to the patient's back—under the direction of the physician, it was the last expedient of science, and it was tried in vain.

"Can you feel them?" asked the physician. But Goriot had caught sight of Rastignac, and answered, "They are coming, are they not?"

"There is hope yet," said the surgeon; "he can speak."

"Yes," said Eugène, "Delphine is coming."

"Oh! that is nothing!" said Bianchon; "he has been talking about his daughters all the time. He calls for them as a man impaled calls for water, they say——"

"We may as well give up," said the physician, addressing the surgeon. "Nothing more can be done now; the case is hopeless."

Bianchon and the house surgeon stretched the dying man out again on his loathsome bed.

"But the sheets ought to be changed," added the physician. "Even if there is no hope left, something is due to human nature. I shall come back again, Bianchon," he said, turning to the medical student. "If he complains again, rub some laudanum over the diaphragm."

He went, and the house surgeon went with him.

"Come, Eugène, pluck up heart, my boy," said Bianchon, as soon as they were alone; "we must set about changing his sheets, and put him into a clean shirt. Go and tell Sylvie to bring up some sheets and come and help us to make the bed."

Eugène went downstairs, and found Mme. Vauquer engaged in setting the table; Sylvie was helping her. Eugène had scarcely opened his mouth before the widow walked up to him with the acidulous sweet smile of a cautious shopkeeper who is anxious neither to lose money nor to offend a customer.

"My dear M. Eugène," she said, when he had spoken, "you know quite as well as I do that old Goriot has not a brass farthing left. If you give out clean linen for a man who is just going to turn up his eyes, you are not likely to see your sheets again, for one is sure to be wanted to wrap him in. Now, you owe me a hundred and forty-four francs as it is, add forty francs to that for the pair of sheets, and then there are several little things, besides the candle that Sylvie will give you; altogether, it will all mount up to at least two hundred francs, which is more than a poor widow like me can afford to lose. Lord! now, M. Eugène, look at it fairly. I have lost quite enough in these five days since this run of ill-luck set in for me. I would rather than ten crowns that the old gentleman had moved out as you said. It sets the other lodgers against the house. It would not take much to make me send him to the workhouse. In short, just put yourself in my place. I have to think of my establishment first, for I have my own living to make."

Eugène hurried up to Goriot's room.

"Bianchon," he cried, "the money or the watch?"

"There it is on the table, or the three hundred and sixty odd francs that are left out of it. I paid up all the old scores out of it before they let me have the things. The pawn ticket lies there under the money."

Rastignac hurried downstairs.

"Here, Madame," he said in disgust, "let us square accounts. M. Goriot will not stay much longer in your house, nor shall I——"

"Yes, he will go out feet foremost, poor old gentleman," she said, counting the francs with a half-facetious, half-lubugrious expression.

"Let us get this over," said Rastignac.

"Sylvie, look out some sheets, and go upstairs to help the gentleman."

"You won't forget Sylvie," said Mme. Vauquer in Eugène's ear; "she has been sitting up these two nights."

As soon as Eugène's back was turned, the old woman hurried after her handmaid.

"Take the sheets that have had the sides turned into the middle, number 7. Lord! they are plenty good enough for a corpse," she said in Sylvie's ear.

Eugène, by this time, was part of the way upstairs, and did not overhear the elderly economist.

"Quick," said Bianchon, "let us change his shirt. Hold him upright."

Eugène went to the head of the bed and supported the dying man, while Bianchon drew off his shirt; and then Goriot made a movement as if he tried to clutch something to his breast, uttering a low inarticulate moaning the while, like some dumb animal in mortal pain.

"Ah yes!" cried Bianchon. "It is the little locket and the chain made of hair that he wants; we took it off a while ago when we put the blisters on him. Poor fellow! he must have it again. There it lies on the chimney-piece."

Eugène went to the chimney-piece and found a little plait of faded golden hair—Mme. Goriot's hair, no doubt. He read the names on the little round locket, ANASTASIE on the one side, DELPHINE on the other. It was the symbol of his own heart that the father always wore on his breast. The curls of hair inside the locket were so fine and soft that it was plain they had been taken from two childish heads. When the old man felt the locket once more, his chest heaved with a long deep sigh of satisfaction, like a groan. It was something terrible to see, for it seemed as if the last quiver of the nerves were laid bare to their eyes, the last communication of sense to the mysterious point within whence our sympathies come and whither they go. A delirious joy lighted up the distorted face. The terrific and vivid force of the feeling that had survived the power of thought made such an impression on the students, that the dying man felt their hot tears falling on him, and gave a shrill cry of delight.

"Nasie! Fifine!"

"There is life in him yet," said Bianchon.

"What does he go on living for?" said Sylvie.

"To suffer," answered Rastignac.

Bianchon made a sign to his friend to follow his example, knelt down and passed his arms under the sick man, and Rastignac on the other side did the same, so that Sylvie, standing in readiness, might draw the sheet from beneath and replace it with the one that she had brought. Those tears, no doubt, had misled Goriot; for he gathered up all his remaining strength in a last effort, stretched out his hands, groped for the students' heads, and as his fingers caught convulsively at their hair, they heard a faint whisper—

"Ah! my angels!"

Two words, two inarticulate murmurs, shaped into words by the soul which fled forth with them as they left his lips.

"Poor dear!" cried Sylvie, melted by that exclamation; the expression of the great love raised for the last time to a sublime height by that most ghastly and involuntary of lies.

The father's last breath must have been a sigh of joy, and in that sigh his whole life was summed up; he was cheated even at the last. They laid Father Goriot upon his wretched bed with reverent hands. Thenceforward there was no expression on his face, only the painful traces of the struggle between life and death that was going on in the machine; for that kind of cerebral consciousness that distinguishes between pleasure and pain in a human being was extinguished; it was only a question of time—and the mechanism itself would be destroyed.

"He will lie like this for several hours, and die so quietly at last, that we shall not know when he goes; there will be no rattle in the throat. The brain must be completely suffused."

As he spoke there was a footstep on the staircase, and a young woman hastened up, panting for breath.

"She has come too late," said Rastignac.

But it was not Delphine; it was Thérèse, her waiting-woman, who stood in the doorway.

"M. Eugène," she said, "Monsieur and Madame have had a terrible scene about some money that Madame (poor thing!) wanted for her father. She fainted, and the doctor came, and she had to be bled, calling out all the while, 'My father is dying; I want to see papa!' It was heartbreaking to hear her——"

"That will do, Thérèse. If she came now, it would be trouble thrown away. M. Goriot cannot recognize anyone now."

"Poor, dear gentleman, is he as bad as that?" said Thérèse.

"You don't want me now, I must go and look after my dinner; it is half-past four," remarked Sylvie. The next instant she all but collided with Mme. de Restaud on the landing outside.

There was something awful and appalling in the sudden apparition of the Countess. She saw the bed of death by the dim light of the single candle, and her tears flowed at the sight of her father's passive features, from which the life had almost ebbed. Bianchon with thoughtful tact left the room.

"I could not escape soon enough," she said to Rastignac.

The student bowed sadly in reply. Mme. de Restaud took her father's hand and kissed it.

"Forgive me, father! You used to say that my voice would call you back from the grave; ah! come back for one moment to bless your penitent daughter. Do you hear me? Oh! this is fearful! No one on earth will ever bless me henceforth; everyone hates me; no one loves me but you in all the world. My own children will hate me. Take me with you, father; I will love you, I will take care of you. He does not hear me . . . I am mad . . ."

She fell on her knees, and gazed wildly at the human wreck before her.

"My cup of misery is full," she said, turning her eyes upon Eugène. "M. de Trailles has fled, leaving enormous debts behind him, and I have found out that he was deceiving me. My husband will never forgive me, and I have left my fortune in his hands. I have lost all my illusions. Alas! I have forsaken the one heart that loved me" (she pointed to her father as she spoke), "and for whom? I have held his kindness cheap, and slighted his affection; many and many a time I have given him pain, ungrateful wretch that I am!"

"He knew it," said Rastignac.

Just then Goriot's eyelids unclosed; it was only a muscular contraction, but the Countess's sudden start of reviving hope was no less dreadful than the dying eyes.

"Is it possible that he can hear me?" cried the Countess. "No," she answered herself, and sat down beside the bed. As Mme. de Restaud seemed to wish to sit by her father, Eugène went down to take a little food. The boarders were already assembled.

"Well," remarked the painter, as he joined them, "it seems that there is to be a death-orama upstairs."

"Charles, I think you might find something less painful to joke about," said Eugène.

"So we may not laugh here?" returned the painter. "What harm does it do? Bianchon said that the old man was quite insensible."

"Well, then," said the employé from the Muséum, "he will die as he has lived."

"My father is dead!" shrieked the Countess.

The terrible cry brought Sylvie, Rastignac, and Bianchon; Mme. de Restaud had fainted away. When she recovered they carried her downstairs, and put her into the cab that stood waiting at the door. Eugène sent Thérèse with her, and bade the maid take the Countess to Mme. de Nucingen.

Bianchon came down to them.

"Yes, he is dead," he said.

"Come, sit down to dinner, gentlemen," said Mme. Vauquer, "or the soup will be cold."

The two students sat down together.

"What is the next thing to be done?" Eugène asked of Bianchon.

"I have closed his eyes and composed his limbs," said Bianchon. "When the certificate has been officially registered at the Mayor's office, we will sew him in his winding sheet and bury him somewhere. What do you think we ought to do?"

"He will not smell at his bread like this any more," said the painter, mimicking the old man's little trick.

"Oh, hang it all!" cried the tutor, "let old Goriot drop, and let us have something else for a change. He is a standing dish, and we have had him with every sauce this hour or more. It is one of the privileges of the good city of Paris that anybody may be born, or live, or die there without attracting any attention whatsoever. Let us profit by the advantages of civilization. There are fifty or sixty deaths every day; if you have a mind to do it, you can sit down at any time and wail over whole hecatombs of dead in Paris. Old Goriot has gone off the hooks, has he? So much the better for him. If you venerate his memory, keep it to yourselves, and let the rest of us feed in peace."

"Oh, to be sure," said the widow, "it is all the better for him that he is dead. It looks as though he had had trouble enough, poor soul, while he was alive."

And this was all the funeral oration delivered over him who had been for Eugène the type and embodiment of fatherhood.

The fifteen lodgers began to talk as usual. When Bianchon and Eugène had satisfied their hunger, the rattle of spoons and forks, the boisterous conversation, the expressions on the faces that bespoke various degrees of want of feeling, gluttony, or indifference, everything about them made them shiver with loathing. They went out to find a priest to watch that night with the dead. It was necessary to measure their last pious cares by the scanty sum of money that remained. Before nine o'clock that evening the body was laid out on the bare sacking of the bedstead in the desolate room; a lighted candle stood on either side, and the priest watched at the foot. Rastignac made inquiries of this latter as to the expenses of the funeral, and wrote to the Baron de Nucingen and the Comte de Restaud, entreating both gentlemen to authorize their man of business to defray the charges of laying their father-in-law in the grave. He sent Christophe with the letters; then he went to bed, tired out, and slept.

Next day Bianchon and Rastignac were obliged to take the certificate to the registrar themselves, and by twelve o'clock the formalities were completed. Two hours went by; no word came from the Count nor from the Baron; nobody appeared to act for them, and Rastignac had already been obliged to pay the priest. Sylvie asked ten francs for sewing the old man in his winding-sheet and making him ready for the grave, and Eugène and Bianchon calculated that they had scarcely sufficient to pay for the funeral, if nothing was forthcoming from the dead man's family. So it was the medical student who laid him in a pauper's coffin, dispatched from Bianchon's hospital, whence he obtained it at a cheaper rate.

"Let us play those wretches a trick," said he. "Go to the cemetery, buy a grave for five years at Père-Lachaise, and arrange with the Church and the undertaker to have a third-class funeral. If the daughters and their husbands decline to repay you, you can carve this on the headstone—*'Here lies M. Goriot, father of the Comtesse de Restaud and the Baronne de Nucingen, interred at the expense of two students.'* "

Eugène took part of his friend's advice, but only after he had gone in person first to M. and Mme. de Nucingen, and then to M. and Mme. de Restaud—a fruitless errand. He went no further than the doorstep in either house. The servants had received strict orders to admit no one.

"Monsieur and Madame can see no visitors. They have just lost their father, and are in deep grief over their loss."

Eugène's Parisian experience told him that it was idle to press the point. Something clutched strangely at his heart when he saw that it was impossible to reach Delphine.

"Sell some of your ornaments," he wrote hastily in the porter's room, "so that your father may be decently laid in his last resting-place."

He sealed the note, and begged the porter to give it to Thérèse for her mistress; but the man took it to the Baron de Nucingen, who flung the note into the fire. Eugène, having finished his errands, returned to the lodging-house about three o'clock. In spite of himself, the tears came into his eyes. The coffin, in its scanty covering of black cloth, was standing there on the pavement before the gate, on two chairs. A withered sprig of hyssop was soaking in the holy water bowl of silver-plated copper; there was not a soul in the street, not a passer-by had stopped to sprinkle the coffin; there was not even an attempt at a black drapery over the wicket. It was a pauper who lay there; no one made a pretense of mourning for him; he had neither friends nor kindred—there was no one to follow him to the grave.

Bianchon's duties compelled him to be at the hospital, but he had left a few lines for Eugène, telling his friend about the arrangements he had made for the burial service. The house student's note told Rastignac that a Mass was beyond their means, that the ordinary office for the dead was cheaper, and must suffice, and that he had sent word to the undertaker by Christophe. Eugène had scarcely finished reading Bianchon's scrawl, when he looked up and saw the little circular gold locket that contained the hair of Goriot's two daughters in Mme. Vauquer's hands.

"How dared you take it?" he asked.

"Good Lord! is that to be buried along with him?" retorted Sylvie. "It is gold."

"Of course it shall!" Eugène answered indignantly; "he shall at any rate take one thing that may represent his daughters into the grave with him."

When the hearse came, Eugène had the coffin carried into the house again, unscrewed the lid, and reverently laid on the old man's breast the token that recalled the days when Delphine and Anastasie were innocent little maidens, before they began "to think for themselves," as he had moaned out in his agony.

Rastignac and Christophe and the two undertaker's men were the only followers of the funeral. The Church of Saint-Etienne du Mont was only a little distance from the Rue Neuve-Sainte-Geneviève. When the coffin had been deposited in a low, dark, little chapel, the law student looked round in vain for Goriot's two daughters or their husbands. Christophe was his only fellow-mourner; Christophe, who appeared to think it was his duty to attend the funeral of the man who had put him in the way of such handsome tips. As they waited there in the chapel for the two priests, the chorister, and the beadle, Rastignac grasped Christophe's hand. He could not utter a word just then.

"Yes, M. Eugène," said Christophe, "he was a good and worthy man, who never said one word louder than another; he never did anyone any harm, and gave nobody any trouble."

The two priests, the chorister, and the beadle came, and said and did as much as could be expected for seventy francs in an age when religion cannot afford to say prayers for nothing.

The ecclesiastics chanted a psalm, the *Liberia nos* and the *De profundis*. The whole service lasted about twenty minutes. There was but one mourning coach, which the priest and chorister agreed to share with Eugène and Christophe.

"There is no one else to follow us," remarked the priest, "so we may as well go quickly, and so save time; it is half-past five."

But just as the coffin was put in the hearse, two empty carriages, with the armorial bearings of the Comte de Restaud and the Baron de Nucingen, arrived and followed in the procession to Père-Lachaise. At six o'clock Goriot's coffin was lowered into the grave, his daughters' servants standing round the while. The ecclesiastic recited the short prayer that the students could afford to pay for, and then both priest and lackeys disappeared at once. The two grave-diggers flung in several spadefuls of earth, and then stopped and asked Rastignac for their fee. Eugène felt in vain in his pocket, and was obliged to borrow five francs of Christophe. This thing, so trifling in itself, gave Rastignac a terrible pang of distress. It was growing dusk, the damp twilight fretted his nerves; he gazed down into the grave, and the tears he shed were drawn from him by the sacred emotion, a single-hearted sorrow. When such tears fall on earth, their radiance reaches heaven. And with that tear that fell on old Goriot's grave, Eugène Rastignac's youth ended. He folded his arms and gazed at the clouded sky; and Christophe, after a glance at him, turned and went—Rastignac was left alone.

He went a few paces further, to the highest point of the cemetery, and looked out over Paris and the windings of the Seine; the lamps were beginning to shine on either side of the river. His eyes turned almost eagerly to the space between the column of the Place Vendôme and the cupola of the Invalides; there lay the shining world that he had wished to reach. He glanced over that humming hive, seeming to draw a foretaste of its honey, and said magniloquently—

"Henceforth there is war between us."

And by way of throwing down the glove to Society, Rastignac went to dine with Mme. de Nucingen.

THE DEVIL'S POOL

BY
GEORGE SAND

BIOGRAPHICAL NOTE

AMANTINE LUCILE AURORE DUPIN, now always known as George Sand, was the daughter of an officer of distinguished if irregular lineage, and a woman of a somewhat low type. She was born at Paris on July 1, 1804, and spent most of her childhood with her aristocratic grandmother at Nohant, a country house in Berry, her education being conducted after the doctrines of Rousseau by the ex-abbé Deschatres. For three years she was an inmate of a convent, where she experienced a mystical conversion; and after her grandmother's death she married a country squire, Casimir Dudevant, who was incapable of intellectual sympathy with her and from whom she was estranged some time after the birth of her son and daughter.

In 1831, Mme. Dudevant cut loose with her husband's consent and went to live in Paris. She formed a literary as well as a more intimate partnership with Jules Sandeau, and in 1832 obtained a marked success with her first independent novel, "Indiana," in which she gives a portrait of M. Dudevant, vivid if disagreeable. "Valentine" and "Lélia" followed, all three dealing with misunderstood women, and implying a protest against the binding force of uncongenial marriages.

Near the end of 1833 she went to Italy with the poet, Alfred de Musset, and later gave an account of their relation, which ended unhappily, in "Elle et Lui." She next came under the influence of Michel de Bourges, the counsel who obtained for her a judicial separation from M. Dudevant, and became a republican. This friend, as well as Liszt, the composer, appears in her "Lettres d'un Voyageur." A phase of religious mysticism under Lamennais, and another of Socialism under Pierre Leroux followed, to be partly eclipsed in turn by her infatuation for the musician, Chopin, with whom she spent the winter of 1837-38 in the island of Majorca. A group of novels, of which the best known is "Consuelo," reflect the period of her interest in schemes of social regeneration.

She now turned to stories of country life, and in "La Mare au Diable," here translated, "François le Champi," and "La Petite Fadette," produced a series of the most charming pastorals—probably the most permanent part of her work. In her last period she wrote some novels of manners, several of which, notably "Les Beaux Messieurs de Bois-Doré" and "Le Marquis de Villemer," were successfully dramatized. After a tranquil old age spent at Nohant, she died there on June 8, 1876.

George Sand is the most prolific of women writers, and her style has the ease and fluidity of actual improvisation. She was not a great or original thinker, and to a large extent she reflected the ideas of the men under whose influence she successively came. But her work has the charm of her enthusiastic if not always very logical idealism, great tenderness, and a genuine love of nature. It would be hard to find in the literature of any country more delightful and touching pictures of peasant life than those of which "The Devil's Pool" is a favorable example. The rustic types are somewhat idealized, and the farm life is seen by a romantic temperament, but the stories have nevertheless a high degree of artistic truth and beauty.

W. A. N.

CRITICISMS AND INTERPRETATIONS

I

By Benjamin W. Wells

HER studies of the peasantry of Berry are probably George Sand's most permanent contribution to literature. They show a feeling for nature, exquisite and till then unparalleled in French fiction. Delicate in style, admirable in composition, deeply poetic, yet simply realistic, "La Mare au diable," "François le champi," "La Petite Fadette," and most original of all, "Les Maîtres sonneurs," have the perpetual charm that belongs to every union of truth and beauty. . . .

Her view of the novelist's art made it essentially the expression of lyric passion. "Nothing is strong in me," she said, "but the necessity of love;" and when this is in question, she will be thoroughly romantic, however realistic she may be elsewhere. Her passion varies, however. It is at first personal, then social and humanitarian. Her central impulse is always an emotion, not an idea, and this is reflected in the composition of her novels, where she is apt to conceive her situation and "let her pen trot" with no clearly defined goal. So the beginning of each story is apt to be the best, and the body of the work better than its close, which occurs, not from any structural necessity, but only because the subject has written itself out in her mind, from which, indeed, she was wont to let it pass so completely that if she chanced to read her own novels after an interval, she found she could not recall so much as the names of the characters.

This composition at haphazard, finishing one novel and beginning another on the same evening, was sustained by a fertile imagination that loved to cradle itself in a rosy optimism. She delighted in "superior beings," in whose magnanimity, gentleness, and passionate devotion the glowing sympathies of her heart alone found satisfaction. Hence her heroes and heroines become less real, and so attract us less than the more genuine creatures of earth that surround them. And here, curiously enough, her strength is just where Balzac, her greatest contemporary, is weakest—in the aristocracy and in her young girls. "You write the 'Comédie humaine,'" she says to him; "I should like to write the *épopée*, the eclogue of humanity." For such real flesh and blood girls as hers, we must go back to Marivaux if not to Molière. "Not the child nor the young wife, but the budding woman, naïve, gentle, timid, with her ingenuous coquetries, her comic little vexations, her timorous ventures, her invincibly romantic disposition, and her constant bashfulness at showing it, her long silent hopes, and discreet waiting, the tempestuous heart and the calm face; all that little world so thrilling, so concentrated, so manifold. All fail here, and George Sand, too sometimes, but not always."[1]

She thought herself "extremely feminine in the inconsequence of her ideas and absolute lack of logic." But she was sensible, though not profound. The romantic girls who took her heroines literally got no comfort from her. "Lélia is not I," she writes to one of them; "I am a better woman than that. It is only a poem, not a doctrine." She could not have spoken more truly. She is preeminently the poet among the novelists of the century. Standing between the romantic novel of adventure and the realistic study of manners, between Dumas and Balzac, she renews the idyl, wins back the lyric from its extreme individualism, unites poetry to reality, and, if she left few descendants in France to walk in her *via media,* the seeds she scattered found fruitful soil in England, and especially in Russia, whence in these last days they have found an acceptance in France that augurs an approaching revival of her own popularity.—From "Modern French Literature."

[1] Faguet, XIX siècle, p. 403.

II

By Matthew Arnold

HOW faithful and close it is, this contact of George Sand with country things, with the life of nature in its vast plenitude and pathos! And always in the end the human interest, as is right, emerges and predominates. What is the central figure in the fresh and calm rural world of George Sand? It is the peasant. And what is the peasant? He is France, life, the future. And this is the strength of George Sand, and of her second movement, after the first movement of energy and revolt was over, towards nature and beauty, towards the country, towards primitive life, the peasant. She regarded nature and beauty, not with the selfish and solitary joy of the artist who but seeks to appropriate them for his own purposes, she regarded them as a treasure of immense and hitherto unknown application, as a vast power of healing and delight for all, and for the peasant first and foremost. Yes, she cries, the simple life is the true one! but the peasant, the great organ of that life, "the minister in that vast temple which only the sky is vast enough to embrace," the peasant is not doomed to toil and moil in it for ever, overdone and unawakened, like Holbein's labourer, and to have for his best comfort the thought that death will set him free. *Non, nous n'avons plus affaire à la mort, mais à la vie* ("Our business henceforth is not with death, but with life").

Whether or not the number of George Sand's works—always fresh, always attractive, but poured out too lavishly and rapidly—is likely to prove a hindrance to her fame, I do not care to consider. Posterity, alarmed at the way in which its literary baggage grows upon it, always seeks to leave behind it as much as it can, as much as it dares—everything but masterpieces. But the immense vibration of George Sand's voice upon the ear of Europe will not soon die away. Her passions and her errors have been abundantly talked of. She left them behind her, and men's memory of her will leave them behind also. There will remain of her to mankind the sense of benefit and stimulus from the passage upon earth of that large and frank nature, of that large and pure utterance—the *large utterance of the early gods.* There will remain an admiring and ever widening report of that great and ingenuous soul, simple, affectionate, without vanity, without pedantry, human, equitable, patient, kind. She believed herself she said, "to be in sympathy, across time and space, with a multitude of honest wills which interrogate their conscience and try to put themselves in accord with it." This chain of sympathy will extend more and more.

It is silent, that eloquent voice! it is sunk, that noble, that speaking head! we sum up, as we best can, what she said to us, and we bid her adieu. From many hearts in many lands a troop of tender and grateful regrets converge towards her humble churchyard in Berry. Let them be joined by these words of sad homage from one of a nation which she esteemed, and which knew her very little and very ill. Her guiding thought, the guiding thought which she did her best to make ours too, "the sentiment of the ideal life, which is none other than man's normal life as we shall one day know it," is in harmony with words and promises familiar to that sacred place where she lies: *Exspectat resurrectionem mortuorum, et vitam venturi sæculi.*—From "Mixed Essays" (1877).

AUTHOR'S PREFACE

WHEN I wrote *The Devil's Pool,* the first of a series of pastoral tales which I meant to bring out together under the title of *Tales of a Hemp-dresser,* I had no system in view, and no design of introducing a revolution into literature. No one man has ever effected a revolution; for a revolution, especially in art, is an unconscious change which everybody has had a hand in. But this is not applicable to tales of rustic life, which have always existed, at all times, and under all forms, and have been sometimes pompous, sometimes affected, and sometimes natural.

I have said somewhere, and must now repeat, that pastoral life has always been the ideal of cities and of the courts of kings. I have attempted nothing new in following the easy path which brings back civilised man to the charms of primitive life. I have not tried to invent a new language nor to affect a new style, though many newspaper articles have told me so. I understand my own intentions better than anybody else can, and I am continually surprised that criticism should be so farseeking, when the simplest ideas and most trivial circumstances are all that inspire the creations of art. Especially as regards *The Devil's Pool,* as I have related in the introduction, an engraving of Holbein, that had struck me, and a real scene that I had before my eyes at the same time, while the men were sowing the crops, were all that induced me to write the modest story laid among the humble landscapes of my daily walks.

If I am asked what I meant to do, I shall answer that I meant to write a very touching and very simple story, and that I have not succeeded to my satisfaction. I have indeed seen and felt the beauty of simplicity, but seeing and describing are not the same thing. The best the artist can hope for is to persuade those who have eyes to see for themselves. Look at what is simple, my kind reader; look at the sky, the fields, the trees, and at what is good and true in the peasants; you will catch a glimpse of them in my book but you will see them much better in nature.

GEORGE SAND.

NOHANT, *the twelfth of April*, 1851.

THE AUTHOR TO THE READER

A la sueur de ton visaige,
  Tu gagnerois ta pauvre vie.
Après long travail et usaige,
  Voicy la *mort* qui te convie.[1]

THIS quaint old French verse, written under one of Holbein's pictures, is profoundly melancholy. The engraving represents a labourer driving his plough through the middle of a field. Beyond him stretches a vast horizon, dotted with wretched huts; the sun is sinking behind the hill. It is the end of a hard day's work. The peasant is old, bent, and clothed in rags. He is urging onward a team of four thin and exhausted horses; the ploughshare sinks into a stony and ungrateful soil. One being only is active and alert in this scene of toil and sorrow. It is a fantastic creature. A skeleton armed with a whip, who acts as ploughboy to the old labourer, and running along through the furrow beside the terrified horses, goads them on. This is the spectre Death, whom Holbein has introduced allegorically into that series of religious and philosophic subjects at once melancholy and grotesque, entitled "The Dance of Death."

In this collection, or rather this mighty composition, where Death, who plays his part on every page, is the connecting link and predominating thought, Holbein has called up kings, popes, lovers, gamesters, drunkards, nuns, courtesans, thieves, warriors, monks, Jews, and travellers—all the people of his time and our own; and everywhere the spectre Death is among them, taunting, threatening, and triumphing. He is absent from one picture only, where Lazarus, lying on a dunghill at the rich man's door, declares that the spectre has no terrors for him; probably because he has nothing to lose, and his existence is already a life in death.

[1] In toil and sorrow thou shalt eat
  The bitter bread of poverty.
After the burden and the heat,
  Lo! it is Death who calls for thee.

Is there comfort in this stoical thought of the half-pagan Christianity of the Renaissance, and does it satisfy religious souls? The upstart, the rogue, the tyrant, the rake, and all those haughty sinners who make an ill use of life, and whose steps are dogged by Death, will be surely punished; but can the reflection that death is no evil make amends for the long hardships of the blind man, the beggar, the madman, and the poor peasant? No! An inexorable sadness, an appalling fatality brood over the artist's work. It is like a bitter curse, hurled against the fate of humanity.

Holbein's faithful delineation of the society in which he lived is, indeed, painful satire. His attention was engrossed by crime and calamity; but what shall we, who are artists of a later date, portray? Shall we look to find the reward of the human beings of to-day in the contemplation of death, and shall we invoke it as the penalty of unrighteousness and the compensation of suffering?

No, henceforth, our business is not with death, but with life. We believe no longer in the nothingness of the grave, nor in safety bought with the price of a forced renunciation; life must be enjoyed in order to be fruitful. Lazarus must leave his dunghill, so that the poor need no longer exult in the death of the rich. All must be made happy, that the good fortune of a few may not be a crime and a curse. As the labourer sows his wheat, he must know that he is helping forward the work of life, instead of rejoicing that Death walks at his side. We may no longer consider death as the chastisement of prosperity or the consolation of distress, for God has decreed it neither as the punishment nor the compensation of life. Life has been blessed by Him, and it is no longer permissible for us to leave the grave as the only refuge for those whom we are unwilling to make happy.

There are some artists of our own day, who, after a serious survey of their surroundings, take pleasure in painting misery, the sordidness of poverty, and the dunghill of Lazarus. This may belong to the domain of art and philosophy; but by depicting poverty as so hideous, so degraded, and sometimes so vicious and criminal, do they gain their end, and is that end as salutary as they would wish? We dare not pronounce judgment. They may answer that they terrify the unjust rich man by pointing out to him the yawning pit that lies beneath the frail covering of wealth; just as in the time of the Dance of Death, they showed him his gaping grave, and Death standing ready to fold him in an impure embrace. Now, they show him the thief breaking open his doors, and the murderer stealthily watching his sleep. We confess we cannot understand how we can reconcile him to the human nature he despises, or make him sensible of the sufferings of the poor wretch whom he dreads, by showing him this wretch in the guise of the escaped convict or the nocturnal burglar. The hideous phantom Death, under the repulsive aspect in which he has been represented by Holbein and his predecessors, gnashing his teeth and playing the fiddle, has been powerless to convert the wicked and console their victims. And does not our literature employ the same means as the artists of the Middle Ages and the Renaissance?

The revellers of Holbein fill their glasses in a frenzy to dispel the idea of Death, who is their cup-bearer, though they do not see him. The unjust rich of our own day demand cannon and barricades to drive out the idea of an insurrection of the people which art shows them as slowly working in the dark, getting ready to burst upon the State. The Church of the Middle Ages met the terrors of the great of the earth with the sale of indulgences. The government of to-day soothes the uneasiness of the rich by exacting from them large sums for the support of policemen, jailers, bayonets, and prisons.

Albert Dürer, Michael Angelo, Holbein, Callot, and Goya have made powerful satires on the evils of their times and countries, and their immortal works are historical documents of unquestionable value. We shall not refuse to artists the right to probe the wounds of society and lay them bare to our eyes; but is the only function of art still to threaten and appal? In the literature of the mysteries of iniquity, which talent and imagination have brought into fashion, we prefer the sweet and gentle characters which can attempt and effect conversions, to the melodramatic villains who inspire terror; for terror never cures selfishness, but increases it.

We believe that the mission of art is a mission of sentiment and love, that the novel of to-day should take the place of the parable and the fable of early times, and that the artist has a larger and more poetic task than that of suggesting certain prudential and conciliatory measures for the purpose of diminishing the fright caused by his pictures. His aim should be to render attractive the objects he has at heart, and, if necessary, I have no objection to his embellishing them a little. Art is not the study of positive reality, but the search for ideal truth, and the *Vicar of Wakefield* was a more useful and healthy book than the *Paysan Perverti* or the *Liaisons Dangereuses*.

Forgive these reflections of mine, kind reader, and let them stand as a preface, for there will be no other to the little story I am going to relate to you. My tale is to be so short and so simple, that I felt obliged to make you my apologies for it beforehand, by telling you what I think of the literature of terror.

I have allowed myself to be drawn into this digression for the sake of a labourer; and it is the story of a labourer which I have been meaning to tell you, and which I shall now tell you at once.

THE DEVIL'S POOL

CHAPTER I

The Tillage of the Soil

I HAD just been looking long and sadly at Holbein's ploughman, and was walking through the fields, musing on rustic life and the destiny of the husbandman. It is certainly tragic for him to spend his days and his strength delving in the jealous earth, that so reluctantly yields up her rich treasures when a morsel of coarse black bread, at the end of the day's work, is the sole reward and profit to be reaped from such arduous toil. The wealth of the soil, the harvests, the fruits, the splendid cattle that grow sleek and fat in the luxuriant grass, are the property of the few, and but instruments of the drudgery and slavery of the many. The man of leisure seldom loves, for their own sake, the fields and meadows, the landscape, or the noble animals which are to be converted into gold for his use. He comes to the country for his health or for change of air, but goes back to town to spend the fruit of his vassal's labour.

On the other hand, the peasant is too abject, too wretched, and too fearful of the future to enjoy the beauty of the country and the charms of pastoral life. To him, also, the yellow harvest-fields, the rich meadows, the fine cattle represent bags of gold; but he knows that only an infinitesimal part of their contents, insufficient for his daily needs, will ever fall to his share. Yet year by year he must fill those accursed bags, to please his master and buy the right of living on his land in sordid wretchedness.

Yet nature is eternally young, beautiful, and generous. She pours forth poetry and beauty on all creatures and all plants that are allowed free development. She owns the secret of happiness, of which no one has ever robbed her.

The happiest of men would be he who, knowing the full meaning of his labour, should, while working with his hands, find his happiness and his freedom in the exercise of his intelligence, and, having his heart in unison with his brain, should at once understand his own work and love that of God. The artist has such delights as these in contemplating and reproducing the beauties of nature; but if his heart be true and tender, his pleasure is disturbed when he sees the miseries of the men who people this paradise of earth. True happiness will be theirs when mind, heart, and hand shall work in concert in the sight of Heaven, and there shall be a sacred harmony between God's goodness and the joys of his creatures. Then, instead of the pitiable and frightful figure of Death stalking, whip in hand, across the fields, the painter of allegories may place beside the peasant a radiant angel, sowing the blessed grain broadcast in the smoking furrow.

The dream of a serene, free, poetic, laborious, and simple life for the tiller of the soil is not so impossible that we should banish it as a chimera. The sweet, sad words of Virgil: "Oh, happy the peasants of the field, if they knew their own blessings!" is a regret, but, like all regrets, it is also a prophecy. The day will come when the labourer too may be an artist, and may at least feel what is beautiful, if he cannot express it—a matter of far less importance. Do not we know that this mysterious poetic intuition is already his, in the form of instinct and vague reverie? Among those peasants who possess some of the comforts of life, and whose moral and intellectual development is not entirely stifled by extreme wretchedness, pure happiness that can be felt and appreciated exists in the elementary stage; and, moreover, since poets have already raised their voices out of the lap of pain and of weariness, why should we say that the labour of the hands excludes the working of the soul? Without doubt this exclusion is the common result of excessive toil and of deep misery; but let it not be said that when men shall work moderately and usefully there will be nothing but bad workers and bad poets. The man who draws in noble joy from the poetic feelings is a true poet, though he has never written a verse all his life.

My thoughts had flown in this direction, without my perceiving that my confidence in the capacity of man for education was strengthened by external influences. I was walking along the edge of a field, which some peasants were preparing to sow. The space was vast as that in Holbein's picture; the landscape, too, was vast and framed in a great sweep of green, slightly reddened by the approach of autumn. Here and there in the great russet field, slender rivulets of water left in the furrows by the late rains sparkled in the sunlight like silver threads. The day was clear and mild, and the soil, freshly cleft by the ploughshare, sent up a light steam. At the other extremity of the field, an old man, whose broad shoulders and stern face recalled Holbein's ploughman, but whose clothes carried no suggestion of poverty, was gravely driving his plough of antique shape, drawn by two placid oxen, true patriarchs of the meadow, tall and rather thin, with pale yellow coats and long, drooping horns. They were those old workers who, through long habit, have grown to be *brothers,* as they are called in our country, and who, when one loses the other, refuse to work with a new comrade, and pine away with grief. People who are unfamiliar with the country call the love of the ox for his yoke-fellow a fable. Let them come and see in the corner of the stable one of these poor beasts, thin and wasted, restlessly lashing his lean flanks with his tail, violently breathing with mingled terror and disdain on the food offered him, his eyes always turned toward the door, scratching with his hoof the empty place at his side, sniffing the yokes and chains which his fellow used to wear, and incessantly calling him with melancholy lowings. The ox-herd will say: "There is a pair of oxen gone; this one will work no more, for his brother is dead. We ought to fatten him for the market, but he will not eat, and will soon starve himself to death."

The old labourer worked slowly, silently, and without waste of effort. His docile team were in no greater haste than he; but, thanks to the undistracted steadiness of his toil and the judicious expenditure of his strength, his furrow was as soon ploughed as that of his son, who was driving, at some distance from him, four less vigorous oxen through a more stubborn and stony piece of ground.

My attention was next caught by a fine spectacle, a truly noble subject for a painter. At the other end of the field a fine-looking youth was driving a magnificent team of four pairs of young oxen, through whose sombre coats glanced a ruddy, glow-like flame. They had the short, curly heads that belong to the wild bull, the same large, fierce eyes and jerky movements; they worked in an abrupt, nervous way that showed how they still rebelled against the yoke and goad and trembled with anger as they obeyed the authority so recently imposed. They were what is called "newly yoked" oxen. The man who drove them had to clear a corner of the field that had formerly been given up to pasture, and was filled with old tree-stumps; and his youth and energy, and his eight half-broken animals, hardly sufficed for the Herculean task.

A child of six or seven years old, lovely as an angel, wearing round his shoulders, over his blouse, a sheepskin that made him look like a little Saint John the Baptist out of a Renaissance picture, was running along in the furrow beside the plough, pricking the flanks of the oxen with a long, light goad but slightly sharpened. The spirited animals quivered under the child's light touch, making their yokes and head-bands creak, and shaking the pole violently, whenever a root stopped the advance of the ploughshare, the labourer would call every animal by name in his powerful voice, trying to calm rather than to excite them; for the oxen, irritated by the sudden resistance, bounded, pawed the ground with their great cloven hoofs, and would have jumped aside and dragged the plough across the fields, if the young man had not kept the first four in order with his voice and goad, while the child controlled the four others. The little fellow shouted too, but the voice which he tried to make of terrible effect, was as sweet as his angelic face. The whole scene was beautiful in its grace and strength; the landscape, the man, the child, the oxen under the yoke; and in spite of the mighty struggle by which the earth was subdued, a deep feeling of peace and sweetness reigned over all. Each time that an obstacle was surmounted and the plough resumed its even solemn progress, the labourer, whose pretended violence was but a trial of his strength, and an outlet for his energy, instantly regained that serenity which is the right of simple souls, and looked with fatherly pleasure toward his child, who turned to smile back at him. Then the young father would raise his manly voice in the solemn and melancholy chant that ancient tradition transmits, not indeed to all ploughmen indiscriminately, but to those who are most perfect in the art of exciting and sustaining the spirit of cattle while at work. This song, which was probably sacred in its origin, and to which mysterious influences must once have been attributed, is still thought to possess the virtue of putting animals on their mettle, allaying their irritation, and of beguiling the weariness of their long, hard toil. It is not enough to guide them skilfully, to trace a perfectly straight furrow, and to lighten their labour by raising the ploughshare or driving it into the earth; no man can be a consummate husbandman who does not know how to sing to his oxen, and that is an art that requires taste and especial gifts.

To tell the truth, this chant is only a recitative, broken off and taken up at pleasure. Its irregular form and its intonations that violate all the rules of musical art make it impossible to describe.

But it is none the less a noble song, and so appropriate is it to the nature of the work it accompanies, to the gait of the oxen, to the peace of the fields, and to the simplicity of the men who sing it, that no genius unfamiliar with the tillage of the earth, and no man except an accomplished labourer of our part of the country, could repeat it. At the season of the year when there is no work or stir afoot except that of the ploughman, this strong, sweet refrain rises like the voice of the breeze, to which the key it is sung in gives it some resemblance. Each phrase ends with a long trill, the final note of which is held with incredible strength of breath, and rises a quarter of a tone, sharping systematically. It is barbaric, but possesses an unspeakable charm, and anybody, once accustomed to hear it, cannot conceive of another song taking its place at the same hour and in the same place, without striking a discord.

So it was that I had before my eyes a picture the reverse of that of Holbein, although the scene was similar. Instead of a wretched old man, a young and active one; instead of a team of weary and emaciated horses, four yoke of robust and fiery oxen; instead of death, a beautiful child; instead of despair and destruction, energy and the possibility of happiness.

Then the old French verse, "A la sueur de ton visaige," etc., and Virgil's "O fortunatos . . . agricolas," returned to my mind, and seeing this lovely child and his father, under such poetic conditions, and with so much grace and strength, accomplish a task full of such grand and solemn suggestions, I was conscious of deep pity and involuntary respect. Happy the peasant of the fields! Yes, and so too should I be in his place, if my arm and voice could be endowed with sudden strength, and I could help to make Nature fruitful, and sing of her gifts, without ceasing to see with my eyes or understand with my brain harmonious colours and sounds, delicate shades and graceful outlines; in short, the mysterious beauty of all things. And above all, if my heart continued to beat in concert with the divine sentiment that presided over the immortal sublimity of creation.

But, alas! this man has never understood the mystery of beauty; this child will never understand it. God forbid that I should not think them superior to the animals which are subject to them, or that they have not moments of rapturous insight to soothe their toil and lull their cares to sleep. I see the seal of the Lord upon their noble brows, for they were born to inherit the earth far more truly than those who have bought and paid for it. The proof that they feel this is that they cannot be exiled with impunity, that they love the soil they have watered with their tears, and that the true peasant dies of homesickness under the arms of a soldier far from his native field. But he lacks some of my enjoyments, those pure delights which should be his by right, as a workman in that immense temple which the sky only is vast enough to embrace. He lacks the consciousness of his sentiment. Those who condemned him to slavery from his mother's womb, being unable to rob him of his vague dreams, took away from him the power of reflection.

Yet, imperfect being that he is, sentenced to eternal childhood, he is nobler than the man in whom knowledge has stifled feeling. Do not set yourselves above him, you who believe yourselves invested with a lawful and inalienable right to rule over him, for your terrible mistake shows that your brain has destroyed your heart, and that you are the blindest and most incomplete of men! I love the simplicity of his soul more than the false lights of yours; and if I had to narrate the story of his life, the pleasure I should take in bringing out the tender and touching side of it would be greater than your merit in painting the degradation and contempt into which he is cast by your social code.

I knew the young man and the beautiful child; I knew their history, for they had a history. Everybody has his own, and could make the romance of his life interesting, if he could but understand it. Although but a peasant and a labourer, Germain had always been aware of his duties and affections. He had related them to me clearly and ingenuously, and I had listened with interest. After some time spent in watching him plough, it occurred to me that I might write his story, though that story were as simple, as straightforward, and unadorned as the furrow he was tracing.

Next year that furrow will be filled and covered by a fresh one. Thus disappear most of the footprints made by man in the field of human life. A little earth obliterates them, and the furrows we have dug succeed one another like graves in a cemetery. Is not the furrow of the labourer of as much value as that of the idler, even if that idler, by some absurd chance, have made a little noise in the world, and left behind him an abiding name?

I mean, if possible, to save from oblivion the furrow of Germain, the skilled husbandman. He will never know nor care, but I shall take pleasure in my task.

CHAPTER II

Father Maurice

"GERMAIN," said his father-in-law one day, "you must decide about marrying again. It is almost two years now since you lost my daughter, and your eldest boy is seven years old. You are almost thirty, my boy, and you know that in our country a man is considered too old to go to housekeeping again after that age; you have three nice children, and thus far they have not proved a burden to us at all. My wife and my daughter-in-law have looked after them as well as they could, and loved them as they ought. Here is Petit-Pierre almost grown up. He goads the oxen very well; he knows how to look after the cattle; and he is strong enough to drive the horses to the trough. So it is not he that worries us. But the other two, love them though we do, God knows the poor little innocents give us trouble enough this year; my daughter-in-law is about to lie in, and she has yet another baby to attend to. When the child we are expecting comes, she will not be able to look after your little Solange, and above all your Sylvain, who is not four years old, and who is never quiet day or night. He has a restless disposition like yours; that will make a good workman of him, but it makes a dreadful child, and my old wife cannot run fast enough to save him when he almost tumbles into the ditch, or when he throws himself in front of the tramping cattle. And then with this other that my daughter-in-law is going to bring into the world, for a month at least her next older child will fall on my wife's hands. Besides, your children worry us, and give us too much to do; we hate to see children badly looked after, and when we think of the accidents that may befall them, for want of care, we cannot rest. So you need another wife, and I another daughter-in-law. Think this over, my son. I have called it to your mind before. Time flies, and the years will not wait a moment for you. It is your duty to your children and to the rest of us, who wish all well at home, to marry as soon as you can."

"Very well, father," answered the son-in-law, "if you really wish it, I must do as you say. But I do not wish to hide it from you that it will make me very sad, and that I hardly wish for anything but to drown myself. We know who it is we lose, we never know whom we find. I had a good wife, a pretty wife, sweet, brave, good to her father and mother, good to her husband, good to her children, good to toil in the fields and in the house, well fitted to work—in short, good for everything; and when you had given her to me, and I took her, we did not place it among our promises that I should go and forget about her if I had the misfortune to lose her."

"What you say shows your good heart, Germain," answered Father Maurice. "I know that you loved my daughter and that you made her happy, and that had you been able to satisfy Death by going in her place, Catherine would be alive to-day, and you would be in the graveyard. She deserved all your love, and if you are not consoled, neither are we. But I do not speak to you of forgetting her. God wished her to leave us, and we do not let a day go by without telling Him in our prayers and thoughts, and words and actions, that we keep her memory and still sorrow for her loss. But if she could speak to you from the other world, and let you know what she wishes, she would tell you to find a mother for her little orphans. So the question is to find a woman who will be worthy to take her place. It will not be easy, but it is not impossible. And when we shall find her for you, you will love her as you used to love my daughter, because you are a good man, and because you will be thankful to her for helping us and for loving your children."

"Very well, Father Maurice, I shall do as you wish, as I have always done."

"It is only justice, my son, to say that you have always listened to the friendly advice and good judgment of the head of the house. So let us consult about your choice of a new wife. First, I don't advise you to take a young girl. That is not what you need. Youth is careless, and, as it is hard work to bring up three children, especially when they are of another bed, you must have a good soul, wise and gentle, and well used to work. If your wife is not about the same age as you, she will have no reason to accept such a duty. She will find you too old and your children too young. She will be complaining, and your children will suffer."

"This is just what makes me uneasy. Suppose the poor little things should be badly treated, hated, beaten?"

"God grant not," answered the old man. "But bad women are more rare with us than good, and we shall be stupid if we cannot pick out somebody who will suit us."

"That is true, father. There are good girls in our village. There is Louise, Sylvaine, Claudie, Marguerite—yes, anybody you want."

"Gently, gently, my boy. All these girls are too young, or too poor, or too pretty; for surely we must think of that too, my son. A pretty woman is not always as well behaved as another!"

"Then you wish me to take an ugly wife?" said Germain, a little uneasy.

"No, not ugly at all, for this woman will bear you other children, and there is nothing more miserable than to have children who are ugly and weak and sickly. But a woman still fresh and in good health, who is neither pretty nor ugly, would suit you exactly."

"I am quite sure," said Germain, smiling rather sadly, "that to get such a woman as you wish, you must have her made to order. All the more because you don't wish her to be poor, and the rich are not easy to get, particularly for a widower."

"And suppose she were a widow herself, Germain? A widow without children and with a good portion?"

"For the moment, I cannot think of anybody like this in our parish."

"Nor I either. But there are others elsewhere."

"You have somebody in mind, father. Then tell me, at once, who it is."

CHAPTER III

Germain, the Skilled Husbandman

"YES, I have somebody in mind," replied Father Maurice. "It is a Leonard, the widow of a Guérin. She lives at Fourche."

"I know neither the woman nor the place," answered Germain, resigned, but growing more and more melancholy.

"Her name is Catherine, like your dead wife's."

"Catherine? Yes, I shall be glad to have to pronounce that name, Catherine; and yet if I cannot love one as much as the other, it will pain me all the more. It will bring her to my mind more often."

"I tell you, you will love her. She is a good soul, a woman with a warm heart. I have not seen her for a long time. She was not an ugly girl then. But she is no longer young. She is thirty-two. She comes of a good family, honest people all of them, and for property she has eight or ten thousand francs in land which she would sell gladly in order to invest in the place where she settles. For she, too, is thinking of marrying again, and I know that if your character pleases her, she will not be dissatisfied with your situation."

"So you have made all the arrangements?"

"Yes, except that I have not had an opinion from either of you, and that is what you must ask each other when you meet. The woman's father is a distant connection of mine, and he has been a good friend to me. You know Father Leonard well?"

"Yes, I have seen you two talking at the market, and at the last you lunched together. Then it was about her that he spoke to you so long?"

"Certainly. He watched you selling your cattle and saw that you drove a shrewd bargain, and that you were a good-looking fellow and appeared active and intelligent; and when I told him what a good fellow you were and how well you have behaved toward us, without one word of vexation or anger during the eight years we have been living and working together, he took it into his head to marry you to his daughter. This suits me, too, I admit, when I think of her good reputation and the honesty of her family and the prosperous condition I know her affairs are in."

"I see, Father Maurice, that you have an eye to money."

"Of course I do; you have, too, have you not?"

"I do look toward it, if you wish, for your sake; but you know that, for my own part, I don't worry whether I gain or not in what we make. I don't understand about profit-sharing; I have no head for that sort of thing. I understand the ground; I understand cattle, horses, carts, sowing, threshing and provender. As for sheep, and vineyards, and vegetables, petty profits, and fine gardening, you know that is your son's business. I don't have much to do with it. As to money, my memory is short, and I should rather give up everything than fight about what is yours and what is mine. I should be afraid of making some mistake and claiming what does not belong to me, and if business were not so clear and simple I should never find my way in it."

"So much the worse, my son; and this is the reason I wish you to have a wife with a clear head to fill my place when I am gone. You never wished to understand our accounts, and this might lead you into a quarrel with my son, when you don't have me any longer to keep you in harmony and decide what is each one's share."

"May you live long, Father Maurice. But do not worry about what will happen when you die. I shall never quarrel with your son. I trust Jacques as I do you; and as I have no property of my own, and all that might accrue to me comes from your daughter and belongs to our children, I can rest easy, and you, too. Jacques would never rob his sister's children for the sake of his own, for he loves them all equally."

"You are right, Germain. Jacques is a good son, a good brother, and a man who loves the truth. But Jacques may die before you, before your children grow up; and in a family we must always remember never to leave children without a head to look after them and govern their disagreements; otherwise, the lawyer-people mix themselves up in it, stir them up to fight, and make them eat up everything in lawsuits. So we ought not to think of bringing home another person, man or woman, without remembering that some day or other that person may have to control the behaviour and business of twenty or thirty children and grandchildren, sons-in-law and daughters-in-law. We never know how big a family can grow, and when a hive is so full that the bees must form new swarms, each one wishes to carry off her share of the honey. When I took you for my son, although my daughter was rich and you were poor, I never reproached her for choosing you. I saw that you were a hard worker, and I knew very well that the best fortune for people in such a country as ours is a pair of arms and a heart like yours. When a man brings these into a family, he brings enough. But with a woman it is different. Her work indoors saves, but it does not gain. Besides, now that you are a father, looking for a second wife, you must remember that your new children will have no claim on the property of your children by another wife; and if you should happen to die they might suffer very much—at least, if your wife had no money in her own right. And then the children which you will add to our colony will cost something to bring up. If that fell on us alone, we should surely take care of them without a word of complaint; but the comfort of everybody would suffer, and your eldest children would bear their share of hardship. When families grow too large, if money does not keep pace, misery comes, no matter how bravely you bear up. This is what I wished to say, Germain; think it over, and try to make the widow Guérin like you; for her discretion and her dollars will help us now and make us feel easy about the future."

"That is true, Father. I shall try to please her and to like her."

"To do that you must go to find her, and see her."

"At her own place? At Fourche? That is a great way from here, is it not? And we scarcely have time to run off at this season of the year."

"When it is a question of a love-match you must make up your mind to lose time, but when it is a sensible marriage of two people, who take no sudden fancies and know what they want, it is very soon decided. To-morrow is Saturday; you will make your day's work a little shorter than usual. You must start after dinner about two o'clock. You will be at Fourche by nightfall. The moon rises early. The roads are good, and it is not more than three leagues distant. It is near Magnier. Besides, you will take the mare."

"I had just as lief go afoot in this cool weather."

"Yes, but the mare is pretty, and a suitor looks better when he comes well mounted. You must put on your new clothes and carry a nice present of game to Father Leonard. You will come from me and talk with him, pass all of Sunday with his daughter, and come back Monday morning with a yes or no."

"Very well," answered Germain calmly, and yet he did not feel very calm.

Germain had always lived soberly, as industrious peasants do. Married at twenty, he had loved but one woman in his life, and after her death, impulsive and gay as his nature was, he had never played nor trifled with another. He had borne a real sorrow faithfully in his heart, and it was not without misgiving nor without sadness that he yielded to his father-in-law; but that father had always governed the family wisely and Germain, entirely devoted as he was to the common welfare, and so, by consequence, to the head of the house, who represented it, could not understand that he might have wronged his own good sense and hurt the interests of all.

Nevertheless, he was sad. Few days went by when he did not cry in secret, for his wife, and although loneliness began to weigh on him, he was more afraid of entering into a new marriage than desirous of finding a support in his sorrow. He had a vague idea that love might have consoled him by coming to him of a sudden, for this is the only way love can console. We never find it when we seek it; it comes over us unawares.

This cold-blooded scheme of marriage that Father Maurice had opened to him, this unknown woman he was to take for his bride, perhaps even all that had been said to him of her virtue and good sense, made him pause to think. And he went away musing as men do whose thoughts are too few to divide into hostile factions, not scraping up fine arguments for rebellion and selfishness, but suffering from a dull grief, submissive to ills from which there is no escape.

Meanwhile, Father Maurice had returned to the farm, while Germain, between sunset and dark, spent the closing hour of the day in repairing gaps the sheep had made in the hedge of a yard near the farm-buildings. He lifted up the branches of the thorn-bushes and held them in place with clods of earth, whilst the thrushes chattered in the neighbouring thicket and seemed to call to him to hurry, for they were eager to come and see his work as soon as he had gone.

CHAPTER IV

Mother Guillette

FATHER MAURICE found at his house an old neighbour who had come to talk with his wife, seeking at the same time to secure a few embers to light her fire. Mother Guillette lived in a wretched hut two gunshots away from the farm. Still she was a willing and an orderly woman. Her poor dwelling was clean and neat and the care with which her clothes were mended showed that she respected herself in the midst of her penury.

"You have come to fetch your evening fire, Mother Guillette," said the old man to her. "Is there anything else you want?"

"No, Father Maurice," answered she; "nothing for the present. I am no beggar, as you know, and I take care not to abuse the kindness of my friends."

"That is very true. Besides, your friends are always ready to do you a service."

"I was just talking to your wife, and I was asking her if Germain had finally decided to marry again."

"You are no gossip," replied Father Maurice; "we can talk in your presence without having any foolish tale-bearing to fear. So I will tell my wife and you that Germain has made up his mind absolutely. To-morrow morning he starts for the farm at Fourche."

"Good enough!" cried Mother Maurice; "poor child! God grant he may find a woman as good and true as he."

"So he is going to Fourche?" remarked Mother Guillette; "how lucky that is! It is exactly what I want. And since you were just asking me if there were anything I wished for, I am going to tell you, Father Maurice, how you can do me a service."

"Tell me what it is; we like to help you."

"I wish Germain would be so kind as to take my daughter along with him."

"Where? To Fourche?"

"No, not to Fourche, but to Ormeaux. She is to stay there the rest of the year."

"What!" exclaimed Mother Maurice, "are you going to separate from your daughter?"

"She must go out to work and earn her living. I am sorry enough, and she is too, poor soul. We could not make up our minds to part Saint John's Day, but now that Saint Martin's is upon us, she finds a good place as shepherdess at the farms at Ormeaux. On his way home from the fair the other day, the farmer passed by here. He caught sight of my little Marie tending her three sheep on the common.

"'You have hardly enough to do, my little girl,' said he; 'three sheep are not enough for a shepherdess: would you like to take care of a hundred? I will take you along. Our shepherdess has fallen sick. She is going back to her family, and if you will be at our farm before a week is over, you shall have fifty francs for the rest of the year up to Saint John's Day.'

"The child refused, but she could not help thinking it over and telling me about it, when she came home in the evening, and found me downhearted and worried about the winter, which was sure to be hard and long; for this year the cranes and wild ducks were seen crossing the sky a whole month before they generally do. We both of us cried, but after a time we took heart. We knew that we could not stay together, since it is hard enough for one person to get a living from our little patch of ground. Then since Marie is old enough—for she is going on to sixteen—she must do like the rest, earn her own living and help her poor mother."

"Mother Guillette," said the old labourer, "if it were only fifty francs you needed to help you out of your trouble, and save you from sending away your daughter, I should certainly find them for you, although fifty francs is no trifle for people like us. But in everything we must consult common sense as well as friendship. To be saved from want this year will not keep you from want in the future, and the longer your daughter takes to make up her mind, the harder you both will find it to part. Little Marie is growing tall and strong. She has not enough at home to keep her busy. She might get into lazy habits——"

"Oh, I am not afraid of that!" exclaimed Mother Guillette. "Marie is as active as a rich girl at the head of a large family can be. She never sits still with her arms folded for an instant, and when we have no work to do, she keeps dusting and polishing our old furniture until it shines like a mirror. The child is worth her weight in gold, and I should much rather have her enter your service as a shepherdess than go so far away to people I don't know. You would have taken her at Saint John's Day; but now you have hired all your hands, and we cannot think of that till Saint John's Day next year."

"Yes, I consent with all my heart, Guillette. I shall be very glad to take her. But in the meantime she will do well to learn her work, and accustom herself to obey others."

"Yes, that is true, no doubt. The die is cast. The farmer at Ormeaux sent to ask about her this morning; we consented, and she must go. But the poor child does not know the way, and I should not like to send her so far alone. Since your son-in-law goes to Fourche to-morrow, perhaps he can take her. It seems that Fourche is close to her journey's end. At least, so they tell me, for I have never made the trip myself."

"It is very near indeed, and my son will show her the way. Naturally, he might even take her up behind him on the mare. That will save her shoes. Here he comes for supper. Tell me, Germain, Mother Guillette's little Marie is going to become a shepherdess at Ormeaux. Will you take her there on your horse?"

"Certainly," answered Germain, who, troubled as he was, never felt indisposed to do a kindness to his neighbour.

In our community a mother would not think of such a thing as to trust a girl of sixteen to a man of twenty-eight. For Germain was really but twenty-eight, and although according to the notions of the country people he was considered rather old to marry, he was still the best-looking man in the neighbourhood. Toil had not wrinkled and worn him as it does most peasants who have passed ten years in tilling the soil. He was strong enough to labour for ten more years without showing signs of age, and the prejudices of her time must have weighed heavily on the mind of a young girl to prevent her from seeing that Germain had a fresh complexion, eyes sparkling and blue as skies in May, ruddy lips, fine teeth, and a body well shaped and lithe as a young horse that has never yet left his pasture.

But purity of manners is a sacred custom in some districts far distant from the corrupted life of great cities, and amongst all the households of Belair, the family of Maurice was known to be honest and truth-loving. Germain was on his way to find a wife. Marie was a child, too young and too poor to be thought of in this light, and unless he were a heartless and a bad man he could not entertain one evil thought concerning her. Father Maurice felt no uneasiness at seeing him take the pretty girl on the crupper. Mother Guillette would have thought herself doing him a wrong had she asked him to respect her daughter as his sister. Marie embraced her mother and her young friends twenty times, and then mounted the mare in tears. Germain, sad on his own account, felt all the more sympathy for her sorrow, and rode away with a melancholy air, while all the people of the neighbourhood waved good-bye to Marie without a thought of harm.

CHAPTER V

Petit-Pierre

THE grey was young, good-looking, and strong. She carried her double burden with ease, laying back her ears and champing her bit like the high-spirited mare she was. Passing in front of the pasture, she caught sight of her mother, whose name was the Old Grey as hers was the Young Grey, and she whinnied in token of goodbye. The Old Grey came nearer the hedge, and striking her shoes together she tried to gallop along the edge of the field in order to follow her daughter; then seeing her fall into a sharp trot, the mare whinnied in her turn and stood in an uneasy attitude, her nose in the air and her mouth filled with grass that she had no thought of eating.

"That poor beast always knows her offspring," said Germain, trying to keep Marie's thoughts from her troubles. "That reminds me, I never kissed Petit-Pierre before I started. The naughty boy was not there. Last night he wished to make me promise to take him along, and he wept for an hour in bed. This morning again, he tried everything to persuade me. Oh, how sly and coaxing he is! But when he saw that he could not gain his point, the young gentleman got into a temper. He went off to the fields, and I have not seen him all day."

"I have seen him," said little Marie, striving to keep back her tears; "he was running toward the clearing with Soulas' children, and I felt sure that he had been away from home a long time, for he was hungry and was eating wild plums and blackberries. I gave him the bread I had for lunch, and he said, 'Thank you, dear Marie; when you come to our house, I will give you some cake.' He is a dear little child, Germain."

"Yes, he is," answered the labourer; "and there is nothing I would not do for him. If his grandmother had not more sense than I, I could not have helped taking him with me, when I saw him crying as though his little heart would burst."

"Then why did you not take him, Germain? He would have been very little trouble. He is so good when you please him."

"He would probably have been in the way in the place where I am going. At least Father Maurice thought so. On the other hand, I should have thought it well to see how they received him. For no one could help being kind to such a nice child. But at home they said that I must not begin by showing off all the cares of the household. I don't know why I speak of this to you, little Marie; you can't understand."

"Oh, yes, I do; I know that you are going away to marry; my mother spoke to me about it, and told me not to mention it to a soul, either at home or at my destination, and you need not be afraid; I shall not breathe a word about it."

"You are very right. For the deed isn't done yet. Perhaps I shall not suit this woman."

"I hope you will, Germain; why should you not suit her?"

"Who knows? I have three children, and that is a heavy burden for a woman who is not their mother."

"Very true. But are not your children like other children?"

"Do you think so?"

"They are lovely as little angels, and so well brought up that you can't find better children."

"There's Sylvain. He is none too obedient."

"He is so very little. He can't help being naughty. But he is very bright."

"He is bright, it is true, and very brave. He is not afraid of cows nor bulls, and if he were given his own way, he would be climbing on horseback already with his elder brother."

"Had I been in your place, I would have taken the eldest boy along. Surely people would have liked you at once for having such a pretty child."

"Yes, if a woman is fond of children. But if she is not."

"Are there women who don't love children?"

"Not many, I think, but still there are some, and that is what troubles me."

"You don't know this woman at all, then?"

"No more than you, and I fear that I shall not know her better after I have seen her. I am not suspicious. When people say nice things to me, I believe them, but more than once I have had good reason to repent, for words are not deeds."

"They say that she is a very good woman."

"Who says so? Father Maurice?"

"Yes, your father-in-law."

"That is all very well. But he knows her no more than I."

"Well, you will soon see. Pay close attention, and let us hope that you will not be deceived."

"I have it. Little Marie, I should be very much obliged if you would come into the house for a minute before you go straight on to Ormeaux. You are quick-witted; you have always shown that you are not stupid, and nothing escapes your notice. Should you see anything to rouse your suspicions, you must warn me of it very quietly."

"Oh! no, Germain, I will not do that; I should be too much afraid of making a mistake; and, besides, if a word lightly spoken were to turn you against this marriage, your family would bear me a grudge, and I have plenty of troubles now without bringing any more on my poor dear mother."

As they were talking thus, the grey pricked up her ears and shied; then returning on her steps, she approached the bushes, where she began to recognise something which had frightened her at first. Germain cast his eye over the thicket, and in a ditch, beneath the branches of a scrub-oak, still thick and green, he saw something which he took for a lamb.

"The little creature is strayed or dead, for it does not move. Perhaps some one is looking for it; we must see."

"It is not an animal," cried little Marie; "it is a sleeping child. It is your Petit-Pierre."

"Heavens!" exclaimed Germain; "see the little scamp asleep so far away from home, and in a ditch where a snake might bite him!"

He lifted up the child, who smiled as he opened his eyes and threw his arms about his father's neck, saying: "Dear little father, you are going to take me with you."

"Oh, yes; always the same tune. What were you doing there, you naughty Pierre?"

"I was waiting for my little father to go by. I was watching the road, and I watched so hard that I fell asleep."

"And if I had passed by without seeing you, you would have been out of doors all night, and a wolf would have eaten you up."

"Oh, I knew very well that you would see me," answered Petit-Pierre, confidently.

"Well, kiss me now, bid me good-bye, and run back quickly to the house, unless you wish them to have supper without you."

"Are you not going to take me, then?" cried the little boy, beginning to rub his eyes to show that he was thinking of tears.

"You know very well that grandpapa and grandmamma do not wish it," said Germain, fortifying himself behind the authority of his elders, like a man who distrusts his own.

The child would not listen. He began to cry with all his might, saying that as long as his father was taking little Marie, he might just as well take him too. They replied that they must pass through great woods filled with wicked beasts who eat up little children. The grey would not carry three people; she had said so when they were starting, and in the country where they were going there was no bed and no supper for little boys. All these good reasons could not persuade Petit-Pierre; he threw himself on the ground, and rolled about, shrieking that his little father did not love him any more, and that if he did not take him he would never go back to the house at all, day or night.

Germain had a father's heart, as soft and weak as a woman's. His wife's death, and the care which he had been obliged to bestow all alone on his little ones, as well as the thought that these poor motherless children needed a great deal of love, combined to make him thus. So, such a sharp struggle went on within him, all the more because he was ashamed of his weakness and tried to hide his confusion from little Marie, that the sweat started out on his forehead, and his eyes grew red and almost ready to weep. At last he tried to get angry, but as he turned toward little Marie in order to let her witness his strength of mind, he saw that the good girl's face was wet with tears; all his courage forsook him and he could not keep back his own, scold and threaten as he would.

"Truly your heart is too hard," said little Marie at last, "and for myself I know that I never could refuse a child who felt so badly. Come, Germain, let's take him. Your mare is well used to carrying two people and a child, for you know that your brother-in-law and his wife, who is much heavier than I, go to market every Saturday with their boy on this good beast's back. Take him on the horse in front of you. Besides, I should rather walk on foot all alone than give this little boy so much pain."

"Never mind," answered Germain, who was dying to allow himself to give way. "The grey is strong, and could carry two more if there were room on her back. But what can we do with this child on the way? He will be cold and hungry, and who will take care of him to-night and to-morrow, put him to bed, wash him, and dress him? I don't dare give this trouble to a woman I don't know, who will think, doubtless, that I am exceedingly free and easy with her to begin with."

"Trust me, Germain, you will know her at once by the kindness or the impatience that she shows. If she does not care to receive your Pierre, I will take charge of him myself. I will go to her house and dress him, and I will take him to the fields with me to-morrow. I will amuse him all day long, and take good care that he does not want for anything."

"He will tire you, my poor girl, and give you trouble. A whole day is a long time."

"Not at all; it will give me pleasure; he will keep me company, and that will make me less sad the first day that

I must pass in a new place. I shall fancy that I am still at home."

Seeing that little Marie was pleading for him, the child seized upon her skirt and held it so tight that they must have hurt him in order to tear it away. When he perceived that his father was weakening, he took Marie's hand in both his tiny sunburned fists and kissed her, leaping for joy, and pulling her toward the mare with the burning impatience children feel in their desires.

"Come along," said the young girl, lifting him in her arms; "let us try to quiet his poor little heart. It is fluttering like a little bird; and if you feel the cold when night comes on, tell me, my Pierre, and I will wrap you in my cape. Kiss your little father, and beg his pardon for being naughty. Tell him that you will never, never be so again. Do you hear?"

"Yes, yes, provided that I always do just as he wishes. Isn't it so?" said Germain, drying the little boy's eyes with his handkerchief. "Marie, you are spoiling the little rascal. But really and truly, you are too good, little Marie. I don't know why you did not come to us as shepherdess last Saint John's Day. You would have taken care of my children, and I should much rather pay a good price for their sake than try to find a woman who will think, perhaps, she is doing me a great kindness if she does not detest them."

"You must not look on the dark side of things," answered little Marie, holding the horse's bridle while Germain placed his son in front of the big pack-saddle covered with goatskin. "If your wife does not care for children, take me into your service next year, and you may be sure I shall amuse them so well that they will not notice anything."

CHAPTER VI

On the Heath

"DEAR me," said Germain, after they had gone a few steps farther, "what will they think at home when they miss the little man? The family will be worried, and will be looking everywhere for him."

"You can tell the man who is mending the road up there that you are taking him along, and ask him to speak to your people."

"That is very true, Marie; you don't forget anything. It never occurred to me that Jeannie must be there."

"He lives close to the farm, and he will not fail to do your errand."

When they had taken this precaution, Germain put the mare to a trot, and Petit-Pierre was so overjoyed that for a time he forgot that he had gone without his dinner; but the motion of the horse gave him a hollow feeling in his stomach, and at the end of a league, he began to gape and grow pale, and confessed that he was dying of hunger.

"This is the way it begins," exclaimed Germain. "I was quite sure that we should not go far without this young gentleman crying with hunger or thirst."

"I am thirsty, too!" said Petit-Pierre.

"Very well, then, let's go to Mother Rebec's tavern at Corlay, the sign of 'The Dawn'—a pretty sign, but a poor lodging. You will take something to drink, too, will you not, Marie?"

"No, no; I don't want anything. I will hold the mare while you go in with the child."

"But I remember, my good girl, that this morning you gave the bread from your own breakfast to my Pierre. You have had nothing to eat. You would not take dinner with us at home; you would do nothing but cry."

"Oh, I was not hungry; I felt too sad, and I give you my word that even now I have no desire to eat."

"You must oblige yourself to eat, little girl, else you will fall sick. We have a long way to go, and it will not do to arrive half-starved and beg for bread before we say how d'ye do. I shall set you a good example myself, although I am not very hungry: and I am sure that I can, for, after all, I did not eat any dinner. I saw you crying, you and your mother, and it made me feel sad. Come along. I am going to tie the grey at the door. Get down; I wish you to."

All three entered the inn, and in less than fifteen minutes the fat, lame hostess was able to place before them a nice-looking omelette, some brown bread, and a bottle of light wine.

Peasants do not eat quickly, and little Pierre had such a good appetite that a whole hour passed before Germain could think of starting out again. At first little Marie ate in order to be obliging; then little by little she grew hungry. For, at sixteen, a girl cannot fast for long, and country air is dictatorial.

The kind words with which Germain knew how to comfort her and strengthen her courage, produced their effect. She tried hard to persuade herself that seven months would soon be over, and to think of the pleasure in store for her when she saw once more her family and her hamlet; for Father Maurice and Germain had both promised to take her into their service. But just as she began to cheer up and play with little Pierre, Germain was so unfortunate as to point out to her from the inn window the lovely view of the valley which can all be seen from this height, and which looks so happy and green and fertile.

Marie looked and asked if the houses of Belair were in sight.

"No doubt," said Germain, "and the farm too, and even your house—see! that tiny grey spot not far from Godard's big poplar, below the belfry."

"Ah, I see it," said the little girl; and then she began to cry.

"I ought not to have made you think of it," said Germain. "I can do nothing but stupid things to-day. Come along, Marie; let's start, and in an hour, when the moon rises, it will not be hot."

They resumed their journey across the great heath, and for fear of tiring the young girl and the child by too rapid a trot, Germain did not make the grey go very fast. The sun had set when they left the road to enter the wood.

Germain knew the way as far as Magnier, but he thought it would be shorter to avoid the Chantaloube road and descend by Presles and La Sépulture, a route he was not in the habit of taking on his way to the fair. He lost his way, and wasted more time before he reached the wood. Even then he did not enter it on the right side, although he did not perceive his mistake, so that he turned his back on Fourche, and took a direction higher up on the way to Ardente.

He was prevented still further from finding his way by a thick mist which rose as the night fell; one of those mists which come on autumn evenings when the whiteness of the moonlight renders them more undefined and more treacherous. The great pools of water scattered through the glades gave forth a vapour so dense that when the grey crossed them, their presence was known only by a splashing noise, and the difficulty with which she drew her feet from the mud.

At last they found a good straight road, and when they came to the end of it, and Germain tried to discover where he was, he saw that he was lost. For Father Maurice had told him, when he explained the way, that on leaving the wood he must descend a very steep hillside, cross a wide meadow, and ford the river twice. He had even warned him to cross this river carefully; for, early in the season, there had been great rains, and the water might still be higher than usual. Seeing neither hillside, nor meadows, nor river, but a heath, level and white as a mantle of snow, Germain stopped, looked about for a house, and waited for a passer-by, but could find nothing to set him right. Then he retraced his steps and re-entered the wood. But the mist thickened yet more, the moon was completely hidden, the roads were execrable, and the quagmires deep. Twice the grey almost fell. Her heavy load made her lose courage, and although she kept enough sagacity to avoid the tree-trunks, she could not prevent her riders from striking the great branches which overhung the road at the height of their heads and caused them great danger. In one of these collisions Germain lost his hat, and only recovered it after much difficulty. Petit-Pierre had fallen asleep, and, lying like a log in his father's arms, hampered him so that he could no longer hold up nor direct the horse.

"I believe we are bewitched," exclaimed Germain, stopping; "for the wood is not large enough to get lost in, if a man is not drunk, and here we have been turning round and round for two hours at least, without finding a way out. The grey has but one idea in her head, and that is to get home. It is she who is deceiving me. If we wish to go home, we have only to give her the bit. But when we are perhaps but two steps from our journey's end, it would be foolish to give up and return such a long road; and yet I am at a loss what to do. I can't see sky or earth, and I am afraid that the child will catch the fever if we remain in this cursed fog, or that he will be crushed beneath our weight if the horse falls forward."

"We must not persist longer," said little Marie. "Let's dismount, Germain. Give me the child; I can carry him perfectly well, and I know better than you how to keep the cloak from falling open and leaving him exposed. You lead the mare by her bridle. Perhaps we shall see more clearly when we are nearer the ground."

This precaution was of service only in saving them from a fall, for the fog hung low and seemed to stick to the damp earth.

Their advance was painfully slow, and they were soon so weary that they halted when they reached a dry spot beneath the great oaks.

Little Marie was in a violent sweat, but she uttered not a word of complaint, nor did she worry about anything. Thinking only of the child, she sat down on the sand and laid it upon her knees, while Germain explored the neighbourhood, after having fastened the grey's reins to the branch of a tree.

But the grey was very dissatisfied with her journey. She reared suddenly, broke the reins loose, burst her girths, and giving, by way of receipt, half a dozen kicks higher than her head, she started across the clearing, showing very plainly that she needed no one to show her the way home.

"Well, here we are afoot," said Germain, after a vain attempt to catch the horse, "and it would do us no good now if we were on the good road, for we should have to ford the river on foot, and since these paths are filled with water, we may be sure that the meadow is wholly submerged. We don't know the other routes. We must wait until this fog clears. It can't last more than an hour or two; as soon as we can see clearly, we shall look about for a house, the first we come to near the edge of the wood. But for the present we can't stir from here. There is a ditch and a pond over there. Heaven knows what is in front of us, and what is behind us is more than I can say now, for I have forgotten which way we came."

CHAPTER VII

Underneath the Big Oaks

"WELL, we must be patient, Germain," said little Marie. "We are not badly off on this little hillock. The rain does not pierce the leaves of these big oaks, and we can light a fire, for I can feel old stumps which stir readily and are dry enough to burn. You have a light, Germain, have you not? You were smoking your pipe a few minutes ago."

"I did have; my tinderbox was in my bag on the saddle with the game that I was bringing to my bride that is to be, but that devilish mare has run away with everything, even with my cloak, which she will lose and tear to bits on every branch she comes to."

"No, no, Germain; saddle and cloak and bag are all there on the ground at your feet. The grey burst her girths, and threw off everything as she ran away."

"That's true, thank God," exclaimed the labourer; "if we can grope about and find a little dead wood, we shall be able to dry ourselves and get warm."

"That's not difficult," said little Marie; "dead wood always cracks when you step on it. But will you give me the saddle?"

"What do you want of it?"

"To make a bed for the child. No, not that way. Upside down. He will not roll off into the hollow, and it is still very warm from the horse's back. Prop it up all around with the stones that you see there."

"I can't see a stone; you must have cat's eyes."

"There, it is all done, Germain. Hand me your cloak so that you can wrap up his little feet, and throw my cape over his body. Just see if he is not as comfortable as though he were in his own bed, and feel how warm he is."

"You certainly know how to take care of children, Marie."

"I need not be a witch to do that; now get your tinderbox from your bag, and I will arrange the wood."

"This wood will never catch fire; it is too damp."

"You are always doubting, Germain. Don't you remember when you were a shepherd, and made big fires in the fields right in the midst of the rain?"

"Yes, that is a knack that belongs to children who take care of sheep; but I was made to drive the oxen as soon as I could walk."

"That is what has made your arms strong and your hands quick! Here, the fire is built; you shall see whether it does not burn. Give me the light and a handful of dry ferns. That is all right. Now blow; you are not consumptive, are you?"

"Not that I know of," said Germain, blowing like a smith's bellows. In an instant the flame leaped up, and throwing out a red glare, it rose finally in pale blue jets under the oak branches, battling with the fog, and gradually drying the atmosphere for ten feet around.

"Now I am going to sit by the child, so that the sparks may not fall on him," said the young girl. "Pile on the wood and stir up the fire, Germain; we shall not catch cold nor fever here, I will answer for it."

"Upon my word, you are a clever girl," said Germain; "and you know how to make a fire like a little fairy of the night. I feel quite revived, and my courage has come back again; for with my legs drenched up to the knees, and with the thought of staying this way till daylight, I was in a very bad temper just now."

"And when people are in a bad temper they don't think of anything," answered little Marie.

"And are you never bad-tempered?"

"No, never; what is the good of it?"

"Oh, of course, there is no good; but how can you help it when you have troubles? Yet Heaven knows that you have not lacked them, my little girl; for you have not always been happy."

"It is true that my mother and I have suffered. We have had sorrows, but we have never lost heart."

"I should never lose heart, no matter how hard my work

was," said Germain, "but poverty would make me very sad; for I have never wanted for anything. My wife made me rich, and I am rich still; I shall be so as long as I work on the farm; and that will be always, I hope. But everybody must suffer his share! I have suffered in another way."

"Yes; you have lost your wife. That is very sad."

"Isn't it?"

"Oh, Germain, I have wept for her many a time. She was so very kind! But don't let us talk about her longer, for I shall burst out crying. All my troubles are ready to come back to me to-day."

"It is true, she loved you dearly, little Marie. She used to make a great deal of you and your mother. Are you crying? Come, my girl, I don't want to cry. . . ."

"But you are crying, Germain. You are crying as hard as I. Why should a man be ashamed to weep for his wife? Don't let me trouble you. That sorrow is mine as well as yours."

"You have a kind heart, Marie, and it does me good to weep with you. Put your feet nearer the fire; your skirts are all soaked, too, poor little girl. I am going to take your place by the boy. You move nearer the fire."

"I am hot enough," said Marie; "and if you wish to sit down, take a corner of the cloak. I am perfectly comfortable."

"The truth is that it is not so bad here," said Germain, as he sat down beside her. "Only I feel very hungry again. It is almost nine o'clock, and I have had such hard work in walking over these vile roads that I feel quite tired out. Are you not hungry, too, little Marie?"

"I?—not at all. I am not accustomed like you to four meals a day, and I have been to bed so often without my supper that once more does not trouble me."

"A woman like you is very convenient; she costs nothing," said Germain, smiling.

"I am not a woman," exclaimed Marie, naïvely, without perceiving the direction the husbandman's ideas had taken. "Are you dreaming?"

"Yes, I believe I must be dreaming," answered Germain. "Perhaps hunger is making my mind wander."

"How greedy you are," answered she, brightening in her turn. "Well, if you can't live five or six hours without eating, have you not game in your bag and fire to cook it?"

"By Jove, that's a good idea! But how about the present to my future father-in-law?"

"You have six partridges and a hare! I suppose you do not need all of them to satisfy your appetite."

"But how can we cook them without a spit or andirons. They will be burned to a cinder!"

"Not at all," said little Marie; "I warrant that I can cook them for you under the cinders without a taste of smoke. Have you never caught larks in the fields, and cooked them between two stones? Oh! that is true—I keep forgetting that you have never been a shepherd. Come, pluck the partridge. Not so hard! You will tear the skin."

"You might be plucking the other to show me how!"

"Then you wish to eat two? What an ogre you are! They are all plucked. I am going to cook them."

"You would make a perfect little sutler's girl, Marie, but unhappily you have no canteen, and I shall have to drink water from this pool!"

"You would like some wine, would you not? Possibly you might prefer coffee. You imagine yourself under the trees at the fair. Call out the host. Some wine for the good husbandman of Belair!"

"You little witch, you are making fun of me! Would not you drink some wine if you had it?"

"I? At Mother Rebec's, with you to-night, I drank some for the second time in my life. But if you are very good, I shall give you a bottle almost full, and excellent too."

"What? Marie, I verily believe you are a witch!"

"Were you not foolish enough to ask for two bottles of wine at the inn? You and your boy drank one, and the other you set before me. I hardly drank three drops, yet you paid for both without looking."

"What then?"

"Why, I put the full one in my basket, because I thought that you or your child would be thirsty on the journey. And here it is."

"You are the most thoughtful girl I have ever met. Although the poor child was crying when we left the inn, that did not prevent her from thinking of others more than of herself. Little Marie, the man who marries you will be no fool."

"I hope not, for I am not fond of fools. Come, eat up your partridges; they are done to a turn; and for want of bread, you must be satisfied with chestnuts."

"Where the deuce did you find chestnuts, too?"

"It is extraordinary! All along the road I picked them off the branches as we went along, and filled my pockets."

"And are they cooked, too?"

"Where would my wits have been had I not had sense enough to put the chestnuts in the fire as soon as it was lighted? That is the way we always do in the fields."

"So we are going to take supper together, little Marie, I want to drink your health and wish you a good husband, just the sort of a man that will suit you. Tell me what kind you want."

"I should find that very difficult, Germain, for I have not thought about it yet."

"What, not at all? Never?" said Germain, as he began to eat with a labourer's appetite, yet stopping to cut off the more tender morsels for his companion, who persisted in refusing them and contented herself with a few chestnuts.

"Tell me, little Marie," he went on, seeing that she had no intention of answering him, "have you never thought of marrying? Yet you are old enough?"

"Perhaps," she said, "but I am too poor. I need at least a hundred crowns to marry, and I must work five or six years to scrape them together."

"Poor girl, I wish Father Maurice were willing to give me a hundred crowns to make you a present of."

"Thank you kindly, Germain. What do you suppose people would say of me?"

"What do you wish them to say of you? They know very well that I am too old to marry you. They would never believe that I—that you——"

"Look, Germain, your child is waking up," said little Marie.

CHAPTER VIII

The Evening Prayer

PETIT-PIERRE had raised his head and was looking about him with a thoughtful air.

"Oh, that is the way he always does, whenever he hears the sound of eating," said Germain. "The explosion of a cannon would not rouse him, but if you work your jaws near him, he opens his eyes at once."

"You must have been just like him at his age," said little Marie, with a sly smile. "See! my Petit-Pierre, you are looking for your canopy. To-night it is made all of green, my child; but your father eats his supper none the less. Do you wish to sup with him? I have not eaten your share; I thought that you might claim it."

"Marie, I wish you to eat," cried the husbandman; "I shall not touch another morsel. I am a greedy glutton. You are depriving yourself for our sake. It is not fair. I am ashamed. It takes away all my appetite. I will not have my son eat his supper unless you take some too."

"Leave us alone," said little Marie; "you have not the key to our appetites. Mine is tight shut to-day, but your Pierre's is as wide open as a little wolf's. Just see how he seizes his food. He will be a strong workman, too, some day!"

In truth, Petit-Pierre showed very soon whose son he was, and though scarcely awake and wholly at a loss to know where he was and how he had come there, he began to eat ravenously. As soon as his hunger was appeased, feeling excited as children do who break loose from their wonted habits, he had more wit, more curiosity, and more good sense than usual. He made them explain to him where he was, and when he found that he was in the midst of a forest, he grew a little frightened.

"Are there wicked beasts in this forest?" he demanded of his father.

"No, none at all. Don't be afraid."

"Then you told a story when you said that if I went with you into the great forest, the wolves would carry me off."

"Just see this logician," said Germain, embarrassed.

"He is right," replied little Marie. "That is what you told him. He has a good memory, and has not forgotten. But, little Pierre, you must learn that your father never tells a story. We passed through the big forest whilst you were sleeping, and now we are in the small forest where there are no wicked beasts."

"Is the little forest very far away from the big one?"

"Far enough; besides, the wolves never go out of the big forest. And then, if some of them should come here, your father would kill them."

"And you too, little Marie?"

"Yes, we, too, for you would help also, my Pierre. You are not frightened, are you? You would beat them soundly?"

"Yes, indeed, I would," said the child, proudly, as he struck an heroic attitude; "we would kill them."

"There is nobody like you for talking to children and for making them listen to reason," said Germain to little Marie. "To be sure, it is not long ago since you were a small child yourself, and you have not forgotten what your mother used to say to you. I believe that the younger one is, the better one gets on with children. I am very much afraid that a woman of thirty who does not yet know what it is to be a mother, would find it hard to prattle to children and reason with them."

"Why, Germain? I don't know why you have such a bad idea of this woman; you will change your mind."

"The devil take the woman!" exclaimed Germain. "I wish I were going away from her forever. What do I want of a wife whom I don't know?"

"Little father," said the child, "why is it that you speak so much of your wife to-day, since she is dead?"

"Then you have not forgotten your poor, dear mother?"

"No; for I saw her placed in a beautiful box of white wood, and my grandmother led me up to her to kiss her and say good-bye. She was very white and very stiff, and every evening my aunt made me pray to God that she might go to

Him in Heaven and be warm. Do you think that she is there now?"

"I hope so, my child; but you must always pray. It shows your mother that you love her."

"I am going to say my prayers," answered the boy. "I forgot them to-night. But I can't say them all alone, for I always forget something. Little Marie must help me."

"Yes, my Pierre, I will help you," said the young girl. "Come and kneel down in my lap."

The child knelt down on the girl's skirt. He clasped his little hands and began to say his prayers, at first with great care and earnestness, for he knew the beginning very well, then slowly and with more hesitation, and finally repeating word by word after Marie, when he came to that place in his prayer where sleep overtook him so invariably that he had never been able to learn the end. This time again the effort of close attention and the monotony of his own accent produced their wonted effect. He pronounced the last syllables with great difficulty, and only after they were thrice repeated. His head grew heavy and fell on Marie's breast; his hands unclasped, divided, and fell open on his knees. By the light of the camp-fire, Germain watched his little darling hushed at the heart of the young girl, who, as she held him in her arms and warmed his fair hair with her sweet breath, had herself fallen into a holy reverie, and prayed in quiet for the soul of Catherine.

Germain was touched. He tried to express to little Marie the grateful esteem which he felt for her, but he could find no fitting words.

He approached her to kiss his son, whom she held close to her breast, and he could scarcely raise his lips from little Pierre's brow.

"You kiss too hard," said Marie, gently pushing away the husbandman's head. "You will wake him. Let me put him back to bed, for the boy has left us already for dreams of paradise."

The child allowed Marie to lay him down, but feeling the goatskin on the saddle, he asked if he were on the grey. Then opening his big blue eyes, and keeping them fixed on the branches for a minute, he seemed to be dreaming, wide-awake as he was, or to be struck with an idea which had slipped his mind during the daytime, and only assumed a distinct form at the approach of sleep.

"Little father," said he, "if you wish to give me a new mother, I hope it will be little Marie."

And without waiting for an answer, he closed his eyes and slept.

CHAPTER IX

Despite the Cold

LITTLE MARIE seemed to give no more heed to the child's odd words than to regard them as a proof of friendship. She wrapped him up with care, stirred the fire, and as the fog resting on the neighbouring pool gave no sign of lifting, she advised Germain to lie near the fire and take a nap.

"I see that you are sleepy already," said she, "for you don't say a word and you gaze into the fire, just as your little boy was doing."

"It is you who must sleep," answered the husbandman, "and I will take care of both of you, for I have never felt less sleepy than I do now. I have fifty things to think of."

"Fifty is a great many," said the little girl, with a mocking accent. "There are lots of people who would be delighted to have one."

"Well, if I am too stupid to have fifty, I have one, at least, which has not left me for the past hour."

"And I shall tell it to you as well as I told you those you thought of before."

"Yes, do tell me if you know, Marie. Tell me yourself. I shall be glad to hear."

"An hour ago," she answered, "your idea was to eat—and now it is to sleep."

"Marie, I am only an ox-driver, but, upon my word, you take me for an ox. You are very perverse, and it is easy to see that you do not care to talk to me, so go to sleep. That will be better than to pick flaws in a man who is out of sorts."

"If you wish to talk, let's talk," said the girl, half reclining near the child and resting her head against the saddle. "You torment yourself, Germain, and you do not show much courage for a man. What wouldn't I say if I didn't do my best to fight my own troubles?"

"Yes, that's very true, and that's just what I am thinking of, my poor child. You are going to live, away from your friends, in a horrid country full of moors and fens, where you will catch the autumn fevers. Sheep do not pay well there, and this is always discouraging for a shepherdess if she means well. Then you will be surrounded by strangers who may not be kind to you and will not know how much you are worth. It makes me more sorry than I can tell you, and I have a great desire to take you home to your mother instead of going on to Fourche."

"You talk very kindly, but there is no reason for your misgivings, my poor Germain. You ought not to lose heart on your friend's account, and instead of showing me the dark side of my lot, you should show me the bright side, as you did after lunch at Rebec's."

"What can I do? That's the way it appeared to me then, and now my ideas are changed. It is best for you to take a husband."

"That cannot be, Germain, and as it is out of the question, I think no more about it."

"Yet such a thing might happen. Perhaps if you told me what kind of a man you want, I might imagine somebody."

"Imagining is not finding. For myself, I never imagine, for it does no good."

"You are not looking for a rich man?"

"Certainly not, for I am as poor as Job."

"But if he were comfortably off, you wouldn't be sorry to have a good house, and good food, and good clothes, and to live with an honest family who would allow you to help your mother."

"Oh, yes, indeed! It is my own wish to help my mother."

"And if this man were to turn up, you would not be too hard to please, even if he were not so very young."

"Ah! There you must excuse me, Germain. That is just the point I insist on. I could never love an old man."

"An old man, of course not; but a man of my age, for example!"

"Your age is too old for me, Germain. I should like Bastien's age, though Bastien is not so good-looking as you."

"Should you rather have Bastien, the swine-herd?" said Germain, indignantly. "A fellow with eyes shaped like those of the pigs he drives!"

"I could excuse his eyes, because he is eighteen."

Germain felt terribly jealous.

"Well," said he, "it's clear that you want Bastien, but, none the less, it's a queer idea."

"Yes, that would be a queer idea," answered little Marie, bursting into shouts of laughter, "and he would make a queer husband. You could gull him to your heart's content. For instance, the other day, I had picked up a tomato in the curate's garden. I told him that it was a fine, red apple, and he bit into it like a glutton. If you had only seen what a face he made. Heavens! how ugly he was!"

"Then you don't love him, since you are making fun of him."

"That wouldn't be a reason. But I don't like him. He is unkind to his little sister, and he is dirty."

"Don't you care for anybody else?"

"How does that concern you, Germain?"

"Not at all, except that it gives me something to talk about. I see very well, little girl, that you have a sweetheart in your mind already."

"No, Germain, you're wrong. I have no sweetheart yet. Perhaps one may come later, but since I cannot marry until I have something laid by, I am destined to marry late in life and with an old man."

"Then take an old man without delay."

"No. When I am no longer young, I shall not care; for the present, it is different."

"I see that I displease you, Marie; that's clear enough," said Germain, impatiently, and without stopping to weigh his words.

Little Marie did not answer. Germain bent over her. She was sleeping. She had fallen back, overcome, stricken down, as it were, by slumber, as children are who sleep before they cease to babble.

Germain was glad that she had not caught his last words. He felt that they were unwise and he turned his back to distract his attention and change his thoughts.

It was all in vain. He could neither sleep nor think of anything except the words he had just spoken. He walked about the fire twenty times; he moved away; he came back. At last, feeling himself tremble as though he had swallowed gunpowder, he leaned against the tree which sheltered the two children, and watched them as they slept.

"I know not how it is," thought he; "I have never noticed that little Marie is the prettiest girl in the countryside. She has not much colour, but her little face is fresh as a wild rose. What a charming mouth she has, and how pretty her little nose is! She is not large for her age, but she is formed like a little quail and is as light as a bird. I cannot understand why they made so much fuss at home over a big, fat woman with a bright red face. My wife was rather slender and pale, and she pleased me more than any one else. This girl is very frail, but she is healthy, and she is pretty to watch as a white kid. And then she has such a gentle, frank expression. You can read her good heart in her eyes even though they are closed in sleep. As to wit, I must confess she has more than ever my dear Catherine had, and she would never become wearisome. She is gay, wise, industrious, loving, and she is amusing. I don't know what more I could wish for. . . .

"But what is the use of thinking of all this?" Germain went on trying to look in another direction. "My father-in-law would not hear of it, and all the family would think me mad! Besides, she would not have me herself, poor child! She thinks me too old; she told me so. She is unselfish, and does not mind poverty and worry, wearing old clothes, and suffering from hunger for two or three months every year, so long as she can satisfy her heart some day and give herself to the man she loves. She is right. I should do the same in her place, and even now, if I had my own way, instead of marrying a wife whom I don't care for, I would choose a girl after my own heart."

The more Germain tried to compose himself by reasoning, the further he was from succeeding. He walked away a dozen steps, to lose himself in the fog; then, all of a sudden, he found himself on his knees beside the two sleeping children. Once he wished to kiss Petit-Pierre, who had one arm about Marie's neck, and made such a mistake that Marie felt a breath, hot as fire, cross her lips, and awakening, looked about her with a bewildered expression totally ignorant of all that was passing within his mind.

"I didn't see you, my poor children," said Germain, retreating rapidly. "I almost stumbled over you and hurt you."

Little Marie was so innocent that she believed him, and fell asleep again. Germain walked to the opposite side of the fire, and swore to God that he would not stir until she had waked. He kept his word, but not without a struggle. He thought that he would go mad.

At length, toward midnight, the fog lifted, and Germain could see the stars shining through the trees. The moon freed herself from the mist which had hidden her, and began to sow her diamonds over the damp moss. The trunks of the oak-trees remained in impressive darkness, but beyond, the white branches of the birch-trees seemed a long line of phantoms in their shrouds. The fire cast its reflection in the pool; and the frogs, growing accustomed to the light, hazarded a few shrill and uneasy notes; the rugged branches of the old trees, bristling with dim-coloured lichens, crossed and intertwined themselves, like great gaunt arms, above the travellers' heads. It was a lovely spot, but so lonely and so sad that Germain, unable to endure it more, began to sing and throw stones into the water to forget the dread weariness of solitude. He was anxious also to wake little Marie, and when he saw her rise and look about at the weather, he proposed that they start on their journey.

"In two hours," said he, "the approach of morning will chill the air so that we can't stay here in spite of our fire. Now we can see our way, and we shall soon find a house which will open its doors to us, or at least a barn where we can pass the rest of the night under shelter."

Marie had no will of her own, and although she was longing to sleep, she made ready to follow Germain. The husbandman took his boy in his arms without waking him, and beckoned Marie to come nearer, in order to cover her with his cloak. For she would not take her own mantle, which was wrapped about the child.

When he felt the young girl so close to him, Germain, who for a time had succeeded in distracting his mind and raising his spirits, began to lose his head once more. Two or three times he strode ahead abruptly, leaving her to walk alone. Then seeing how hard it was for her to follow, he waited, drew her quickly to his side, and pressed her so tight that she was surprised, and even angry, though she dared not say so.

As they knew not the direction whence they had come, they had no idea of that in which they were going. So they crossed the wood once more, and found themselves afresh before the lonely moor. Then they retraced their steps, and after much turning and twisting they spied a light across the branches.

"Good enough! Here's a house," exclaimed Germain. "And the people are already astir, for the fire is lighted. It must be very late."

It was no house, but the camp-fire, which they had covered before they left, and which had sprung up in the breeze.

They had tramped for two hours, only to find themselves at the very place from which they had started.

CHAPTER X

Beneath the Stars

"THIS time I give up," said Germain, stamping his foot. "We are bewitched, that is certain, and we shall not get away from here before broad day. The devil is in this place!"

"Well, it's of no use to get angry," said Marie. "We must take what is given us. Let us make a big fire. The child is so well wrapped up that he is in no danger, and we shall not die from a single night out of doors. Where have you hidden the saddle, Germain? Right in the midst of the holly-bushes,—what a goose you are! It's very convenient to get it from there!"

"Stop, child; hold the boy while I pull his bed from the thorns. I didn't want you to scratch your hands."

"It's all done. Here's the bed, and a few scratches are not sabre-cuts," replied the brave girl.

She proceeded to put the child to bed again, and Petit-Pierre was so sound asleep this time that he knew nothing of his last journey. Germain piled so much wood on the fire that the forest all about glowed with the light.

Little Marie had come to the end of her powers, and although she did not complain, her legs would support her no longer. She was white, and her teeth chattered with cold and weakness. Germain took her in his arms to warm her. The uneasiness, the compassion, the tenderness of movement he could not repress, took possession of his heart and stilled his senses. As by a miracle his tongue was loosened, and every feeling of shame vanished.

"Marie," said he, "I like you, and I am very sorry that you don't like me. If you would take me for your husband, there are no fathers, nor family, nor neighbours, nor arguments which could prevent me from giving myself to you. I know how happy you would make my children, and that you would teach them to love the memory of their mother, and with a quiet conscience I could satisfy the wishes of my heart. I have always been fond of you, and now I love you so well that were you to ask me to spend all my life in doing your pleasure, I would swear to do it on the instant. Please think how much I love you, and try to forget my age. Think that it is a wrong notion to believe that a man of thirty is old. Besides, I am but twenty-eight. A young girl is afraid that people will talk about her if she takes a man ten or twelve years older than she, simply because that is not the custom in our country, but I have heard say that in other countries people don't look at it in this light, and that they had rather allow a sensible man of approved courage to support a young girl, than trust her to a mere boy, who may go astray, and, from the honest fellow they thought him, turn into a good-for-nothing. And then years don't always make age. That depends on the health and strength a person has. When a man is used up by overwork and poverty, or by a bad life, he is old before twenty-five. While I—but Marie, you are not listening. . . ."

"Yes, I am, Germain; I hear you perfectly," answered little Marie, "but I am thinking over what my mother used to tell me so often: that a woman of sixty is to be pitied greatly when her husband is seventy or seventy-five and can no longer work to support her. He grows feeble, and it becomes her duty to nurse him at the very age when she begins to feel great need of care and rest herself, and so it is that the end comes in a garret."

"Parents do well to say so, I admit," answered Germain, "but then they would sacrifice all their youth, the best years of their life, to calculating what will become of them at the age when a person is no longer good for anything, and when it is a matter of indifference which way death comes. But I am in no danger of starving in my old age. I am even going to lay by something, since I live with my wife's parents and spend nothing. And then, you see, I shall love you so well that I can never grow old. They say that when a man is happy he keeps sound, and I know well that in love for you

I am younger than Bastien; for he does not love you; he is too stupid, too much of a child to understand how pretty and how good you are, and how you were made for people to court. Do not hate me, Marie. I am not a bad man. I made my Catherine happy, and on her death-bed she swore before God that she had had only happiness of me, and she asked me to marry again. Her spirit must have spoken to her child to-night. Did you not hear the words he said? How his little lips quivered as his eyes stared upward, watching something that we could not see! He was surely looking at his mother, and it was she who made him say that he wished you to take her place."

"Germain," answered Marie, amazed and yet thoughtful, "you speak frankly, and everything that you say is true. I am sure that I should do well to love you if it did not displease your parents too much. But what can I do? My heart does not speak for you. I am very fond of you, but though your age does not make you ugly, it makes me afraid. It seems as if you were some such relation to me, as an uncle or a godfather, that I must be respectful toward you, and that there might be moments when you would treat me like a little girl rather than like your wife and your equal. And perhaps my friends would make fun of me, and although it would be silly to give heed to that, I think that I should be a little sad on my wedding-day."

"Those are but childish reasons, Marie; you speak like a child."

"Yes, that is true; I am a child," said she, "and it is on that account I am afraid of too sensible a man. You must see that I am too young for you, since you just found fault with me for speaking foolishly. I can't have more sense than my age allows."

"O Heavens! how unlucky I am to be so clumsy and to express so ill what I think!" cried Germain. "Marie, you don't love me. That is the long and short of it. You find me too simple and too dull. If you loved me at all, you would not see my faults so clearly. But you do not love me. That is the whole story."

"That is not my fault," answered she, a little hurt that he was speaking with less tenderness. "I am doing my best to hear you, but the more I try the less I can get it into my head that we ought to be husband and wife."

Germain did not answer. His head dropped into his hands, and little Marie could not tell whether he wept or sulked or was fast asleep. She felt uneasy when she saw him so cast down, and could not guess what was passing in his mind. But she dared not speak to him more, and as she was too astonished at what had passed to have any desire to sleep, she waited impatiently for dawn, tending the fire with care and watching over the child, whose existence Germain appeared to forget. Yet Germain was not asleep. He did not mope over his lot. He made no plans to encourage himself, nor schemes to entrap the girl. He suffered; he felt a great weight of grief at his heart. He wished that he were dead.

The world seemed to turn against him, and if he could have wept at all, his tears would have come in floods. But mingled with his sorrow there was a feeling of anger against himself, and he felt choked, without the power or the wish to complain.

When morning came, and the sounds of the country brought it to Germain's senses, he lifted his head from his hands and rose. He saw that little Marie had slept no more than he, but he knew no words in which to tell her of his anxiety. He was very discouraged. Hiding the grey's saddle once more in the thicket, he slung his sack over his shoulder and took his son by the hand.

"Now, Marie," said he, "we are going to try to end our journey. Do you wish me to take you to Ormeaux?"

"Let us leave the woods together," answered she, "and when we know where we are, we shall separate, and go our different ways."

Germain did not answer. He felt hurt that the girl did not ask him to take her as far as Ormeaux, and he did not notice that he had asked her in a tone well fitted to provoke a refusal.

After a few hundred steps, they met a wood-cutter, who pointed out the high road, and told them that when they had crossed the plain, one must turn to the right, the other to the left to gain their different destinations, which were so near together that the houses of Fourche were in plain sight from the farm of Ormeaux, and *vice versa.*

When they had thanked him and passed on, the wood-cutter called them back to ask whether they had not lost a horse.

"Yes," he said, "I found a pretty grey mare in my yard, where perhaps a wolf had driven her to seek refuge; my dogs barked the whole night long, and at daybreak I saw the mare under my shed. She is there now. Come along with me, and if you recognise her, you may take her."

When Germain had given a description of the grey, and felt convinced that it was really she, he started back to find his saddle. Little Marie offered to take his child to Ormeaux, whither he might go to get him after he had introduced himself at Fourche.

"He's rather dirty after the night that we have passed," said she. "I will brush his clothes, wash his pretty face, and comb his hair, and when he looks neat and clean, you can present him to your new family."

"Who told you that I wish to go to Fourche?" answered Germain, petulantly. "Perhaps I shall not go."

"But truly, Germain, it is your duty to go there. You will go there," replied the girl.

"You seem very anxious to have me married off, so that you may be quite sure that I shall not trouble you again?"

"Germain, you must not think of that any more. It is an idea which came to you in the night, because this unfortunate mishap took away your spirits. But now you must come to your senses. I promise you to forget everything that you said to me, and not breathe it to a soul."

"Oh, say what you wish. It is not my custom to deny what I have spoken. What I told you was true and honest, and I shall not blush for it before anybody."

"Yes, but if your wife were to know that just before you came you were thinking of another woman, it would prejudice her against you. So take care how you speak now. Don't look at me before everybody with such a rapt expression. Think of Father Maurice, who relies on your obedience, and who would be enraged at me if I were to turn you from his will. Good-bye, Germain. I take Petit-

Pierre in order to force you to go to Fourche. He is a pledge which I keep on your behalf."

"So you want to go with her?" said the husbandman to his son, seeing that the boy had clasped Marie's hands and was following her resolutely.

"Yes, father," answered the child, who had heard the conversation and understood after his own fashion the words spoken so unguardedly before him. "I am going away with my dearest little Marie. You shall come to find me when you have done marrying, but I wish Marie to be my little mother."

"You see how much he wishes it," said Germain to the girl. "Listen to me, Petit-Pierre," he added. "I wish her to be your mother and to stay with you always. It is she who does not wish to. Try to make her grant you what she has denied me."

"Don't be afraid, father, I shall make her say yes. Little Marie does everything that I wish."

He walked away with the young girl. Germain stood alone, sadder and more irresolute than ever.

XI

The Belle of the Village

AND after all, when he had brushed the dust of travel from his clothes and from his horse's harness, when he had mounted the grey, and when he had learned the road, he felt that there was no retreat and that he must forget that anxious night as though it had been a dangerous dream.

He found Father Leonard seated on a trim bench of spinach-green. The six stone steps leading up to the door showed that the house had a cellar. The walls of the garden and of the hemp-field were plastered with lime and sand. It was a handsome house, and might almost have been mistaken for the dwelling of a bourgeois.

Germain's future father-in-law came forward to meet him, and having plied him, for five minutes, with questions concerning his entire family, he added that conventional phrase with which one passer-by addresses another concerning the object of his journey: "So you are taking a little trip in this part of the country?"

"I have come to see you," replied the husbandman, "to give you this little present of game with my father's compliments, and to tell you from him that you ought to know with what intentions I come to your house."

"Oh, ho!" said Father Leonard, laughing and tapping his capacious stomach, "I see, I understand, I am with you, and," he added with a wink "you will not be the only one to pay your court, young man. There are three already in the house dancing attendance like you. I never turn anybody away, and I should find it hard to say yes or no to any of them, for they are all good matches. Yet, on account of Father Maurice and for the sake of the rich fields you till, I hope that it may be you. But my daughter is of age and mistress of her own affairs. She will do as she likes.

Go in and introduce yourself. I hope that you will draw the prize."

"I beg your pardon," answered Germain, amazed to find himself an extra when he had counted on being alone in the field. "I was not aware that your daughter was supplied already with suitors, and I did not come to quarrel over her."

"If you supposed that because you were slow in coming, my daughter would be left unprovided for, you were greatly mistaken, my son," replied Father Leonard with unshaken good humour. "Catherine has the wherewithal to attract suitors, and her only difficulty lies in choosing. But come in; don't lose heart. The woman is worth a struggle."

And pushing in Germain by the shoulders with boisterous gaiety, he called to his daughter as they entered the house:

"So, Catherine, here is another!"

This cordial but unmannerly method of introduction to the widow, in the presence of her other devotees, completed Germain's distress and embarrassment. He felt the awkwardness of his position, and stood for a few moments without daring to look upon the beauty and her court.

The Widow Guérin had a good figure and did not lack freshness, but her expression and her dress displeased Germain the instant he saw her. She had a bold, self-satisfied look, and her cap, edged with three lace flounces, her silk apron, and her fichu of fine black lace were little in accord with the staid and sober widow he had pictured to himself.

Her elaborate dress and forward manner inclined Germain to judge the widow old and ugly, although she was certainly not either. He thought that such finery and playful manners might well suit little Marie's years and wit, but that the widow's fun was laboured and over bold, and that she wore her fine clothes in bad taste.

The three suitors were seated at a table loaded with wines and meats which were spread out for their use throughout the Sunday morning; for Father Leonard liked to show off his wealth, and the widow was not sorry to display her pretty china and keep a table like a rich lady. Germain, simple and unsuspecting as he was, watched everything with a penetrating glance, and for the first time in his life he kept on the defensive when he drank. Father Leonard obliged him to sit down with his rivals, and taking a chair opposite he treated him with great politeness, and talked to him rather than to the others.

The present of game, despite the breach Germain had made on his own account, was still plenteous enough to produce its effect. The widow did not look unaware of its presence, and the suitors cast disdainful glances in its direction.

Germain felt ill at ease in this company, and did not eat heartily. Father Leonard poked fun at him.

"You look very melancholy," said he, "and you are ill-using your glass. You must not allow love to spoil your appetite, for a fasting lover can make no such pretty speeches as he whose ideas are brightened with a drop of wine."

Germain was mortified at being thought already in love, and the artificial manner of the widow, who kept lowering her eyes with a smile as a woman does who is sure of her calculations, made him long to protest against his pretended surrender; but fearing to appear uncivil, he smiled and held his peace.

He thought the widow's beaus, three bumpkins. They must have been rich for her to admit of their pretensions. One was over forty, and fat as Father Leonard; another had lost an eye, and drank like a sot. The third was a young fellow, and nice-looking; but he kept insisting on displaying his wit, and would say things so silly that they were painful to hear. Yet the widow laughed as though she admired all his foolishness, and made small proof of her good taste thereby. At first Germain thought her infatuated with him, but soon he perceived that he himself was especially encouraged, and that they wished him to make fresh advances. For this reason he felt an increasing stiffness and severity which he took no pains to conceal.

The time came for mass, and they rose from table to go thither in company. It was necessary to walk as far as Mers, a good half-league away, and Germain was so tired that he longed to take a nap before they went; but he was not in the habit of missing mass, and he started with the others.

The roads were filled with people, and the widow marched proudly along, escorted by her three suitors, taking an arm, first of one and then of another, and carrying her head high with an air of importance. She was eager to display the fourth to the eyes of the passers-by; but Germain felt so ridiculous to be dragged along in the train of a petticoat where all the world might see, that he kept at a respectable distance, chatting with Father Leonard, and succeeded in occupying his attention so well that they did not look at all as if they belonged to the party.

XII

The Master

WHEN they reached the village, the widow halted to allow them to catch up. She was bent upon making her entry with all her train; but Germain, denying her this pleasure, deserted Father Leonard, and after conversing with several acquaintances, he entered the church by another door. The widow was vexed.

When mass was over, she made her appearance in triumph on the lawn, where dancing was going on, and she began her dance with her three lovers in turn. Germain watched her and saw that she danced well, but with affectation.

"So, you don't ask my daughter?" said Leonard, tapping him on the shoulder. "You are too easily frightened."

"I have not danced since I lost my wife," answered the husbandman.

"But now that you are looking for another, mourning's over in heart as well as in clothes."

"That's no reason, Father Leonard. Besides, I am too old and I don't care for dancing."

"Listen," said Father Leonard, drawing him toward a retired corner, "when you entered my house you were vexed to see the place already besieged, and I see that you are very proud. But that is not reasonable, my boy. My daughter is used to a great deal of attention, particularly since she left off her mourning two years ago, and it is not her place to lead you on."

"Has your daughter been thinking of marrying for two years already without making her choice?" asked Germain.

"She doesn't wish to hurry, and she is right. Although she has lively manners, and although you may not think that she reflects a great deal, she is a woman of excellent common sense, and knows very well what she is about."

"It does not appear to me so," said Germain ingenuously, "for she has three suitors in her train, and if she knew her own mind, there are two of them, at least, whom she would find superfluous and request to stay at home."

"Why, Germain, you don't understand at all. She doesn't wish the old man, nor the blind man, nor the young man, I am quite certain; yet if she were to turn them off, people would think that she wished to remain a widow and nobody else would come."

"Oh, I see. These three are used for a guide-post."

"As you like. What is the harm if they are satisfied?"

"Every man to his taste," said Germain.

"I see that yours is different. Now supposing that you are chosen, then they would leave the coast clear."

"Yes, supposing! and meanwhile how much time should I have to whistle?"

"That depends on your persuasive tongue, I suppose. Until now, my daughter has always thought that she would pass the best part of her life while she was being courted, and she is in no hurry to become the servant of one man when she can order so many others about. So she will please herself as long as the game amuses her; but if you please her more than the game, the game will cease. Only you must not lose courage. Come back every Sunday, dance with her, let me know that you are amongst her followers, and if she finds you more agreeable and better bred than the others, some fine day she will tell you so, no doubt."

"Excuse me, Father Leonard. Your daughter has the right to do as she pleases, and it is not my business to blame her. If I were in her place, I should do differently. I should be more frank, and should not waste the time of men who have, doubtless, something better to do than dancing attendance on a woman who makes fun of them. Still, if that is what amuses her and makes her happy, it is no affair of mine. Only there is one thing I must tell you which is a little embarrassing, since you have mistaken my intentions from the start, for you are so sure of what is not so, that you have given me no chance to explain. You must know, then, that I did not come here to ask for your daughter in marriage, but merely to buy a pair of oxen which you are going to take to market next week, and which my father-in-law thinks will suit him."

"I understand, Germain," answered Leonard very calmly; "you changed your plans when you saw my daughter with her admirers. It is as you please. It seems that what attracts some people repels others, and you are perfectly welcome to withdraw, for you have not declared your intentions. If you wish seriously to buy my cattle, come and see them in the pasture, and whether we make a bargain or not, you will come back to dinner with us before you return."

"I don't wish to trouble you," answered Germain. "Perhaps you have something to do here. I myself am tired of watching the dancing and standing idle. I will go to see your cattle, and I will soon join you at your house."

Then Germain made his escape, and walked away toward the meadows where Leonard had pointed out to him some of his cattle. It was true that Father Maurice intended to buy, and Germain thought that if he were to bring home a fine pair of oxen at a reasonable price, he might more easily receive a pardon for wilfully relinquishing the purpose of his journey. He walked rapidly, and soon found himself at some distance from Ormeaux. Then of a sudden, he felt a desire to kiss his son and to see little Marie once again, although he had lost all hope and even had chased away the thought that he might some day owe his happiness to her. Everything that he had heard and seen: this woman, flirtatious and vain; this father, at once shrewd and short-sighted, encouraging his daughter in habits of pride and untruth; this city luxury, which seemed to him a transgression against the dignity of country manners; this time wasted in foolish, empty words; this home so different from his own; and, above all, that deep uneasiness which comes to a labourer of the fields when he leaves his accustomed toil: all the trouble and annoyance of the past few hours made Germain long to be with his child and with his little neighbour. Even had he not been in love, he would have sought her to divert his mind and raise his spirits to their wonted level.

But he looked in vain over the neighbouring meadows,

He saw neither little Marie nor little Pierre, and yet it was the hour when shepherds are in the fields. There was a large flock in a pasture. He asked of a young boy who tended them whether the sheep belonged to the farm of Ormeaux.

"Yes," said the child.

"Are you the shepherd? Do boys tend the flocks of the farm, amongst you?"

"No, I am taking care of them to-day, because the shepherdess went away. She was ill."

"But have you not a new shepherdess, who came this morning?"

"Yes, surely; but she, too, has gone already."

"What! gone? Did she not have a child with her?"

"Yes, a little boy who cried. They both went away after they had been here two hours."

"Went away! Where?"

"Where they came from, I suppose. I didn't ask them."

"But why did they go away?" asked Germain, growing more and more uneasy.

"How the deuce do I know?"

"Did they not agree about wages? Yet that must have been settled before."

"I can tell you nothing about it. I saw them come and go, nothing more."

Germain walked toward the farm and questioned the farmer. Nobody could give him an explanation; but after speaking with the farmer, he felt sure that the girl had gone without saying a word, and had taken the weeping child with her.

"Can they have been ill-treating my son?" cried Germain.

"It was your son, then? How did he happen to be with the little girl? Where do you come from, and what is your name?"

Germain, seeing that after the fashion of the country they were answering him with questions, stamped his foot impatiently, and asked to speak with the master.

The master was away. Usually, he did not spend the whole day when he came to the farm. He was on horseback, and he had ridden off to one of his other farms.

"But honestly," said Germain, growing very anxious, "can't you tell me why this girl left?"

The farmer and his wife exchanged an odd smile. Then the former answered that he knew nothing, and that it was no business of his. All that Germain could learn was that both girl and child had started off toward Fourche. He rushed back to Fourche. The widow and her lovers were still away; so was Father Leonard. The maid told him that a girl and a child had come to ask for him, but that as she did not know them, she did not wish to let them in, and had advised them to go to Mers.

"And why did you refuse to let them in?" said Germain, angrily. "People are very suspicious in this country, where nobody opens the door to a neighbour."

"But you see," answered the maid, "in a house as rich as this, I must keep my eyes open. When the master is away, I am responsible for everything, and I cannot open the door to the first person that comes along."

"It is a bad custom," said Germain, "and I had rather be poor than to live in constant fear like that. Good-bye to you, young woman, and good-bye to your vile country."

He made inquiries at the neighbouring house. The shepherdess and child had been seen. As the boy had left Belair suddenly, carelessly dressed, with his blouse torn, and his little lambskin over his shoulders, and as little Marie was necessarily poorly clad at all times, they had been taken for beggars. People had offered them bread. The girl had accepted a crust for the child, who was hungry, then she had walked away with him very quickly, and had entered the forest.

Germain thought a minute, then he asked whether the farmer of Ormeaux had not been at Fourche.

"Yes," they answered, "he passed on horseback a few seconds after the girl."

"Was he chasing her?"

"Oh, so you understand?" answered the village publican, with a laugh. "Certain it is that he is the devil of a fellow for running after girls. But I don't believe that he caught her; though, after all, if he had seen her——"

"That is enough, thank you!" And he flew rather than ran to Leonard's stable. Throwing the saddle on the grey's back, he leaped upon it, and set off at full gallop toward the wood of Chanteloube.

His heart beat hard with fear and anger; the sweat poured down his forehead; he spurred the mare till the blood came, though the grey needed no pressing when she felt herself on the road to her stable.

CHAPTER XIII

The Old Woman

GERMAIN came soon to the spot where he had passed the night on the border of the pool. The fire was smoking still. An old woman was gathering the remnants of the wood little Marie had piled there. Germain stopped to question her. She was deaf and mistook his inquiries.

"Yes, my son," said she, "this is the Devil's Pool. It is an evil spot, and you must not approach it without throwing in three stones with your left hand, while you cross yourself with the right. That drives away the spirits. Otherwise trouble comes to those who go around it."

"I am not asking about that," said Germain, moving nearer her, and screaming at the top of his lungs. "Have you seen a girl and a child walking through the wood?"

"Yes," said the old woman, "a little child was drowned there."

Germain shook from head to foot; but happily the hag added:

"That happened a long time ago. In memory of the accident they raised a handsome cross there. But one stormy night, the bad spirits threw it into the water. You can still see one end of it. If anybody were unlucky enough to pass the night here, he could never find his way out before daylight. He must walk and walk, and though he went two hundred leagues into the forest, he must always return to the same place."

The peasant's imagination was aroused in spite of himself, and the thought of the evils that must come in order that the old woman's assertions might be vindicated, took so firm a hold of his mind that he felt chilled through and through. Hopeless of obtaining more news, he remounted, and traversed the woods afresh, calling Pierre with all his might, whistling, cracking his whip, and snapping the branches that the whole forest might re-echo with the noise of his coming; then he listened for an answering voice, but he heard no sound save the cow-bells scattered through the glades, and the wild cries of the swine as they fought over the acorns.

At length Germain heard behind him the noise of a horse following in his traces, and a man of middle age, dark, sturdy, and dressed after the city fashion, called to him to stop. Germain had never seen the farmer of Ormeaux, but his instinctive rage told him at once that this was the man. He turned, and eyeing him from head to foot, waited for him to speak.

"Have not you seen a young girl of fifteen or sixteen go by with a small boy?" asked the farmer, with an assumed air of indifference, although he was evidently ill at ease.

"What do you want of her?" answered Germain, taking no pains to conceal his anger.

"I might tell you that that is none of your business, my friend. But as I have no reason for secrecy, I shall tell you that she is a shepherdess whom I engaged for a year, before I knew her. When I saw her, she looked too young and frail to work on the farm. I thanked her, but I wished to pay the expenses of her short journey, and while my back was turned, she went off in a huff. She was in such a hurry that she forgot even some of her belongings and her purse, which has certainly not much in it, probably but a few pennies; but since I was going in this direction, I hoped to meet her, and give her back the things which she left behind, as well as what I owe her."

Germain had too honest a heart not to pause at hearing a story which, however unlikely, was not impossible. He fastened his penetrating gaze on the farmer, who submitted to the examination with a plentiful supply of impudence or of good faith.

"I wish to get at the bottom of this matter," said Germain; "and," continued he, suppressing his indignation, "the girl lives in my village. I know her. She can't be far away. Let's ride on together; we shall find her, no doubt."

"You are right," said the farmer; "let's move on; but if we do not find her before we reach the end of this road, I shall give up, for I must turn off toward the Ardentes."

"Oh, oh!" thought the peasant, "I shall not part with you, even if I have to follow you around the Devil's Pool for twenty-four hours."

"Stop," said Germain suddenly, fixing his eyes on a clump of broom which waved in a peculiar manner. "Halloa! halloa! Petit-Pierre, is that you, my child?"

The boy recognised his father's voice, and came out from the broom leaping like a young deer; but when he saw Germain in company with the farmer, he stopped dismayed, and stood resolute.

"Come, my Pierre, come. It is I," cried the husbandman, as he leaped from his horse and ran toward his boy to take him in his arms; "and where is little Marie?"

"She is hiding there, because she is afraid of that dreadful black man, and so am I."

"You needn't be afraid. I am here. Marie, Marie. It is I."

Marie crept toward them, but the moment she saw Germain with the farmer close behind, she sprang forward, and throwing herself into his arms, clung to him as a daughter to her father.

"Oh, my brave Germain!" she cried, "you will defend me. I am not afraid when you are near."

Germain shuddered. He looked at Marie. She was pale; her clothes were torn by the thorns which had scratched her as she passed, rushing toward the brake like a stag chased by the hunters. But neither shame nor despair were in her face.

"Your master wishes to speak to you," said he, his eyes fixed on her features.

"My master!" she exclaimed fiercely; "that man is no master of mine, and he never shall be. You, Germain, you are my master. I want you to take me home with you. I will be your servant for nothing."

The farmer advanced, feigning impatience. "Little girl," said he, "you left something behind at the farm, which I am bringing back to you."

"No, you are not, sir," answered little Marie. "I didn't forget anything, and I have nothing to ask of you."

"Listen a moment," returned the farmer. "It's I who have something to tell you. Come with me. Don't be afraid. It's only a word or two."

"You may say them aloud. I have no secrets with you."

"At any rate do take your money."

"My money? You owe me nothing, thank God!"

"I suspected as much," said Germain under his breath, "but I don't care, Marie. Listen to what he has to say to you, for—I am curious to know. You can tell me afterward. Go up to his horse. I shall not lose sight of you."

Marie took three steps toward the farmer. He bent over the pommel of his saddle, and lowering his voice he said:

"Little girl, here is a bright golden louis for you. Don't say anything about it; do you hear? I shall say that I found you too frail to work on my farm. There will be no more talk about that. I shall be passing by your house one of these days; and if you have not said anything, I will give you something more; and then if you are more sensible, you have only to speak. I will take you home with me, or I will come at dusk and talk with you in the meadows. What present would you like me to bring you?"

"Here, sir, is the present I have for you," answered little Marie, aloud, as she threw the golden louis in his face with all her might. "I thank you heartily and I beg that if you come anywhere near our house, you will be good enough to let me know. All the boys in the neigbourhood will go out to welcome you, because, where I live, we are very fond of gentlemen who try to make love to poor girls. You shall see. They will be on the lookout for you."

"You lie with your dirty tongue," cried the farmer, raising his stick with a dangerous air. "You wish to make people believe what is not so, but you shall never get a penny out of me. We know what kind of a girl you are."

Marie drew back, frightened, and Germain sprang to the bridle of the farmer's horse and shook it violently.

"I understand now," said he; "it is easy to see what is going on. Get down, my man, get down; I want to talk to you."

The farmer was not eager to take up the quarrel. Anxious to escape, he set spurs to his horse and tried to loosen the peasant's grasp by striking down his hands with a cane; but Germain dodged the blow, and seizing hold of his antagonist's leg, he unseated him and flung him to the earth. The farmer regained his feet, but although he defended himself vigorously, he was knocked down once more. Germain held him to the ground. Then he said:

"Poor coward, I could thrash you if I wished. But I don't want to do you an injury, and, besides, no amount of punishment would help your conscience—but you shall not stir from this spot until you beg the girl's pardon, on your knees."

The farmer understood this sort of thing and wished to take it all as a joke. He made believe that his offence was not serious, since it lay in words alone, and protested that he was perfectly willing to ask her pardon, provided he might kiss the girl afterward. Finally, he proposed that they go and drink a pint of wine at the nearest tavern, and so part good friends.

"You are disgusting!" answered Germain, rubbing his victim's head in the dirt, "and I never wish to see your nasty face again. So blush, if you are able, and when you come to our village, you had better slink along Sneak's Alley."[1]

He picked up the farmer's holly-stick, broke it over his knee to show the strength of his wrists, and threw away the pieces with disgust. Then giving one hand to his son and the other to little Marie, he walked away, still trembling with anger.

[1] This is the road, which, diverging from the principal street at the entrance of villages, makes a circuit about them. Persons who are in dread of receiving some well-deserved insult, are supposed to take this route to escape attention.

CHAPTER XIV

The Return to the Farm

At the end of fifteen minutes they had left the heath behind them. They trotted along the high road, and the grey whinnied at each familiar object. Petit-Pierre told his father as much as he could understand of what had passed.

"When we reached the farm," said he, "*that man* came to speak to my Marie in the fold where we had gone to see the pretty sheep. I had climbed into the manger to play, and *that man* did not see me. Then he said good morning to Marie, and he kissed her."

"You allowed him to kiss you, Marie?" said Germain, trembling with anger.

"I thought it was a civility, a custom of the place to new-comers, just as at your farm the grandmother kisses the young girls who enter her service to show that she adopts them and will be a mother to them."

"And next," went on little Pierre, who was proud to have an adventure to tell of, "*that man* told you something wicked, which you have told me never to repeat and not even remember; so I forgot it right away. Still, if father wishes, I will tell him what it was——"

"No, Pierre, I don't wish to hear, and I don't wish you ever to think of it again."

"Then I will forget it all over again," replied the child. "Next, *that man* seemed to be growing angry because Marie told him that she was going away. He told her he would give her whatever she wanted—a hundred francs! And my Marie grew angry too. Then he came toward her as if he wished to hurt her. I was afraid, and I ran to Marie and cried. Then *that man* said: 'What's that? Where did that child come from? Put it out,' and he raised his cane to beat me. But my Marie prevented him, and she spoke to him this way: 'We will talk later, sir; now I must take this child back to Fourche, and then I shall return.' And as soon as he had left the fold, my Marie spoke to me this way: 'We must run, my Pierre; we must get away as quickly as we can, for this is a wicked man and he is trying to do us harm.' Then when we had gone back of the farmhouses, we crossed a little meadow, and we went to Fourche to find you. But you were not there, and they wouldn't let us wait. And then *that man,* riding his black horse, came behind us, and we ran on as fast as we could and hid in the woods. And then he followed us, and when we heard him coming, we hid again. And then, when he had passed, we began to run toward home, and then you came and found us, and that is how it all happened. I haven't forgotten anything, have I, my Marie?"

"No, my Pierre, that is the whole truth. Now, Germain, you must be my witness, and tell everybody in the village that if I did not stay there it was not from want of courage and industry."

"And, Marie, I want to ask of you whether a man of twenty-eight is too old when there is a woman to be defended and an insult to be revenged. I should like to know whether Bastien or any other pretty boy, ten years better off than I, would not have been knocked to pieces by *that man,* as Petit-Pierre says. What do you think?"

"I think, Germain, that you have done me a great service, and that I shall be grateful all my life."

"Is that all?"

"Little Father," said the child, "I forgot to ask little Marie what I promised. I have not had time yet, but I will speak to her at home, and I will speak to my grandmother too."

The child's promise set Germain to thinking. He must explain his conduct to his family and give his objections to the widow Guérin, and all the while conceal the true reasons which had made him so judicious and so decided. When a man is proud and happy, it seems an easy task to thrust his happiness upon others, but to be repulsed on one side and blamed on the other is not a very pleasant position.

Fortunately, Petit-Pierre was fast asleep when they reached the farm, and Germain put him to bed undisturbed. Then he began upon all sorts of explanations. Father Maurice, seated on a three-legged stool before the door, listened with gravity; and, although he was ill-content with the result of the journey, when Germain told him about the widow's systematic coquetry, and demanded of his father-in-law whether he had the time to go and pay his court fifty-two Sundays in the year at the risk of being dismissed in the end, the old man nodded his head in assent and answered: "You were not wrong, Germain; that could never be." And then, when Germain described how he had been obliged to bring back little Marie, with the utmost haste, in order to protect her from the insults or perhaps from the violence of a wicked master, Father Maurice nodded approvingly again and said: "You were not wrong, Germain, that was right."

When Germain had told his story, and had set forth all his reasons, the old farmer and his wife heaved deep, simultaneous sighs of resignation, and looked at each other. Then the head of the house rose and said: "God's will be done. Love can't be made to order."

"Come to supper, Germain," said his mother-in-law. "It is unfortunate that this did not come to a better end, but, after all, it seems that God did not wish it. We must look elsewhere."

"Yes," added the old man, "as my wife says, we must look elsewhere."

There was no more noise at the house, and on the morrow, when Petit-Pierre rose with the larks at dawn, he was no longer excited by the extraordinary events of the preceding days. Like other little peasants of his age, he became indifferent, forgot everything that had been running in his head, and thought only of playing with his brothers, and of pretending to drive the horses and oxen like a man.

Germain plunged into his work, and tried to forget, too; but he became so absent-minded and so sad that everybody noticed it. He never spoke to little Marie, he never even looked at her, and yet had anybody asked him in what meadow she was, or by what road she had passed, there was not a moment in the day when he could not have answered if he would. He dared not ask his family to take her in at the farm during the winter, and yet he knew well how she must suffer from want. But she did not suffer; and Mother Guillette could not understand how her little store of wood never grew less, and how her shed was full in the morning, although she had left it almost empty at night. It was the same with the wheat and potatoes. Somebody entered by the garret window, and emptied a sack on the floor without awaking a soul or leaving a trace of his coming. The widow was at once uneasy and delighted. She made her daughter promise to tell nobody, and said that were people to know of the miracle performed at her house they would take her for a witch. She felt confident that the devil had a share in it, but she was in no hurry to pick a quarrel with him by calling down the priest's exorcisms on the house. It would be time enough, she said, when Satan should come to demand her soul in return for his gifts.

Little Marie understood the truth better, but she dared not speak to Germain, for fear of seeing him return to his dreams of marriage, and, before him, she pretended to perceive nothing.

CHAPTER XV

Mother Maurice

ONE day, Mother Maurice was alone in the orchard with Germain, and spoke to him kindly:

"My poor son, I believe you are not well. You don't eat as well as usual; you never laugh; you talk less and less. Perhaps one of us, or all of us, have hurt your feelings, without knowing and without wishing it."

"No, my mother," answered Germain, "you have always been as kind to me as the mother who brought me into the world, and I should be very ungrateful if I were to complain of you or your husband, or of anybody in the household."

"Then, my child, it is the sorrow for your wife's death which comes back to you. Instead of growing lighter with time, your grief becomes worse, and as your father has said very wisely, it is absolutely necessary for you to marry again."

"Yes, my mother, that is my opinion, but the women whom you advised me to ask don't suit me. Whenever I see them, instead of forgetting my Catherine, I think of her all the more."

"Apparently that's because we haven't been able to understand your taste. You must help us by telling us the truth. There must be a woman somewhere who is made for you, for God doesn't make anybody without placing his happiness in somebody else. So if you know where to find this woman whom you need, take her, and be she pretty or ugly, young or old, rich or poor, we have made up our minds, my husband and I, to give our consent, for we are tired of seeing you so sad, we can never be happy while you are sorrowful."

"My mother, you are as kind as the kind Lord, and so is my father," answered Germain; "but your compassion brings small help to my troubles, for the girl I love doesn't care for me."

"She is too young, then? It's foolish for you to love a young girl."

"Yes, mother dear, I have been foolish enough to love a young girl, and it's my fault. I do my best to stop thinking of it, but, working or sleeping, at mass or in bed, with my children or with you, I can think of nothing else."

"Then it's like a fate cast over you, Germain. There's but one remedy, and it is that this girl must change her mind and listen to you. It's my duty to look into this, and see whether it's practicable. Tell me where she lives, and what's her name."

"Oh, my dear mother, I dare not," said Germain, "because you will make fun of me."

"I shall not make fun of you, Germain, because you are in trouble, and I don't wish to make it harder for you. Is it Fanchette?"

"No, mother, of course not."

"Or Rosette?"

"No."

"Tell me, then, for I shall never finish if I must name every girl in the country-side."

Germain bowed his head, and could not bring himself to answer.

"Very good," said Mother Maurice, "I shall let you alone for to-day; to-morrow, perhaps, you will be more confidential with me, or possibly your sister-in-law will question you more cleverly."

And she picked up her basket to go and spread her linen on the bushes.

Germain acted like children who make up their minds when they see that they are no longer attracting attention. He followed his mother, and at length, trembling, he named Marie of Guillette.

Great was the surprise of Mother Maurice. Marie was the last person she would have dreamed of. But she had the delicacy not to cry out, and made her comments to herself. Then seeing that her silence hurt Germain, she stretched out her basket toward him and said:

"Is there any reason for not helping me at my work?

Carry this load, and come and talk with me. Have you reflected well, Germain? Are you fully decided?"

"Alas, dear mother, you mustn't speak in that way. I should be decided if I had a chance of success, but as I could never be heard, I have only made up my mind to cure myself, if I can."

"And if you can't?"

"There is an end to everything, Mother Maurice: when the horse is laden too heavily, he falls, and when the cow has nothing to eat, she dies."

"Do you mean to say that you will die, if you do not succeed? God grant not, Germain. I don't like to hear a man like you talk of those things; for what he says, he thinks. You are very brave, and weakness is dangerous for strong men. Take heart; I can't conceive that a poverty-stricken girl, whom you have honoured so much as to ask her to marry you, will refuse you."

"Yet it's the truth: she does refuse me."

"And what reasons does she give you?"

"That you have always been kind to her, and that her family owes a great deal to yours, and that she doesn't wish to displease you by turning me away from a rich marriage."

"If she says that, she proves her good sense, and shows what an honest girl she is. But, Germain, she doesn't cure you; for of course she tells you that she loves you and would marry you if we were willing?"

"That's the worst part of all. She says that her heart can never be mine."

"If she says what she doesn't think in order to keep you at a safer distance, the child deserves our love, and we should pass over her youth on account of her great good sense."

"Yes," said Germain, struck by a hope he had never held before; "that would be very wise and right of her! But if she is so sensible, I am sure it is because I displease her."

"Germain," said Mother Maurice, "you must promise me not to worry for a whole week. Keep from tormenting yourself, eat, sleep, and be as gay as you used to be. For my part, I'll speak to my husband, and if I gain his consent, you shall know the girl's real feelings toward you."

Germain promised, and the week passed without a single word in private from Father Maurice, who seemed to suspect nothing. The husbandman did his best to look calm, but he grew ever paler and more troubled.

CHAPTER XVI

Little Marie

AT length, on Sunday morning, when mass was over, his mother-in-law asked Germain what encouragement he had had from his sweetheart since the conversation in the orchard.

"Why, none at all," answered he; "I haven't spoken to her."

"How can you expect to win her if you don't speak to her?"

"I have spoken to her but once," replied Germain. "That was when we were together at Fourche, and since then I haven't said a single word. Her refusal gave me so much pain that I had rather not hear her begin again to tell me that she doesn't love me."

"But, my son, you must speak to her now; your father gives his approval. So make up your mind. I tell you to do it, and, if need be, I shall order you to do it, for you can't rest in this uncertainty."

Germain obeyed. He reached Mother Guillette's house, hanging his head with a hopeless air. Little Marie sat alone before the hearth so thoughtful that she did not hear Germain's step. When she saw him before her, she started from her chair in surprise and grew very red.

"Little Marie," said he, sitting down near her, "I come to trouble you and to give you pain. I know it very well, but the man and his wife at home [it was thus after the peasant fashion that he designated the heads of the house] wish me to speak to you, and beg you to marry me. You don't care for me. I am prepared for it."

"Germain," answered little Marie, "are you sure that you love me?"

"It pains you, I know, but it isn't my fault. If you could change your mind, I should be so very happy, and certain it is that I don't deserve it. Look at me, Marie; am I very terrible?"

"No, Germain," she answered, with a smile, "you are better looking than I."

"Don't make fun of me; look at me charitably; as yet, I have never lost a single hair nor a single tooth. My eyes tell you plainly how much I love you. Look straight in my eyes. It is written there, and every girl knows how to read that writing."

Marie looked into Germain's eyes with playful boldness; then of a sudden she turned away her head and trembled.

"Good God," exclaimed Germain, "I make you afraid; you look at me as though I were the farmer at Ormeaux, Don't be afraid of me, please don't; that hurts me too much. I shall not say any bad words to you, I shall not kiss you if you will not have me, and when you wish me to go away, you have only to show me the door. Must I go in order to stop your trembling?"

Marie held out her hand toward the husbandman, but without turning her head, which was bent on the fireplace, and without saying a word.

"I understand," said Germain. "You pity me, for you are kind; you are sorry to make me unhappy; but you can't love me."

"Why do you say these things to me, Germain?" answered little Marie, after a pause. "Do you wish to make me cry?"

"Poor little girl, you have a kind heart, I know; but you don't love me, and you are hiding your face for fear of letting me see your dislike and your repugnance. And I? I dare not even clasp your hand! In the forest, when my boy was asleep and you were sleeping too, I almost kissed you very gently. But I would have died of shame rather than ask it of you, and that night I suffered as a man burning over a slow fire. Since that time I have dreamed of you every night. Ah! how I have kissed you, Marie! Yet during all that time you have slept without a dream. And now, do you know what I think? I think that were you to turn and look at me with the eyes I have for you, and were you to move your face close to mine, I believe I should fall dead for joy. And you, you think that if such a thing were to happen, you would die of anger and shame!"

Germain spoke as in a dream, not hearing the words he said. Little Marie was trembling all the time, but he was shaking yet more and did not notice it. Of a sudden, she turned. Her eyes were filled with tears, and she looked at him reproachfully. The poor husbandman thought that this was the last blow, and without waiting for his sentence he rose to go, but the girl stopped him, and throwing both her arms about him, she hid her face in his breast.

"Oh, Germain," she sobbed, "didn't you feel that I loved you?"

Then Germain had gone mad, if his son, who came galloping into the cottage on a stick, with his little sister on the crupper, scourging the imaginary steed with a willow branch, had not brought him to his senses. He lifted the boy and placed him in the girl's arms.

"See," said he, "by loving me, you have made more than one person happy."

APPENDIX

CHAPTER I

A Country Wedding

HERE ends the history of Germain's marriage as he told it to me himself, good husbandman that he is. I ask your forgiveness, kind reader, that I know not how to translate it better; for it is a real translation that is needed by this old-fashioned and artless language of the peasants of the country "that I sing," as they used to say. These people speak French that is too true for us, and since Rabelais and Montaigne, the advance of the language has lost for us many of its old riches. Thus it is with every advance, and we must make the best of it. Yet it is a pleasure still to hear those picturesque idioms used in the old districts in the centre of France; all the more because it is the genuine expression of the laughing, quiet, and delightfully talkative character of the people who make use of it. Touraine has preserved a certain precious number of patriarchal phrases. But Touraine was civilised greatly during the Renaissance, and since its decline she is filled with fine houses and high roads, with foreigners and traffic. Berry remained as she was, and I think that after Brittany and a few provinces in the far south of France, it is the best preserved district to be found at the present day. Some of the customs are so strange and so curious that I hope to amuse you a few minutes more, kind reader, if you will allow me to describe to you in detail a country wedding—Germain's, for example—at which I had the pleasure of assisting several years ago.

For, alas! everything passes. During my life alone, more change has taken place in the ideas and in the customs of my village than had been seen in the centuries before the

Revolution. Already half the ceremonies, Celtic, Pagan, or of the Middle Ages, that in my childhood I have seen in their full vigour, have disappeared. In a year or two more, perhaps the railroads will lay their level tracks across our deep valleys, and will carry away, with the swiftness of lightning, all our old traditions and our wonderful legends.

It was in winter about the carnival season, the time of year when, in our country, it is fitting and proper to have weddings. In summer the time can hardly be spared, and the work of the farm cannot suffer three days' delay, not to speak of the additional days impaired to a greater or to a less degree by the moral and physical drunkenness which follows a gala-day. I was seated beneath the great mantelpiece of the old-fashioned kitchen fireplace when shots of pistols, barking of dogs, and the piercing notes of the bagpipe told me that the bridal pair were approaching. Very soon Father and Mother Maurice, Germain, and little Marie, followed by Jacques and his wife, the closer relatives, and the godfathers and godmothers of the bride and groom, all made their entry into the yard.

Little Marie had not yet received her wedding-gifts—favours, as they call them—and was dressed in the best of her simple clothes, a dress of dark, heavy cloth, a white fichu with great spots of brilliant colour, an apron of carnation—an Indian red much in vogue at the time, but despised nowadays—a cap of very white muslin after that pattern, happily still preserved, which calls to mind the head-dress of Anne Boleyn and of Agnes Sorel. She was fresh and laughing, but not at all vain, though she had good reason to be so. Beside her was Germain, serious and tender, like young Jacob greeting Rebecca at the wells of Laban. Another girl would have assumed an important air and struck an attitude of triumph, for in every rank it is something to be married for a fair face alone. Yet the girl's eyes were moist and shone with tenderness. It was plain that she was deep in love and had no time to think of the opinions of others. Her little air of determination was not absent, but everything about her denoted frankness and good-will There was nothing impertinent in her success, nothing selfish in her sense of power. Never have I seen so lovely a bride, when she answered with frankness her young friends who asked if she were happy:

"Surely I have nothing to complain of the good Lord."

Father Maurice was spokesman. He came forward to pay his compliments, and give the customary invitations. First he fastened to the mantelpiece a branch of laurel decked out with ribbons; this is known as the *writ*—that is to say, the letter of announcement. Next he gave to every guest a tiny cross made of a bit of blue ribbon sewn to a transverse bit of pink ribbon—pink for the bride, blue for the groom. The guests of both sexes were expected to keep this badge to adorn their caps or their button-holes on the wedding-day. This is the letter of invitation, the admission ticket.

Then Father Maurice paid his congratulations. He invited the head of the house and all his *company*—that is to say, all his children, all his friends, and all his servants—to the benediction, *to the feast, to the sports, to the dance, and to everything that follows.* He did not fail to say, "I have come *to do you the honour of inviting you;*" a very right manner of speech, even though it appears to us to convey the wrong meaning, for it expresses the idea of doing honour to those who seem worthy of it.

Despite the generosity of the invitation carried from house to house throughout the parish, politeness, which is very cautious amongst peasants, demands that only two persons from each family take advantage of it—one of the heads of the house, and one from the number of their children.

After the invitations were made, the betrothed couple and their families took dinner together at the farm.

Little Marie kept her three sheep on the common, and Germain tilled the soil as though nothing had happened.

About two in the afternoon before the day set for the wedding, the music came. The music means the players of the bagpipe and hurdy-gurdy, their instruments decorated with long streaming ribbons, playing an appropriate march to a measure which would have been rather slow for feet foreign to the soil, but admirably adapted to the heavy ground and hilly roads of the country.

Pistol-shots, fired by the young people and the children, announced the beginning of the wedding ceremonies. Little by little the guests assembled and danced on the grass-plot before the house in order to enter into the spirit of the occasion. When evening was come they began strange preparations; they divided into two bands, and when night had settled down they proceeded to the ceremony of the *favours*.

All this passed at the dwelling of the bride, Mother Guillette's cottage. Mother Guillette took with her her daughter, a dozen pretty shepherdesses, friends and relatives of her daughter, two or three respectable housewives, talkative neighbours, quick of wit and strict guardians of ancient customs. Next she chose a dozen stout fellows, her relatives and friends; and last of all the parish hemp-dresser, a garrulous old man. and as good a talker as ever there was.

The part which, in Brittany, is played by the bazvalon, the village tailor, is taken in our part of the country by the hemp-dresser and the wool-carder, two professions which are unusually combined in one. He is present at all ceremonies, sad or good, for he is very learned and a fluent talker, and on these occasions he must always figure as spokesman, in order to fulfil with exactitude certain formalities used from time immemorial. Travelling occupations, which bring a man into the midst of other families, without allowing him to shut himself up within his own, are well fitted to make him talker, wit, story-teller, and singer.

The hemp-dresser is peculiarly sceptical. He and another village functionary, of whom we have spoken before, the grave-digger, are always the daring spirits of the neighbourhood. They have talked so much about ghosts, and they know so well all the tricks of which these malicious spirits are capable, that they fear them scarcely at all. It is especially at night that all of them—grave-diggers, hemp-dressers, and ghosts—do their work. It is also at night when the hemp-dresser tells his melancholy stories. Permit me to make a digression.

When the hemp has reached the right stage, that is to say, when it has been steeped sufficiently in running water, and half dried on the bank, it is brought into the yard and arranged in little upright sheaves, which, with their stalks divided at the base, and their heads bound in balls, bear in the dusk some small resemblance to a long procession of little white phantoms, standing on their slender legs, and moving noiselessly along the wall.

It is at the end of September, when the nights are still warm, that they begin to beat it by the pale light of the moon. By day the hemp has been heated in the oven; at night they take it out to beat it while it is still hot. For this they use a kind of horse surmounted by a wooden lever which falls into grooves and breaks the plant without cutting it. It is then that you hear in the night that sudden, sharp noise of three blows in quick succession. Then there is silence; it is the movement of the arm drawing out the handful of hemp to break it in a fresh spot. The three blows begin again; the other arm works the lever, and thus it goes on until the moon is hidden by the early streaks of dawn. As the work continues but a few days in the year, the dogs are not accustomed to it, and yelp their plaintive howls toward every point of the horizon.

It is the time of unwonted and mysterious sounds in the country. The migrating cranes fly so high that by day they are scarcely visible. By night they are only heard, and their hoarse wailing voices, lost in the clouds, sound like the parting cry of souls in torment, striving to find the road to heaven, yet forced by an unconquerable fate to wander near the earth about the haunts of men; for these errant birds have strange uncertainties, and many a mysterious anxiety in the course of their airy flight. Sometimes they lose the wind when the capricious gusts battle, or come and go in the upper regions. When this confusion comes by day, you can see the leader of the file fluttering aimlessly in the air, then turn about and take his place at the tail of the triangular phalanx, while a skilful manœuvre of his companions forms them soon in good order behind him. Often, after vain efforts, the exhausted leader relinquishes the guidance of the caravan; another comes forward, tries in his turn, and yields his place to a third, who finds the breeze, and continues the march in triumph. But what cries, what reproaches, what protests, what wild curses or anxious questionings are exchanged in an unknown tongue amongst these winged pilgrims!

Sometimes, in the resonant night, you can hear these sinister noises whirling for a long time above the housetops, and as you can see nothing, you feel, despite your efforts, a kind of dread and kindred discomfort, until the sobbing multitude is lost in boundless space.

There are other noises too which belong to this time of year, and which sound usually in the orchards. Gathering the fruit is not yet over, and the thousand unaccustomed cracklings make the tree seem alive. A branch groans as it bends beneath a burden which has reached, of a sudden, the last stage of growth; or perhaps an apple breaks from the twig, and falls on the damp earth at your feet with a dull sound. Then you hear rush by, brushing the branches and the grass, a creature you cannot see; it is the peasant's dog, that prowling and uneasy rover, at once impudent and cowardly, always wandering, never sleeping, ever seeking you know not what, spying upon you, hiding in the brush, and taking flight at the sound of a falling apple, which he thinks a stone that you are throwing at him.

It is during those nights, nights misty and grey, that the hemp-dresser tells his weird stories of will-o'-the-wisps and milk-white hares, of souls in torment and wizards changed to wolves, of witches' vigils at the cross-roads, and screech-owls, prophetesses of the graveyard. I remember passing the early hours of such a night while the hemp-dressing was going on, and the pitiless strokes, interrupting the dresser's story at its most awful place, sent icy shivers through our veins.

And often too the good man continued his story as he worked, and four or five words were lost, terrible words, no doubt, which we dared not make him repeat, and whose omission added a mystery yet more fearful to the dark mysteries of the story which had gone before. It was in vain the servants warned us that it was too late to stay without doors, and that bedtime had sounded for us long since; they too were dying to hear more; and then with what terror we crossed the hamlet on our way home! How deep did the church porch appear to us, and how thick and black the shadows of the old trees! The graveyard we dared not see; we shut our eyes tight as we passed it.

But no more than the sacristan is the hemp-dresser gifted solely with the desire of frightening; he loves to make people laugh; he is sarcastic and sentimental at need, when love and marriage are to be sung. It is he who collects and keeps stored in his memory the oldest songs, and who transmits them to posterity. And so it is he who acts at weddings the part we shall see him play at the presentation of little Marie's favours.

CHAPTER II

The Wedding Favours

WHEN all the guests were met together in the house, the doors and windows were closed with the utmost care; even the garret window was barricaded; boards and benches, logs and tables were placed behind every entrance, just as if the inhabitants were making ready to sustain a siege; and within these fortifications solemn stillness prevailed until at a distance were heard songs and laughter and the sounds of rustic music. It was the band of the bridegroom, Germain at the head, followed by his most trusty companions and by the grave-digger, relatives, friends, and servants, who formed a compact and merry train. Meanwhile, as they came nearer the house they slackened their pace, held a council of war, and became silent. The girls, shut up in the house, had arranged little loop-holes at the windows by which they could see the enemy approach and deploy in battle array. A fine, cold rain was falling, which added zest to the situation, while a great fire blazed on the hearth within. Marie wished to cut short the inevitable slowness of this well-ordered siege; she had no desire to see her lover catch cold, but not being in authority she had to take an ostensible share in the mischievous cruelty of her companions.

When the two armies met, a discharge of fire-arms on the part of the besiegers set all the dogs in the neighbourhood to barking. Those within the house dashed at the door with loud yelps, thinking that the attack was in earnest, and the children, little reassured by the efforts of their mothers, began to weep and to tremble. The whole scene was played so well that a stranger would have been deceived, and would have made his preparations to fight a band of brigands. Then the grave-digger, bard and orator of the groom, took his stand before the door, and with a rueful voice exchanged the following dialogue with the hemp-dresser, who was stationed above the same door:

The Grave-digger: "Ah, my good people, my fellow-townsmen, for the love of Heaven, open the door."

The Hemp-dresser: "Who are you, and what right have you to call us your dear fellow-townsmen? We don't know you."

The Grave-digger: "We are worthy folk in great distress. Don't be afraid of us, my friends. Extend us your hospitality. Sleet is falling; our poor feet are frozen, and our journey home has been so long that our sabots are split."

The Hemp-dresser: "If your sabots are split, you can look on the ground; you will find very soon a sprig of willow to make some *arcelets* [small curved blades of iron which are fastened on split sabots to hold them together]."

The Grave-digger: "Willow *arclets* are scarcely strong enough. You are making fun of us, good people, and you would do better to open your doors. We can see a splendid fire blazing in your dwelling. The spit must be turning, and we can make merry with you, heart and belly. So open your doors to poor pilgrims who will die on the threshold if you are not merciful."

The Hemp-dresser: "Ah ha! so you are pilgrims? You never told us that. And what pilgrimage do you come from, may I ask?"

The Grave-digger: "We shall tell you that when you open the door, for we come from so far that you would never believe it."

The Hemp-dresser: "Open the door to you? I rather think not. We can't trust you. Tell us, is it from Saint Sylvain of Pouligny that you come?"

The Grave-digger: "We have been at Saint Sylvain of Pouligny, but we have been farther still."

The Hemp-dresser: "Then you have been as far as Saint Solange?"

The Grave-digger: "At Saint Solange we have been, sure enough, but we have been farther yet."

The Hemp-dresser: "You are lying. You have never been as far as Saint Solange."

The Grave-digger: "We have been farther, for now we are come from Saint Jacques of Compostelle."

The Hemp-dresser: "What absurdity are you telling us? We don't know that parish. We can easily see that you are bad people, brigands, nobodies, and liars. Go away with your nonsense. We are on our guard. You can't come in."

The Grave-digger: "Ah, my poor fellow, take pity on us. We are not pilgrims, as you have guessed, but we are unlucky poachers pursued by the keepers. Even the police are after us, and if you don't hide us in your hay-loft, we shall be taken and led off to prison."

The Hemp-dresser: "And who will prove you are what you say you are, this time? For you have told us one lie already that you can't maintain."

The Grave-digger: "If you will let us in, we shall show you a pretty piece of game we have killed."

The Hemp-dresser: "Show it right away, for we have our suspicions."

The Grave-digger: "All right, open the door or a window to let us pass the creature in."

The Hemp-dresser: "Oh, no, not quite so foolish. I am looking at you through a little chink, and I can see neither hunters nor game amongst you."

Here an ox-driver, a thick-set fellow of herculean strength, detached himself from a group where he had stood unperceived, and raised toward the window a plucked goose, spitted on a strong iron bar decorated with tufts of straw and ribbons.

"Ho, ho!" cried the hemp-dresser, after cautiously extending an arm to feel the roast. "That isn't a quail nor a partridge; it isn't a hare nor a rabbit; it's something like a goose or a turkey. Upon my word you're clever hunters, and that game didn't make you run very far. Move on, you rogues; we know all your lies, and you had best go home and cook your supper. You are not going to eat ours."

The Grave-digger: "O Heavens, where can we go to cook our game? It is very little for so many as we, and, besides, we have neither place nor fire. At this time every door is closed, and every soul asleep. You are the only people who are celebrating a wedding at home, and you must be hard-hearted indeed to let us freeze outside. Once again, good people, open the door; we shall not cost you anything. You can see that we bring our own meat; only a little room at your hearth, a little blaze to cook with, and we shall go on our way rejoicing."

The Hemp-dresser: "Do you suppose that we have too much room here, and that wood is bought for nothing?"

The Grave-digger: "We have here a small bundle of hay to make the fire. We shall be satisfied with that; only grant us leave to place the spit across your fireplace."

The Hemp-dresser: "That will never do. We are disgusted and don't pity you at all. It is my opinion that you are drunk, that you need nothing, and that you only wish to come in and steal away our fire and our daughters."

The Grave-digger: "Since you won't listen to reason, we shall make our way in by force."

The Hemp-dresser: "Try, if you want; we are shut in well enough to have no fear of you, and since you are impudent fellows, we shall not answer you again."

Thereupon the hemp-dresser shut the garret window with a bang, and came down into the room below by a step-ladder. Then he took the bride by the hand, the young people of both sexes followed, and they all began to sing and chatter merrily, while the matrons sang in piercing voices, and shrieked with laughter in derision and bravado at those without who were attempting an attack.

The besiegers, on their side, made a great hubbub. They discharged their pistols at the doors, made the dogs growl, whacked the walls, shook the blinds, and uttered frightful shrieks. In short, there was such a pandemonium that nobody could hear, and such a cloud of dust that nobody could see.

And yet this attack was all a sham. The time had not come for breaking through the etiquette. If, in prowling about, anybody were to find an unguarded aperture, or any opening whatsoever, he might try to slip in unobserved, and then, if the carrier of the spit succeeded in placing his roast before the fire, and thus prove the capture of the hearth, the comedy was over and the bridegroom had conquered.

The entrances of the house, however, were not numerous enough for any to be neglected in the customary precautions, and nobody might use violence before the moment fixed for the struggle.

When they were weary of dancing and screams, the hemp-dresser began to think of capitulation. He went up to his window, opened it with precaution, and greeted the baffled assailants with a burst of laughter.

"Well, my boys," said he, "you look very sheep-faced. You thought there was nothing easier than to come in, and you see that our defence is good. But we are beginning to have pity on you, if you will submit and accept our conditions."

The Grave-digger: "Speak, good people. Tell us what we must do to approach your hearth."

The Hemp-dresser: "You must sing, my friends; but sing a song we don't know—one that we can't answer by a better."

"That's not hard to do," answered the grave-digger, and he thundered in a powerful voice:

"'Six months ago, 'twas in the spring . . .'"

"'I wandered through the sprouting grass,'"

answered the hemp-dresser in a slightly hoarse but terrible voice. "You must be jesting, my poor friends, singing us such time-worn songs. You see very well that we can stop you at the first word."

"'She was a prince's daughter . . .'"

"'Right gladly would she wed,'"

answered the hemp-dresser. "Come, move on to the next; we know that a little too well."

The Grave-digger: "How do you like this one?—

"'As I was journeying home from Nantes.'"

The Hemp-dresser:

"'Weary, oh, weary, was I, was I.'"

"That dates from my grandmother's time. Let's have another."

The Grave-digger:

"'One day I went a-walking . . .'"

The Hemp-dresser:

"'Along a lovely wood!'"

"That one is too stupid! Our little children wouldn't take the trouble to answer you. What! Are these all you know?"

The Grave-digger: "Oh, we shall sing you so many that you will never be able to hear them all."

In this way a full hour passed. As the two antagonists were champions of the country round in the matter of songs, and as their store seemed inexhaustible, the contest might last all night with ease, all the more because the hemp-dresser, with a touch of malice, allowed several ballads of ten, twenty, or thirty couplets to be sung through, feigning by his silence to admit his defeat. Then the bridegroom's camp rejoiced and sang aloud in chorus, and thought that this time the foe was worsted; but at the first line of the last couplet, they heard the hoarse croaking of the old hemp-dresser bellow forth the second rhyme. Then he cried:

"You need not tire yourselves by singing such a long one, my children—we know that one to our finger-tips."

Once or twice, however, the hemp-dresser made a wry face, contracted his brow, and turned toward the expectant housewives with a baffled air. The grave-digger was singing something so old that his adversary had forgotten it, or perhaps had never even heard it; but instantly the good gossips chanted the victorious refrain through their noses with voices shrill as a sea-mew's, and the grave-digger, forced to surrender, went on to fresh attempts.

It would have taken too long to wait for a decision of the victory. The bride's party declared itself disposed to be merciful, provided that the bride were given a present worthy of her.

Then began the song of the favours to a tune solemn as a church chant.

The men without sang together in bass voice:

"'Open the door, true love,
Open the door;
I have presents for you, love,
Oh, say not adieu, love.'"

To this the women answered from within falsetto, with mournful voices:

> "'My father is sorry, my mother is sad,
> And I am a maiden too kind by far
> At such an hour my gate to unbar.'"

The men took up the first verse as far as the fourth line and modified it thus:

> "'And a handkerchief new, love.'"

But, on behalf of the bride, the women answered in the same way as at first.

For twenty couplets, at least, the men enumerated all the wedding-presents, always mentioning something new in the last line: a handsome apron, pretty ribbons, a cloth dress, laces, a golden cross, and even a hundred pins to complete the modest list of wedding-presents. The refusal of the women could not be shaken, but at length the men decided to speak of

> "A good husband, too, love."

And the women answered, turning toward the bride and singing in unison with the men:

> "'Open the door, true love,
> Open the door;
> Here's a sweetheart for you, love,
> Pray let us enter, too, love.'"

CHAPTER III

THE WEDDING

IMMEDIATELY the hemp-dresser drew back the wooden bolt which barred the door within. At this time it was still the only fastening known in most of the dwellings of our hamlet. The groom's band burst into the bride's house, but not without a struggle; for the young men quartered within, and even the old hemp-dresser and the gossips, made it their duty to defend the hearth. The spit-bearer, upheld by his supporters, had to plant the roast before the fire-place. It was a regular battle, although people abstained from striking, and there was no anger shown in this struggle. But everybody was pushing and shoving so hard, and there was so much playful pride in this display of muscular strength, that the results might well have been serious, although they did not appear so across the laughs and songs. The poor old hemp-dresser, fighting like a lion, was pinned to the wall and squeezed by the crowd until his breath almost left him. More than one champion was upset and trodden under foot involuntarily; more than one hand, jammed against the spit, was covered with blood. These games are dangerous, and latterly the accidents have been so severe that our peasants have determined to allow the ceremony of the favours to fall into disuse; I believe we saw the last at the marriage of François Meillant, although there was no real struggle on that occasion.

The battle was earnest enough, however, at Germain's wedding. It was a point of honour on one side to invade, on the other to defend, Mother Guillette's hearth. The great spit was twisted like a screw beneath the strong fists which fought for it. A pistol-shot set fire to a small quantity of hemp arranged in sheaves and laid on a wicker shelf near the ceiling. This incident created a diversion, and while some of the company crowded about to extinguish the sparks, the grave-digger, who had climbed unbeknown into the garret, came down the chimney and seized the spit, at the very moment when the ox-driver, who was defending it near the hearth, raised it above his head to prevent it from being torn away. Some time before the attack, the women had taken the precaution to put out the fire lest in the struggle somebody should fall in and get burned. The jocular grave-digger, in league with the ox-driver, grasped the trophy and tossed it easily across the andirons. It was done! Nobody might interfere. The grave-digger sprang to the middle of the room and lighted a few wisps of straw, which he placed about the spit under pretence of cooking the roast, for the goose was in pieces and the floor was strewn with its scattered fragments.

Then there was a great deal of laughter and much boastful dispute. Everybody showed the marks of the blows he had received, and as it was often a friend's hand that had struck them, there was no word of complaint nor of quarrelling. The hemp-dresser, half flattened out, kept rubbing the small of his back and saying that, although it made small difference to him, he protested against the ruse of his friend, the grave-digger, and that if he had not been half dead, the hearth had never been captured so easily. The women swept the floor and order was restored. The table was covered with jugs of new wine. When the contestants had drunk together and taken breath, the bridegroom was led to the middle of the chamber, and, armed with a wand, he was obliged to submit to a fresh trial.

During the struggle, the bride and three of her companions had been hidden by her mother, godmother, and aunts, who had made the four girls sit down in a remote corner of the room while they covered them with a large white cloth. Three friends of Marie's height, with caps of a uniform size, were chosen, so that when they were enveloped from head to toe by the cloth it was impossible to tell them apart.

The bridegroom might not touch them, except with the tip of his staff, and then merely to designate which he thought to be his wife. They allowed him time enough to make an examination with no other help than his eyes afforded, and the women, placed on either side, kept zealous watch lest cheating should occur. Should he guess wrong, he might not dance with his bride, but only with her he had chosen by mistake.

When Germain stood in front of these ghosts wrapped in the same shroud, he feared he should make a wrong choice; and, in truth, that had happened to many another, so carefully and conscientiously were the precautions made. His heart beat loud. Little Marie did her best to breathe hard and shake the cloth a little, but her malicious companions followed her example, and kept poking the cloth with their fingers, so that there was as many mysterious signals as there were girls beneath the canopy. The square headdresses upheld the cloth so evenly that it was impossible to discern the contour of a brow outlined by its folds.

Aften ten minutes' hesitation, Germain shut his eyes, commended his soul to God, and stretched out the wand at random. It touched the forehead of little Marie, who cast the cloth from her, and shouted with triumph. Then it was his right to kiss her, and lifting her in his strong arms, he bore her to the middle of the room, where together they opened the dance, which lasted until two in the morning. The company separated to meet again at eight. As many people had come from the country round, and as there were not beds enough for everybody, each of the village maidens took to her bed two or three other girls, while the men spread themselves pell-mell on the hay in the barn-loft. You can imagine well that they had little sleep, for they did nothing but wrestle and joke, and tell foolish stories. Properly, there were three sleepless nights at weddings, and these we cannot regret.

At the time appointed for departure, when they had partaken of milk-soup, seasoned with a strong dose of pepper to stimulate the appetite—for the wedding feast gave promise of great bounty—the guests assembled in the farmyard. Since our parish had been abolished, we had to go half a league from home to receive the marriage blessing. It was cool and pleasant weather, but the roads were in such wretched condition that everybody was on horseback, and each man took a companion on his crupper, whether she were young or old. Germain started on the grey, and the mare, well-groomed, freshly shod, and decked out with ribbons, pranced about and snorted fire from her nostrils. The husbandman went to the cottage for his bride in company with his brother-in-law, Jacques, who rode the old grey, and carried Mother Guillette on the crupper, while Germain returned from the farm-yard in triumph, holding his dear little wife before him.

Then the merry cavalcade set out, escorted by the children, who ran ahead and fired off their pistols to make the horses jump. Mother Maurice was seated in a small cart, with Germain's three children and the fiddlers. They led the march to the sound of their instruments. Petit-Pierre was so handsome that his old grandmother was pride itself. But the eager child did not stay long at her side. During a moment's halt made on the journey, before passing through a difficult piece of road, he slipped away and ran to beg his father to carry him in front on the grey.

"No, no," replied Germain, "that will call forth some disagreeable joke; we mustn't do it."

"It's little that I care what the people of Saint Chartier say," said little Marie. "Take him up, Germain, please do; I shall be prouder of him than I am of my wedding-gown."

Germain yielded, and the pretty trio darted into the crowd borne by the triumphant gallop of the grey.

And so it was; the people of Saint Chartier, although they were very sarcastic, and somewhat disdainful of the neighbouring parishes which had been annexed to theirs, never thought of laughing when they saw such a handsome husband, such a lovely wife, and a child that a king's wife might court. Petit-Pierre was all dressed in light blue cloth, with a smart red waistcoat so short that it descended scarcely below his chin. The village tailor had fitted his armholes so tight that he could not bring his two little hands together. But, oh, how proud he was! He wore a round hat, with a black-and-gold cord, and a peacock's plume which stuck out proudly from a tuft of guinea feathers. A bunch of flowers, bigger than his head, covered his shoulder, and ribbons fluttered to his feet. The hemp-dresser, who was also the barber and hair-dresser of the district, had cut his hair evenly, by covering his head with a bowl, and clipping off the protruding locks, an infallible method for guiding the shears. Thus arrayed, the poor child was less poetic, certainly, than with his curls streaming in the wind, and his Saint John Baptist's sheepskin about him; but he knew nothing of this, and everybody admired him and said that he had quite the air of a little man. His beauty triumphed over everything, for what is there over which the exceeding beauty of childhood could not triumph?

His little sister, Solange, had, for the first time in her life, a peasant's cap in place of the calico hood which little girls wear until they are two or three years old. And what a cap it was! Longer and larger than the poor little thing's whole body. How beautiful she thought it! She dared not even turn her head; so she kept quite still and thought the people would take her for the bride.

As for little Sylvain, he was still in long clothes, and, fast asleep on his grandmother's knees, he did not even know what a wedding was.

Germain looked at his children tenderly, and when they reached the town hall, he said to his bride:

"Marie, I have come here with a happier heart than I had the day when I brought you home from the forest of Chanteloube, thinking that you could never love me. I took you in my arms to put you on the ground as I do here; but I thought that never again should we be mounted on the good grey with the child on our knees. I love you so dearly, I love these little creatures so dearly, I am so happy that you love me and that you love them, and that my family love you, and I love your mother so well and all my friends so well, and everybody else so well to-day, that I wish I had three or four hearts to fill all of them; for surely one is too small to hold so much love and so much happiness. It almost makes my stomach ache."

There was a crowd at the door of the town hall and another at the church to see the pretty bride. Why should we not tell about her dress? it became her so well. Her muslin cap, without spot and covered with embroidery, had lappets trimmed with lace. At that time peasant women never allowed a single lock to be seen, and, although they conceal beneath their caps splendid coils of hair tied up with tape to hold the coif in place, even to-day it would be thought a scandal and a shame for them to show themselves bareheaded to men. Nowadays, however, they allow a slender braid to appear over their foreheads, and this improves their appearance very much. Yet I regret the classic head-dress of my time; its spotless laces next the bare skin gave an effect of pristine purity which seemed to me very solemn; and when a face looked beautiful thus, it was with a beauty of which nothing can express the charm and unaffected majesty.

Little Marie wore her cap thus, and her forehead was so white and so pure that it defied the whiteness of linen to cast it in the shade. Although she had not closed an eye the night before, the morning air and, yet more, the joy within of a soul pure as the heaven, and, more than all, a small secret flame guarded with the modesty of girlhood, caused a bloom to mount to her cheeks delicate as the peach-blossom in the first beams of an April sun.

Her white scarf, modestly crossed over her breast, left visible only the soft curves of a neck rounded like a turtle-dove's; her home-made cloth gown of myrtle-green outlined her pretty figure, which looked already perfect, yet which must still grow and develop, for she was but seventeen. She wore an apron of violet silk with the bib our peasant women were so foolish as to suppress, which added so much elegance and decency to the breast. Nowadays they display their scarfs more proudly, but there is no longer in their dress that delicate flower of the purity of long ago, which made them look like Holbein's virgins. They are more forward and more profuse in their courtesies. The good old custom used to be a kind of staid reserve which made their rare smile deeper and more ideal.

During the offertory, after the fashion of the day, Germain placed the "thirteen"—that is to say, thirteen pieces of silver—in his bride's hand. He slipped over her finger a silver ring of a form unchanged for centuries, but which is replaced for henceforth by the golden wedding-ring. As they walked out of church, Marie said in a low voice:

"Is this really the ring I wanted? Is it the one I asked you for, Germain?"

"Yes," answered he, "my Catherine wore it on her finger when she died. There is but one ring for both my weddings."

"Thank you, Germain," said the young woman, in a serious and impressive tone. "I shall die with it on, and if I go before you, you must keep it for the marriage of your little Solange."

CHAPTER IV

The Cabbage

THEY mounted and returned very quickly to Belair. The feast was bountiful, and, mingled with songs and dances, it lasted until midnight. For fourteen hours the old people did not leave the table. The grave-digger did the cooking, and did it very well. He was celebrated for this, and he would leave his fire to come in and dance and sing before and after every course. And yet this poor Father Bontemps was epileptic. Who would have thought it? He was fresh and strong, and merry as a young man. One day we found him in a ditch, struck down by his malady at nightfall. We carried him home with us, in a wheelbarrow, and we spent all night in caring for him. Three days afterward, he was at a wedding, singing like a thrush, jumping like a kid, and bustling about after his old fashion. When he left a marriage, he would go to dig a grave and nail up a coffin. Then he would become very grave, and though nothing of this appeared in his gay humour, it left a melancholy impression which hastened the return of his attacks. His wife was paralysed, and had not stirred from her chair for twenty years. His mother is living yet, at a hundred and forty, but he, poor man, so happy and good and amusing, was killed last year by falling from his loft to the sidewalk. Doubtless he died a victim to a fatal attack of his disease, and, as was his habit, had hidden in the hay, so as not to frighten and distress his family. In this tragic manner he ended a life strange as his disposition—a medley of things sad and mad, awful and gay; and, in the midst of all, his heart was ever good and his nature kind.

Now we come to the third day of the wedding, the most curious of all, which is kept to-day in all its vigour. We shall not speak of the roast which they carry to the bridal bed; it is a very silly custom, and hurts the self-respect of the bride, while it tends to ruin the modesty of the attendant girls. Besides, I believe that it is practised in all the provinces, and does not belong peculiarly to our own.

Just as the ceremony of the wedding favours is a symbol that the heart and home of the bride are won, that of the cabbage is a symbol of the fruitfulness of marriage. When breakfast is over on the day after the wedding, this fantastic representation begins. Originally of Gallic derivation, it has passed through primitive Christianity, and little by little it has become a kind of mystery, or droll morality-play of the Middle Ages.

Two boys, the merriest and most intelligent of the company, disappear from breakfast, and after costuming themselves, return escorted by dogs, children, and pistol-shots. They represent a pair of beggars—husband and wife—dressed in rags. The husband is the filthier of the two; it is vice which has brought him so low; the wife is unhappy and degraded only through the misdeeds of her husband.

They are called the gardener and the gardener's wife, and they pretend it is their duty to guard and care for the sacred cabbage. The husband has several names, each with a meaning. Sometimes they call him the "scarecrow," because his head is covered with straw or hemp, and because his legs and a portion of his body are surrounded with straw to hide his nakedness, ill concealed by his rags. He has also a great belly, or hump, constructed of straw or hay underneath his blouse. Then he is known as the "ragamuffin," on account of his covering of rags. Lastly he is termed the "infidel," and this is most significant of all, because by his cynicism and his debauchery he is supposed to typify the opposite of every Christian virtue.

He comes with his face all smeared with soot and the lees of wine, and sometimes made yet more hideous by a grotesque mask. An earthenware cup, notched and broken, or an old sabot attached to his girdle by a cord, shows that he has come to beg for alms of wine. Nobody refuses him, and he pretends to drink; then he pours the wine on the ground by way of libation. At every step he falls, rolls in the mud, and feigns to be a prey to the most shameful drunkenness. His poor wife runs after him, picks him up, calls for help, arranges his hempen locks, which struggle forth in unkempt wisps from beneath his filthy hat, sheds tears over her husband's degradation, and pours forth pathetic reproaches.

"Wretched man," she cries, "see the misery to which your wickedness has brought us. I have to spend all my time sewing and working for you, mending your clothes. You tear and bedraggle yourself incessantly. You have eaten up all my little property; our six children lie on straw, and we are living in a stable with the beasts. Here we are forced to beg for alms, and, besides, you are so ugly and vile and despicable that very soon they will be tossing us bread as if we were dogs. Ah, my poor people, take pity on us! Take pity on me! I haven't deserved my lot, and never had woman a more dirty and detestable husband. Help me to pick him up, else the waggons will run over him as they run over broken bottles, and I shall be a widow, and that will end by killing me with grief, though all the world says it would be an excellent riddance for me."

Such is the part of the gardener's wife, and her continued lamentations last during the entire play. For it is a genuine spontaneous comedy acted on the spur of the moment in the open air, along the roads and across the fields, aided by every chance occurrence that presents itself. Everybody shares in the acting, people within the wedding-party and people without, wayfarers and dwellers in houses, for three or four hours of the day, as we shall see. The theme is always the same, but the variations are infinite; and it is here that we can see the instinct of mimicry, the abundance of droll ideas, the fluency, the wit at repartee, and even the natural eloquence of our peasants.

The rôle of gardener's wife is intrusted commonly to a slender man, beardless and fresh of face, who can give a great appearance of truth to his personification and plays the burlesque despair naturally enough to make people sad and glad at once, as they are in real life. These thin, beardless men are not rare among us, and, strangely enough, they are sometimes most remarkable for their muscular strength.

When the wife's misfortunes have been explained, the young men of the company try to persuade her to leave her drunken husband and amuse herself with them. They offer her their arms and drag her away. Little by little she gives way; her spirits rise, and she begins to run about, first with one and then with another, and grows more scandalous in her behaviour: a fresh "morality;" the ill-conduct of the husband excites and aggravates the evil in the wife.

Then the "infidel" wakes from his drunkenness. He looks about for his companion, arms himself with a rope and a stick, and rushes after her. They make him run, they hide, they pass the wife from one to another, they try to divert her attention and to deceive her jealous spouse. His friends try to get him drunk. At length he catches his unfaithful wife, and wishes to beat her. What is truest and most carefully portrayed in this play is that the jealous husband never attacks the men who carry off his wife. He is very polite and prudent with them, and wishes only to take vengeance on the sinning woman, because she is supposed to be too feeble to offer resistance.

At the moment, however, when he raises his stick and prepares his cord to strike the delinquent, all the men in the party interpose and throw themselves between husband and wife.

"Don't strike her! Never strike your wife," is the formula repeated to satiety during these scenes. They disarm the husband, and force him to pardon and to kiss his wife, and soon he pretends to love her better than ever. He walks along, his arm linked in hers, singing and dancing until, in a new access of drunkenness, he rolls upon the ground, and then begin all over again the lamentations of the wife, her discouragements, her pretended unfaithfulness, her husband's jealousy, the interference of the neighbours, and the reconciliation. In all this there is a simple and even coarse lesson, which, though it savours strongly of its Middle-Age origin, does not fail to fix its impression if not on the married folk, who are too loving or too sensible to have need of it, at least upon the children and the young people. The "infidel," racing after young girls and pretending to wish to kiss them, frightens and disgusts them to such a degree that they fly in unaffected terror. His dirty face and his great stick, harmless as it is, make the children shriek aloud. It is the comedy of customs in their most elementary but their most striking state.

When this farce is well under way, people make ready to hunt for the cabbage. They bring a stretcher and place upon it the "infidel," armed with a spade, a cord, and a large basket. Four powerful men raise him on their shoulders. His wife follows on foot, and after her come the "elders" in a body with serious and thoughtful looks; then the wedding-march begins by couples to a step tuned to music. Pistol-shots begin anew, and dogs bark louder than ever at the sight of the filthy "infidel" borne aloft in triumph. The children swing incense in derision with sabots fastened at the end of a cord.

But why this ovation to an object so repulsive? They are marching to the capture of the sacred cabbage, emblem of the fruitfulness of marriage, and it is this drunkard alone who can bear the symbolic plant in his hand. Doubtless, there is in it a pre-Christian mystery which recalls the Saturnalian feasts or some rout of the Bacchanals. Perhaps this "infidel," who is, at the same time, pre-eminently a gardener, is none other than Priapus himself, god of gardens and of drunkenness, a divinity who must have been pure and serious in his origin as is the mystery of birth, but who has been degraded bit by bit through licence of manners and distraction of thought.

However this may be, the triumphal procession arrives at the bride's house, and enters the garden. Then they select the choicest cabbage, and this is not done very quickly, for the old people keep consulting and disputing interminably, each one pleading for the cabbage he thinks most suitable. They put it to vote, and when the choice is made the gardener fastens his cord to the stalk, and moves away as far as the size of the garden permits. The gardener's wife takes care that the sacred vegetable shall not be hurt in its fall. The wits of the wedding, the hemp-dresser, the grave-digger, the carpenter, and the sabot-maker, form a ring about the cabbage, for men who do not till the soil, but pass their lives in other people's houses, are thought to be, and are really, wittier and more talkative than simple farm-hands. One digs, with a spade, a ditch deep enough to uproot an oak. Another places on his nose a pair of wooden or cardboard spectacles. He fulfils the duties of "engineer," walks up and down, constructs a plan, stares at the workmen through his glasses, plays the pedant, cries out that everything will be spoiled, has the work stopped and begun afresh as his fancy directs, and makes the whole performance as long and ridiculous as he can. This is an addition to the formula of an ancient ceremony held in mockery of theorists in general, for peasants despise them royally, or from hatred of the surveyors who decide boundaries and regulate taxes, or of the workmen employed on bridges and causeways, who transform commons into highways, and suppress old abuses which the peasants love. Be this as it may, this character in the comedy is called the "geometrician," and does his best to make himself unbearable to those who are toiling with pickaxe and shovel.

After a quarter of an hour spent in mummery, and difficulties raised in order to avoid cutting the roots, and to transplant the cabbage without injury, while shovelfuls of dirt are tossed into the faces of the onlookers—so much the worse for him who does not retreat in time, for were he bishop or prince he must receive the baptism of earth—the "infidel" pulls the rope, the "infidel's wife" holds her apron, and the cabbage falls majestically amidst the applause of the spectators. Then a basket is brought, and the "infidel" pair plant the cabbage therein with every care and precaution. They surround it with fresh earth, and support it with sticks and strings, such as city florists use for their splendid potted camellias; they fix red apples to the points of the sticks, and twist sprigs of thyme, sage, and laurel all about them; they bedeck the whole with ribbons and streamers; they place the trophy upon the stretcher with the "infidel," whose duty it is to maintain its equilibrium and preserve it from harm; and at length, they move away from the garden in good order and in marching step.

But when they are about to pass the gate, and again when they enter the yard of the bridegroom's house, an imaginary obstacle blocks the way. The bearers of the burden stagger, utter loud cries, retreat, advance once more, and, as though crushed by a resistless force, they pretend to sink beneath its weight. While this is going on, the bystanders shout loudly, exciting and steadying this human team.

"Slowly, slowly, my child. There, there, courage! Look out! Be patient! Lower your head; the door is too low! Close up; it's too narrow! A little more to the left; now to the right; on with you; don't be afraid; you're almost there."

Thus it is that in years of plentiful harvest, the ox-cart, loaded to overflowing with hay or corn, is too broad or too high to enter the barn door. Thus it is that the driver shouts at the strong beasts, to restrain them or to urge them on; thus it is that with skill and mighty efforts they force this mountain of riches beneath the rustic arch of triumph. It is, above all, the last load, called "the cart of sheaves," which requires these precautions, for this is a rural festival, and the last sheaf lifted from the last furrow is placed on the top of the cart-load ornamented with ribbons and flowers, while the foreheads of the oxen and the whip of the driver are decorated also. The triumphant and toilsome entry of the cabbage into the house is a symbol of the prosperity and fruitfulness it represents.

Safe within the bridegroom's yard, the cabbage is taken from its stretcher and borne to the topmost peak of the house or barn. Whether it be a chimney, a gable, or a dove-cot that crowns the roof, the burden must, at any risk, be carried to the very highest point of the building. The "infidel" accompanies it as far as this, sets it down securely, and waters it with a great pitcher of wine, while a salvo of pistol-shots and demonstrations of joy from the "infidel's wife" proclaim its inauguration.

Without delay, the same ceremony is repeated all over again. Another cabbage is dug from the garden of the husband and is carried with the same formalities and laid upon the roof which his wife has deserted to follow him. These trophies remain in their places until the wind and the rain destroy the baskets and carry away the cabbage. Yet their lives are long enough to give some chance of fulfilment to the prophecies which the old men and women make with bows and courtesies.

"Beautiful cabbage," they say, "live and flourish that our young bride may have a fine baby before a year is over; for if you die too quickly it is a sign of barrenness, and you will stick up there like an ill omen."

The day is already far gone when all these things are accomplished. All that remains undone is to take home the godfathers and godmothers of the newly married couple. When the so-called parents dwell at a distance, they are accompanied by the music and the whole wedding procession as far as the limits of the parish; there they dance anew on the high road, and everybody kisses them good-bye. The "infidel" and his wife are then washed and dressed decently, if the fatigue of their parts has not already driven them away to take a nap.

Everybody was still dancing and singing and eating in the Town Hall of Belair at midnight on this third day of the wedding when Germain was married. The old men at table could not stir, and for good reason. They recovered neither their legs nor their wits until dawn on the morrow. While they were regaining their dwellings, silently and with uncertain steps, Germain, proud and active, went out to hitch his oxen, leaving his young wife to slumber until daylight. The lark, carolling as it mounted to the skies, seemed to him the voice of his heart returning thanks to Providence. The hoar-frost, sparkling on the leafless bushes, seemed to him the whiteness of April flowers that comes before the budding leaves. Everything in nature was laughing and happy for him. Little Pierre had laughed and jumped so much the evening before that he did not come to help lead his oxen; but Germain was glad to be alone. He fell on his knees in the furrow he was about to plough afresh, and said his morning prayer with such a burst of feeling that two tears rolled down his cheeks, still moist with sweat.

Afar off he heard the songs of the boys from neighbouring villages, who were starting on their return home, singing again in their hoarse voices the happy tunes of the night before.

THE STORY OF A WHITE BLACKBIRD

BY

ALFRED DE MUSSET

TRANSLATED BY

KATHARINE ROYCE

BIOGRAPHICAL NOTE

LOUIS CHARLES ALFRED DE MUSSET was born in the heart of old Paris on November 11, 1810. His father, who held various important state offices, is remembered chiefly as the editor and biographer of Rousseau. Alfred was brought up in a literary atmosphere and his early experiments in poetry and the drama convinced Sainte-Beuve that he possessed genius. When he was nineteen his "Contes d'Espagne et d'Italie" had a sensational success. Though he is reckoned a member of the romantic school, he was sufficiently detached and critical to be aware of its foibles, and in his "Ballade à la lune," contained in this first volume, he poked fun at the romantic worship of the moon, comparing it as it shone above a steeple to the dot over an *i*. He had a strong admiration for certain elements in classicism, and it seemed at one time that he might found a new school combining the virtues of both the old and new. But his drama, "Une nuit vénitienne," was a failure on the stage, and in the future he wrote only to be read and so missed much of the influence he might have had on the theatre of his day. Many of his plays reached the stage years after they were written, notable among them being "Les Caprices de Marianne," "Il ne faut jurer de rien," "Il faut qu'une porte soit ouverte ou fermée," "Un Caprice," and "Bettine."

In 1833 De Musset went to Italy with George Sand, and that tempestuous and typically romantic love affair left him a wreck. The traces of it are to be found not only in his elegiac love poetry, but also in prose work like his "Confession d'un enfant du siècle," and in drama like "On ne badine pas avec l'amour," where one is shown the danger of trifling with love.

The gaiety and irresponsibility which marked the earlier years of his production had now given place to pain and bitterness. His later years were lightened by popular appreciation, but he suffered much from illness. He wrote little of importance after he was forty, and he died on May 2, 1857.

De Musset's reputation is primarily that of a poet, and he ranks among the greatest in French literature. His "Nuits" reveal with great beauty of expression all the passion and suffering of which a soul of extreme sensitiveness is capable. Though he resented the suggestion that he imitated Byron, he shows some resemblance to him in his self-pity; but in the delicacy and variety of the phases of sentiment and passion displayed in his poems he far surpasses the English poet. His plays and his reflective writings are often brilliant, and he had a fine satiric power.

His fiction is subordinate in importance to both his poetry and his dramas, yet it exemplifies some of his characteristic qualities. His first success was won in this field, and his "Confession" contains much besides the other side of the story told in George Sand's "Elle et Lui." "The White Blackbird" is a charming satire on the literary life of his time, exposing not merely the ease with which popular taste is imposed upon and some current types of literary humbugs, but also the universal tendency to confound mere eccentricity with genius. The allegorical form in which it is clothed is well sustained in the earlier part; but as the satire becomes more pronounced the blackbird and his pretended affinity tend to discard their disguise as birds and become frankly human beings—perhaps even human beings who can be identified. Yet, on the whole, the blackbird's story holds our attention, and in the telling of it there is a delightful mingling of grace, sentiment, and wit.

W. A. N.

CRITICISM AND INTERPRETATION

By George Pellissier

Alfred de Musset was above all else the poet of youth. Smiling upon life, the elect of genius, the betrothed of love, he appears with a candid, haughty eye, the bloom of spring on his cheek, a song on his lips. What gayety, what youthful freshness! What turbulent ardor in pleasure and dissipation! Back with "decrepit age!" Give room to eager, impetuous, triumphant adolescence! Make way for the poet of eighteen whose heart beats at the first summons, whose forehead is gilded by the first rays of glory! His heart opens; he suffers; he sings of his pain. The volatile ballads of the Cherubim are followed by Don Juan's impassioned accents. Every wave lures him, even the most impure, where he hopes to find a remote reflection of his adored ideal. And when love no longer blossoms on a prematurely withered stalk, he feels that all the charm of life has vanished with the spring, that genius itself cannot survive the incapacity to love. Eleven years after the petulant fervors and cavalier graces of his début, when his years had scarcely sounded thirty, he sits down at his desk with his head in his hands to dream of a past of tarnished memories, of a future that favors no hope. For others, thirty is the age of vigorous, productive maturity; for Cherubim, it is the period of decline and lassitude. After several always more rare efforts to reform, follows a precocious old age, both idle and sterile, with no work assigned, no duty to accomplish. All is finished; he resigns himself to existence, lacking interest in life, rather detesting it. He assists in his own ruin, furthering it by recourse to fictitious intoxications. He seeks the waters of Jouvence even in the muddy pools of the gutters, always sinking lower into the depths of a mournful silence. With youth, the poet of youth had lost all; when he died to love, he was also dead to poetry.

Alfred de Musset abandoned his life to the hazards of fancy, and his genius to the caprices of inspiration. Later the poet bore the penance of a natural inconstancy, indolence, and aversion to all discipline, already foreshadowed by an idle, desultory youth. Nervous and whimsical as a child, he continues to allow himself to drift without the power to restrain himself. His youth is scattered to all winds, and his soul's treasures are squandered. He makes his entire life consist in the delirium of a morbid, exalted passion, which, although it at first feeds his genius, is not long in consuming it. . . .

Of all our poets he has brought the most passionate fervor into poetry. He voices his emotion while it is still expanding, allowing it to gush forth in its eager violence, unreservedly surrendering it vibrating with ardent sincerity. Pain or joy—everything seeks to escape from his breast, and that immediately. Others part with their most personal impressions when the moment arrives; but, like the pelican whose anguish he has celebrated, he delivers up his own entrails for food. He allows not only his tears to flow, but also the blood from his wound.—From "The Literary Movement in France in the Nineteenth Century" (1893).

THE STORY OF A WHITE BLACKBIRD

CHAPTER I

HOW glorious it is, but how difficult, to be an unusual blackbird in this world! I certainly am not a fabulous bird, and Monsieur de Buffon has described me. But, alas! I am extremely rare, and very difficult to find. Would to God that I were entirely impossible!

My father and mother were an excellent couple who had been living for a number of years in the depths of a retired old garden of the Marais. Their family life was exemplary. While my mother, sitting in a thick bush, laid regularly three times a year, and while she slept, kept her eggs warm with a truly patriarchal fervor, my father, who was still very neat and very impatient, in spite of his great age, picked busily around her all day, bringing her nice insects which he took delicately by the tip of the tail so as not to disgust his wife, and, when night came on, he never failed, if the weather was fine, to treat her to a song which delighted the whole neighborhood. Not the slightest quarrel, not the slightest cloud, had ever troubled this peaceful union.

I had scarcely come into the world, when, for the first time in his life, my father began to show ill humor. Although I was as yet only a doubtful gray, he could not recognize in me either the color or the appearance of his numerous progeny.

"Look at that dirty child," he would sometimes say, with a cross glance at me; "it seems as if the young rascal must go and stick himself into all the old plaster and mud holes he can find, he always looks so ugly and dirty."

"Heavens, my dear," my mother would answer, as she sat rolled up like a ball in an old porringer where she had made her nest, "don't you see that it is because of his age? And you too, in your younger days, were not you a charming scapegrace? Just let our little blackbird grow up, and you will see how handsome he will be; he is one of the best that I ever hatched."

Although she spoke up bravely in my defense, my mother had no illusions about me; she saw my wretched plumage starting and it seemed to her a monstrosity; but she followed the custom of all mothers, who often love their children better just because nature has used them unkindly, as if they themselves were to blame, or as if they must try to resist in advance the injustice of the fate that may sometime overtake their children.

When it was time for my first moulting, my father grew very pensive and examined me carefully. As long as my feathers were falling, he still treated me rather kindly and even fed me when he saw me shivering almost naked in a corner; but as soon as my poor little trembling wings began to be covered with down, my father got so angry every time he saw a white feather appear that I was afraid he would pluck me bare for the rest of my life. Alas! I had no mirror; I did not know the cause of this fury, and I wondered and wondered why the best of fathers should be so cruel to me.

One day when the sunshine and my new feathers had made my heart rejoice, in spite of myself, as I was fluttering along a path, I began to sing, unfortunately for me. At the first note that he heard, my father sprang into the air like a rocket.

"What is that I hear?" he cried. "Is that the way a blackbird whistles? Is that the way I whistle? Is that any way to whistle?"

And, throwing himself down beside my mother with the most terrible expression on his face:

"Wretched bird!" said he, "who has been laying in your nest?"

At these words, my mother was so indignant that she threw herself out of her porringer, hurting one of her claws as she did so; she tried to speak, but her sobbing suffocated her; she fell to the ground half swooning. I saw her apparently dying; horrified and trembling with fear, I threw myself at my father's feet.

"Oh father!" I said, "if I whistle all wrong, and if I am ill dressed, do not let my mother be punished for it! Is it her fault if nature has denied me a voice like yours? Is it her fault that I have not your fine yellow beak and your handsome French-looking black coat, which makes you look like a church warden swallowing an omelette? If the powers above have made me a monster, and if some one must bear the blame, let me at least be the only one to suffer!"

"That is not the question," said my father. "What do you mean by daring to whistle in that absurd fashion? Who taught you to whistle like that, contrary to all rules and customs?"

"Alas, Sir," I answered humbly, "I whistled as I could, because the fine weather made me feel gay, and perhaps I had eaten too many flies."

"No one whistles like that in my family," replied my father, beside himself. "For centuries we have been whistling from father to son, and I would have you know that right here, there is an old gentleman on the first story, and a young grisette in the attic, who open their windows to hear me whenever I sing at night. Is it not enough that I must always have before my eyes the hideous color of your foolish feathers which makes you look as if you were covered with flour like a clown at the circus? If I were not the most peaceful of blackbirds, I should have plucked you bare a hundred times before now, like a chicken ready for roasting."

"Very well!" I cried, indignant at my father's injustice, "if that is how you feel, so be it! I will take my departure, I will relieve you of the sight of my unfortunate white tail by which you pull me about all day. I will leave you, Sir, I will fly; there will be enough other children to comfort you in your old age, since my mother lays three times a year; I will go far away and hide my misery from you, and perhaps," I added sobbing, "perhaps I shall find, in our neighbor's garden or in the gutters, some worms or spiders wherewith to support my sad existence."

"As you please," replied my father, who was not at all propitiated by my words. "Only let me see no more of you! You are no son of mine; you are no blackbird."

"And what am I then, if you please, Sir?"

"I have not the slightest idea, but you are no blackbird."

After pronouncing these astounding words, my father went slowly away. My mother picked herself up sorrowfully, and, limping as she went, returned to her porringer to weep her fill. As for me, sad and bewildered, I flew away as best I could, and as I had threatened to do, I went and perched on the gutter of a neighboring house.

CHAPTER II

MY father was so inhumane as to leave me for several days in this humiliating situation. In spite of his violent temper, he was good hearted, and I could tell from the sidelong glances that he cast at me, that he would have been glad to pardon me and call me back; and my mother, still more, constantly gazed up at me with eye full of tenderness, and even dared, from time to time, to call me with a little plaintive cry; but my horrible white plumage filled them in spite of themselves with terror and repugnance which I saw were wholly beyond remedy.

"I am not a blackbird!" I kept repeating; and in fact, when I was pluming myself in the morning, using the water in the gutter for a mirror, I could see only too clearly how little resemblance I bore to the rest of my family. "Oh heavens!" I repeated once more, "tell me then what I am!"

One night when there was a pouring rain, I was just ready to fall asleep, worn out with grief and hunger, when I saw alighting near me a bird wetter, paler, and thinner than I could have believed possible. He was almost the same color as I, as well as I could see through the rain which was pouring over us; he had scarcely enough feathers on his whole body to cover a sparrow, and he was bigger than I. At the first glance, he seemed to me a very poor and needy bird; but in spite of the storm which deluged his nearly bald head, he still had a proud air which fascinated me. With becoming modesty, I made him a low bow, to which he responded with a peck that almost knocked me off the gutter. When he saw that I was scratching my ear and that I was retiring ruefully without attempting to reply to him in his own language:

"Who are you?" he asked in a voice as hoarse as his head was bald.

"Alas! my Lord," I answered (fearing a second jab), "I have not the slightest idea. I thought I was a blackbird, but I have been convinced that I am not."

My unusual answer and my air of sincerity aroused his interest. He came close to me and made me tell him my story, which I did with all the sorrow and humility befitting my position and the terrible weather.

"If you were a carrier pigeon like me," said he after he had heard my tale, "the foolish things that you grieve over would not give you a moment's trouble. We travel, that is our whole life. And although we have our love affairs, I do not know who my father is. Our pleasure, indeed our very existence, is rushing through the air, flying through space, seeing mountains and plains at our feet, breathing the very azure of heaven, and not the exhalations of the earth, darting like an arrow towards an end which we never miss. I can travel farther in one day than a man can in ten."

"Upon my word, Sir," said I, plucking up a little more courage, "you are a gipsy bird."

"That is another thing that I care nothing about," answered he. "I am a bird without a country; I know only three things: my journeys, my wife, and my little ones. Wherever my wife is, there is my country."

"But what have you there hanging around your neck? It looks like a ragged old curl paper."

"Those are important papers," answered he, puffing himself up proudly. "I am now on way to Brussels, and I am carrying a message to the celebrated banker —— which will lower the rate of exchange by one franc and seventy-eight centimes."

"Good Lord," I cried, "you certainly lead a fine life, and I am sure that Brussels must be a very interesting city to see. Could you not take me with you? Since I am not a blackbird, perhaps I am a carrier pigeon."

"If you were," he replied, "you would have struck back when I pecked you just now."

"Very well, Sir, that's easily remedied; let us not quarrel for so small a matter. Morning is coming and the storm is clearing away. I beg you to let me follow you! I am ruined, I have nothing left in the world—if you refuse me, there is nothing left for me to do but to drown myself in this gutter."

"Very well, let us start. Follow me if you can."

I cast one last glance at the garden where my mother was sleeping. A tear flowed from my eyes; the wind and the rain carried it away. I spread my wings, and I started.

CHAPTER III

I HAVE already said that my wings were not yet very strong. While my leader went like the wind, I was out of breath trying to keep up with him; I held out for some time, but presently I became so dizzy, that I felt as if I should soon faint away.

"Is it much further?" I asked in a weak voice.

"No," answered he, "we have reached Bourget; we only have to go sixty leagues more."

I tried to pluck up courage, not wanting to look like a wet hen, and I flew for another quarter of an hour, but for the time being, I was exhausted.

"Monsieur," I stammered once more, "couldn't we stop a moment? I am frightfully thirsty, and, if we should perch on a tree . . ."

"Go to the devil! You are nothing but a blackbird!" the carrier pigeon answered angrily.

And without condescending to turn his head, he continued his furious flight. As for me, stunned and half blind, I fell into a wheat field.

I do not know how long my swoon lasted. When I recovered consciousness, the first thing that I remembered was the pigeon's parting word: "You are nothing but a blackbird," he had said. Oh my dear parents, I thought, you were mistaken, then! I will go home to you; you will recognize me as your own legitimate child, and you will allow me a place in that nice little pile of leaves under my mother's porringer.

I made an effort to rise; but the fatigue of the voyage and the pain caused by my fall paralyzed all my limbs. As soon as I stood upon my feet, my faintness returned, and I fell back on my side.

My mind was already fixed upon the terrible thought of death, when I saw two charming ladies coming towards me on tiptoes, between the poppies and corn-flowers. One was a very prettily spotted and extremely coquettish little magpie, and the other a rose colored turtle dove. The dove paused a few steps from me, looking very modest and sympathetic; but the magpie came skipping towards me in the most delightful way.

"Heaven above! What are you doing there, my poor child?" she asked caressingly in a silvery voice.

"Alas! Madame la Marquise," I replied (for she must have been at least a Marquise), "I am a poor devil of a traveller whose postilion has abandoned him on the road, and I am dying of hunger."

"Holy Virgin! What are you telling me?" replied she.

And she began immediately to fly here and there among the bushes near by, going and coming this way and that, and bringing me a quantity of berries and fruits, which she put in a heap near me, all the while asking me questions.

"But who are you? Where did you come from? Your adventure seems perfectly unbelievable! And where were you going? Travelling alone, so young, for you are only getting through with your first moulting! What are your parents about? Where do they belong? How could they let you go in such a state? Why, it is enough to make one's feathers stand on end!"

While she was talking, I had raised myself a little on my elbow, and was eating greedily. The turtle dove still stood motionless, gazing at me with pitying eyes. However, she noticed that I kept turning my head with a languid air, and she realized that I was thirsty. A drop of the rain that had fallen during the night still lingered on a sprig of chickweed; she took this drop timidly in her beak, and brought it to me quite fresh. Surely, if I had not been so ill, such a modest person would never have done such a thing.

I did not yet know what love was, but my heart beat violently. Torn between two conflicting emotions, I was overpowered by an inexplicable charm. She who had brought my food was so gay, and my cup bearer was so gentle and affectionate, that I could have wished my breakfast to last through all eternity. Unfortunately, all things come to an end, even the appetite of a convalescent. When the meal was finished and my strength had returned, I satisfied the little magpie's curiosity, and told her my troubles just as truthfully as I had told them to the pigeon the evening before. The magpie listened more attentively than one would have expected her to do, and the turtle dove showed the most charming signs of emotion. But, when I came to touch upon the principal cause of all my trouble, that is, my ignorance about myself:

"Are you joking?" exclaimed the magpie. "You, a blackbird! You, a pigeon! For shame! You are a magpie, my dear child, if ever there was one, and a very pretty magpie," she added, touching me lightly with her wing, as one might wave a fan.

"But, Madame la Marquise," I replied, "it seems to me that, for a magpie, I am such a color, saving your presence . . ."

"A Russian magpie, my dear, you are a Russian pie! Did you not know that they are white? Poor boy, what innocence!"

"But, Madame," I replied, "how could I be a Russian magpie, when I was born in the heart of the Marais, in an old broken porringer?"

"Ah, how simple you are! You belong to the invasion, my dear; do you imagine that you are the only one? Trust to me, and let yourself go; I will take you away with me at once and show you the most beautiful things in the world."

"And where shall we go, Madame, if you please?"

"To my green palace, my darling; you shall see how we live there. By the time you have been a magpie for a quarter of an hour, you will never want to hear of anything else. There are about a hundred of us there, not those big, village magpies who beg for alms along the public roads, but noble, well-bred society birds, quick and slender, and no larger than one's fist. Not one of us has either more or less than seven black marks and five white marks; that is invariable, and we despise the rest of the world. To be sure, you have not the black marks, but your standing as a Russian will suffice to gain you admission. Our life consists of two things: chattering and prinking. From morning till noon, we adorn ourselves, and from noon till evening, we chatter. Each of us perches on a tree, the highest and oldest that we can find. In the midst of the forest there stands an immense oak, which, alas, is uninhabited! It was the dwelling of the late King Pie X, the goal of all our pilgrimages which cost us so many sighs; but apart from this mild sorrow, we enjoy ourselves wonderfully. With us, the wives are not prudish nor the husbands jealous, but our pleasures are pure and honest, because our hearts are as noble as our language is free and joyous. Our pride knows no bounds, and, if a jay or any other plebeian bird happens to come amongst us, we pluck him mercilessly. But for all that, we are the best people in the world, and the sparrows, the tom-tits, and the goldfinches, that live in our thicket, find us always ready to help, or feed, or defend them. There is no more constant chattering anywhere than we keep up, and nowhere is there less slanderous talk. Of course we have some religious old pies who say their prayers all day long, but the giddiest of our young females can pass close by the severest old dowager without any fear of being pecked. In a word, our life is made up of pleasure, honor, small-talk, glory, and finery."

"All that is certainly very fine, Madame," I replied, "and I should certainly be very ill bred not to obey the commands of such a person as you. But before I permit myself the honor of following you, allow me, if you please, to say a word to this sweet young lady.—Mademoiselle," I continued, addressing the turtle dove, "tell me frankly, I beg you; do you think that I am really a Russian magpie?"

At this question, the dove hung her head, and turned pale red, like Lolotte's ribbons.

"But, Monsieur," said she, "I don't know if I can . . ."

"For heaven's sake, speak, Mademoiselle! My intentions are not such as to offend you, quite the contrary. Both of you seem to me so charming, that I register a vow to offer my hand and my heart to whichever will accept me, the moment I succeed in finding out whether I am a magpie or some other kind of bird. Because, when I am looking at you," I added, speaking a little more softly to the young lady, "I feel a sensation curiously like a turtle dove, and it troubles me strangely."

"But, truly," said the turtle dove blushing still more deeply, "I do not know whether it is the sunlight reflected upon you from the poppies, but your plumage seems to me to have a slight tinge . . ."

She dared to say no more.

"Oh perplexity!" I cried, "how can I tell what to believe? How can I give my heart to either one of you, when it is so cruelly torn asunder? Oh Socrates! how admirable is your precept: 'Know thyself!' but how difficult it is to follow."

Since the day when my unfortunate song had made my father so terribly angry, I had never used my voice again. But now, it occurred to me to try it as a means of finding out the truth. "Good gracious!" thought I, "since my father turned me out of doors at the very first couplet, the least I can expect is, that the second will produce some sort of an effect upon these ladies!" Therefore, after having bowed politely, as if to ask them to make allowances because of the rain to which I had been exposed, I began first to whistle, then to warble, then to trill, and then to sing with all my might like a Spanish muleteer in the open air.

The more I sang, the more the little magpie moved away from me with an air of surprise which soon changed to astonishment, and then to fright and annoyance. She circled around me like a cat around a bit of hot bacon which has just burned her, but which she is tempted to taste once more. Observing the effects of my experiment, and desiring to carry it to a conclusion, the more impatient the poor Marquise seemed, the louder I sang. She held out for twenty-five minutes in spite of my melodious efforts; finally, being unable to stand it any longer, she flew away with a rush, and went back to her green palace. As for the turtle dove, she had fallen sound asleep almost at the beginning of my song.

"Wonderful effect of harmony!" thought I. "I am more than ever determined to return to the Marais, to my mother's porringer."

Just as I was starting to fly away, the turtle dove opened her eyes again.

"Farewell" said she, "farewell, charming stranger, so charming and yet so troublesome! My name is Gourouli; remember me!"

"Lovely Gourouli," I answered, "you are good, gentle, and charming; I wish that I could live and die for you. But you are *couleur de rose*. So much happiness is not for me!"

CHAPTER IV

THE sad effect produced by my singing naturally saddened me also. "Alas, music! Alas, poetry!" I said to myself as I started for Paris once more, "how few are the hearts that understand you!"

As these reflections passed through my mind, I hit my head against that of a bird who was flying in the opposite direction. The blow was so severe and so unexpected, that we both fell into the top of a tree, which fortunately happened to be there. After we had shaken ourselves once or twice, I looked at the new comer, expecting a fight. I saw to my surprise that he was white. In fact, his head was a little bigger than mine, and he had a sort of plume on his forehead which gave him a mock-heroic air. Also he carried his tail very high, in quite a noble style; for the rest, I could not see that he had any disposition to fight. We accosted each other very civilly, and excused ourselves, after which we entered into conversation. I took the liberty of asking his name and from what country he came.

"I am astonished," said he, "that you do not know me. Are you not one of us?"

"In fact, monsieur," I replied, "I do not know to whom I belong. Every one asks me the same question and tells me the same thing; I think they must have made a wager."

"You are joking," replied he; "your plumage is too becoming for me to fail to recognize you as one of our fraternity. You certainly belong to the ancient and honorable race which is called in Latin *cacatua,* in the language of the learned *kakatoës,* and in the vulgar tongue cockatoo."

"Faith, Sir, that is possible, and I should consider it a great honor. But let us suppose, for the moment, that I do not belong to that kindred, and pray tell me whom I have the honor of addressing."

"I am," answered the stranger, "the great poet Kacatogan. I have made long voyages, Monsieur, I have crossed arid tracts, and my wanderings have been cruelly difficult. I have been dealing with rhymes for a long, long time, and my muse has been through many vicissitudes. I sang softly under Louis XVI, Monsieur, I shouted for the Republic, I sang of the Empire in the noble style, I praised the Restoration cautiously, and I have even made an effort recently, and have adapted myself, not without difficulty, to the requirements of this tasteless age. I have given to the world piquant couplets, sublime hymns, graceful dithyrambs, pious elegies, dramas with long hair, romances with curly hair, vaudevilles with powdered hair, and tragedies with bald heads. In a word, I flatter myself that I have added some gay festoons, some somber battlements, and some ingenious arabesques to the temple of the muses. What more could you expect? I have grown old. But my rhymes still flow copiously, Monsieur, and just now, I was dreaming of a poem in one canto, which should have no less than six pages, when you gave me this bump on my forehead. For the rest, if I can be of any use to you, I am entirely at your service."

"Indeed, Monsieur, you can help me," I replied, "for at this very moment I am seriously embarrassed as to a poetical matter. I dare not call myself a poet, certainly not a great poet like you," I added, with a bow, "but nature has given me a throat which torments me with the longing to sing whenever I am very happy or very sad. To tell you the truth, I know absolutely nothing of the rules."

"I have forgotten them myself," said Kacatogan, "do not give yourself any concern about that."

"But something disagreeable always happens to me. My voice produces the same effect upon those who hear it as that of a certain Jean de Nivelle upon. . . . You know what I mean?"

"I know," said Kacatogan; "I know that peculiar effect by my own experience. I am not acquainted with the cause, but the effect is indisputable."

"Very well, Monsieur, do you not know of any remedy for this serious annoyance—you who seem to be the Nestor of poetry?"

"No," said Kacatogan, "for my part, I have never been able to find a remedy. When I was young, I was very much troubled because I was always hissed; but now, I never think of it any more. I fancy that the repugnance of the audience arises from the fact that they read other writers than ourselves: that distracts their attention."

"I agree with you; but you must admit, Monsieur, that it is hard for a well meaning creature to have people run away whenever he has a pleasant impulse. Would you please be so good as to listen to me, and give me your candid opinion?"

"Willingly," said Kacatogan; "I am all ears."

I began to sing, and had the satisfaction of seeing that Kacatogan neither flew away nor fell asleep. He gazed at me steadily, and, from time to time, nodded his head with an air of approval, or murmured some flattering words. But I soon saw that he was not listening, but only dreaming of his own poem. Taking advantage of a moment when I paused for breath, he suddenly interrupted me.

"I have found the rhyme I wanted, now!" said he, smiling and shaking his head. "It is the sixty thousand seven hundred and fourteenth that my brain has produced! And they dare to say that I am growing old! I shall read this poem to some of my good friends. I shall read it to them, and we shall see what they will say!"

So saying, he spread his wings and flew away, seeming to have no further remembrance of having met me.

CHAPTER V

BEING left solitary and disappointed, I had nothing better to do than to profit by the remainder of the day and to fly at full speed towards Paris. Unfortunately, I did not know my way. My voyage with the pigeon had been so trying that I was unable to remember the route exactly; so that, instead of turning sharply to the right, I turned to the left at Bourget, and, being overtaken by night, I was obliged to seek shelter in the woods of Morfontaine.

All the birds were going to bed when I arrived. The pies and jays, who, as everyone knows, are the most uneasy creatures in the world at bedtime, were pushing and scuffling in every direction. The sparrows were scolding and treading on each other in the bushes. At the water's edge two herons were walking solemnly, balancing themselves on their long stilts, in a meditative attitude, the George Dandins of the place, patiently awaiting their wives. Huge crows, already half asleep, were perching clumsily on the tops of the tallest trees, and saying their evening prayers in nasal tones. Lower down, some amorous tom-tits were still chasing each other through the thicket, while a woodpecker with ruffled plumage was pushing his family from behind, to drive them into a hole in a tree. Whole flocks of hedge-sparrows were coming in from the fields, dancing in the air like puffs of smoke, and alighting on a shrub, covering it completely. Chaffinches, linnets, and robin redbreasts had grouped themselves lightly on some pruned branches like crystals on a chandelier. Voices sounded in every direction, saying quite plainly: "—Come, wife! — Come, daughter! — This way, sweetheart! — Come here, dearest!—Here I am, my dear!—Goodnight, my love! —Goodby, friends!— Sleep well, children!"

What a position for a bachelor, to lodge in such a tavern! I felt tempted to accost some birds of about my size and ask for their hospitality.—At night, I thought, all birds are gray;

and, for that matter, does it do people any harm to sleep quietly near them?

I turned first toward a ditch where some starlings were assembled. They were making their evening toilette with special care, and I noticed that most of them had golden wings and varnished claws: these were the dandies of the forest. They were good-natured enough, but did not pay me the compliment of noticing me at all. But their talk was so silly, they recounted their quarrels and their successes with such self conceit, and they pressed against each other so closely, that I really could not stand it.

I then went and perched on a branch where there were half a dozen birds of different kinds sitting in a row. I modestly took the last place at the extreme end of the branch, hoping to be tolerated there. Unfortunately, my neighbor was an old dove, as dry as a rusty weather vane. As I approached her, the few feathers which covered her bones were the object of her tenderest care; she was pretending to plume them, but she was too much afraid of pulling one out: she was merely counting them over, to see if she still had the proper number. I had scarcely touched her with the tip of my wing, when she stood erect, with freezing dignity.

"What are you doing, Monsieur?" she said, pinching her beak together, with British modesty.

And, giving me a great push with her elbow, she threw me off the branch with a vigor that would have done credit to a porter.

I fell into a furze bush where a big wood hen was sleeping. Even my mother in her porringer had not such an air of complete beatitude. She was so plump, so well grown, so comfortably seated on her own fat stomach, that one might have taken her for a pasty which had had its crust eaten off. I slipped up to her furtively.—"She will not wake up," I said to myself, "and, in any case, such a nice fat mother cannot be very spiteful." In point of fact she was not. She half opened her eyes, and said with a little sigh:

"You are bothering me, little one, do go away."

Just then I heard some one calling me. It was some thrushes, in the top of a service tree, who were making signs to me to come to them.—"There are some good souls at last," I thought. They made room for me, laughing wildly, and I slipped into the feathery group as swiftly as a love letter into a muff. But it did not take long to find out that those ladies had eaten more grapes than were good for them; they could scarcely hold on to the branches on which they were sitting, and their highly spiced pleasantries, their peals of laughter, and their ribald songs drove me to move on.

I was beginning to despair, and was about to go to sleep in a solitary corner, when a nightingale began to sing. Every one kept silence at once. Ah me! how pure his voice was! how sweet even his melancholy seemed! Instead of disturbing any one's sleep, his notes seemed only to soothe it. No one dreamed of telling him to be quiet, no one found fault with his singing at such an hour; his father did not beat him and his friends did not take to flight.

"I, then, am the only one who is forbidden to be happy! I will go away, I will fly from this cruel company! I would rather try to find my way in the dark, at the risk of being eaten by some owl, than to have my heart torn by the sight of others' happiness!"

Moved by this thought, I started once more and wandered for a long time at random. At daybreak I saw the towers of Notre Dame. In the twinkling of an eye I was there, and I soon recognized our garden. I flew to it quicker than lightning . . . Alas it was empty . . . In vain did I call my parents. Nobody answered. The tree where my father used to sit, my mother's bush, the precious porringer, all had disappeared. The axe had destroyed everything; instead of the green bordered path where I was born, nothing was left but a pile of fagots.

CHAPTER VI

I WENT at once in search of my parents through all the gardens in the neighborhood, but my trouble was in vain. They must doubtless have taken refuge in some distant place, and I have never been able to learn what became of them.

Overwhelmed with sorrow, I went and perched on the gutter to which my father's anger had exiled me. There I passed whole days and nights lamenting my sad life. I could no longer sleep, I ate scarcely anything, and I came very near dying of hunger.

One day when I was bemoaning my fate as usual, I said aloud: "So then, I am neither a blackbird, since my father used to pluck out my feathers; nor a pigeon, since I fell by the way when I was trying to fly over to Belgium; nor a Russian magpie, since the little Marquise stopped up her ears as soon as I opened my mouth; nor a turtle dove, since Gourouli herself, gentle Gourouli, snored like a monk while I was singing; nor a cockatoo, since Kacatogan would not condescend to listen to me; nor any kind of a bird, in fact, since at Morfontaine they left me to sleep all alone. But nevertheless I am covered with feathers and I have claws and wings. I am certainly not a monster, as was proved by Gourouli and the little Marquise herself, for they found me pleasing enough. By what inexplicable mystery is it, that these feathers, wings, and claws do not form a whole to which one could give a name? May I not be, perhaps . . ."

I was about to continue my lamentations, when I was interrupted by two porters' wives, who were quarreling in the street.

"Goodness gracious!" said one of them to the other, "if you ever succeed, I will make you a present of a white blackbird!"

"The Lord be praised!" I cried. "Now I have it. Oh heavens! I am the son of a blackbird, and I am white: I am a white blackbird!"

This discovery, I must confess, modified my ideas considerably. Instead of pitying myself as I used, I began to puff myself up and walked proudly up and down the gutter, gazing forth into space with a victorious air.

"It is something," I said to myself, "to be a white blackbird. It is more worth while than the jog trot of a donkey. I did not need to grieve over not meeting with others like myself: it is the fate of genius, and it is my fate! I meant to flee from the world, I will astonish it! Since I am that unique bird whose very existence is denied by the vulgar, it is both my right and my duty to behave accordingly, as the Phoenix does, and to despise all other birds. I must buy Alfieri's memoirs and Lord Byron's poems. Such substantial nourishment will inspire me with a noble pride, to say nothing of that with which the Lord has endowed me. Yes, I will try, if possible, to increase the prestige given me by my birth. Nature made me rare, I will make myself mysterious. It shall be regarded as a favor, an honor to see me.—And, in fact," I added in a lower tone, "how if I should actually exhibit myself for money?"

"For shame! What an unworthy idea! I will write a poem like Kacatogan, not in one canto, but in twenty-four, like all the great men; but that is not enough, there must be forty-eight, with notes and an appendix! The universe must be made to realize the fact of my existence. In my verses, I shall not fail to deplore my isolation; but I shall do it in such a way, that even the happiest people will envy me. Since Providence has denied me a mate, I will say the most dreadful things about other peoples. I will prove that all grapes are sour except those that I eat. The nightingales had better look out for their laurels; I will prove, as clearly as two and two make four, that their complaints make one's heart ache, and that their wares are of no value. I must go and see Charpentier. First of all I must win a real foothold in the world of letters. I mean to surround myself with a court composed, not merely of journalists, but of real authors, and even of literary women. I shall write a rôle for Mademoiselle Rachel, and, if she refuses to play it, I will publish with a great flourish of trumpets that her talent is quite inferior to that of some old provincial actress. I will go to Venice, and rent the beautiful palace Mocenigo, which is on the Grand Canal, in the midst of that fairy-like city, and costs four livres and ten sous a day. I shall find inspiration in all the souvenirs which the author of Lara must have left there. From the depths of my solitude, I shall flood the world with a deluge of interlocking rhymes, modeled after Spenser's strophes, in which I shall relieve my great soul; I shall make all the tom-tits sigh, all the turtle doves coo, all the woodpeckers weep, and all the old owls screech. But, as for my own person, I shall be inexorable and unbeguiled by the wiles of love. In vain they may urge and entreat me to take pity on the unhappy mortals who have been won by my sublime songs. To all such advances I shall simply reply: 'Fiddlesticks.' Oh, it will be too much glory! My manuscripts will sell for their weight in gold, my books will cross the ocean; fame and fortune will pursue me wherever I go; still alone, I shall seem indifferent to the murmurs of the crowd that will surround me. In a word, I shall be a perfect white blackbird, a genuine eccentric author, fêted, spoiled, admired, envied, but perfectly churlish and unbearable.

CHAPTER VII

IT did not take me more than six weeks to bring out my first work. It was, as I had intended, a poem in forty-eight cantos. There was, indeed, some careless work here and there, owing to the great rapidity of my production; but I thought that the public of today, being used to the literature which is printed at the foot of the page in the papers, would not criticize me for that.

My success was worthy of me, that is to say, it was unparalleled. The subject of my work was simply myself: In this choice of subject I was following the usual custom of the present time. I narrated my past sufferings with charming fatuity; I acquainted the reader with a thousand of the most intimate domestic details. The description of my mother's porringer filled no less than fourteen cantos: I counted the grooves, the holes, the lumps, the splinters, the slivers, the nails, the spots, the various tints, the reflections; I pictured the inside, the outside, the edges, the bottom, the sides, the sloping surfaces, the straight surfaces; passing on to the contents, I made a study of the blades of grass, the straws, the dead leaves, the bits of wood, the pebbles, the drops of water, the fragments of dead flies, the broken legs of June bugs which were in the nest; it was a ravishing description. But don't imagine that I printed it all in one place; some readers would have had the impertinence to skip it. I skillfully cut it in pieces, and mixed it in with the story, in order that nothing should be lost; so that, at the most interesting and dramatic moment, you would suddenly find fifteen pages of porringer. I believe that this is one of the great secrets of art, and as I am not avaricious, any one who wishes may profit by it.

All Europe was in an uproar over the appearance of my book; and devoured the intimate revelations which I had condescended to make. How could it have been otherwise? I not only gave all the facts relating to my own person, but

I gave the public a complete picture of all the reveries that had passed through my head since the age of two months; I even interpolated, in one of the most beautiful passages, an ode composed when I was in the egg. And, as a matter of course, I did not neglect to touch, in passing, on the great subject which is now occupying the attention of so many; that is to say, the future of humanity. This problem appeared interesting to me, and in a leisure moment, I outlined a solution which was generally considered satisfactory.

Every day I received complimentary verses, letters of congratulation, and anonymous declarations of love. As to visits, I followed strictly the plan that I had formed; my door was closed to all the world. Nevertheless I could not refuse to receive two strangers who had sent word that they were relatives of mine. One was a blackbird from Senegal, and the other a blackbird from China.

"Ah, Monsieur," said they, smothering me with caresses, "what a great blackbird you are! How well you have painted, in your immortal poem, the profound sufferings of misunderstood genius! If we were not already as little understood as possible, we should be so after having read your work. How we sympathize with your sorrows, with your sublime contempt of the commonplace! We too, Monsieur, we know by our own experience, the secret sufferings which you have sung! Here are two sonnets which we have written, the one supplementing the other. We beg you to accept them."

"And here is something more," added the Chinese bird, "some music which my wife composed to a passage in your preface. She renders the author's meaning wonderfully."

"Gentlemen," said I, "as far as I can judge, you seem to be endowed with generous hearts and enlightened minds. But pardon me if I ask you a question. What is the cause of your melancholy?"

"Eh! Monsieur," answered the native of Senegal, "look how I am built. My plumage, indeed, is good to look at, and my coat is of that fine green color that you see glistening on the backs of ducks; but my beak is too short and my feet are too big; and see what a tail I am encumbered with!

My body is not two-thirds the length of my tail. Isn't that enough to make any one go to the devil?"

"And as for me, Monsieur," said the Chinese, "my misfortune is still more distressing. My friend's tail sweeps the street; but the little scalawags make fun of me because I have none at all."

"Gentlemen," I replied, "I pity you with all my heart. It is always troublesome to have too much or too little of anything whatever. But allow me to inform you that there are in the Jardin des Plantes several persons who resemble you, and who have already been there for some time, quite peaceably stuffed. Just as mere shamelessness is not sufficient to enable a literary woman to write a good book, so mere discontent is not enough to turn a blackbird into a genius. I am the only one of my kind, and I grieve for it; I may be wrong, but I have a right to my opinion. Gentlemen, I am white; turn white, and we will see what you can manage to say then."

rather hastily, complaining bitterly of my persistence. I noticed, as I went in, a large bottle full of a sort of paste made of flour and whiting. I asked my wife what she did with this medicine; she answered that it was an opiate for her chilblains.

This opiate struck me as being a trifle suspicious; but yet how could one suspect so gentle and good a person, who had given herself to me with such warmth and sincerity? I had not known at first that my beloved was a literary lady; she confessed it to me after a while, and even showed me the manuscript of a novel which she had imitated both from Walter Scott and from Scarron. I leave you to imagine how delighted I was with this pleasant surprise. I not only found myself possessed of an incomparable beauty, but I now felt sure that my companion's intelligence was fully worthy of my own genius. From that time on, we worked together. While I was composing my poems, she scrawled over reams of paper. I would recite my verses aloud to her, and that did not hinder her from writing at the same time. She hatched out her romances with an ease almost equal to my own, always choosing the most dramatic subjects, such as parricides, seductions, murders, and even pocket-picking, always taking care, in passing, to attack the government and to preach the emancipation of female blackbirds. In a word; no effort was too much for her mind, no *tour de force* was too much for her modesty; she never crossed out a line, nor formed a plan before beginning to work. She was the very type of a literary blackbird.

One day when she was working with unusual zeal, I noticed she was perspiring freely, and I was surprised to see a big black spot on her back at the same time.

"Heavens above!" said I, "what is the matter? Are you sick?"

At first she seemed a little startled and almost embarrassed, but her training and her society manners soon came to her aid and she recovered her admirable self control. She told me that it was an ink spot, and that she was very apt to get them in her moments of inspiration.

"Is it possible that my wife is changing color?" I said softly to myself. This thought would not let me sleep. The bottle of paste recurred to my mind. "Oh heavens!" I cried. "What a suspicion! this heavenly being only a daubed and painted creature? Has she been whitening herself to deceive me? . . . When I thought I was pressing to my heart a sister soul, a privileged being created for me alone, was I wedded to nothing but flour?"

Haunted by this horrible thought, I formed a plan to allay my doubts. I purchased a barometer, and waited impatiently for it to bring a rainy day. I meant to take my wife into the country, choosing a doubtful Sunday, and try the experiment of a washing. But it was the middle of July and the weather was terribly fine.

The outward signs of happiness and my habit of writing had greatly excited my sensibilities. As I was rather simple, it sometimes happened, while I was working, that my sentiments were more powerful than my ideas, and I would begin to weep while I was waiting for a rhyme. My wife was very fond of these rare occasions: any masculine weakness flatters a woman's pride. On a certain night, when I was smoothing over an erasure, according to Boileau's precept, I felt that I must open my heart.

"Oh my only beloved!" said I to my dear mate, "without whom my life is but a dream, who can change the whole world for me with a glance or a smile, heart of my heart, do you know how I love you? A little care and study will easily help me to find words to put into verse some trivial idea that has already been used by other poets; but where shall I ever find words to express to you the inspiration with which your beauty fills me? I do not know whether even the remembrance of my past sufferings could provide me with words with which I could tell you of my present happiness. Before you came to me, my isolation was that of an exiled orphan; today it is that of a king. Do you know, my angel, my beauty, that in this frail body whose semblance I bear until death destroys it, in this feverish little brain where useless thoughts arise, there can be nothing, nothing that is not for you? Only listen to what my brain can tell you, and then feel how much greater is my love! Oh that my genius were a pearl, and that you were Cleopatra!"

As I was expressing this lover's folly, I wept over my wife, and she changed color before my eyes. At every tear that I shed, there appeared a feather, not even a good black, but dingy and rusty (I believe that she must have changed color somewhere else already). After some minutes of tender folly, I found myself confronted by a bird quite free from paste and flour, and precisely like the most tiresome and ordinary blackbirds.

What should I do? What should I say? Reproaches were useless. It is true, I could have considered the case as a legal impediment, and annulled my marriage; but how could I dare to publish my disgrace? Was not my sorrow in itself trouble enough? I took my courage in my two claws and resolved to leave the world, to abandon the career of letters, to flee to the desert, and if possible, to avoid forevermore the sight of any living creature, and to seek, like Alceste,

. . . A region remote,
Where a blackbird is free to be white if he choose!

CHAPTER IX

THEREUPON I flew away, still weeping; and the wind, which is the good or ill luck of birds, carried me to a branch in Morfontaine. This time, every one had gone to bed.—"What a marriage!" said I to myself. "What a trick! The poor child certainly whitened herself with the best of intentions; but I am none the less to be pitied, nor is her color less rusty."

The nightingale was still singing. Alone, in the deep night, he was enjoying with all his heart that gift of God which makes him so superior to poets, and was expressing himself freely to the surrounding silence. I could not resist the temptation of going to speak to him.

"How fortunate you are!" I said: "Not only have you the privilege of singing all you like, and finely too, and every one listens; but you have a wife and children, a nest, and friends, a good pillow made of moss, a full moon, and no newspapers. Rubini and Rossini are nothing, compared to you: you are the equal of the one and you foretell the other. I too have sung, Monsieur, and it was pitiful. I arranged words in battle array like Prussian soldiers, and I was stringing my foolishness together while you were here in the woods. Can you teach your secret?"

"Yes," replied the nightingale, "but it is not what you think. My wife bores me, and I do not love her; I am in love with the rose: Sadi, the Persian poet wrote about it. All night long I sing my best for her, but she sleeps and does not hear me. Her calyx is closed now, and she is cradling an old beetle in it,—and tomorrow morning, when I have gone back to bed, worn out with suffering and fatigue, she will open, and let some bee suck from her very heart!"

THE SIEGE OF BERLIN

THE LAST CLASS

THE CHILD SPY

THE GAME OF BILLIARDS

THE BAD ZOUAVE

BY

ALPHONSE DAUDET

BIOGRAPHICAL NOTE

ALPHONSE DAUDET was born at Nîmes in the south of France on May 13, 1840. His father was an unsuccessful silk manufacturer, and his boyhood was far from happy. After a period of schooling at Lyons, he became at sixteen usher in a school, but before the end of the following year he abandoned a profession in which he found only misery. Going up to Paris he joined his elder brother, Ernest, who was then trying to get a foothold in journalism. At eighteen he published a volume of poems, "Les Amoureuses," wrote for the "Figaro," and began experimenting with playwriting. He attracted the attention of the Duc de Morny, who made him one of his secretaries and in various ways helped him to a start in life.

His first notable success came in 1866 with his "Lettres de mon Moulin," a series of sketches and stories of great charm and delicacy, and this was followed up by a longer work, "Le petit chose," a pathetic fiction based upon his own unhappy youth. In 1872 he produced the first of his three volumes on the amazing "Tartarin of Tarascon," probably the most vital of all his creations. In "Fromont jeune et Risler aîné" he created another great character, Delobelle, the broken-down actor, and he took captive the reading world by his combination of humor and pathos, and the vividness of his portraits of types. Pathos was again the chief characteristic of "Jack," in which the life of a neglected boy at a school which recalls the establishment of Mr. Squeers is not the only parallel between Daudet and Dickens.

Daudet was now a successful writer of established reputation, and through the seventies and eighties he wrote a succession of novels of a considerable variety of theme. Thus he dealt with the Paris of dethroned monarchs in "Les Rois en exil"; with new millionaires in "Le Nabab";

with the talkative type of his native South in "Numa Roumestan," satirizing the statesman Gambetta; with the demimonde in "Sapho"; while in "L'Immortel" he drew a scathing picture of the French Academy, which never honored itself by electing him to membership. "Tartarin" reappeared in all his buoyancy in "Tartarin sur les Alpes," and, less successfully as a colonist in "Port-Tarascon." Some volumes of reminiscences, a considerable number of short stories, some delightful tales for children, and a few plays complete the list of his more important writings. He died at Paris on December 17, 1897.

Daudet was especially distinguished for his style. He wrote with a great impression of ease, yet he obtained an effect of great brilliance and felicity. He belonged to the realistic school, and though he achieved a very living sense of actuality he escaped the cynicism and brutality that marked the work of some of his colleagues.

None of his work is more perfect of its kind than his short stories, and the collection called "Contes du lundi" from which the following examples are taken exhibit his power of restrained pathos at its height. The horrors of the Franco-Prussian War have been more terribly pictured on some larger canvases, but no one has etched with more delicacy and sensitiveness the small private tragedies of that great disaster. "The Siege of Berlin," "The Last Class," and "The Bad Zouave" are not only classics of the art of the short story; they contain the essence of French patriotism.

W. A. N.

CRITICISMS AND INTERPRETATIONS

I

By Henry James

THE charm of Daudet's talent comes from its being charged to an extraordinary degree with his temperament, his feelings, his instincts, his natural qualities. This, of course, is a charm in a style only when nature has been generous. To Alphonse Daudet she has been exceptionally so; she has placed in his hand an instrument of many chords. A delicate nervous organisation, active and indefatigable in spite of its delicacy, and familiar with emotion of almost every kind, equally acquainted with pleasure and with pain; a light, quick, joyous, yet reflective, imagination, a faculty of seeing images, making images, at every turn, of conceiving everything in the visible form, in the plastic spirit; an extraordinary sensibility to all the impressions of life and a faculty of language which is in perfect harmony with his wonderful fineness of perception—these are some of the qualities of which he is the happy possessor, and which make his equipment for the work he has undertaken exceedingly rich.—From "Partial Portraits" (1888).

II

By George Pellissier

DAUDET works in a sort of fever. Even before beginning to write his books, he has related, acted, and almost "lived" them. This habit responds to a necessity of his nature, and this he also constitutes his process of composition. The original sketch is only an improvisation, but with the second version begins what he calls the painful part of his labor. He first abandons himself to his fancy, giving free rein to his troubadour instincts. The subject urges him on and outstrips him; his hand glides rapidly over the paper without writing all the words, or even pausing to punctuate, in the effort to follow the fever of his toiling brain by hastily stenographing ideas and sentiments. Only with that "trembling of the fingers," with him a sign of inspiration, does he take up his pen. He at once launches into the full current of the action. As his figures are already "on foot in his mind," he loses no time in introducing them in full activity. The greater part of his novels consists in a series of pictures or episodes which pass in file beneath our eyes. There are no preludes either at the outset or in passing from one chapter to another; he explains the situation by a word, leaving the reader to imagine such events as are not adapted to an entirely actual *mise en scène.* He renders only what moves his heart and sets his nerves in vibration—what is dramatic, picturesque, and animated in human affairs.—From "The Literary Movement in France in the Nineteenth Century" (1893).

THE SIEGE OF BERLIN

WE were going up Avenue des Champs-Elysées with Dr. V——, asking the shell-riddled walls, and the sidewalks torn up by grape-shot, for the story of the siege of Paris, when, just before we reached the Rond-point de l'Etoile, the doctor stopped and, pointing to one of the great corner houses so proudly grouped about the Arc de Triomphe, said to me:

"Do you see those four closed windows up there on that balcony? In the early days of August, that terrible August of last year, so heavily laden with storms and disasters, I was called there to see a case of apoplexy. It was the apartment of Colonel Jouve, a cuirassier of the First Empire, an old enthusiast on the subject of glory and patriotism, who had come to live on the Champs-Élysées, in an apartment with a balcony, at the outbreak of the war. Guess why? In order to witness the triumphant return of our troops. Poor old fellow! The news of Wissembourg reached him just as he was leaving the table. When he read the name of Napoleon at the foot of that bulletin of defeat, he fell like a log.

"I found the former cuirassier stretched out at full length on the carpet, his face covered with blood, and as lifeless as if he had received a blow on the head from a poleaxe. He must have been very tall when he was standing; lying there, he looked enormous. Handsome features, magnificent teeth, a fleece of curly white hair, eighty years with the appearance of sixty. Beside him was his granddaughter, on her knees and bathed in tears. She looked like him. One who saw them side by side might have taken them for two beautiful Greek medallions, struck from the same die, one of which was old and earth-coloured, a little roughened on the edges, the other resplendent and clean-cut, in all the brilliancy and smoothness of a fresh impression.

"The child's grief touched me. Daughter and granddaughter of soldiers, her father was on MacMahon's staff, and the image of that tall old man stretched out before her evoked in her mind another image no less terrible. I comforted her as best I could, but in reality I had little hope. We had to do with a case of complete paralysis on one side, and at eighty years of age few people recover from it. For three days the patient lay in the same state of inanition and stupor. Then the news of Reichshofen reached Paris. You remember in what a strange way it came. Up to the evening, we all believed in a great victory, twenty thousand Prussians killed and the Prince Royal a prisoner. I know not by what miracle, what magnetic current, an echo of that national rejoicing sought out our poor deaf-mute in the depths of his paralysis; but the fact is that on that evening, when I approached his bed, I did not find the same man there. His eye was almost clear, his tongue less heavy. He had the strength to smile at me, and he stammered twice:

" 'Vic-to-ry!'

"And as I gave him details of the grand exploit of MacMahon, I saw that his features relaxed and his face lighted up.

"When I left the room, the girl was waiting for me at the door, pale as death. She was sobbing.

" 'But he is saved!' I said, taking her hands.

"The unhappy child hardly had the courage to reply. The true report of Reichshofen had been placarded; MacMahon in retreat, the whole army crushed. We gazed at each other in consternation. She was in despair, thinking of her father. I trembled, thinking of the old man. He certainly could not stand this fresh shock. And yet what were we to do? Leave him his joy, and the illusions which had revived him? But in that case we must lie.

" 'Very well, I will lie!' said the heroic girl, quickly wiping away her tears; and with radiant face she entered her grandfather's chamber.

"It was a hard task that she had undertaken. The first few days she had no great difficulty. The good man's brain was feeble, and he allowed himself to be deceived like a child. But with returning health his ideas became clearer. We had to keep him posted concerning the movement of the armies, to draw up military bulletins for him. Really, it was pitiful to see that lovely child leaning night and day over her map of Germany, pinning little flags upon it, and struggling to lay out a glorious campaign: Bazaine besieging Berlin, Froissart in Bavaria, MacMahon on the Baltic. For all this she asked my advice, and I assisted her as well as I could; but it was the grandfather who was especially useful to us in that imaginary invasion. He had conquered Germany so many times under the First Empire! He knew all the strokes beforehand: 'Now this is where they will go. Now this is what they will do'; and his anticipations were always realised, which did not fail to make him very proud.

"Unlucky it was of no avail for us to take cities and win battles; we never went quickly enough for him. That old man was insatiable! Every day, when I arrived, I learned of some new military exploit.

"'Doctor, we have taken Mayence,' the girl would say to me, coming to meet me with a heart-broken smile, and I would hear through the door a joyous voice shouting to me:

"'They are getting on! They are getting on! In a week we shall be in Berlin!'

"At that moment the Prussians were only a week's march from Paris. We asked ourselves at first if it would be better to take him into the provinces; but as soon as we were outside the city, the state of the country would have told him everything, and I considered him still too weak, too much benumbed by his great shock, to let him know the truth. So we decided to remain.

"The first day of the investment of Paris, I went up to their rooms, I remember, deeply moved, with that agony at the heart which the closed gates, the fighting under the walls, and our suburbs turned into frontiers, gave us all. I found the good man seated on his bed, proud and jubilant.

"'Well,' he said, 'so the siege has begun!'

"I gazed at him in blank amazement.

"'What, colonel! you know?'

"His granddaughter turned towards me:

"'Why, yes, doctor, that's the great news. The siege of Berlin has begun.'

"As she said this, she plied her needle with such a sedate and placid air! How could he have suspected anything? He could not hear the guns of the forts. He could not see our unfortunate Paris, all in confusion and dreadful to behold. What he saw from his bed was a section of the Arc de Triomphe, and in his room, about him, a collection of bric-a-brac of the First Empire, well adapted to maintain his illusion. Portraits of marshals, engravings of battles, the King of Rome in a baby's dress, tall consoles adorned with copper trophies, laden with imperial relics, medals, bronzes, a miniature of St. Helena, under a globe, pictures representing the same lady all becurled, in a ball-dress of yellow, with leg-of-mutton sleeves and bright eyes;—and all these things: consoles, King of Rome, marshals, yellow ladies, with the high-necked, short-waisted dresses, the bestarched stiffness, which was the charm of 1806. Gallant colonel! It was that atmosphere of victories and conquests, even more than anything we could say to him, that made him believe so innocently in the siege of Berlin.

"From that day our military operations were much simplified. To take Berlin was only a matter of patience. From time to time, when the old man was too much bored, we would read him a letter from his son—an imaginary letter, of course, for nothing was allowed to enter Paris, and since Sedan, MacMahon's aide-de-camp had been sent to a German fortress. You can imagine the despair of that poor child, without news from her father, knowing that he was a prisoner, in need of everything, perhaps sick, and she obliged to represent him as writing joyful letters, a little short, perhaps, but such as a soldier on the field might be expected to write, always marching forward through a conquered country. Sometimes her strength gave way; then they were without news for weeks. But the old man became anxious, could not sleep. Thereupon a letter from Germany would speedily arrive, which she would bring to his bedside and read joyously, forcing back her tears. The colonel would listen religiously, smile with a knowing air, approve, criticise, and explain to us the passages that seemed a little confused. But where he was especially grand was in the replies that he sent to his son. 'Never forget that you are a Frenchman,' he would say to him. 'Be generous to those poor people. Don't make the invasion too hard for them.' And there were recommendations without end, admirable preachments upon respect for the proprieties, the courtesy which should be shown to the ladies, a complete code of military honour for the use of conquerors. He interspersed also some general considerations upon politics, the conditions of peace to be imposed upon the vanquished. Thereupon I must say that he was not exacting.

"'A war indemnity, and nothing more. What is the use of taking their provinces? Is it possible to turn Germany into France?'

"He dictated this in a firm voice; and one was conscious of such candour in his words, of such a noble, patriotic faith, that it was impossible not to be moved while listening to him.

"Meanwhile the siege went on—not the siege of Berlin, alas! It was the time of intense cold, of the bombardment, of epidemics and of famine. But, thanks to our care, to our efforts, to the unwearying affection which multiplied itself about him, the old man's serenity was not disturbed for an instant. To the very end I was able to obtain white bread and fresh meat for him. There was none for anybody but him, to be sure; and you can imagine nothing more touching than those breakfasts of the grandfather, so innocently selfish—the old man seated on his bed, fresh and smiling, with a napkin at his chin, and his granddaughter beside him, a little pale because of privations, guiding his hand, helping him to drink, and to eat all those forbidden good things. Then, enlivened by the repast, in the comfort of his warm room, the winter wind whistling outside and the snow eddying about his windows, the ex-cuirassier would recall his campaigns in the north, and would describe to us for the hundredth time that terrible retreat from Russia, when they had nothing to eat but frozen biscuit and horseflesh.

"'Do you understand that, my love? We had horseflesh!'

"I rather think that she did understand it. For two months she had had nothing else. From that day, however, as the period of convalescence drew near, our task about the patient became more difficult. That numbness of all his senses, of all his members, which had served us so well hitherto, began to disappear. Two or three times, the terrible volleys from Porte Maillot had made him jump, with his ears pricked up like a hunting-dog; we were obliged to invent a final victory of Bazaine under the walls of Berlin, and guns fired in his honour at the Invalides. Another day when his bed had been moved to the window—it was, I believe, the Thursday of Buzenval—he saw large numbers of National Guards collected on Avenue de la Grande Armée.

"'What are all those troops?' asked the good man; and we heard him mutter between his teeth:

"'Poorly set up! Poorly set up!'

"That was all; but we understood that we must take great precautions thenceforth. Unluckily we did not take enough.

"One evening when I arrived, the girl came to me in great trouble.

"'They are to march into the city to-morrow,' she said.

"Was the grandfather's door open? In truth, on thinking it over afterwards, I remembered that his face wore an extraordinary expression that night. It is probable that he had overheard us. But we were talking of the Prussians; and the good man was thinking of the French, of that triumphal entry which he had been awaiting so long—MacMahon marching down the avenue amid flowers and flourishes of trumpets, his son beside him, and he, the old colonel, on his balcony, in full uniform as at Lutzen, saluting the torn flags and the eagles blackened by powder.

"Poor Father Jouve! He had imagined doubtless that we intended to prevent him from witnessing that parade of our troops, in order to avoid too great excitement. So he was very careful not to mention it to any one; but the next day, at the very hour when the Prussian battalions entered hesitatingly upon the long road which leads from Porte Maillot to the Tuileries, the window up there opened softly, and the colonel appeared on the balcony, with his helmet, his long sword, all the glorious old array of one of Milhaud's cuirassiers. I wonder still what effort of the will, what sudden outburst of life had placed him thus upon his feet and in his harness. This much is sure, that he was there, standing behind the rail, amazed to find the broad avenues so silent, the blinds of the houses closed, Paris as gloomy as a huge lazaretto, flags everywhere, but such strange flags, white with little crosses, and no one to go to meet our soldiers.

"For a moment he might have thought that he was mistaken.

"But no! Yonder, behind the Arc de Triomphe, there was a confused rumbling, a black line approaching in the rising sunlight. Then, little by little, the points of the helmets gleamed, the little drums of Jena began to beat, and beneath the Arc de Triomphe, while the heavy tramp of the regiments and the clashing of the sabres beat time, Schubert's *Triumphal March* burst forth!

"Thereupon in the deathlike silence of the square, a cry rang out, a terrible cry: 'To arms! To arms! The Prussians!' and the four uhlans of the vanguard saw up yonder, on the balcony, a tall old man wave his arms, stagger, and fall. That time, Colonel Jouve was really dead."

THE LAST CLASS

THE STORY OF A LITTLE ALSATIAN

I WAS very late for school that morning, and I was terribly afraid of being scolded, especially as Monsieur Hamel had told us that he should examine us on participles, and I did not know the first thing about them. For a moment I thought of staying away from school and wandering about the fields. It was such a warm, lovely day. I could hear the blackbirds whistling on the edge of the wood, and in the Rippert field, behind the sawmill, the Prussians going through their drill. All that was much more tempting to me than the rules concerning participles; but I had the strength to resist, and I ran as fast as I could to school.

As I passed the mayor's office, I saw that there were people gathered about the little board on which notices were posted. For two years all our bad news had come from that board—battles lost, conscriptions, orders from headquarters; and I thought without stopping:

"What can it be now?"

Then, as I ran across the square, Wachter the blacksmith, who stood there with his apprentice, reading the placard, called out to me:

"Don't hurry so, my boy; you'll get to your school soon enough!"

I thought that he was making fun of me, and I ran into Monsieur Hamel's little yard all out of breath.

Usually, at the beginning of school, there was a great uproar which could be heard in the street, desks opening and closing, lessons repeated aloud in unison, with our ears stuffed in order to learn quicker, and the teacher's stout ruler beating on the desk:

"A little more quiet!"

I counted on all this noise to reach my bench unnoticed; but as it happened, that day everything was quiet, like a Sunday morning. Through the open window I saw my comrades already in their places, and Monsieur Hamel walking back and forth with the terrible iron ruler under his arm. I had to open the door and enter, in the midst of that perfect silence. You can imagine whether I blushed and whether I was afraid!

But no! Monsieur Hamel looked at me with no sign of anger and said very gently:

"Go at once to your seat, my little Frantz; we were going to begin without you."

I stepped over the bench and sat down at once at my desk. Not until then, when I had partly recovered from my fright, did I notice that our teacher had on his handsome blue coat, his plaited ruff, and the black silk embroidered breeches, which he wore only on days of inspection or of distribution of prizes. Moreover, there was something extraordinary, something solemn about the whole class. But what surprised me most was to see at the back of the room, on the benches which were usually empty, some people from the village sitting, as silent as we were: old Hauser with his three-cornered hat, the ex-mayor, the ex-postman, and others besides. They all seemed depressed; and Hauser had brought an old spelling-book with gnawed edges, which he held wide-open on his knee, with his great spectacles askew.

While I was wondering at all this, Monsieur Hamel had mounted his platform, and in the same gentle and serious voice with which he had welcomed me, he said to us:

"My children, this is the last time that I shall teach you. Orders have come from Berlin to teach nothing but German in the schools of Alsace and Lorraine. The new teacher arrives to-morrow. This is the last class in French, so I beg you to be very attentive."

Those few words overwhelmed me. Ah! the villains! that was what they had posted at the mayor's office.

My last class in French!

And I barely knew how to write! So I should never learn! I must stop short where I was! How angry I was with myself because of the time I had wasted, the lessons I had missed, running about after nests, or sliding on the Saar! My books, which only a moment before I thought so tiresome, so heavy to carry—my grammar, my sacred history—seemed to me now like old friends, from whom I should be terribly grieved to part. And it was the same about Monsieur Hamel. The thought that he was going away, that I should never see him again, made me forget the punishments, the blows with the ruler.

Poor man! It was in honour of that last lesson that he had put on his fine Sunday clothes; and I understood now why those old fellows from the village were sitting at the end of the room. It seemed to mean that they regretted not having come oftener to the school. It was also a way of thanking our teacher for his forty years of faithful service, and of paying their respects to the fatherland which was vanishing.

I was at that point in my reflections, when I heard my name called. It was my turn to recite. What would I not have given to be able to say from beginning to end that famous rule about participles, in a loud, distinct voice, without a slip! But I got mixed up at the first words, and I stood there swaying against my bench, with a full heart, afraid to raise my head. I heard Monsieur Hamel speaking to me:

"I will not scold you, my little Frantz; you must be punished enough; that is the way it goes; every day we say to ourselves: 'Pshaw! I have time enough. I will learn to-morrow.' And then you see what happens. Ah! it has been the great misfortune of our Alsace always to postpone its lessons until to-morrow. Now those people are entitled to say to us: 'What! you claim to be French, and you can neither speak nor write your language!' In all this, my poor Frantz, you are not the guiltiest one. We all have our fair share of reproaches to address to ourselves.

"Your parents have not been careful enough to see that you were educated. They preferred to send you to work in the fields or in the factories, in order to have a few more sous. And have I nothing to reproach myself for? Have I not often made you water my garden instead of studying?

And when I wanted to go fishing for trout, have I ever hesitated to dismiss you?"

Then, passing from one thing to another, Monsieur Hamel began to talk to us about the French language, saying that it was the most beautiful language in the world, the most clear, the most substantial; that we must always retain it among ourselves, and never forget it, because when a people falls into servitude, "so long as it clings to its language, it is as if it held the key to its prison."[1] Then he took the grammar and read us our lesson. I was amazed to see how readily I understood. Everything that he said seemed so easy to me, so easy. I believed, too, that I had never listened so closely, and that he, for his part, had never been so patient with his explanations. One would have said that, before going away, the poor man desired to give us all his knowledge, to force it all into our heads at a single blow.

When the lesson was at an end, we passed to writing. For that day Monsieur Hamel had prepared some entirely new examples, on which was written in a fine, round hand: "France, Alsace, France, Alsace." They were like little flags, waving all about the class, hanging from the rods of our desks. You should have seen how hard we all worked and how silent it was! Nothing could be heard save the grinding of the pens over the paper. At one time some cock-chafers flew in; but no one paid any attention to them, not even the little fellows who were struggling with their straight lines, with a will and conscientious application, as if even the lines were French. On the roof of the schoolhouse, pigeons cooed in low tones, and I said to myself as I listened to them:

"I wonder if they are going to compel them to sing in German too!"

From time to time, when I raised my eyes from my paper, I saw Monsieur Hamel sitting motionless in his chair and staring at the objects about him as if he wished to carry away in his glance the whole of his little schoolhouse. Think of it! For forty years he had been there in the same place, with his yard in front of him and his class just as it

[1] "S'il tient sa langue, il tient la clé qui de ses chaines le délivre." —Mistral.

was! But the benches and desks were polished and rubbed by use; the walnuts in the yard had grown, and the hop-vine which he himself had planted now festooned the windows even to the roof. What a heart-rending thing it must have been for that poor man to leave all those things, and to hear his sister walking back and forth in the room overhead, packing their trunks! For they were to go away the next day—to leave the province forever.

However, he had the courage to keep the class to the end. After the writing, we had the lesson in history; then the little ones sang all together the *ba, be, bi, bo, bu.* Yonder, at the back of the room, old Hauser had put on his spectacles, and, holding his spelling-book in both hands, he spelled out the letters with them. I could see that he too was applying himself. His voice shook with emotion, and it was so funny to hear him, that we all longed to laugh and to cry. Ah! I shall remember that last class.

Suddenly the church clock struck twelve, then the Angelus rang. At the same moment, the bugles of the Prussians returning from drill blared under our windows. Monsieur Hamel rose, pale as death, from his chair. Never had he seemed to me so tall.

"My friends," he said, "my friends, I—I——"

But something suffocated him. He could not finish the sentence.

Thereupon he turned to the blackboard, took a piece of chalk, and, bearing on with all his might, he wrote in the largest letters he could:

"VIVE LA FRANCE!"

Then he stood there, with his head resting against the wall, and without speaking, he motioned to us with his hand:

"That is all; go."

THE CHILD SPY

HIS name was Stenne, little Stenne.

He was a child of Paris, sickly and pale, who might have been ten years old, perhaps fifteen; with those urchins one can never tell. His mother was dead; his father, formerly in the navy, was keeper of a square in the Temple quarter. Babies, nurse-maids, old ladies in reclining-chairs, poor mothers, all of toddling Paris that seeks shelter from vehicles in those flower-gardens bordered by paths, knew Father Stenne and adored him. They knew that beneath that rough mustache, the terror of dogs and of loiterers, lay concealed a kind, melting, almost maternal smile, and that, in order to see that smile one had only to ask the good man:

"How's your little boy?"

Father Stenne was so fond of his boy! He was so happy in the afternoon, after school, when the little fellow came for him and they made together the circuit of the paths, stopping at each bench to salute the occupants and to answer their kind words.

Unfortunately with the siege everything changed. Father Stenne's square was closed, petroleum was stored there, and the poor man, forced to keep watch all the time, passed his life among the deserted and neglected shrubs, alone, unable to smoke, and without the company of his boy except very late at night, at home. So that you should have seen his mustache when he mentioned the Prussians. As for little Stenne, he did not complain very much of that new life.

A siege! It is such an amusing thing for urchins. No school! No lessons! Vacation all the time and the street like a fair.

The child stayed out of doors, wandering about until night. He followed the battalions of the quarter when they went to the fortifications, choosing by preference those which had a good band; and upon that subject little Stenne was well posted. He could tell you that the band of the 96th did not amount to much, but that in the 55th they had a fine one. At other times he watched the troops go through the drill; then there were the lines at the shop-doors.

With his basket on his arm, he stood in the long lines that formed in the dark winter mornings, without gas, at the doors of the butchers' and bakers' shops. There, with their feet in the water, people became acquainted, talked politics, and every one asked his advice, as M. Stenne's son. But the games of *bouchon* were the most amusing thing of all, and that famous game of *galoche*, which the Breton militia had brought into fashion during the siege. When little Stenne was not at the fortifications, or at the baker's, you were sure to find him at the game on Place du Château d'Eau. He did not play, you understand; it required too much money. He contented himself with watching the players, with such eyes!

One especially, a tall youth in a blue blouse, who bet nothing less than five-franc pieces, aroused his admiration. When he ran you could hear the money jingling in his pockets.

One day, as he picked up a coin which had rolled to little Stenne's feet, the tall youth said to him in an undertone:

"That makes you squint, eh? Well, I will tell you where they are to be found, if you want."

When the game was ended he led him to a corner of the square and proposed to him to go with him to sell newspapers to the Prussians; he received thirty francs per trip. At first Stenne refused, highly indignant; and he actually stayed away from the game for three days. Three terrible days. He did not eat, he did not sleep. At night, he saw piles of *galoches* at the foot of his bed, and five-franc pieces lying flat, all glistening. The temptation was too great. On the fourth day he returned to the Château d'Eau, saw the tall youth again, and allowed himself to be persuaded.

They set out one snowy morning, a canvas bag over their shoulders and newspapers hidden under their blouses.

When they reached the Flanders gate it was barely light. The tall youth took Stenne by the hand, and, approaching the sentry—an honest volunteer with a red nose and a good-natured expression—he said to him in the whining voice of a pauper:

"Let us pass, my kind monsieur. Our mother is sick, papa is dead, I am going out with my little brother to pick up potatoes in the fields."

And he wept. Stenne, covered with shame, hung his head. The sentry looked at them a moment, and cast a glance at the deserted road.

"Hurry up," he said, stepping aside; and there they were upon the Aubervilliers Road. How the tall fellow laughed!

Confusedly, as in a dream, little Stenne saw factories transformed into barracks, abandoned barricades covered with wet rags, long chimneys cutting the mist and rising into the sky, smokeless and broken. At intervals, a sentry, beplumed officers looking into the distance with field-glasses, and small tents drenched with melted snow in front of dying fires. The tall fellow knew the roads and cut across the fields to avoid the outposts. However, they fell in with a patrol of sharp-shooters, whom they could not avoid. The sharp-shooters were in their little cabins, perched on the edge of a ditch filled with water, along the Soissons railroad. That time the tall fellow repeated his story in vain; they would not allow them to pass. Then, while he was complaining, an old sergeant, all wrinkled and grizzled, who resembled Father Stenne, came out of the guard-house to the road.

"Come, little brats, I wouldn't cry!" he said to the children; "we'll let you go to get your potatoes, but come in and warm yourselves a little first. This little fellow looks as if he was frozen!"

Alas! It was not with cold that little Stenne was trembling—it was with fear, with shame. In the guard-house they found several soldiers crouching about a paltry fire, a genuine widow's fire, by the heat of which they were thawing out biscuit on the points of their bayonets. They moved closer together to make room for the children. They gave them a little coffee. While they were drinking, an officer came to the door, called to the sergeant, spoke to him in an undertone and hurried away.

"My boys," said the sergeant, returning with a radiant face, "there will be something up to-night. They have found out the Prussians' countersign. I believe that this time we shall capture that infernal Bourget again."

There was an explosion of cheers and laughter. They danced and sang and brandished their sword-bayonets; and the children, taking advantage of the tumult, disappeared.

When they had passed the railway there was nothing before them but a level plain, and in the distance a long, blank wall, riddled with loopholes. It was towards that wall that they bent their steps, stooping constantly to make it appear that they were picking up potatoes.

"Let's go back, let's not go on," said little Stenne again and again.

The other shrugged his shoulders and kept on. Suddenly they heard the click of a gun being cocked.

"Lie down!" said the tall fellow, throwing himself on the ground.

When they were down, he whistled. Another whistle answered over the snow. They crawled on. In front of the wall, level with the ground, appeared a pair of yellow mustaches beneath a soiled cap. The tall youth jumped into the trench, beside the Prussian.

"This is my brother," he said, pointing to his companion.

Little Stenne was so little, that at the sight of him the Prussian began to laugh, and he was obliged to take him in his arms to lift him up to the breach.

On the other side of the wall were great piles of earth, felled trees, black holes in the snow, and in each hole the same dirty cap and the same yellow mustaches, laughing when they saw the children pass.

In the corner was a gardener's house casemated with trunks of trees. The lower room was full of soldiers playing cards, and cooking soup over a big, blazing fire. The cabbages and pork smelled good; what a contrast to the bivouac of the sharp-shooters! Above were the officers. They could hear them playing the piano and opening champagne. When the Parisians entered, a joyous cheer greeted them. They produced their newspapers; then they were given drink and were induced to talk. All the officers had a haughty and disdainful manner; but the tall youth amused them with his faubourgian wit, his street Arab's vocabulary. They laughed, repeated his phrases after him, and wallowed with delight in the Parisian mud which he brought them.

Little Stenne would have liked to talk too, to prove that he was not stupid, but something embarrassed him. Opposite him, apart from the rest, was an older and graver Prussian, who was reading, or rather seemed to be reading, for his eyes did not leave little Stenne. Affection and reproach were in his glance as if he had at home a child of the same age as Stenne, and as if he were saying to himself:

"I would rather die than see my son engaged in such business."

From that moment Stenne felt as it were a hand resting on his heart, which prevented it from beating.

To escape that torture, he began to drink. Soon everything about him whirled around. He heard vaguely, amid loud laughter, his comrade making fun of the National Guards, of their manner of drilling; he imitated a call to arms in the Marais, a night alarm on the ramparts. Then the tall fellow lowered his voice, the officers drew nearer to him, and their faces became serious. The villain was warning them of the attack of the sharp-shooters.

At that little Stenne sprang to his feet in a rage, thoroughly sober:

"Not that! I won't have it!"

But the other simply laughed and kept on. Before he had finished, all the officers were standing. One of them pointed to the door and said to the children:

"Clear out!"

And they began to talk among themselves very rapidly, in German.

The tall youth went out as proud as a prince, jingling his money. Stenne followed him, hanging his head; and when he passed the Prussian whose glance had embarrassed him so, he heard a sad voice say:

"Not a nice thing to do, that. Not a nice thing."

Tears came to his eyes.

Once in the field, the children began to run and returned quickly to the city. Their bag was full of potatoes which the Prussians had given them. With them they passed unhindered to the trench of the sharp-shooters. There they were preparing for the night attack. Troops came up silently and massed behind the walls. The old sergeant was there, busily engaged in posting his men, with such a happy expression. When the children passed, he recognised them and bestowed a pleasant smile upon them.

Oh! how that smile hurt little Stenne! For a moment he was tempted to call out:

"Don't go there; we have betrayed you."

But the other had told him: "If you speak we shall be shot"; and fear restrained him.

At La Courneuve, they entered an abandoned house to divide the money. Truth compels me to state that the division was made honestly, and that little Stenne's crime did not seem so terrible to him when he heard the coins jingling under his blouse, and thought of the games of *galoche* which he had in prospect.

But when he was alone, the wretched child! When the tall fellow had left him at the gate, then his pockets began to be very heavy, and the hand that grasped his heart grasped it tighter than ever. Paris did not seem the same to him. The people who passed gazed sternly at him as if they knew whence he came. He heard the word "spy" in the rumbling of the wheels, in the beating of the drums along the canal. At last he reached home, and, overjoyed to find that his father was not there, he went quickly up to their room, to hide under his pillow that money that weighed so heavily upon him.

Never had Father Stenne been so joyous and so good-humoured as when he returned that night. News had been received from the provinces: affairs were looking better. As he ate, the old soldier looked at his musket hanging on the wall, and said to the child with his hearty laugh:

"I say, my boy, how you would go at the Prussians if you were big!"

About eight o'clock, they heard cannon.

"That is Aubervilliers. They are fighting at Bourget," said the good man, who knew all the forts. Little Stenne turned pale, and, on the plea that he was very tired, he went to bed; but he did not sleep. The cannon still roared. He imagined the sharp-shooters arriving in the dark to surprise the Prussians, and themselves falling into an ambush. He remembered the sergeant who had smiled at him and he saw him stretched out on the snow, and many others with him. The price of all that blood was concealed there under his pillow, and it was he, the son of Monsieur Stenne, of a soldier—tears choked him. In the adjoining room he heard his father walk to the window and open it. Below on the square, the recall was sounding; and a battalion was forming to leave the city. Evidently it was a real battle. The unhappy child could not restrain a sob.

"What's the matter with you?" asked Father Stenne as he entered the room.

The child could not stand it any longer; he leaped out of bed and threw himself at his father's feet. At the movement that he made the silver pieces rolled on the floor.

"What is all this? Have you been stealing?" demanded the old man, trembling.

Thereupon, without pausing for breath, little Stenne told him that he had been to the Prussian quarters and of what he had done there.

As he spoke, his heart felt freer; it relieved him to accuse himself. Father Stenne listened, with a terrible face. When it was at an end, he hid his face in his hands and wept.

"Father, father—" the child began.

The old man pushed him away without replying, and picked up the money.

"Is this all?" he asked.

Little Stenne motioned that it was all. The old man took down his musket and cartridge box, and said as he put the money in his pocket:

"All right; I am going to return it to them."

And without another word, without even turning his head, he went down and joined the troops who were marching away in the darkness. He was never seen again.

THE GAME OF BILLIARDS

AS they have been fighting two days, and have passed the night with their knapsacks on, beneath a flood of rain, the soldiers are completely exhausted. And yet for three mortal hours they have been left waiting, with grounded arms, in the puddles of the highroads and the mud of the saturated fields.

Benumbed by fatigue, by sleepless nights, and with their uniforms drenched with rain, they crowd together to warm and comfort one another. There are some who sleep standing, leaning against a neighbour's knapsack, and weariness and privations can be read distinctly upon those relaxed faces, overcome with sleep. Rain, mud, no fire, nothing to eat, a low, black sky, and the enemy in the air about. It is funereal.

What are they doing there? What is going on? The guns, with their muzzles pointed towards the wood, have the appearance of watching something. The mitrailleurs in ambush stare fixedly at the horizon. Everything seems ready for an attack. Why do they not attack? What are they waiting for?

They are awaiting orders, and headquarters sends none.

And yet the headquarters are not far away. They are at yonder stately Louis-Treize château, whose red bricks, scoured by the rain, glisten among the trees half-way up the hill. Truly a princely dwelling, quite worthy to bear the banner of a marshal of France. Behind a broad moat and a stone wall which separate them from the road, smooth green lawns, lined with vases of flowers, extend to the porch. On the other side, the private side of the house, the hornbeam hedges show luminous gaps; the pond in which swans are swimming lies like a mirror, and beneath the pagodalike roof of an enormous aviary, peacocks and golden pheasants flash their wings and display their plumage, uttering shrill cries amid the foliage. Although the owners have gone away, one does not feel the abandonment, the desolation of war. The oriflamme of the leader of the army has safeguarded even the tiniest flowers in the lawns, and it is an impressive thing to find so near the battle-field that opulent tranquillity that is born of perfect order, of the accurate alignment of the shrubbery, of the silent depths of the avenues.

The rain, which fills the roads yonder with such disgusting mud, and digs such deep ruts, here is nothing more than an elegant, aristocratic shower, reviving the red of the bricks and the green of the lawns, polishing the leaves of the orange-trees and the white feathers of the swans. Everything glistens, everything is peaceful. Really, but for the flag floating on the roof, but for the two soldiers on sentry-go before the gate, one would never suspect that it is the headquarters of an army. The horses are resting in the stables. Here and there one sees a groom, or an orderly in undress uniform, loitering about the kitchen, or a gardener in red trousers placidly drawing his rake over the gravel in the great courtyards.

The dining-room, the windows of which look upon the porch, discloses a half-cleared table; uncorked bottles, soiled and empty glasses on the rumpled cloth; the end of a banquet, after the guests have gone. In the adjoining room one may hear loud voices, laughter, the clicking of balls and the clinking of glasses. The marshal is playing his game of billiards, and that is why the army is waiting for orders. When the marshal had begun his game, the heavens might fall, but nothing in the world could prevent him from finishing it.

Billiards! that is the weakness of that great warrior. He stands there, as grave as in battle, in full uniform, his breast covered with medals, with kindled eyes, flushed cheeks, excited by feasting, grog, and the game. His aides-de-camp surround him, zealous and respectful, uttering admiring exclamations at each of his strokes. When the marshal makes a point, they all hasten to mark it; when the marshal is thirsty, they all rush to prepare his grog. There is a constant rustling of epaulettes and plumes, a jingling of medals; and to see all those sweet smiles, those artful, courtierlike reverences, all those new uniforms and embroidery in that lofty apartment, with its oaken wainscoting, looking upon parks and courts of honour, recalls the autumn days at Compiègne, and affords the eyes a little rest from the stained cloaks that shiver yonder along the roads, forming such sombre groups in the rain.

The marshal's opponent is a young captain of the staff, belted and curled and light-gloved, who is in the first rank of billiard-players and capable of beating all the marshals on earth; but he has the tact to keep a respectful distance behind his chief, and devotes his energies to the task of not winning, and at the same time not losing too easily. He is what is called an officer with a future.

Attention, young man, let us be on our guard! The marshal has fifteen, and you ten. The point is to keep the game in that condition to the end; then you will have done more for your promotion than if you were outside with the others, beneath those torrents of water which drown the horizon, soiling your natty uniform, tarnishing the gold of your aiguillettes, awaiting orders which do not come.

It is really an interesting game. The balls roll and clash and mingle their colours. The cushions send them merrily back; the cloth waxes hot. Suddenly the flash of a cannon-shot passes across the sky. A dull sound rattles the windows. Everybody starts, and they look at each other anxiously. The marshal alone has neither seen nor heard anything; leaning over the table, he is busily engaged in planning a magnificent draw-shot; draw-shots are his strong point.

But there comes another flash, then another. The cannon-shots succeed each other in hot haste. The aides-de-camp run to the windows. Can it be that the Prussians are attacking.

"Very well, let them attack!" says the marshal, chalking his cue. "It's your turn, captain."

The staff quivers with admiration. Turenne asleep upon a gun-carriage was nothing compared to this marshal, who plays billiards so tranquilly at the moment of going into action. Meanwhile the uproar redoubles. With the roar of the cannon is mingled the tearing sound of the mitrailleuses, the rattle of musketry. A red steam, black at the edges, rises around the lawns. The whole park is on fire. The terrified peacocks and pheasants shriek in the aviary; the Arabian horses, smelling the powder, rear in the stables. The headquarters begins to be excited. Despatch after despatch. Couriers arrive at full speed. They ask for the marshal.

The marshal cannot be seen. Did I not tell you that nothing could prevent him from finishing his game?

"It is your turn, captain."

But the captain is distraught. That is what it is to be young. Behold he loses his head, forgets his tactics, and makes two runs in succession, which almost give him the game. Thereupon the marshal becomes furious. Surprise and indignation animate his manly face. Just at this moment a horse ridden at a hard gallop rushes into the courtyard. An aide-de-camp covered with mud forces his way past the sentries and ascends the steps at one bound. "Marshal, marshal!" You should see how he is greeted. Puffing with anger and red as a rooster, the marshal appears at the window, his billiard-cue in his hand:

"What's the matter? What's all this? Isn't there any sentry there?"

"But, marshal——"

"All right, in a moment; wait for my orders, in God's name!"

And the window is violently closed.

Wait for his orders! That is just what they are doing, the poor fellows. The wind drives the rain and the grapeshot full in their faces. Whole battalions are wiped out, while others stand useless, with their arms in readiness, utterly unable to understand their inaction. Nothing to do. They are awaiting orders. However, as one needs no orders to die, the men fall by hundreds behind the shrubs, in the moats, in front of the great silent château. Even after they have fallen, the grape tears them still, and from the open wounds the generous blood of France flows noiselessly. Above, in the billiard-room, it is getting terribly warm too; the marshal has recovered his lead, but the little captain is defending himself like a lion.

Seventeen! eighteen! nineteen!

They hardly have time to mark the points. The roar of the battle draws nearer. The marshal has but one more to go. Already shells are falling in the park. Suddenly one bursts over the pond. The mirror is shattered; a swan in deadly alarm swims wildly about amid an eddy of bloody feathers. That is the last stroke.

Then, a profound silence. Only the rain falling on the hedges, a confused rumbling at the foot of the hill, and, along the muddy roads, a sound like the trampling of a hurrying flock. The army is in full retreat. The marshal has won his game.

THE BAD ZOUAVE

THAT evening the big blacksmith, Lory of Sainte-Marie-aux-Mines, was not happy.

When the smithy fire had gone down and the sun had set, it was his custom to sit on a bench before his door, tasting that grateful weariness which is the reward of heavy labor and of a hot day's work. Before he sent home his apprentices, he would drink several deep glasses of cool beer with them, while he watched the workers coming out of the factories.

But that evening the good blacksmith remained at his forge until it was time for his supper, and even then he went as if he regretted to leave. As his old wife looked at him, she thought,

"What can have happened to him? Can he have received bad news from the regiment and be hiding it from me? Perhaps the older of the boys is sick——"

But she dared not question him, and busied herself quieting three little tow-headed rascals, brown as ears of parched corn, who were laughing around the table as they crunched their good salad of black radishes and cream.

At last the blacksmith pushed back his plate in a rage and cried,

"Ah, what brutes, what curs!"

"Come, Lory, who are you talking about?" said his wife.

He shouted,

"I am talking of five or six scamps who were seen this morning parading the town in their French uniforms, arm in arm with the Bavarians—more of those fellows who have —how do they say it?—'chosen Prussian citizenship.' And to think that every day we are seeing such false Alsatians come back! What can they have given the scoundrels to drink anyway?"

The mother tried to defend them.

"My poor husband, what do you expect? Those boys are not entirely to blame. They are sent to Algeria, so far away in Africa! They get home-sick out there, and their temptation is very strong to come back and not be soldiers any longer."

Lory struck the table a heavy blow with his fist.

"Be still, mother! You women-folk understand nothing at all. You live so much with children and so little for anything else that you become exactly the size of your cubs. I tell you, those fellows are ragamuffins, renegades, the worst sort of scoundrels! If bad luck ever made our own Christian capable of such infamous conduct, as surely as my name is George Lory, seven years chasseur in the army of France, I would run him through the body with my saber!"

Terrible to look upon, he half rose from his chair and pointed to his long chasseur's saber, which hung under a picture of his son in the uniform of a zouave, taken out there in Africa.

But merely to look at that honest Alsatian face,—burned almost black by the sun, the strong light making the colours stand out vividly against the blank whiteness around —that was enough to quiet him suddenly. He began to laugh.

"I am a fine fellow to be losing my head this way! As if our Christian could dream of turning Prussian—Christian, who bowled over such a lot of them in the war!"

Brought back to good humour by this idea, the good smith managed to make a cheerful meal, and set out right after it to empty a couple of glasses at the *Ville de Strasbourg.*

The old woman was now left alone. She had put the small blond scamps to bed; they could be heard twittering in the next room like a nestful of birds getting ready for sleep. She picked up her work, and set to darning before the door on the garden side of the house. Once in a while she sighed, and she thought,

"Of course—there can be no doubt of it—they are scoundrels and renegades—but, what of it? Their mothers are glad to see them again."

And she thought of the time when her own boy had not yet gone to join the army and stood there just at that hour of the day, getting ready to work in the garden. She looked at the well where he refilled his watering cans: her boy, in his blouse, with his long hair, that beautiful hair which had been cut short when he entered the Zouaves.

Suddenly she trembled. The little gate at the back—the gate which led to the fields,—had been opened. The dogs had not barked, though the man who had just entered slunk along the walk like a thief, and slipped in among the bee-hives.

"Good-day, mother!"

His uniform all awry, there stood before her Christian, her son, anxious, shame-faced, and thick-tongued. The wretched boy had come back with the others and for the last hour had been prowling about the house, waiting for his father to go out. She wanted to scold him, but she had not the courage. How long it was since she had seen him, had hugged him! And then he went on to give her such good reasons for his return!—how he had grown weary for his native countryside, for the smithy:—weary of living always so far away from them all, and of the discipline—much harsher of late—as well as of his comrades, who called him "Prussian" because of his Alsatian accent. She believed every word he said. She had only to look at him to believe him. Deep in their talk, they went into the lower room. The little ones woke up, and ran in their nightshirts and bare feet to embrace the big brother. He was urged to eat, but he was not hungry. He was only thirsty, always thirsty; and he gulped great draughts of water on top of all the beer and white wine for which he had paid that morning at the inn.

But some one was coming into the yard. It was the blacksmith returning.

"Christian, here comes your father. Quick, hide until I have time to talk with him and explain."

She pushed the boy behind the great porcelain stove and again set herself to sewing with trembling hands. But as ill fortune would have it, the Zouave's cap lay upon the table, and it was the first thing Lory noticed as he entered. The mother's pallor, and her agitation—he understood it all.

"Christian is here!" he cried, in a terrible voice. Taking

down his saber with a mad gesture, he rushed towards the stove where crouched the Zouave, pale, sobered, and steadying himself against the wall to keep from falling.

The mother threw herself between them.

"Lory, Lory! Don't kill him! He came back because I wrote that you needed him at the forge!"

She riveted her hold upon his arm, and dragged him back, sobbing. The children, in the darkness of their room, began to cry when they heard those voices full of anger and tears, and so thick that they did not know them.

The smith stood still and looked at his wife.

"Oh!" he said. "So it was you who made him come back! Very well. It is time he went to bed. I shall decide to-morrow what I must do."

Christian woke next morning from a sleep filled with nightmares and broken by causeless terrors, to find himself in the room he had used as a child. Already warm and well up in the sky, the sun sent its rays across the blossoming hops and through the small leaded panes of the window. Hammers were ringing on the anvil below. His mother sat by his pillow: she had been so afraid of her husband's anger that she had not stirred from there all night. Nor had the father gone to bed. Till the first dawn, he had walked through the house weeping, sighing, opening and closing closets. He now entered his son's room. He was very grave and dressed for a journey. He wore his high gaiters and his big hat, and carried his heavy mountain stick with its iron ferule. He went straight to the bed.

"Come, get up!"

Dazed, the boy made as if to get his Zouave equipment.

"No, not that!" said the father, sternly.

The mother, all apprehension, said,

"But, my dear, he has no other things."

"Give him mine. I shall not need them again."

While the boy dressed, Lory carefully packed the uniform, with its little vest and its huge red trousers. As soon as he had made the package, he slung about his neck the tin box which contained the schedule of coaches.

"Now let us go down," he said; and all three without a word descended to the smithy.

The blast roared. Everyone was at work. When Christian saw once more that great open shed of which he had so often thought off there in Algeria, he recalled his childhood and the long hours he had played out there, between the heat of the road and the sparks from the forge that glittered amid the black dust. He felt a sudden flood of tenderness, a great longing to be pardoned by his father; but whenever he raised his eyes, he met an inexorable look.

At last the blacksmith made up his mind to speak.

"Boy," he said, "there stands the anvil with the tools. They are all yours. And so is all this." He indicated the little garden which lay beyond, filled with sunshine and with bees, and framed by the sooty square of the door.

"The hives, the vine, the house itself,—they are all yours. You sacrificed your honour for these things. The least you can do is to take care of them. Now you are master here. As for myself, I shall go away. You owe five years to France: I am going to pay them for you."

"Lory, Lory!' cried the poor old wife, "where are you going?"

"Father!" begged the son.

But the blacksmith was already on his way. He walked with great strides and did not turn back.

At Sidi-bel-Abbés, the dépôt of the Third Zouaves, there enlisted some days later a volunteer who gave his age as fifty-five years.

WALTER SCHNAFFS' ADVENTURE

TWO FRIENDS

THE CRIPPLE

BY

GUY DE MAUPASSANT

BIOGRAPHICAL NOTE

HENRI RENÉ ALBERT GUY DE MAUPASSANT, the supreme master of the short story as a form of art, was born of a landed family at the Château of Miromesnil in Normandy on August 5, 1850. He was educated at Yvetot and Rouen, and entered the government service, holding positions in the ministries of marine and of public instruction. His recreation he found in rowing and attending gatherings of literary men. Gustave Flaubert, the novelist, was an old friend of De Maupassant's mother's, and at his house the young man met Turgenev, Daudet, Zola, and other distinguished men of letters. His first publication was a volume of poems which appeared in 1880 and which led to proceedings being begun against the author by the public prosecutor. It is said that De Maupassant recognized that his verses lacked melody, and he turned definitely to prose, which he had been cultivating for some years under the tutelage of Flaubert. In the same year he joined with Zola, Huysmans, and three others in the publication of a collection of stories called the "Soirées de Médan," to which De Maupassant's contribution was the now famous "Boule de suif." The consummate art of this masterpiece was recognized at once, and the author's position was soon assured. He produced with great fertility for the next ten years; but about 1887 some of his writings began to suggest that he was suffering from hallucinations. A sea-voyage seemed to bring him back to normal condition; but before long it appeared that he was subject to inherited nervous disease which he aggravated by the use of drugs. He had besides injured his constitution by excessive physical exercise. He became more and more melancholy and misanthropic, and gradually sank into paralysis and insanity. He tried to take his life in 1892 and on July 6 of the following year he died at Paris in distressing circumstances.

De Maupassant's longer works include "Une Vie" (1883) a pitiful story of the disastrous life of an innocent girl; "Mont-Oriol," the description of the exploiting of a medicinal spring and the "promoting" of a fashionable watering-place; "Bon Ami," the career of a handsome but heartless adventurer in financial and journalistic circles; "Pierre et Jean," one of the most penetrating of his studies of family life; "Fort comme la mort," and "Notre cœur" (1890). His short stories, on which his fame principally rests, deal with phases of life with which he had himself come into contact. Thus one group is concerned with the peasantry of the Normandy where he spent his youth; another with the life of clerks in government offices; another with society at sea-coast resorts; another with journalism. They are almost without exception the outcome of observation rather than invention; and it is primarily to the quality of his observation that they owe their distinction. He carried "naturalism" to the farthest point it could reach, describing life as he saw it without prejudice and usually without pity. No man ever wrote with less bias in favor of either good or evil, with less of dominating theory, philosophical, ethical, or social. His aim was to find in life materials for art, and to treat these materials without prepossession of any kind. Under Flaubert he had trained himself to great fastidiousness in the choice of the absolutely right word, and he practised a severe economy, using only the kind and amount of detail requisite to bring out the essence of a character or situation. The extent to which, in spite of all this, his work bears the stamp of his personality shows how impossible it is to achieve absolute objectivity so long as art implies selection. But as far as man can go in this direction, De Maupassant went; and he left, after his ten years of feverish activity, a mass of short stories, the best of which are unsurpassed for their firmness of outline, economy of means of expression, and exactness of description. What he pictures is seldom joyous, often ugly and even base and brutal; but his work has the vividness and precision of the most masterly etching.

W. A. N.

CRITICISM AND INTERPRETATION

By Arthur Symons

EVERY artist has his own vision of the world. Maupassant's vision was of solid superficies, of texture which his hands could touch, of action which his mind could comprehend from the mere sight of its incidents. He saw the world as the Dutch painters saw it, and he was as great a master of form, of rich and sober colour, of the imitation of the outward gestures of life, and of the fashion of external things. He had the same view of humanity, and shows us, with the same indifference, the same violent ferment of life, the life of full-blooded people who have to elbow their way through the world. His sense of desire, of greed, of all the baser passions, was profound; he had the terrible logic of animalism. Love-making, drunkenness, cheating, quarrelling the mere idleness of sitting drowsily in a chair, the gross life of the farmyard and the fields, civic dissensions, the sordid provincial dance of the seven deadly sins, he saw in the same direct, unilluminating way as the Dutch painters; finding, indeed, no beauty in any of these things, but getting his beauty in the deft arrangement of them, in the mere act of placing them in a picture. The world existed for him as something formless which could be cut up into little pictures. He saw no further than the lines of his frame. The interest of the thing began inside that frame, and what remained outside was merely material.

As a writer, Maupassant was *de race,* as the French say; he was the lineal descendant of the early *conteurs.* Trained under the severe eye of the impeccable Flaubert, he owed infinitely, no doubt, to that training, and much to the actual influence of the great novelist, who, in "L'Education sentimentale," has given us the type of the modern novel. But his style is quite different from that of Flaubert, of which it has none of the splendid, subdued richness, the harmonious movement; it is clear, precise, sharply cut, without ornament or elaboration; with much art, certainly in its deliberate plainness, and with the admirable skill of an art which conceals art. . . .

Not Swift himself had a surer eye or hand for the exact, brief, malicious notation of things and ideas. He seems to use the first words that come to hand, in the order in which they naturally fall; and when he has reached this point he stops, not conceiving that there is anything more to be done. . . .

A story of Maupassant, more than almost anything in the world, gives you the impression of manual dexterity. It is adequately thought out, but it does not impress you by its thought; it is clearly seen, but it does not impress you especially by the fidelity of its detail; it has just enough of ordinary human feeling for the limits it has imposed on itself. What impresses you is the extreme ingenuity of its handling; the way in which this juggler keeps his billiard-balls harmoniously rising and falling in the air. Often, indeed, you cannot help noticing the conscious smile which precedes the trick, and the confident bow which concludes it. He does not let you into the secret of the trick, but he prevents you from ignoring that it is after all only a trick which you have been watching.—From "Studies in Prose and Verse" (1899).

WALTER SCHNAFFS' ADVENTURE

EVER since he entered France with the invading army Walter Schnaffs had considered himself the most unfortunate of men. He was large, had difficulty in walking, was short of breath and suffered frightfully with his feet, which were very flat and very fat. But he was a peaceful, benevolent man, not warlike or sanguinary, the father of four children whom he adored, and married to a little blonde whose little tendernesses, attentions and kisses he recalled with despair every evening. He liked to rise late and retire early, to eat good things in a leisurely manner and to drink beer in the saloon. He reflected, besides, that all that is sweet in existence vanishes with life, and he maintained in his heart a fearful hatred, instinctive as well as logical, for cannon, rifles, revolvers and swords, but especially for bayonets, feeling that he was unable to dodge this dangerous weapon rapidly enough to protect his big paunch.

And when night fell and he lay on the ground wrapped in his cape beside his comrades who were snoring, he thought long and deeply about those he had left behind and of the dangers in his path. "If he were killed what would become of the little ones? Who would provide for them and bring them up?" Just at present they were not rich, although he had borrowed when he left so as to leave them some money. And Walter Schnaffs wept when he thought of all this.

At the beginning of a battle his legs became so weak that he would have fallen if he had not reflected that the entire army would pass over his body. The whistling of the bullets gave him goose-flesh.

For months he had lived thus in terror and anguish.

His company was marching on Normandy, and one day he was sent to reconnoitre with a small detachment, simply to explore a portion of the territory and to return at once. All seemed quiet in the country; nothing indicated an armed resistance.

But as the Prussians were quietly descending into a little valley traversed by deep ravines a sharp fusillade made them halt suddenly, killing twenty of their men, and a company of sharpshooters, suddenly emerging from a little wood as large as your hand, darted forward with bayonets at the end of their rifles.

Walter Schnaffs remained motionless at first, so surprised and bewildered that he did not even think of making his escape. Then he was seized with a wild desire to run away, but he remembered at once that he ran like a tortoise compared with those thin Frenchmen, who came bounding along like a lot of goats. Perceiving a large ditch full of brushwood covered with dead leaves about six paces in front of him, he sprang into it with both feet together, without stopping to think of its depth, just as one jumps from a bridge into the river.

He fell like an arrow through a thick layer of vines and thorny brambles that tore his face and hands and landed heavily in a sitting posture on a bed of stones. Raising his eyes, he saw the sky through the hole he had made in falling through. This aperture might betray him, and he crawled along carefully on hands and knees at the bottom of this ditch beneath the covering of interlacing branches, going as fast as he could and getting away from the scene of the skirmish. Presently he stopped and sat down, crouched like a hare amid the tall dry grass.

He heard firing and cries and groans going on for some time. Then the noise of fighting grew fainter and ceased. All was quiet and silent.

Suddenly something stirred beside him. He was frightfully startled. It was a little bird which had perched on a branch and was moving the dead leaves. For almost an hour Walter Schnaffs' heart beat loud and rapidly.

Night fell, filling the ravine with its shadows. The soldier began to think. What was he to do? What was to become of him? Should he rejoin the army? But how? By what road? And he began over again the horrible life of anguish, of terror, of fatigue and suffering that he had led since the commencement of the war. No! He no longer had the courage! He would not have the energy necessary to endure long marches and to face the dangers to which one was exposed at every moment.

But what should he do? He could not stay in this ravine in concealment until the end of hostilities. No, indeed! If it were not for having to eat, this prospect would not have daunted him greatly. But he had to eat, to eat every day.

And here he was, alone, armed and in uniform, on the enemy's territory, far from those who would protect him. A shiver ran over him.

All at once he thought: "If I were only a prisoner!" And his heart quivered with a longing, an intense desire to be taken prisoner by the French. A prisoner, he would be saved, fed, housed, sheltered from bullets and swords, without any apprehension whatever, in a good well-kept prison. A prisoner! What a dream!

His resolution was formed at once.

"I will constitute myself a prisoner."

He rose determined to put this plan into execution without a moment's delay. But he stood motionless, suddenly a prey to disturbing reflections and fresh terrors.

Where would he make himself a prisoner and how? In what direction? And frightful pictures, pictures of death came into his mind.

He would run terrible danger in venturing alone through the country with his pointed helmet.

Supposing he should meet some peasants. These peasants seeing a Prussian who had lost his way, an unprotected Prussian, would kill him as if he were a stray dog! They would murder him with their forks, their picks, their scythes and their shovels. They would make a stew of him, a pie with the frenzy of exasperated, conquered enemies.

If he should meet the sharpshooters! These sharpshooters, madmen without law or discipline, would shoot him just for amusement to pass an hour; it would make them laugh to see his head. And he fancied he was already leaning against a wall in front of four rifles whose little black apertures seemed to be gazing at him.

Supposing he should meet the French army itself. The vanguard would take him for a scout, for some bold and sly trooper who had set off alone to reconnoitre, and they would fire at him. And he could already hear, in imagination, the irregular shots of soldiers lying in the brush, while he himself, standing in the middle of the field, was sinking to the earth, riddled like a sieve with bullets which he felt piercing his flesh.

He sat down again in despair. His situation seemed hopeless.

It was quite a dark, black and silent night. He no longer budged, trembling at all the slight and unfamiliar sounds that occur at night. The sound of a rabbit crouching at the edge of his burrow almost made him run. The cry of an owl caused him positive anguish, giving him a nervous shock that pained like a wound. He opened his big eyes as wide as possible to try and see through the darkness, and he imagined every moment that he heard someone walking close beside him.

After interminable hours in which he suffered the tortures of the damned, he noticed through his leafy cover that the sky was becoming bright. He at once felt an intense relief. His limbs stretched out, suddenly relaxed, his heart quieted down, his eyes closed; he fell asleep.

When he awoke the sun appeared to be almost at the meridian. It must be noon. No sound disturbed the gloomy silence. Walter Schnaffs noticed that he was exceedingly hungry.

He yawned, his mouth watering at the thought of sausage, the good sausage the soldiers have, and he felt a gnawing at his stomach.

He rose from the ground, walked a few steps, found that his legs were weak and sat down to reflect. For two or three hours he again considered the pros and cons, changing his mind every moment, baffled, unhappy, torn by the most conflicting motives.

Finally he had an idea that seemed logical and practical. It was to watch for a villager passing by alone, unarmed and with no dangerous tools of his trade, and to run to him and give himself up, making him understand that he was surrendering.

He took off his helmet, the point of which might betray him, and put his head out of his hiding place with the utmost caution.

No solitary pedestrian could be perceived on the horizon. Yonder, to the right, smoke rose from the chimney of a little village, smoke from kitchen fires! And yonder, to the left, he saw at the end of an avenue of trees a large turreted château. He waited till evening, suffering frightfully from hunger, seeing nothing but flights of crows, hearing nothing but the silent expostulation of his empty stomach.

And darkness once more fell on him.

He stretched himself out in his retreat and slept a feverish sleep, haunted by nightmares, the sleep of a starving man.

Dawn again broke above his head and he began to take his observations. But the landscape was deserted as on the previous day, and a new fear came into Walter Schnaffs' mind—the fear of death by hunger! He pictured himself lying at full length on his back at the bottom of his hiding place, with his two eyes closed, and animals, little creatures of all kinds, approached and began to feed on his dead body, attacking it all over at once, gliding beneath his clothing to bite his cold flesh, and a big crow pecked out his eyes with its sharp beak.

He almost became crazy, thinking he was going to faint and would not be able to walk. And he was just preparing to rush off to the village, determined to dare anything, to brave everything, when he perceived three peasants walking to the fields with their forks across their shoulders, and he dived back into his hiding place.

But as soon as it grew dark he slowly emerged from the ditch and started off, stooping and fearful, with beating heart, towards the distant château, preferring to go there rather than to the village, which seemed to him as formidable as a den of tigers.

The lower windows were brilliantly lighted. One of them was open and from it escaped a strong odor of roast meat, an odor which suddenly penetrated to the olfactories and to the stomach of Walter Schnaffs, tickling his nerves, making him breathe quickly, attracting him irresistibly and inspiring his heart with the boldness of desperation.

And abruptly, without reflection, he placed himself, helmet on head, in front of the window.

Eight servants were at dinner around a large table. But suddenly one of the maids sat there, her mouth agape, her eyes fixed and letting fall her glass. They all followed the direction of her gaze.

They saw the enemy!

Good God! The Prussians were attacking the château!

There was a shriek, only one shriek made up of eight shrieks uttered in eight different keys, a terrific screaming of terror, then a tumultuous rising from their seats, a jostling, a scrimmage and a wild rush to the door at the farther end. Chairs fell over, the men knocked the women down and walked over them. In two seconds the room was empty, deserted, and the table, covered with eatables, stood in front of Walter Schnaffs, lost in amazement and still standing at the window.

After some moments of hesitation he climbed in at the window and approached the table. His fierce hunger caused him to tremble as if he were in a fever, but fear still held him back, numbed him. He listened. The entire house seemed to shudder. Doors closed, quick steps ran along the floor above. The uneasy Prussian listened eagerly to these confused sounds. Then he heard dull sounds, as though bodies were falling to the ground at the foot of the walls, human beings jumping from the first floor.

Then all motion, all disturbance ceased, and the great château became as silent as the grave.

Walter Schnaffs sat down before a clean plate and began to eat. He took great mouthfuls, as if he feared he might be interrupted before he had swallowed enough. He shovelled the food into his mouth, open like a trap, with both hands, and chunks of food went into his stomach, swelling out his throat as it passed down. Now and then he stopped, almost ready to burst like a stopped-up pipe. Then he would take the cider jug and wash down his œsophagus as one washes out a clogged rain pipe.

He emptied all the plates, all the dishes and all the bottles. Then, intoxicated with drink and food, besotted, red in the face, shaken by hiccoughs, his mind clouded and his speech thick he unbuttoned his uniform in order to breathe or he could not have taken a step. His eyes closed, his mind became torpid; he leaned his heavy forehead on his folded arms on the table and gradually lost all consciousness of things and events.

The last quarter of the moon above the trees in the park shed a faint light on the landscape. It was the chill hour that precedes the dawn.

Numerous silent shadows glided among the trees and occasionally a blade of steel gleamed in the shadow as a ray of moonlight struck it.

The quiet château stood there in dark outline. Only two windows were still lighted up on the ground floor.

Suddenly a voice thundered:

"Forward! nom d'un nom! To the breach, my lads!"

And in an instant the doors, shutters and window panes fell in beneath a wave of men who rushed in, breaking, destroying everything, and took the house by storm. In a moment fifty soldiers, armed to the teeth, bounded into the kitchen, where Walter Schnaffs was peacefully sleeping, and placing to his breast fifty loaded rifles, they overturned him, rolled him on the floor, seized him and tied his head and feet together.

He gasped in amazement, too besotted to understand, perplexed, bruised and wild with fear.

Suddenly a big soldier, covered with gold lace, put his foot on his stomach, shouting:

"You are my prisoner. Surrender!"

The Prussian heard only the one word "prisoner" and he sighed, "Ya, ya, ya."

He was raised from the floor, tied in a chair and examined with lively curiosity by his victors, who were blowing like whales. Several of them sat down, done up with excitement and fatigue.

He smiled, actually smiled, secure now that he was at last a prisoner.

Another officer came into the room and said:

"Colonel, the enemy has escaped; several seem to have been wounded. We are in possession."

The big officer, who was wiping his forehead, exclaimed: "Victory!"

And he wrote in a little business memorandum book which he took from his pocket:

"After a desperate encounter the Prussians were obliged to beat a retreat, carrying with them their dead and wounded, the number of whom is estimated at fifty men. Several were taken prisoners."

The young officer inquired:

"What steps shall I take, colonel?"

"We will retire in good order," replied the colonel, "to avoid having to return and make another attack with artillery and a larger force of men."

And he gave the command to set out.

The column drew up in line in the darkness beneath the walls of the château and filed out, a guard of six soldiers with revolvers in their hands surrounding Walter Schnaffs, who was firmly bound.

Scouts were sent ahead to reconnoitre. They advanced cautiously, halting from time to time.

At daybreak they arrived at the district of La Roche-Oysel, whose national guard had accomplished this feat of arms.

The uneasy and excited inhabitants were expecting them. When they saw the prisoner's helmet tremendous shouts arose. The women raised their arms in wonder, the old people wept. An old grandfather threw his crutch at the Prussian and struck the nose of one of their own defenders.

The colonel roared:

"See that the prisoner is secure!"

At length they reached the town hall. The prison was opened and Walter Schnaffs, freed from his bonds, cast into it. Two hundred armed men mounted guard outside the building.

Then, in spite of the indigestion that had been troubling him for some time, the Prussian, wild with joy, began to dance about, to dance frantically, throwing out his arms and legs and uttering wild shouts until he fell down exhausted beside the wall.

He was a prisoner—saved!

That was how the Château de Champignet was taken from the enemy after only six hours of occupation.

Colonel Ratier a cloth merchant, who had led the assault at the head of a body of the national guard of La Roche-Oysel, was decorated with an order.

TWO FRIENDS

BESIEGED Paris was in the throes of famine. Even the sparrows on the roofs and the rats in the sewers were growing scarce. People were eating anything they could get.

As Monsieur Morissot, watchmaker by profession and idler for the nonce, was strolling along the boulevard one bright January morning, his hands in his trousers pockets and stomach empty, he suddenly came face to face with an acquaintance—Monsieur Sauvage, a fishing chum.

Before the war broke out Morissot had been in the habit, every Sunday morning, of setting forth with a bamboo rod in his hand and a tin box on his back. He took the Argenteuil train, got out at Colombes, and walked thence to the Ile Marante. The moment he arrived at this place of his dreams he began fishing, and fished till nightfall.

Every Sunday he met in this very spot Monsieur Sauvage, a stout, jolly, little man, a draper in the Rue Notre Dame de Lorette, and also an ardent fisherman. They often spent half the day side by side, rod in hand and feet dangling over the water, and a warm friendship had sprung up between the two.

Some days they did not speak; at other times they chatted; but they understood each other perfectly without the aid of words, having similar tastes and feelings.

In the spring, about ten o'clock in the morning, when the early sun caused a light mist to float on the water and gently warmed the backs of the two enthusiastic anglers, Morissot would occasionally remark to his neighbor:

"My, but it's pleasant here."

To which the other would reply:

"I can't imagine anything better!"

And these few words sufficed to make them understand and appreciate each other.

In the autumn, toward the close of day, when the setting sun shed a blood-red glow over the western sky, and the reflection of the crimson clouds tinged the whole river with red, brought a glow to the faces of the two friends, and gilded the trees, whose leaves were already turning at the first chill touch of winter, Monsieur Sauvage would sometimes smile at Morissot, and say:

"What a glorious spectacle!"

And Morissot would answer, without taking his eyes from his float:

"This is much better than the boulevard, isn't it?"

As soon as they recognized each other they shook hands cordially, affected at the thought of meeting under such changed circumstances.

Monsieur Sauvage, with a sigh, murmured:

"These are sad times!"

Morissot shook his head mournfully.

"And such weather! This is the first fine day of the year."

The sky was, in fact, of a bright, cloudless blue.

They walked along, side by side, reflective and sad.

"And to think of the fishing!" said Morissot. "What good times we used to have!"

"When shall we be able to fish again?" asked Monsieur Sauvage.

They entered a small café and took an absinthe together, then resumed their walk along the pavement.

Morissot stopped suddenly.

"Shall we have another absinthe?" he said.

"If you like," agreed Monsieur Sauvage.

And they entered another wine shop.

They were quite unsteady when they came out, owing to the effect of the alcohol on their empty stomachs. It was a fine, mild day, and a gentle breeze fanned their faces.

The fresh air completed the effect of the alcohol on Monsieur Sauvage. He stopped suddenly, saying:

"Suppose we go there?"

"Where?"

"Fishing."

"But where?"

"Why, to the old place. The French outposts are close to Colombes. I know Colonel Dumoulin, and we shall easily get leave to pass."

Morissot trembled with desire.

"Very well. I agree."

And they separated, to fetch their rods and lines.

An hour later they were walking side by side on the highroad. Presently they reached the villa occupied by the colonel. He smiled at their request, and granted it. They resumed their walk, furnished with a password.

Soon they left the outposts behind them, made their way through deserted Colombes, and found themselves on the outskirts of the small vineyards which border the Seine. It was about eleven o'clock.

Before them lay the village of Argenteuil, apparently lifeless. The heights of Orgement and Sannois dominated the landscape. The great plain, extending as far as Nanterre, was empty, quite empty—a waste of dun-colored soil and bare cherry trees.

Monsieur Sauvage, pointing to the heights, murmured:

"The Prussians are up yonder!"

And the sight of the deserted country filled the two friends with vague misgivings.

The Prussians! They had never seen them as yet, but they had felt their presence in the neighborhood of Paris for months past—ruining France, pillaging, massacring, starving them. And a kind of superstitious terror mingled with the hatred they already felt toward this unknown, victorious nation.

"Suppose we were to meet any of them?" said Morissot.

"We'd offer them some fish," replied Monsieur Sauvage, with that Parisian light-heartedness which nothing can wholly quench.

Still, they hesitated to show themselves in the open country, overawed by the utter silence which reigned around them.

At last Monsieur Sauvage said boldly:

"Come, we'll make a start; only let us be careful!"

And they made their way through one of the vineyards bent double, creeping along beneath the cover afforded by the vines, with eye and ear alert.

A strip of bare ground remained to be crossed before they could gain the river bank. They ran across this, and, as soon as they were at the water's edge, concealed themselves among the dry reeds.

Morissot placed his ear the ground, to ascertain, if possible, whether footsteps were coming their way. He heard nothing. They seemed to be utterly alone.

Their confidence was restored, and they began to fish.

Before them the deserted Ile Marante hid them from the farther shore. The little restaurant was closed, and looked as if it had been deserted for years.

Monsieur Sauvage caught the first gudgeon, Monsieur Morissot the second, and almost every moment one or other raised his line with a little, glittering, silvery fish wriggling at the end; they were having excellent sport.

They slipped their catch gently into a close-meshed bag lying at their feet; they were filled with joy—the joy of once more indulging in a pastime of which they had long been deprived.

The sun poured its rays on their backs; they no longer heard anything or thought of anything. They ignored the rest of the world; they were fishing.

But suddenly a rumbling sound, which seemed to come from the bowels of the earth, shook the ground beneath them: the cannon were resuming their thunder.

Morissot turned his head and could see toward the left, beyond the banks of the river, the formidable outline of Mont-Valérien, from whose summit arose a white puff of smoke.

The next instant a second puff followed the first, and in a few moments a fresh detonation made the earth tremble.

Others followed, and minute by minute the mountain gave forth its deadly breath and a white puff of smoke, which rose slowly into the peaceful heaven and floated above the summit of the cliff.

Monsieur Sauvage shrugged his shoulders.

"They are at it again!" he said.

Morissot, who was anxiously watching his float bobbing up and down, was suddenly seized with the angry impatience of a peaceful man toward the madmen who were firing thus, and remarked indignantly:

"What fools they are to kill one another like that!"

"They're worse than animals," replied Monsieur Sauvage.

And Morissot, who had just caught a bleak, declared:

"And to think that it will be just the same so long as there are governments!"

"The Republic would not have declared war," interposed Monsieur Sauvage.

Morissot interrupted him:

"Under a king we have foreign wars; under a republic we have civil war."

And the two began placidly discussing political problems with the sound common sense of peaceful, matter-of-fact citizens—agreeing on one point: that they would never be free. And Mont-Valérien thundered ceaselessly, demolishing the houses of the French with its cannon balls, grinding lives of men to powder, destroying many a dream, many a cherished hope, many a prospective happiness; ruthlessly causing endless woe and suffering in the hearts of wives, of daughters, of mothers, in other lands. "Such is life!" declared Monsieur Sauvage.

"Say, rather, such is death!" replied Morissot, laughing.

But they suddenly trembled with alarm at the sound of footsteps behind them, and, turning round, they perceived close at hand four tall, bearded men, dressed after the manner of livery servants and wearing flat caps on their heads. They were covering the two anglers with their rifles.

The rods slipped from their owners' grasp and floated away down the river.

In the space of a few seconds they were seized, bound, thrown into a boat, and taken across to the Ile Marante.

And behind the house they had thought deserted were about a score of German soldiers.

A shaggy-looking giant, who was bestriding a chair and smoking a long clay pipe, addressed them in excellent French with the words:

"Well, gentlemen, have you had good luck with your fishing?"

Then a soldier deposited at the officer's feet the bag full of fish, which he had taken care to bring away. The Prussian smiled.

"Not bad, I see. But we have something else to talk about. Listen to me, and don't be alarmed:

"You must know that, in my eyes, you are two spies sent to reconnoitre me and my movements. Naturally, I capture you and I shoot you. You pretended to be fishing, the better to disguise your real errand. You have fallen into my hands, and must take the consequences. Such is war.

"But as you came here through the outposts you must have a password for your return. Tell me that password and I will let you go."

The two friends, pale as death, stood silently side by side, a slight fluttering of the hands alone betraying their emotion.

"No one will ever know," continued the officer. "You will return peacefully to your homes, and the secret will disappear with you. If you refuse, it means death—instant death. Choose!"

They stood motionless, and did not open their lips.

The Prussian, perfectly calm, went on, with hand outstretched toward the river:

"Just think that in five minutes you will be at the bottom of that water. In five minutes! You have relations, I presume?"

Mont-Valérien still thundered.

The two fishermen remained silent. The German turned and gave an order in his own language. Then he moved his chair a little way off, that he might not be so near the prisoners, and a dozen men stepped forward, rifle in hand, and took up a position twenty paces off.

"I give you one minute," said the officer; "not a second longer."

Then he rose quickly, went over to the two Frenchmen, took Morissot by the arm, led him a short distance off, and said in a low voice:

"Quick! the password! Your friend will know nothing. I will pretend to relent."

Morissot answered not a word.

Then the Prussian took Monsieur Sauvage aside in like manner, and made him the same proposal.

Monsieur Sauvage made no reply.

Again they stood side by side.

The officer issued his orders; the soldiers raised their rifles.

Then by chance Morissot's eyes fell on the bag full of gudgeons lying in the grass a few feet from him.

A ray of sunlight made the still quivering fish glisten like silver. And Morissot's heart sank. Despite his efforts at self-control his eyes filled with tears.

"Good-by, Monsieur Sauvage," he faltered.

"Good-by, Monsieur Morissot," replied Sauvage.

They shook hands, trembling from head to foot with a dread beyond their mastery.

The officer cried:

"Fire!"

The twelve shots were as one.

Monsieur Sauvage fell forward instantaneously. Morissot, being the taller, swayed slightly and fell across his friend with face turned skyward and blood oozing from a rent in the breast of his coat.

The German issued fresh orders.

His men dispersed, and presently returned with ropes and large stones, which they attached to the feet of the two friends; then they carried them to the river bank.

Mont-Valérien, its summit now enshrouded in smoke, still continued to thunder.

Two soldiers took Morissot by the head and the feet; two others did the same with Sauvage. The bodies, swung lustily by strong hands, were cast to a distance, and, describing a curve, fell feet foremost into the stream.

The water splashed high, foamed, eddied, then grew calm; tiny waves lapped the shore.

A few streaks of blood flecked the surface of the river.

The officer, calm throughout, remarked, with grim humor:

"It's the fishes' turn now!"

Then he retraced his way to the house.

Suddenly he caught sight of the net full of gudgeons, lying forgotten in the grass. He picked it up, examined it, smiled, and called:

"Wilhelm!"

A white-aproned soldier responded to the summons, and the Prussian, tossing him the catch of the two murdered men, said:

"Have these fish fried for me at once, while they are still alive; they'll make a tasty dish."

Then he resumed his pipe.

THE CRIPPLE

THE following adventure happened to me about 1882. I had just taken the train and settled down in a corner, hoping that I should be left alone, when the door suddenly opened again and I heard a voice say: "Take care, monsieur, we are just at a crossing; the step is very high."

Another voice answered: "That's all right, Laurent, I have a firm hold on the handle."

Then a head appeared, and two hands seized the leather straps hanging on either side of the door and slowly pulled up an enormous body, whose feet striking on the step, sounded like two canes. When the man had hoisted his torso into the compartment I noticed, at the loose edge of his trousers, the end of a wooden leg, which was soon followed by its mate. A head appeared behind this traveller and asked: "Are you all right, monsieur?"

"Yes, my boy."

"Then here are your packages and crutches."

And a servant, who looked like an old soldier, climbed in, carrying in his arms a stack of bundles wrapped in black and yellow papers and carefully tied; he placed one after the other in the net over his master's head. Then he said: "There, monsieur, that is all. There are five of them—the candy, the doll, the drum, the gun, and the *pâté de foies gras.*"

"Very well, my boy."

"Thank you, Laurent; good health!"

The man closed the door and walked away, and I looked at my neighbor. He was about thirty-five, although his hair was almost white; he wore the ribbon of the Legion of Honor; he had a heavy mustache and was quite stout, with the stoutness of a strong and active man who is kept motionless on account of some infirmity. He wiped his brow, sighed, and, looking me full in the face, he asked: "Does smoking annoy you, monsieur?"

"No, monsieur."

Surely I knew that eye, that voice, that face. But when and where had I seen them? I had certainly met that man, spoken to him, shaken his hand. That was a long, long time ago. It was lost in the haze wherein the mind seems to feel around blindly for memories and pursues them like fleeing phantoms without being able to seize them. He, too, was observing me, staring me out of countenance, with the persistence of a man who remembers slightly but not completely. Our eyes, embarrassed by this persistent contact, turned away; then, after a few minutes, drawn together again by the obscure and tenacious will of working memory, they met once more, and I said: "Monsieur, instead of staring at each other for an hour or so, would it not be better to try to discover where we have known each other?"

My neighbor answered graciously: "You are quite right, monsieur."

I named myself: "I am Henri Bonclair, a magistrate."

He hesitated for a few moments; then, with the vague look and voice which accompany great mental tension, he said: "Oh, I remember perfectly. I met you twelve years ago, before the war, at the Poincels!"

"Yes, monsieur. Ah! Ah! You are Lieutenant Revalière?"

"Yes. I was Captain Revalière even up to the time when I lost my feet—both of them together from one cannon ball."

Now that we knew each other's identity we looked at each other again. I remembered perfectly the handsome, slender youth who led the cotillons with such frenzied agility and gracefulness that he had been nicknamed "the fury." Going back into the dim, distant past, I recalled a story which I had heard and forgotten, one of those stories to which one listens but forgets, and which leave but a faint impression upon the memory.

There was something about love in it. Little by little the shadows cleared up, and the face of a young girl appeared before my eyes. Then her name struck me with the force of an explosion: Mademoiselle de Mandel. I remembered everything now. It was indeed a love story, but quite commonplace. The young girl loved this young man, and when I had met them there was already talk of the approaching wedding. The youth seemed to be very much in love, very happy.

I raised my eye to the net, where all the packages which had been brought in by the servant were trembling from the motion of the train, and the voice of the servant came back to me, as if he had just finished speaking. He had said: "There, monsieur, that is all. There are five of them: the candy, the doll, the drum, the gun, and the *pâté de foies gras.*"

Then, in a second, a whole romance unfolded itself in my head. It was like all those which I had already read, where the young lady married notwithstanding the catastrophe, whether physical or financial; therefore, this officer who had been mained in the war had returned, after the campaign, to the young girl who had given him her promise, and she had kept her word.

I considered that very beautiful, but simple, just as one considers simple all devotions and climaxes in books or in plays. It always seems, when one reads or listens to these stories of magnanimity, that one could sacrifice one's self with enthusiastic pleasure and overwhelming joy. But the following day, when an unfortunate friend comes to borrow some money, there is a strange revulsion of feeling.

But, suddenly, another supposition, less poetic and more realistic, replaced the first one. Perhaps he had married before the war, before this frightful accident, and she, in despair and resignation, had been forced to receive, care for, cheer, and support this husband, who had departed, a handsome man, and had returned without his feet, a frightful wreck, forced into immobility, powerless anger, and fatal obesity.

Was he happy or in torture? I was seized with an irresistible desire to know his story, or, at least, the principal points, which would permit me to guess that which he could not or would not tell me. Still thinking the matter over, I began talking to him. We had exchanged a few commonplace words; and I raised my eyes to the net, and thought: "He must have three children: the bonbons are for his wife, the doll for his little girl, the drum and the gun for his sons, and this *pâté de foies gras* for himself."

Suddenly I asked him: "Are you a father, monsieur?"

He answered: "No, monsieur."

I suddenly felt confused, as if I had been guilty of some breach of etiquette, and I continued: "I beg your pardon. I had thought that you were when I heard your servant speaking about the toys. One listens and draws conclusions unconsciously."

He smiled and then murmured: "No, I am not even married. I am still at the preliminary stage."

I pretended suddenly to remember, and said: "Oh! that's true! When I knew you, you were engaged to Mademoiselle de Mandel, I believe."

"Yes, monsieur, your memory is excellent."

I grew very bold and added: "I also seem to remember hearing that Mademoiselle de Mandel married Monsieur—Monsieur——"

He calmly mentioned the name: "Monsieur de Fleurel."

"Yes, that's it! I remember it was on that occasion that I heard of your wound."

I looked him full in the face, and he blushed. His full face, which was already red from the over-supply of blood, turned crimson. He answered quickly, with a sudden ardor of a man who is pleading a cause which is lost in his mind and in his heart, but which he does not wish to admit:

"It is wrong, monsieur, to couple my name with that of Madame de Fleurel. When I returned from the war—without my feet, alas! I never would have permitted her to become my wife. Was it possible? When one marries, monsieur, it is not in order to parade one's generosity; it is in order to live every day, every hour, every minute, every second beside a man; and if this man is disfigured, as I am, it is a death sentence to marry him! Oh, I understand, I admire all sacrifices and devotions when they have a limit, but I do not admit that a woman should give up her whole life, all joy, all her dreams, in order to satisfy the admiration of the gallery. When I hear, on the floor of my room, the tapping of my wooden legs and of my crutches, I grow angry enough to strangle my servant. Do you think that I would permit a woman to do what I myself am unable to tolerate? And, then, do you think that my stumps are pretty?"

He was silent. What could I say? He certainly was right. Could I blame her, hold her in contempt, even say that she was wrong? No. However, the end which conformed to the rule, to the truth, did not satisfy my poetic appetite. These herioc deeds demand a beautiful sacrifice, which seemed to be lacking, and I felt a certain disappointment. I suddenly asked: "Has Madame de Fleurel any children?"

"Yes, one girl and two boys. It is for them that I am bringing these toys. She and her husband are very kind to me."

The train was going up the incline to Saint-Germain. It passed through the tunnels, entered the station, and stopped. I was about to offer my arm to the wounded officer, in order to help him descend, when two hands were stretched up to him through the open door.

"Hello! my dear Revalière!"

"Ah! Hello, Fleurel!"

Standing behind the man, the woman, still beautiful, was smiling and waving her hands to him. A little girl, standing beside her, was jumping for joy, and two young boys were eagerly watching the drum and the gun, which were passing from the car into their father's hands.

When the cripple was on the ground, all the children kissed him. Then they set off, the little girl holding in her hand the small varnished rung of a crutch, just as she might walk beside her big friend and hold his thumb.